A l

Cole's husky voice filled the room as he asked, "You're not afraid of anything, are you, Sarah?"

The hairbrush stilled in midair as she found his reflection in the mirror. "I'm afraid of everything."

"I don't believe you."

She shrugged her shoulders.

"You're a remarkable woman, Sarah Beth Hogan."

Laying the brush on the washstand, he drew her back against him and slowly lowered his head, his mouth claiming hers in a gentle, searching kiss.

Lifting her hands, she clasped his neck, her fingers entwining in his thick hair. She answered his kiss boldly, her own feverish passion unlike anything she had ever experienced . . .

HEARTFIRE ROMANCES

SWEET TEXAS NIGHTS   (2610, $3.75)
by Vivian Vaughan

Meg Britton grew up on the railroads, working proudly at her father's side. Nothing was going to stop them from setting the rails clear to Silver Creek, Texas—certainly not some crazy prospector. As Meg set out to confront the old coot, she planned her strategy with cool precision. But soon she was speechless with shock. For instead of a harmless geezer, she found a boldly handsome stranger whose determination matched her own.

CAPTIVE DESIRE   (2612, $3.75)
by Jane Archer

Victoria Malone fancied herself a great adventuress, but being kidnapped was too much excitement for even Victoria! Especially when her arrogant kidnapper thought she was part of Red Duke's outlaw gang. Trying to convince the overbearing, handsome stranger that she had been an innocent bystander when the stagecoach was robbed, proved futile. But when he thought he could maker her confess by crushing her to his warm, broad chest, by caressing her with his strong, capable hands, Victoria was willing to admit to anything. . . .

LAWLESS ECSTASY   (2613, $3.75)
by Susan Sackett

Abra Beaumont could spot a thief a mile away. After all, her father was once one of the best. But he'd been on the right side of the law for years now, and she wasn't about to let a man like Dash Thorne lead him astray with some wild plan for stealing the Tear of Allah, the world's most fabulous ruby. Dash was just the sort of man she most distrusted—sophisticated, handsome, and altogether too sure of his considerable charm. Abra shivered at the devilish gleam in his blue eyes and swore he would need more than smooth kisses and skilled caresses to rob her of her virtue . . . and much more than sweet promises to steal her heart!

LINDSEY HANKS
LONG TEXAS NIGHT

ZEBRA BOOKS
KENSINGTON PUBLISHING CORP.

ZEBRA BOOKS

are published by

Kensington Publishing Corp.
475 Park Avenue South
New York, NY 10016

First printing: September, 1991

Printed in the United States of America

Prologue

Sarah Beth Hogan faced the small gathering with her head held high. The rigid stances and grim expressions of the group's members boded ill for anyone unwise enough to disagree with them—and Sarah had.

The Reverend J. T. Mullins stepped from the crowd and clasped Sarah's hand, slightly shaking his head. "Sarah, Sarah," he whispered, "what have you done?"

"Only my Christian duty, sir."

"You see it as your duty to go against the word of an upstanding member of our gathering and blaspheme her character in the eyes of the community?"

"What about the false accusation of Orie Wheeler? Does his innocence count for naught?" Sarah asked, hardly above a whisper.

Murmurs swiftly passed through the crowd. The Reverend Mullins held up his hand to silence the people.

"My dear, Orie Wheeler is not one of us. Mae Riley is. And if she said he stole her purse with her husband's wages in it, there is no reason to doubt her word."

"Reverend, it is not my intention to be disrespectful. Yet, you force me to speak the truth. Mrs. Riley said she was

5

returning from town around noon when Orie Wheeler pushed her down and grabbed her purse. Orie has helped me every Tuesday for six weeks. On that particular Tuesday, Orie was busy until late afternoon helping me replace flowers in the cemetery," Sarah said, a bit louder.

"I've meant to address this issue long before now and in the privacy of my chamber. But since you brought it up, we will discuss it now." He drew a long breath. "Sarah, you are the widow of a fine Christian man. I didn't know your late husband, but the congregation speaks highly of him, as does your mother and grandparents. That you would have any dealings whatsoever with the likes of Orie Wheeler is a blemish on your husband's memory, not to mention the teachings of this church."

"I thought we as members of this flock were to minister to the sinners and disbelievers, teaching them the error of their ways. Have I misinterpreted the doctrine, Reverend Mullins?"

A roar of shocked disapproval swept through the crowd.

"Young lady, don't you dare speak with such disrespect to me. It is only by the grace of the members of this church that you have had a roof over your head and food on your table since your husband's death."

Sarah's exemplary life was above reproach. She'd moved from her grandparent's strict home to her husband's. The desire to escape her grandfather's puritanical authority had been her only sin. She'd married the man of her grandfather's choosing, hoping for a freer existence. Yet, in truth, her vows had only bound her firmly to a man who had then exercised the same rigid control over her life. Eli, her late husband, had been the minister of this same church until his passing. And after his death, when Sarah had refused to move back into her grandfather's home, the new minister had moved her from the parsonage to a one-room shelter adjacent to the church. She'd lived in the strictest terms on their succor. How could Reverend Mullins throw it up in her face? she thought. She hated to think ill of her fellowman, but their benevolence was a bit tightfisted by any standard. Regardless of what they thought, she'd earned her keep by the sweat of her brow.

The only bright spot in her existence was the company of Orie Wheeler as they worked together. She worked from sunup until sundown doing the bidding of the congregation. She'd taken on the task of weeding and planting the cemetery. Orie Wheeler helped her with the never-ending chore. In return, she was teaching him how to read and to do his sums. The good Lord knew she wasn't a teacher by any standard. Still, she had an uncanny memory for numbers, and to help Orie she'd tackled the job. In the eyes of the church, he was a no-good drifter—drinking, gambling, and womanizing his way straight to hell. "Live and let live" was his belief. He was the one person in all the world who didn't preach or lecture her. Even his ribald humor brought a chuckle from her more often than she liked to admit. She realized he was a far cry from the members of the church. Yet, he was the only friend she had who was close to her age. She loved to hear the stories he told of all the places he'd seen. And she knew that Mae Riley accused him falsely.

"I'm waiting, Mrs. Hogan," the reverend grated.

"For what?" she asked.

"Your apology!" He yanked the Bible from under his arm and began flipping through the pages until he found the passage he was looking for. " 'Thou shall not bear false witness against thy neighbor.' "

Sarah Beth Hogan completely lost control, her calm evaporating like fog in a ray of sunshine. Before the minister could stop her, she grabbed the Bible from his hand. Scanning the scripture the reverend had read from, she pointed to a passage. Lifting her head, she quoted, clear and precise: " 'Thou shalt not covet thy neighbor's house; thou shalt not covet thy neighbor's wife, nor his ox, nor his ass, *nor anything that is thy neighbor's.*' " She shut the Bible, handing it back to a slack-jawed J. T. Mullins.

7

"Reverend Mullins, if you will check your facts, you will learn that Miss Irene Bishop just ordered a new suit of lamb's wool and emerald silk. She also ordered a hat and cape to match. Mae Riley cannot stand for anyone to have anything better than she has. On the Tuesday in question, she learned of Miss Bishop's order. Not to be outdone, she placed an order for the same suit in lamb's wool and blue silk, also with a matching cape and hat. The only way to cover herself for spending her husband's money was to concoct the story of Orie Wheeler robbing her."

At the close of her long narrative, Sarah squared her shoulders and stiffened her back. Her chest heaving with emotion, she took her leave from the room of loose-lipped faces and the condemning eyes of J. T. Mullins.

Chapter One

Sarah squinted into the fading light and rammed the needle home. She jumped, and a tiny drop of blood appeared on the crooked seam. Her finger flew to her mouth, and she sucked on the injury. Tears pooled in her eyes and rolled down her cheeks to fall onto the droplet of blood. A feeling of complete helplessness enveloped her. Couldn't she do anything right? She'd made a complete shambles of her poor, wretched life. She'd alienated everyone who had anything to do with her except Orie Wheeler and Irene Bishop.

As she studied the situation, it was clear that other than her two friends, no one else cared for her—not unless she was working for them unfailingly. She had shamed her mother and grandparents by her behavior. They'd made it clear they would have nothing more to do with her until she made a formal apology to the Reverend Mullins, the congregation, and Mae Riley.

Laying aside her mending, she stood up and walked to the window. A gray ball of fur wiggled from the fabric and followed her. She leaned down and scooped up the cat. "What's to become of us, Mr. Herman?"

His answer was a contented purr as he nosed her neck.

She had one week to vacate her room. Being twenty-four years old, widowed, and destitute was not a comforting thought.

Orie had come by and offered to rob a bank for her if she wanted him to. Irene Bishop had clapped her on the back and praised her courage, then offered her a room in the home she shared with her invalid brother. Sarah knew that if she accepted, the people of the church would ostracize Irene. For better or worse, they were Irene's only social life.

Her tears fell freely onto Mr. Herman's shimmering coat. He purred loudly, and with his sandpaper tongue licked away the drops of sadness.

Shadows merged as night descended, enclosing the town of Highridge, Tennessee, in a blanket of darkness. The fragrant smell of pipe tobacco encircled a bushy head of silver-white hair. Indecision marked the features of Wesley Calvin Norman, attorney at law, as he tapped the bowl of the pipe. He studied the dim light coming from the tiny room. Words that could change Sarah Hogan's life rested in his breast pocket. He knocked the fire from his pipe and pushed from the tree.

He and James Moore had been friends since the day he'd come into Hazard, Texas, to set up his law practice. James had been in need of an attorney; and he, in need of a client. It was a first for each of them. James was devastated. His wife had left him, taking their infant daughter with her.

Unlike other men, when James had found out he was going to be a father, he'd wanted a daughter above all else. His wife had turned his dream into a nightmare when she'd packed her bags and returned to her parents' home in Tennessee, vowing Hazard, Texas, was no fit place to rear a daughter.

Once, when James had been really down and out, he had confided in his friend. He didn't know how he'd ever persuaded Ellen Moore to marry him. She had been so different from any female he'd ever known. He'd sworn someone spiked the punch the night he'd met her. Nothing else could have explained it. She was deeply religious; her prune-faced parents were fanatical in their beliefs. And it tore at his soul to know they were rearing his daughter. Through the years, he had kept tabs on his daughter, deeply troubled by

10

the way she had turned out. Her grandparents had made every effort to hide her beauty.

When James had learned that his son-in-law, the preacher, had died, he'd had enough. One way or another, his daughter was coming to Texas, even if he had to kidnap her. Wes had dissuaded his friend from such drastic measures.

James Moore, a rich man, could afford to indulge the desire to see his daughter settled happily in Hazard, Texas. But if she had one drop of her father's blood in her, force would not work. By her own free will, she had to agree to come to Hazard. Wes and James had put their heads together and studied long and hard. Eventually they'd devised a plan that was foolproof—if Sarah Beth Hogan would go along with it.

Wes Norman ended his reminiscences about what he knew of Sarah's life. Tomorrow, I'll see the deed through, he thought. She's suffered enough persecution from these hypocritical dimwits. Let's see what she does with this opportunity. She might throw the document in my face, or she might take up the challenge and change the course of her life.

Sarah stepped from the milliner's shop, her shoulders slumped and head lowered dejectedly. She moved slowly up the street, pondering her future. The last few days had left her little hope of supporting herself. She'd applied for work everywhere, only to be turned down flatly. She was the bad apple in an otherwise bountiful harvest.

"Mrs. Sarah Hogan?"

Her head snapped up. "Yes?"

"My name is Wes Norman." He extended his hand to her. "I realize you don't know me, but you will very soon."

She placed her gloved hand in his, hoping he wouldn't notice the mended fingers. "Mr. Norman?"

"Is there somewhere we can talk? I have some important matters we must discuss. I represent the estate of James Moore."

"Estate? You mean my father's dead?"

The attorney nodded.

Tears pooled in her eyes, rolling under the frames of her glasses and down her cheeks before she could blink them away.

Taking her elbow, he guided her down the street, ignoring the stares of passersby. "I'm sorry. I should have been more tactful. We can talk in the dining room of the hotel, if that's okay?"

"Yes," she said. Sniffling, she removed her glasses and dabbed at her eyes.

After they sat down, Wes ordered coffee for them and gave her a few moments to compose herself.

As the waitress served the coffee, Sarah removed her gloves, all the while studying the attorney.

"I'm sorry, Mr. Norman. I didn't know my father, but I'd always hoped one day I would have that pleasure."

"He was a fine man, Mrs. Hogan, and a very good friend. His passing has left me with the delicate job of carrying out his wishes."

"What happened to him?" she asked.

He thumped his chest. "His heart just gave out, I'm afraid."

"Is . . . is there anything I can do?"

"As a matter of fact, there is." Mr. Norman pulled a sheaf of papers from his breast pocket. "Your father was a wealthy man, Mrs. Hogan. You are his heir."

"But he didn't even know me."

"That's where you're wrong. Your father never lost track of you. He loved you very much, and his concern for your welfare never diminished. He would have done anything for you, but your mother wouldn't allow it."

"My mother had contact with my father all these years and never told me?"

"I'm sorry. I didn't realize she hadn't told you." He pulled several yellowed photographs from his other pocket and placed them on the table.

Amazement enveloped her as she fingered the frayed

edges of the pictures. They were all of her at one stage or another in her life. "Why didn't she tell me? All my life I've wondered about him, and why he never came to see me."

"I believe your mother and grandparents thought he would be a bad influence on you."

"Why? Was he a bad person?"

"No, not at all, but they didn't agree with his way of life."

She smiled slightly. "Then, I take it he wasn't a preacher?"

Wes laughed. "No. Although, at the time he met your mother, he was a Bible salesman. In all honesty, he was a gambler, and later became the owner of a very prosperous saloon, the only saloon in Hazard."

"Oh no, Mr. Norman, don't tell me he has left me this saloon . . . this . . . den of iniquity."

"In a roundabout way, yes."

"What do you mean?"

"Your father's will is very clear about his wishes. He felt that your mother and grandparents influenced you in every aspect of your upbringing. Now that you are of age, it is his turn, although his presence will be missing. He wanted you to experience life in a different light. He knew of your strict religious training. He agreed with that to a point, but not to the exclusion of all else."

"If he left me a saloon, I will simply sell it and give the money to charity. There are no ifs, ands, or buts about it. I would never have anything to do with something so foreign to my beliefs."

"I'm afraid, Mrs. Hogan, that it's not that simple."

"It's not?" she asked weakly.

"As I said, your father's will is very clear. In order for you to claim your inheritance—which entails quite a bit of land, a ranch, railroad stock, cattle, and a substantial amount of cash—you must live in Hazard." Wes drew a deep breath and plunged ahead. "And operate the saloon for a period of one year."

"Well, I won't. It's simply out of the question."

"Very well, Mrs. Hogan. Then, if you will just sign these papers, our business will be concluded."

"How much cash?" she asked as visions of herself and a bony Mr. Herman begging on the street swam before her eyes.

"About fifty thousand dollars, give or take a thousand or so."

"Fifty thousand!" She clasped her hand over her mouth and darted a glance around the deserted room. "Fifty thousand, you said?"

Joy jumped in the attorney's eyes as he nodded his head.

"And all I have to do is run the saloon for one year?"

Again he nodded.

For just a tiny second she imagined herself swathed in emerald silk. Of course, she couldn't forget Mr. Herman. He napped before a warm fire, near a dish overflowing with flaked fish and a bowl of rich cream.

The attorney watched her closely. He could just imagine what was going on in her head. Her appearance spoke volumes. The shapeless black dress had seen better days. He smiled. If it was brand-new, it still wouldn't have any redeeming qualities. Her chestnut hair was dull and lifeless — what he could see of it. The rest was in a tight bun that rode low on the back of her head and was covered with a black net. Warped wire-framed glasses did little to hide the startling green of her eyes. Yet their presence seemed to cause her to squint. Her hands were a shame, red and chapped, the nails clean but cut bluntly, some to the quick. Various scratches and cuts marred her skin. No wonder James wanted her away from this influence. She was twenty-four, he thought James had told him.

"Mr. Norman?" she asked, interrupting his thoughts. "How does one go about running a saloon?"

"It's not a difficult job. If you decide to take it, I will aid you in any way I can. And you already have several people in your employ."

"I do?"

"Yes, Gunter, the bartender, and two hostesses who see

to the customers. A man named Billy Ward cleans up, and Fancy Fingers Floyd plays the piano. You'd have to take care of the books and the ordering, but Gunter and I will help you with that until you get the hang of it."

"Where would I live, Mr. Norman?"

"Above the saloon is a very nice apartment. Also on the outskirts of town is a ranch with a small house, which at the time the sheriff is renting. I'm sure the apartment will please you." He smiled. "Oh, and please call me Wes."

"Oh, Mr. Norman . . . Wes, I feel the temptation you've placed before me will send me posthaste to hell in a handbasket."

Wes reached across the table and lifted her hand. "My dear Sarah, the only hell you need fear is the hell of remaining in this shortsighted community. I must admit that I'm aware of your situation, financial and otherwise."

A grimace darted across her face. "I'm afraid I've done a terrible thing, shamed myself and my family."

"You've done no such thing. It took a very brave person to face the wrath of J. T. Mullins. After enduring that encounter, running a saloon will be like child's play." Gently tracing an angry scratch on the back of her hand, he asked, "What happened to your hands?"

Embarrassed, she pulled her hands away and tucked them in the folds of her dress. "I've been weeding the cemetery."

"And is the pay good?"

"Oh, I don't get paid. The congregation requested that I do it. I work for my room and board."

"Let me ask you another question. Before you moved into your room, did anyone else live there?"

She shook her head. "It was a storage room."

"I see," he answered as a volley of anger swept through him. Damn them and damn their attempts to turn Sarah into nothing more than a wretched servant, having her at their beck and call for meager crumbs from their tables. To hell with the lot of them. He had the power and the means to help this young lady, and by god, he would do it, if he had to kidnap her and drag her away.

· She saw the anger flash across his face and wondered if it was directed at her. "I'm sorry I can't make up my mind, but I'm torn with the decision of right and wrong. Yet, I wonder, could it be so terrible if it were my father's wish that I do it?"

"My sentiments exactly. Give it a try, Sarah. How long can a year possibly last?"

She smiled brightly.

In the months to come, that question would haunt Sarah.

Chapter Two

Hazard, Texas, 1885

Coleman Blade punched the pillow and adjusted it behind his head. His rumpled hair, as black as a raven's wing, draped his brow, and beads of sweat rolled down his neck into the springy curls covering his chest. His deep, slate-gray eyes watched with appreciation as his companion disrobed with trained sensuality. She bent from the waist to slide her stockings slowly down her legs. With her bottom airborne, she turned her head toward the bed, sending her hair over her shoulder in a curtain of shimmering ebony. When Coleman sucked in his breath, she laughed, and tossed the stockings onto the chair, with his discarded clothing. She slid across the mattress beside him.

"Took me long enough, didn't it?"

"What do you mean?" he drawled, cupping her breasts in the palms of his hands.

She tossed her hair. "To get a response from you other than your usual cynicism. You're a hard, cold man."

He smiled lazily. "Hard, yes, but cold, I don't know."

"That's not what I mean and you know it." Her hand wrapped around the hardness he spoke of, and began to stroke him. The teasing glimmer in her eyes diminished as desire sparked and flamed.

Later as she dozed beside him, he studied the sleek lines of her body. It was so reminiscent of his way of life—a dif-

17

ferent face, a different body, but the words whispered in passion were always the same. Yet none of it meant anything to him. Absently he twirled an ebony strand of her hair around his finger. He knew he frightened her, at least until passion drove the fear from her mind. She was also curious, and had tried to question him until his lips had silenced her.

He was aware of the rumors and the fear he generated. Tales of bloody brawls and a fast gun followed him like a shadow. That he tempted death on a daily basis and mocked his own mortality sent chills coursing along the spine of many an opportunist who wanted to take him down. This suited him just fine; he had a job to do, and if his reputation gave him a slight edge, then more power to the gossip mongers.

He'd paid his dues and made his own way. His reputation was like his name—Cole Blade; it suited him perfectly. How ironic. On many occasions he'd had to rely on a deadly blade to see a job completed.

During the past few months, a bad element had spread through Hazard, Texas. The once-safe streets were littered with guns for hire, and the town's saloon had become a nest of card-cheaters, and itchy triggerfingers. Fights broke out at the drop of a hat, and blood flowed as freely as the cheap whiskey.

Rumors of a railroad spur linking Hazard to outlying areas were the cause of the upheaval. Everyone wanted a piece of the pie, and there was just so much pie. Dusty Mills, a new landowner, seemed to be the link behind the bad element. He was buying up property with the same eagerness that some of his hired hands apparently had for using their guns. Murder plagued the residents of Hazard, and outlandish property deals were whispered about behind closed doors.

Cole's friendship with James Moore had come about unexpectedly. James had loved Hazard, and when the trouble began, it hadn't taken him long to get his fill of corruption. He wouldn't stand for it—this was his home, these people were his friends, and he'd be damned if he'd watch his community disintegrate into nothing more than a memory. At the onset, he'd learned that talking did little more than exercise his mouth. He'd then decided to fight fire with fire.

A smile tugged Cole's mouth as he thought of James Moore. James had tracked him down. Before he'd introduced himself, he'd asked, "Are you the man with no conscience—the meanest, fastest gun in Texas?"

"That depends on who's asking," Cole had responded.

James had made him an offer he couldn't refuse. And to beat it all, they discovered they really liked and respected each other.

For a while everything settled down, until James Moore disappeared. There was a new grave in the cemetery and a marker bearing his name. Some said he'd died from a heart attack and his closest friend buried him without any fanfare. Others said a sniper put a bullet in his back and dumped his body in the river. Whatever, he was sorely missed.

Cole listened as the squalling of cats and the lonely baying of a dog joined choruses. His companion snuggled closely and nudged her chin into his neck. He mumbled softly and patted her naked leg. Moonlight streamed into the room and bounced on the chair holding Cole's clothes, glimmering off the five-star badge and the slightly raised lettering. *Sheriff, Hazard, Texas.*

He smiled into the darkness.

Wide potholes marred the dusty street, and the driver managed to hit every single one dead center. Sarah braced herself for the next jolt while trying to see everything that lined the streets of her new home. Her head slammed against the back of the coach, tilting her hat askew and sending hairpins into her scalp. Her thick hair tumbled around her shoulders in disarray.

Wes Norman hid his mirth behind his hand with an exaggerated yawn. But there was nothing he could do about the sparkle in his eyes. This journey had been a new experience for him. Sarah Beth Hogan had never been out of Highridge, Tennessee, that she could remember, so everything she saw was an adventure. Watching her, he felt the same anticipation he would have had if he were reading a wonderful new book. He couldn't wait to turn the pages to see what would happen next. And just when he thought he'd figured out the plot, a new twist would lead him astray. Their journey had been arduous, to say the least. But Sarah, with eyes as big as saucers and her excitement infectious, had made it a wondrous adventure. She'd asked a thousand questions and had tried to see everything they'd passed. Wes had immediately become captured by her warm smile and dry humor. The only blemish to mar their venture had been the fit her mother and grandparents had pitched. They'd lamented the shame she'd brought on them and vowed they were washing their hands of her if she continued her hell-bound journey. They'd spouted dire predictions on the future of her soul and quoted scripture until Wes had become furious. He'd wanted to hogtie her grandfather and dump him in the nearest creek, then gag the grandmother and mother. When Wes had quoted a few verses of his own, they finally shut up. Still, they'd stolen the joy of her parting.

A bellowing shout from the driver, and the bone-jarring halt of the carriage, sent Sarah scooting across the seat. Before she could adjust her person, the coach door swung open and the excited face of the driver peered inside. "Sorry for the delay, but it looks like you're gonna get to witness your first gunfight, Mrs. Hogan. We'll have to wait here until it's over. They're squaring off now." He lifted his hand and motioned toward the street.

Leaning from her seat, she could see people hurriedly moving from the street to gather on the boardwalks. Suddenly it became very quiet, the only sound the ringing of spurs as the two men faced off against each other. She could see the back of one man, his stance stiff and his hand poised above the butt of his gun. The man approaching him was facing the sun, yet it appeared not to bother him. His hat rested low on his brow and his eyes were narrowed. If he was nervous, it didn't show.

Sarah heard him clearly when he asked, "Are you sure this is what you want to do?"

"What's the matter, Blade? You worried that I'll take you down?"

"It never crossed my mind."

"Well, it better, 'cause I'm talkin' to a dead man."

"Mind telling me your name? I want to get it right on your tombstone."

For an instant the man seemed to falter and his hand trembled above his gun. Then just as quickly he stiffened his back and bellowed, "Tom Rivers!" His hand closed around the notched handle. His arm began an upward arch as his identity reached the ears of the bystanders.

A gunshot shattered the air. Tom Rivers, gunslinger, wilted in a dead heap in the potholed street of Hazard, Texas, his legend echoing distantly with the many that had gone before him.

Cole Blade was a hard man to kill.

Sarah couldn't believe her eyes. She'd actually thought they wouldn't do something so barbaric. She slumped into the seat. "Why?" she whispered.

Wes patted her hand. "I'm sorry you had to witness a killing before your feet even touched the ground. I know it's hard, Sarah, but try not to let it bother you. He was a gunslinger. All he'd wanted was to add another notch to his gun and make a name for himself. By killing Cole Blade, he would have become famous."

"Is this Blade man a gunslinger?"

Wes laughed. "Yes. He's also the sheriff of Hazard."

"Oh," was her weak reply.

The coach jolted forward. As they passed the spot where the gunfight had taken place, she saw several men lifting the body. The sheriff called to them. Sarah watched as the sheriff pulled his hand from his pocket and flipped a coin through the air. "See that he gets a nice tombstone."

"Sure thing, Sheriff," one of the men answered, snapping the coin from the air.

In only a few moments, the coach halted and the door swung open. The beaming face of the driver appeared in the opening. "I hope you enjoyed your ride, Mrs. Hogan."

"Yes," she answered as she accepted his large callused hand. What else could she say?

While she waited for Wes to make arrangements for their baggage and a very disgruntled Mr. Herman, her head swung as though it were on a pivot. It was over, with no one seeming bothered by the death. Instead, the crowd had cleared and the people were going about their business. The town was a beehive of activity. Women dressed in full-skirted calico and gingham dresses with shopping baskets on their arms mingled with shopkeepers, or directed errand boys to their wagons or buggies. Others, in beautiful dresses of satin and lace, were escorted by men dressed to the nines in dark sack coats, sparkling white shirts, and black string ties. Not all the men dressed so richly. Most wore homespun shirts and favored the rough denim pants. Yet, one and all wore sturdy leather boots, and had a weapon strapped to their hips.

Across the street from the stage depot was Chapel's Hotel. Next door was a barbershop with a large sign on the side of the building advertising a bathhouse. Hazard's bank and the hardware store sat like roosting hens on a small rise overlooking the main thoroughfare. Beautiful horses carried riders slowly down the street, and one and all peered curiously at Sarah.

"Ready?" Wes asked, taking her arm. As he guided her down the boardwalk, a multitude of dread filled her. Could she do what her father intended?

When they reached the saloon, Sarah stopped and cast Wes a weak smile.

He squeezed her arm and whispered, "Chin up, everything will be fine."

She could hear the sound of the piano as someone pounded out the tune of "Camp Town Races." As she peeked above the swinging doors, all she saw was a haze of smoke. After pushing her wire-framed spectacles to the bridge of her nose, she mopped her neck with a threadbare hanky and took a deep fortifying breath. With a last glance at Wes, she placed her gloved hand on the batwing door and took a step forward. Suddenly, without warning, Sarah was tumbling through the air. She landed with a dull thud in the dusty road, and her breath whooshed from her. When she could get her breath, the first thing she noticed was a smelly body untangling his limbs from hers.

"Ma' am, I'm terrible sorry," the man offered, picking up his hat and slapping it against his dusty pants, his right eye suspiciously red and beginning to swell. "I had no idea you was standin' there. Curly pushed me and I pushed him, then one thing just led to another."

She pulled herself up on her elbows and adjusted her glasses. To her utter dismay, her skirt rode up around her knees, showing anyone who dared to look an uncommon amount of leg and the hem of her plain drawers. And it seemed that everyone in Hazard dared to look, because spectators were pushing in for a closer view.

Shame flooded her. At that moment, she would have crawled back on the stage and headed straight for Tennessee, even if she had to beg her way back into the Reverend Mullins's flock.

Now, Sarah, you're not a quitter, are you? An inner voice questioned.

I most certainly am! she thought right back. I've never been so humiliated in my life, sprawled in the middle of the road in Hazard, Texas. What a way to make an entrance to my new home.

Then, from deep inside her, the spirit she'd inherited from her father (the same spirit her grandparents and mother had feared) began to sweep through her. She would not let this incident crush her. Her very existence depended on her ability to run the saloon.

The man who'd tumbled her to the ground clasped her arm and hauled her to her feet.

"Some welcoming committee ya'll have here in Hazard," she said dryly.

Everyone laughed and tried to help her brush the dust and dirt from her dress.

Wes stepped forward with her hat dangling from his fingers. "I'd like you all to meet Sarah Beth Hogan, James Moore's daughter and the new owner of the Do Drop In."

"Truly," she announced with humor sparkling in her eyes, "it was not my intention to 'drop in' in such a fashion."

Again the men laughed and stepped forward, doffing their hats and pumping her hand as though they were trying to get water.

"Let's get you settled in," Wes whispered, moving her through the spectators.

This time Wes stepped through the doors first, making sure the path was clear.

Without his arm to steady her, Sarah was sure she would have fainted dead away. Her first impression was of sin, pure and simple. Pictures of naked women adorned the walls, one even boasting a brass nameplate identifying the woman. A long bar with a dirty mirrored wall behind it was the focal point of the large room. Several men lingered against the bar while others sat at tables scattered around the room. At one table, a card game was taking place. Sarah's eyes shot back to the card game. Two women, one in fiery red, the other in emerald, stood behind two of the players. They laughed with ease and let their hands rest casually on the men's shoulders. When the woman in the fiery red leaned forward and dropped a handful of coins on the table, Sarah's breath caught in her throat. If the woman's breasts had joined the money littering the table, it would not have surprised Sarah. The cut of the dress was indeed designed to please a man.

Wes struggled to keep a straight face. He'd followed her gaze and could just imagine what was going on in her head. Damn it, he was proud. She was handling it well.

Dragging her attention from the blatant display of flesh,

24

she continued her inspection of the room. A battered piano stood at one end of the room near a small stage. At that, she cocked a brow. "A stage?"

"Sometimes a traveling troupe comes through. This is the only place large enough to accommodate a crowd," he answered.

Wes escorted her around the room amidst curious stares and the tipping of hats. One by one, he introduced her to her employees. Gunter, the bartender, came from behind the bar, wiping his hands on his dirty apron before clasping her hand.

"Ma'am, I'm pleased to at last meet James Moore's daughter. This is a fine place we have here, but as you can see, we are sadly lacking the touch of a woman's hand."

Gunter's warm reception pleased her. "My hand may not be as welcome as you think. If anyone has any ideas, I would like to hear them."

"Yes, ma' am. And, ma' am? I want you to know that you have good employees. We all thought a lot of your father, and we're anxious to see you succeed."

"Thank you."

Sarah was more hesitant when she met the two women. She wasn't comfortable at all. But they soon put her at ease with their friendly smiles and smooth charm. Belle was the one dressed in red. She had glorious black hair and a creamy complexion. Collie was the one dressed in emerald. She was friendly, but there was a sadness deep in her eyes that reached out to Sarah.

"Collie?" Sarah asked.

"Yes, just like the dog. It's my hair."

"It's beautiful," Sarah said, admiring the lustrous mixture of brown hair streaked heavily with blond strands.

It would take some getting used to, but Sarah knew she would never say anything about the way the girls dressed. If it didn't bother them, why should it bother her? She made up her mind right then to try to follow Orie's philosophy of Live and Let Live. She'd had enough of someone always telling her every move to make. She wouldn't make the same mistake and turn the girls against her by trying to tell them how to dress.

Fancy Fingers Floyd was the biggest disappointment. No wonder there were no tables close to the piano. He smelled like something that had been dead for a week. His clothes desperately needed a good washing, as did he. He was a jaunty fellow, and his fingers flew over the keys like honey on a hot biscuit. Still, Sarah knew a lot of work faced her where he was concerned. It would take some deep thought before she could tactfully approach the bathing issue.

Then there was Billy Ward, a man of undetermined age who cleaned up the place. He slouched forward, balancing himself on the handle of a stubby broom. A bushy beard and mustache covered the lower portion of his face, and a black patch covered one eye. The brim of his hat rested low on his brow. His dark hair was long and uneven, in desperate need of a cut.

His hands in fingerless gloves clasped hers warmly and his eye sparkled with merriment. "So, this is James's daughter? Well, you're not at all what I expected."

Sarah smiled softly at the man. "I'm afraid to ask what you expected, Mr. Ward."

He scratched his face and peered at her intently. "Well, I don't rightly know myself. Being reared by them Bible-thumpers is sorta like being reared by the Indians. They can sneak up on you when your back is turned and have you in their clutches before you can say jack rabbit."

"I'll keep that in mind, Mr. Ward, and I'll keep my eyes peeled for Indians, too."

He laughed loudly and pounded the stubby broom against the floor, sending a cloud of dust around their feet. "You've got spunk, missy, I'll have to say that for you. Maybe with your spunk and my good looks we can get this place in shape again."

It was Sarah's turn to laugh. Before she could control it, bubbling laughter shook her shoulders. "You can count on it, Mr. Ward."

Chapter Three

Wes led Sarah up the gracefully curving stairs and along a wide hallway, pointing out Collie's and Belle's rooms as he directed Sarah to the end of the hall. Taking a key from his pocket, he unlocked the door and pushed it open, inviting her to precede him.

She stepped inside.

Unlike the saloon, the apartment was clean and orderly. Sunshine splashed through the windows, lending a bright cheerfulness to the room. A small sitting room with a matching parlor suite upholstered in a brocatelle of blues and browns occupied one end of the room. Sarah lowered herself to the sofa, smoothing her hand across the fine fabric. "Good springs," she said, bouncing slightly on the sofa. A large curtain-top desk and chair rested in the corner. Atop the desk was a lamp, an inkwell, and a stack of papers.

Wes pointed out that her father had worked here on the saloon's books and his other business interests.

Sarah moved among the furnishings, running her hands along the polished wood and across the back of her father's chair.

The bedroom boasted a high four-poster bed, a dresser, and chifforobe. A folding screen with a shirred fabric insert stood to the side of a copper bathing tub. The windows, with light cotton curtains, faced the busy main street, and a thick carpet of blue covered the floors.

27

"I can't believe this is mine."

"It is." Wes beamed proudly.

She moved from one room to another again, touching everything. "I never expected anything like this. It's beautiful—and my father left it all to me?"

"Everything he had is yours. He loved you very much."

"I wish I had known him."

"Maybe by being around his things and his friends you'll have a better understanding of him. He was a good man, Sarah."

Sarah sat down on the sofa and patted the cushion beside her. Wes joined her.

"What am I going to do about the saloon? I don't know anything about telling people what to do. The place is filthy. I know if it was up to me I'd take a broom, a new broom—" she laughed—"and a bucket of water with strong soap, and clean the place from top to bottom."

"It is up to you, Sarah. You can do whatever you want, as long as the saloon stays open and makes a profit."

Sarah rolled her eyes and slumped against the sofa. "I assure you, you have more faith in my ability than I do."

"You're James Moore's daughter. I don't believe you've begun to tap the energy and drive that's inside you."

"I hope you're right."

"Can I be perfectly frank?"

"You mean you haven't been so far?" Again a smile wreathed her face.

"For starters, you need to feel good about yourself. All of your life you've obeyed your mother and grandparents, then your husband. Now you're on your own. Take charge and believe in yourself, and everything else will come easier. In the meantime, a little self-indulgence and a new wardrobe would do wonders for your self-confidence."

"But I could never dress like Collie and Belle."

"You don't have to dress like the girls. How do you want to present yourself?"

"I don't know. You must remember I'm in mourning and must dress accordingly."

28

"Who says?"

"But—" she began.

"Sarah, were you faithful to your husband?"

"Of course," she gasped.

"And I'm sure you were obedient?"

"By all means."

"Then you did your duty as a wife, but he's dead. Now you need to get on with your life." Wes lifted her hand and traced the frayed seams of her gloves. "Sarah, Sarah, you've a wonderful opportunity ahead of you. Don't ruin it by clinging to the past. It tires me to see you constantly dressed in cheap black garments, your hair worn in a style befitting someone three times your age. Your face and hands are rough; you've cut your nails to the quick. Spoil yourself a little. You can afford it."

"Wes, I don't know the first thing about nice clothing. And I've never been spoiled."

"You should have been," he answered bitterly, thinking of her coldhearted grandfather. "We have a wonderful dressmaker here in Hazard, Ida Flowers. Won't you please stop by and see her?"

"Yes, as soon as I get things in order here."

Wes rose and smiled down at her. "I'll go so you can get some rest. But, please keep in mind the things I've said. You've got your work cut out for you, and anything you can do to make the adjustment easier will make you stronger in the long run."

"Thank you, Wes, and please don't give up on me."

"You'll do fine. Rest now, and I'll send Gunter up with your supper later."

As Wes opened the door, a red-faced boy was standing there, his hand poised to knock. At his feet sat Sarah's carpetbag, and in his other hand was the cage bearing a squalling Mr. Herman.

"Thank God," the youth mumbled, shoving the cage into Wes's hand. "I haven't heard such caterwauling since Mrs. Long's old tom got his tail caught under the rocker. I tell ya, this is a very unhappy puss, and I'm proud to get him off my hands."

"Oh, Mr. Herman, I'd forgotten all about you," Sarah said, taking the cage from Wes and releasing the hinge. Mr. Herman darted out and eyed Sarah momentarily, then proceeded to make himself at home.

Later, when Sarah entered the bedroom, Mr. Herman was in the middle of the bed meticulously grooming his rumpled coat. She sat before the mirror and unpinned her hair, pulling her fingers through its length until it unfurled around her shoulders. Taking her time, she eyed her dingy hair and her dry complexion. Wes was right; she was a mess. What was she supposed to do? She didn't know anything about creams and ointments. The only luxury she'd known was a heavenly scented bar of soap Irene Bishop had given her for her last birthday. She used it only on special occasions. The Reverend Mullins called such luxuries tools of the devil. Oh well, she was too tired to think about that now. Tomorrow she would figure out what to do. After opening the window, in case Mr. Herman needed to go out, she stripped down to her mended drawers and chemise, and climbed into bed. The cool crisp sheets felt wonderful. She pulled Mr. Herman next to her and scratched his ears.

"I declare, Mr. Herman, going to bed in broad daylight . . . why, I'd think we'd died and gone to heaven if I didn't know what faced me downstairs."

Mr. Herman purred contentedly.

Sarah lay with excitement roiling through her, thinking of all the things she'd experienced in such a short span. The wonderful travel—she'd seen things she'd only dreamed about. The town of Hazard looked prosperous, the people friendly. She'd already made some friends. The gunfight had unnerved her, yet everyone seemed to accept such things as common occurrences. On a lighter note, she thought she'd handled herself very well after being tumbled into the dusty street in front of half the people of Hazard.

The rigorous journey had taken its toll. As she gave thanks for all her blessings, she drifted off to sleep. She slept deeply and didn't hear Gunter knock when he brought her supper. Nor did she hear the fight that broke out in the saloon about midnight. Somewhere just at the break of dawn, a rooster crowed proudly. Sarah heard this and stumbled to her feet, dreading the backbreaking job of weeding the cemetery. Only when her feet hit the soft carpet did she remember where she was.

She dressed quickly and hurried from her room. As she slipped down the stairs, all was quiet. The place smelled of stale smoke and whiskey. As she moved about the room deciding the best course of action, she noticed someone had covered the canvasses. With a quick look around the room to make sure she was absolutely alone, she approached one of the paintings. With a trembling hand, she lifted the sheet draping the lady. In due time, she'd faced each nude rendering. The lady with the brassplate identifying her as Katy was the most beautiful and the more daring. Sarah's eyes fastened on the voluptuous breasts. She stared at the large dark nipples in fascination, wondering if the woman was a figment of some artist's imagination, or if she truly had existed. Her eyes scaled the length of the reclined figure where only a narrow swatch of sheer fabric covered her privates. She couldn't understand why the artist had even bothered to cover her; why, one could see straight through the material.

With a fiery blush staining her cheeks, she pondered the ladies at her leisure, deciding quickly she had nothing to fear from the garish displays.

She began rolling up her sleeves. To the covered paintings, she said, "Okay, ladies — and I use the term loosely — this place looks like a pigsty and smells just about as bad. I might not know about men or the pleasure of their drink, but I do know about clean. And this place is as far from clean as I've ever seen."

"Mornin', Mrs. Hogan," came a gravelly voice behind her.

Sarah turned and saw Billy Ward standing in the back doorway with his broom. "Good morning, Mr. Ward," she said grimly. With the patch over one eye and the bushy beard, he reminded her of a pirate. She wished she had the nerve to ask him to shave off the beard or at least tidy it up a bit. "I'm glad to see you." She was about to make a comment concerning his cleaning procedure, but waited, watching as his eye darted from one covered painting to another.

Shaking his head and clucking his tongue, Billy said, "Sidewinder Sam ain't gonna like this, no sir, he ain't."

"Sidewinder Sam? Who's he?"

"A gunslinger. At least, he was, until someone blowed off his trigger finger."

Sarah's eyes shot open. "A gunslinger?"

Seeing Sarah's pale face, he added quickly, "Oh, he don't bother anybody unless you rile him. He comes to the Do Drop In just to see Katy."

"The woman in the painting?" Sarah asked, lifting her hand toward the covered canvas.

Billy nodded. "Sam orders a bottle and moons over Katy, saying she was his woman at one time. 'Course, we don't know if there's any truth to it, but you don't argue with Sam. He has a mean temper. Yessiree, when he sees her covered up, no tellin' what he might do."

"Does he come here often?" Sarah asked worriedly.

"He's a drifter. Sometimes weeks go by and we don't see him."

For a moment Sarah studied the draped painting. "Well, I certainly don't want to cause problems. We could uncover Katy, and when I have time, I'll replace the other paintings with some pretty landscape scenes. That should please everyone."

She heard Billy groan behind her, and turned around.

"We're a saloon, ma'am, not a minister's parlor. Before we know it, you'll be puttin' vases of flowers on the tables and servin' tea and cookies."

His remark brought her up short. "Mr. Ward, I was planning no such thing. Give me time to adjust."

Billy hitched up his pants and ambled toward her. Stopping in front of her, he rested his weight on the handle of the broom. "Just a word of advice, ma'am. Don't take too long adjustin', or someone'll open a new saloon and run us out of business."

Drawing in a deep breath, she sighed. "Then by all means, Mr. Ward, please uncover Katy."

"Thank you, ma'am," he said, a grin breaking through his beard. "I'll get the ladder."

Sarah pushed the tables into a corner and stacked the chairs on them while Billy removed the sheet.

After he finished the chore, he stepped back proudly and perused the painting.

"Billy, will you go to the store and get a couple of new brooms? I fear yours has seen better days."

After Billy left, she opened the front doors and swung them wide, then propped open the batwing doors until the fresh morning air filled the room.

She discovered a room in the back with a small four-eye stove and a water closet. She put kindling in the stove and lit it, then put coffee on to boil and an extra pan of water for her cleaning. While she waited for the water to heat, she prowled until she had an armful of cleaning rags and soap. From sheer habit, she knotted a towel around her waist to protect the front of her dress. For an instant, she wondered why she was protecting her threadbare dress. After a quick cup of coffee, she carried her cleaning supplies into the saloon. Kicking off her shoes and balancing herself on a chair, she began washing the grime from the beautiful mirror, humming softly while she worked.

Chapter Four

Coleman Blade stood in the doorway and watched the woman stretch to reach the top of the mirror. His eyes gleamed in appreciation as her breasts pressed against the glass. Her apron had shifted until the knot rode her hip like a holster. But it wasn't a holster Cole had in mind as he watched the fabric slide across her slim hip. When she stretched just so, a length of bare leg caught his attention. He'd never dreamed watching someone clean a mirror could be so stirring. He shifted restlessly.

Sarah leaned to one side to examine the mirror. The reflection of a man standing in the doorway startled her and she lost her balance. She grabbed for support as her fingers swept down the cool clean glass. Before she hit the floor, strong arms caught her. Trembling from the near disaster, she rested her head against the wide chest until her heart slowed its frightful pounding. When she lifted her head, it was to encounter the most beautiful man she'd ever seen. Her breath caught in her chest, and her tongue stilled in her mouth. Eyes the color of a stormy day examined her with concern.

"You okay?" the beautiful mouth said.

She could only nod dumbly.

"You're sure?"

Again she nodded. His teeth were sparkling white and as even as a picket fence.

He sat her on her feet and looked her up and down. She

looked like a ragamuffin. Her hair was plastered against her head and a few loosened strands clung like flypaper to her neck. Her complexion was sunbrowned like that of a field hand, and the wire-framed glasses she wore rested almost on the tip of her dirt-smudged nose. Her high-neck dress was stained with dust and grime and spotted in places with water. The towel apron hugging her waist was dingy and lopsided. The hands she held primly before her were rough and red. And to beat it all, she was barefooted, her naked toes peeking at him from beneath her skirt. She bore his scrutiny in silence; the only indication of nervousness was the rubbing of one bare foot atop the other. This couldn't be James Moore's daughter, the sparkling beauty he'd heard James speak of so often. There had to be some mistake. He was tempted to swing her around to make sure she was the same female he'd been admiring from the backside.

But no, the curves were there amidst the folds of drab fabric. Had James told him she was a widow? Or was it old maid? Hell, it didn't matter. She would fit either mold. Probably has a house full of cats to boot, he thought disgustedly.

Cole wasn't the only one doing some powerful scrutinizing.

Sarah looked her fill, from the top of his black hat down the strong chiseled lines of his jaws. His thickly lashed eyes were a storm gray. A slim nose and perfectly carved lips decorated his sunbronzed face. She shifted her weight and sighed deeply, wishing she could melt into a puddle on the floor. She wondered what Beautiful was thinking. Did the pounding of her heart echo in the room, or was it only her imagination? She lifted her hand and pushed her glasses upon her nose, and immediately squinted. At last, she worked up the courage to smile.

She stepped back. "Thank you. If you hadn't caught me, I'm sure I would've broken something."

"It's my fault that you lost your balance. I startled you. I'm not used to seeing any signs of life around here for several more hours. I was curious when I saw the doors standing open."

His voice was smooth and flowed over her like cool spring water.

"I'm Sarah Beth Hogan, James Moore's daughter," she informed, whipping out her hand, barely missing the buckle on his gunbelt.

"Cole Blade, ma'am."

When Beautiful took her red, chapped hand into his, she thought a whole passel of butterflies were trying to take flight in her stomach.

Oh god, it's true. She is his daughter, he thought, groaning inwardly as she squinted up at him. She had a nice smile, and when she wasn't squinting, her eyes were large and a brilliant green. But two redeeming qualities couldn't possibly compensate for her overall appearance. Be kind, he warned himself. James had been a friend. The least he could do was befriend his plain daughter.

"Cole Blade," she repeated. She shifted her gaze to the leather vest he wore and the badge attached there. Lifting her hand to her cheek, she felt the impression where the badge had rested against her face. "You're the sheriff?"

"Yes, ma'am."

She snapped to attention like a drill sergeant. "You're the sheriff!"

"Yes, ma'am, I thought we'd already decided that." He wondered if she might have a hearing problem in addition to not being able to see.

"No, no . . . you're the man who was in the gunfight."

"Which one?"

"You mean there's been more than one?"

"I'm afraid so, ma'am."

"Yesterday when I arrived there was a gunfight taking place in the middle of town."

"Yes, that was me.

"You—you m-mean it d-do-esn't . . . bother you?"

"Should it?" Did she also have a stuttering problem? She couldn't say half a dozen words without repeating herself.

36

"What about the golden rule: 'Do unto others as you would have them do unto you'?"

"I did, only I did it first. He meant to kill me, not that I wanted him to, but he had his heart set on it. I was only defending myself."

"Oh."

"Morning Sheriff . . . Sarah," Belle and Collie called as they entered the saloon.

"We brought you some breakfast, Sarah."

"Thank you."

"We've come to help you clean. My, but you've been busy," Collie added, noticing the chairs stacked atop the tables and the partially cleaned mirror.

Sarah smiled softly. "Thank you, but it really isn't necessary. Billy can help. I've sent him after some new brooms. I'm sure you all need to sleep after staying up half the night."

"We don't need much sleep," Belle lied, knowing they would be dragging their feet by late afternoon when the crowd spilled into the saloon.

Sarah watched as the girls talked and laughed with the sheriff, their manner light and casual. How Sarah wished for the self-confidence to speak so carefree and teasingly with a man. Her grandfather had insisted she speak only when addressed to speak. Not even her late husband had encouraged frivolous conversation. Orie Wheeler was the only person of the male sex she'd ever been completely comfortable talking with. And only because he'd teased and battered her until she had no choice. She'd asked him a thousand questions and had listened raptly as he patiently answered her. Some of his answers had sharply conflicted with those of her grandfather and her late husband. Instead of relieving her mind, his answers had only confused her.

"Hey, what's this? Who uncovered Katy?" Belle called, interrupting Sarah's thoughts. "Collie and I stayed after closing and covered them. We thought you might feel more comfortable."

"That was very thoughtful, but Mr. Ward told me a gunslinger by the name of Sidewinder Sam might cause problems if he sees that particular painting covered."

"Sidewinder Sam!" they exclaimed in unison.

"Are you thinkin' what I'm thinkin'?" Collie asked Belle with a suspicious gleam in her eyes.

"Yep, sure am," Belle replied laughingly.

"There is no Sidewinder Sam, Sarah."

"But Mr. Ward said this gunslinger was in love with Katy at one time, and that—"

"Forget what Billy said. Your father had that painting delivered here just a few weeks before he . . . he—" she cleared her throat—"before he died. He called her Katy, and some say he might have even known her at one time or another. He never said, and we never asked."

"Billy just made up this tale to scare you into uncovering it," Collie said. "If anyone's in love with Katy, it's him. We catch him staring at her all the time."

"Yeah, that Billy's a strange one," Belle added. "He showed up here shortly after your father's death and asked for a job. Mr. Norman hired him to keep the saloon clean and relieve Gunter from time to time. No one knows where Billy came from, and he hasn't offered any information about himself."

"Well," Sarah said, miffed, "the very nerve of him scaring me like that. I've a mind to cover her out of sheer meanness."

Three pairs of eyes gazed conspiringly from one to the other and wicked grins broke across their faces.

"I'll get the ladder," Collie offered.

"He needs more than a lesson in housecleaning, and I'm going to teach him."

Collie returned with the ladder and propped it against the wall. "Well, shall we?" Sarah asked, picking up the sheet and climbing the ladder.

Leaning against the end of the bar, Cole watched the girls with a broad smile. He scanned the length of the painting, then shifted his gaze to Sarah.

"May I make a suggestion, Mrs. Hogan?"

Sarah liked the sound of his deep, husky voice. "Of course, Sheriff."

"Put a fig leaf over her."

Belle replied laughingly, "I doubt we can find fig leaves in Hazard, Sheriff."

"Besides," Sarah mumbled, "it'd probably take the whole tree."

Belle and Collie giggled.

Cole's laughter rumbled deep in his chest. "You've got a point there."

"Oh, I might as well just uncover them."

"Oh no, you don't," Belle interjected. "It won't hurt the men to live with it this way for a day or two — probably be good for them." She winked, then added, "Us too. Maybe they'll pay more attention to Collie and me. Tips have been lousy lately."

Cole pushed away from the bar. "Well, whatever, it doesn't matter to me what you do." He tipped his hat. "Good day, ladies. I'll leave you to your cleaning. If you need me for anything, I'm just across the street."

"No offense intended, but I hope the sheriff is the last person I need," Sarah intoned.

"I know what you mean. Nice meeting you, ma'am." He nodded his head and tipped his thumb to the brim of his hat.

What a handsome man, Sarah thought as she watched him turn and leave. "Does he come by every morning?" she asked, her eyes still on the swinging door.

Belle and Collie had not missed Sarah's interest in the sheriff. Belle winked at Collie. "When he makes his rounds," Belle offered.

"Oh," she said softly. "Well, let's get to work."

When Billy returned, he immediately noticed the covered painting and cast Sarah a sour look. In turn, she wrote out the duties she expected him to complete each night after closing and handed him the list. "Your chores, Mr. Ward."

"Sorry, I can't read," he announced, handing her back the list.

"Then, I will read them to you." She held the list at arm's length and squinted. By degrees, she moved it closer. Finally, she slid her glasses near the tip of her nose and looked at the paper over the wire frames. "Empty ashtrays and sweep the floor; wipe off the tables and chairs; carry out the trash."

When she finished reading, Billy turned a questioning eye on Sarah. Fingering his beard, he regarded her shrewdly. "You expect me to do this every night after closing, huh?"

She returned his gaze with a look of cool scrutiny. "Yes, I do, Mr. Ward."

After a moment, Billy snorted, "Humph, ain't never took no orders from a woman before."

"Do you have a problem with that?"

"Me? Hell no!"

"Mr. Ward! Watch your language."

Billy picked up the new broom and began sweeping, the dust billowing around him as he grumbled, "Ain't no Katy, ain't no swearin', just a friggin' new broom and more work to do."

Sarah had to turn her back to keep him from seeing the smile that spread across her face.

By working together, they managed to have everything in order an hour before the afternoon crowd began trickling in. Belle and Collie had plenty of time to freshen up and change clothing. Pleased with the way the place looked, Sarah took Gunter aside and asked his advice about talking to the piano player. He agreed totally with her suggestions and asked that she trust his judgment in dealing with Floyd. She happily left it up to him and made herself scarce. She didn't want to face the customers yet.

Sarah pored over her father's books until she had a grasp of the business. Yet, as hard as she worked, she couldn't get her mind off the sheriff. Cole Blade, oh my, what a man. Of all the things she'd seen, why was his image clearer than any of the others? How can that be? she wondered, picturing him again as he stood before her. The memory of his strong arms and sparkling smile played havoc with her good intentions.

Chapter Five

"It's time," Sarah said, a shiver of anticipation coursing through her. Turning, she walked to her bedroom and opened the door of the wardrobe. Selecting the best of her black dresses, she laid it on the bed. Mr. Herman napped belly-up within the crevice of the joined pillows, his legs and paws limp, his face turned toward the window. The first time she had seen him sleeping that way, she had thought he'd died, until she rushed to his side and shook him awake, only to receive a disgruntled growl.

After undressing, she donned the dress, her fingers trembling as she buttoned the bodice. All day she had dreaded this moment, but she couldn't put off her responsibility any longer. Tonight she would manage the Do Drop In, and meet the people her father had known for years. Would they accept her?

Standing before the mirror, she viewed herself with a critical eye. Would her hair look better down and gathered at the back with a ribbon, the way Collie had worn hers this morning? Unpinning her hair, she let the mass of dull brown hair fall over her shoulders. Picking up her brush, she drew it through the unruly waves, curlier than usual because of the hot, clammy weather. The more she brushed, the frizzier it became. Giving up, she coiled it into the usual wad at the nape of her neck. Taking off her glasses, she leaned close to the mirror and pinched her cheeks to add color to her pale face. Next, she raked her teeth across her lips, biting them gently to redden them.

There, much better, she thought, slipping her glasses back on her nose.

After rubbing Mr. Herman on his soft belly, Sarah left her room. Only the Power Above could hear the frightened words that half rose to her lips as she gazed over the balcony at the raucous crowd celebrating beneath her.

Belle saw Sarah at the top of the stairs first, and then Collie. One pair of eyes followed another, each wondering what held the other's attention. Little by little, the din diminished as the boisterous chattering stilled, dealers stopped shuffling the cards, and the music ended in the middle of a song. Everyone suddenly stared up at her, waiting. Her muscles suddenly went limp; she clutched the banister to support herself. Trying to gather her composure, she took a deep breath, almost coughing as a thick cloud of tobacco smoke filled her lungs. After exhaling slowly, her mouth slightly trembled as she smiled down on the crowd.

Squinting, she scanned the room of unfamiliar upturned faces until she settled on the man at the foot of the stairway. Her heart stampeded as her green eyes met a pair of steel-gray eyes. Cole Blade leaned casually against the end of the bar, his long, muscled legs crossed at his ankles. A mocking smile curled one corner of his mouth and one black brow arched inquisitively as he studied her with keen curiosity. Was it a challenge she read in their dark depths? He thinks I'm a coward, she thought, licking her suddenly dry lips. Well, I'm not, her inner voice countered. Drawing from his strength, she focused her attention on Cole's silent encouragement. Squaring her shoulders, she lifted her skirt and, with hard-won grace, began descending the stairway.

As she neared the foot of the steps, the hem of her skirt caught on the toe of her shoe, tripping her. Her arm flailed the air as she tried to grab the banister, hitting the rim of her glasses and sending them sailing from her head.

Gripping her shoulders, Cole righted her, then gazed down into a red-faced, green-eyed Sarah Hogan. Behind them, roars of laughter shook the rafters. Cole watched her face turn from a deep red to startling white.

43

Swallowing rapidly, she quickly placed her hand over her mouth and spoke through her fingers. "I've . . . I've got . . . to get out of here. I'm . . . I'm going . . . to be sick."

"Like hell you are," he countered with a whisper, lightly squeezing her shoulders. "Turn tail now, and you'll never be able to face them. Get a hold of yourself, Mrs. Hogan," he ordered.

Panting with fright, she took a deep breath to calm herself, and stiffened her back.

Cole watched her with tender regard. What a hellacious chore she had before her. As she steadied herself he could see the strength flowing into her, and for the first time, she reminded him of James Moore. Stubborn to a fault. He could see the fire leaping in her eyes and suddenly he knew she could handle any situation.

"Where are my glasses? I need them."

He looked down at her, laughing a little. "Maybe you don't need them as badly as you think. You haven't squinted once since they came off."

"But I have to have them," she pleaded.

"Do you know what I think?"

She looked around his wide shoulders at the people. The room had quieted; everyone seemed to be waiting expectantly. "I don't have time for you to tell me what you think. Everyone's watching us."

"How would you know, if you can't see them?" he taunted. "I think you wear glasses to hide behind, Mrs. Hogan."

"I do not," she hissed.

"Prove it. You have such nice big green eyes. Don't hide them behind those hideous spectacles." Until now, he hadn't noticed the golden highlights that tipped her long dark lashes.

Sarah swallowed deeply. "Oh, all right, I'll welcome my customers without them. Now, are you satisfied?"

"Very," he answered with a crooked grin.

A hush filled the room when Cole repositioned himself at the bar. Sarah glanced quickly over at him and he nodded. She hesitated, then slowly turned her head toward the sea of faces. She could see every face clearly, but, merciful heavens, she wished she couldn't. She laced her hands in front of her skirt and tried to recall the speech she had rehearsed time and again. All she could remember was the first line.

"G-g-ood—" As she spoke, her voice choked up as though a wad of cotton were in her throat. She licked her dry lips, swallowed, and tried again. "Good evening, welcome to the Do Drop In."

Belle and Collie nodded and gave her smiles of encouragement.

"In case you don't know, I'm Sarah Beth Hogan, James Moore's daughter. Though I never knew my father, I understand he was one of the first citizens here in Hazard and helped develop the community. Those are hard shoes for anyone to fill. For some strange reason, he wanted me to try to fill them, and I intend to give it my best." She laughed uneasily, and looked at Cole for support. Unconcerned, he struck a match on the sole of his boot and touched the flame to his cigarette, drawing deeply.

Facing the men again, she saw the doubtful expressions on their faces as they looked from one to the other. She could understand their reluctance to accept her.

"I realize more strongly than any of you that I don't exactly have glowing qualifications for a saloonkeeper."

Murmurs swept through the room until suddenly it quieted, and she saw their smiling faces. "I promise you, you are no less shocked now than I was when Mr. Norman read me my father's will. At any rate, I am here, and will do the best job I can. We have a fine staff here, and with their help, I know the saloon will run as smoothly as it always has. I'm only asking you to give me a chance." She drew a deep breath, then sighed. "That's all I have to say, so please go ahead and enjoy yourselves."

Shock and disbelief coursed through her when they began clapping and cheering. Sarah beamed. They were accepting her; they would wade through her inexperience with her.

As the familiar sounds picked up again, Belle and Collie came forward, each taking one of her hands and gently squeezing it, noticing her damp palms. "You did real good, Sarah."

"I've never been so nervous in my life."

"Don't worry, we're behind you all the way," Collie said. "Everyone is."

"You bet," Belle agreed, giving her hand a warm little squeeze before releasing it. "We'd better get back to work, Collie. The men want their drinks."

Sarah turned toward Cole, her heart sinking when she saw he had left. Then suddenly she remembered her glasses. Where were they? What if someone had stepped on them? She asked Gunter if he had seen them. He hadn't. As they searched the area around the bar, a guffaw of laughter burst from several men at a nearby table.

Then suddenly silence hung in the room as Sarah watched a man walking her way. Coming to a halt in front of her, he offered her a drink, filled with amber liquid.

Her heart tripped several beats. "I . . . I don't drink, but . . . thank you."

He threw back his head and laughed—as did everyone else in the room. "I ain't offerin' you no drink, Mrs. Hogan." He held his glass beneath her eyes. "Just lookee thar."

Frowning, Sarah looked down inside it and saw her glasses. She felt her face burning in embarrassment. "Oh my goodness!"

"Now, ma' am, I'll admit I've had too much to drink a time or two and seen double, but I ain't never had it starin' back at me."

Again laughter erupted in the room. Suddenly her shoulders started shaking, and with a good-natured grin, she joined them in laughter.

Removing her glasses from his drink, she held them out from her, letting the whiskey drip to the floor. "I think you need a new drink, Mr. . . ."

"Simpson, Gil Simpson, ma'am."

"Gunter?" she called over her shoulder, "fix Mr. Simpson

46

another drink, would you please?"

"Sure thing, Mrs. Hogan."

"Thank you, ma'am," Mr. Simpson replied as he went to the bar to replace his drink.

Sarah cleaned her glasses and, feeling a spark of confidence, slipped them into a pocket on her dress. Next, she helped the girls by carrying a tray of drinks to one of the tables. On her way back to the bar, she saw Cole and Wes sitting at a table near the front door. She felt a tremor of happiness surge through her, vaguely wondering why she should feel so pleased that Cole had not left. She made her way toward their table, noticing Cole watching her as he crushed his cigarette in the ashtray.

Wes slid back his chair and politely rose from his seat to greet her. "Good evening, Sarah. Won't you join us?"

Her eyes were riveted on Cole. "If I won't be intruding."

"Intruding? Of course not," Wes said, seating her across from Cole and then taking his own seat. "Cole tells me you delivered quite a speech tonight. Sorry I wasn't here."

"Yes, you missed my grand entrance, too." She gave Cole her most charming smile. "I never thanked you." She lowered her head demurely and laughed embarrassed. "That's the second time you've saved me."

He shrugged his broad shoulders indifferently. "Forget it. I'll just put *Rescue Widow Woman* on my list of expected duties to perform each day."

Sarah stared at him, speechless, trying to decide if he was teasing her or insulting her. When he didn't smile, she took it as the latter and became angry. The cords in her neck and temple stood out and worked convulsively. Before she could think of a retort, he slid back his chair and stood up.

"If you two will excuse me, I need to get back to the jail and relieve Johnny." He glanced down at Sarah's fuming face. "See you tomorrow, widow woman," he said with a wink.

Her eyes shot through him like red-hot arrows. Chuckling softly, he pushed through the swinging door and left, a teasing smile on his handsome face.

47

"Did you hear what he called me?" her voice shrieked.

Wes reached over, placing his hand on her clenched fist. "Now, Sarah, he was only teasing you."

With a stubborn thrust of her chin, she announced, "I don't like him calling me Widow Woman."

Wes's shaggy eyebrow lifted askance. "You are a widow, and you are a woman, aren't you?"

"Yes, but when *he* puts the two words together, it sounds vulgar."

Wes's shoulders shook in laughter. "Vulgar? I've heard women called worse than that."

"Humph," Sarah snorted, putting an end to that particular subject.

An argument broke out between two men at a gaming table nearby. Sarah jerked around in her chair, her eyes widening with fear as the men stood facing one another from across the table. She noticed both were armed with guns, yet neither indicated they planned to use them.

"You lyin', cheatin' son of a bitch!"

Sarah flinched.

"Damn it to hell, Chet," the other man drawled drunkenly, "watch yore mouth. Yo're in a 'spectable place now."

"Then, let's step outside where it ain't," the other man demanded, placing one hand on the hilt of his six-shooter.

"Oh heavens no," Sarah wailed, clutching her throat. Leaning toward Wes, she whispered frantically, "Go get Sheriff Blade."

"No need to, Sarah. They're brothers."

"So what? Remember what Cain did to his brother, Abel?" she screeched in alarm.

"They do this all the time, don't worry."

Digging in her pocket, she retrieved her glasses and put them on her nose. Sliding back her chair, she announced, "Well, if you won't go, then I will!"

"Wait a minute," Wes shouted, too late.

Sarah was out the door and running toward the jail. *My first night and this happens,* she thought, panic-stricken.

Chapter Six

Cole propped his chair against the wall and crossed his booted feet atop the desk. Pulling his knife from the sheath at his waist, he worked the gleaming blade over the whetstone with quick, skillful movements. Well, the widow woman had pulled off her introduction, and she a minister's wife, no less. Why it came as a surprise, he didn't know. But when Wes told him she was the widow of a preacher, it had taken him back. How the devil must be laughing now, he thought, his upper lip curved up ironically. It had taken a hell of a lot of courage for a woman of her background to speak before what she considered a room full of sinners. What really impressed him had been her honesty.

Cole leaned forward, setting the whetstone on the desk. Settling back once again in his chair, he raked his thumb lightly against the sharp edge of the blade, testing its sharpness. He glanced at the cell across from him. He knew his prisoner was feigning sleep. Sooner or later, his brothers would try to break him out.

Unexpectedly, the door swung open, and a hint of black sleeve caught his eye. With an incredibly swift movement, he hurled the knife, nailing the sleeve to the doorjamb.

From the corner of his eye, he saw his prisoner leap from his cot. "I told you they'd come."

"Let 'em," Cole said in a deadly voice, whipping his gun from its holster. Directing the Colt .45 toward the partially opened door, his eyes fastened on the black sleeve. They sure were taking their good sweet time, he thought restlessly.

Lowering the chair to the floor, he slowly slid it back, and rose. Moving cautiously across the room, he stopped behind the door and peered around it. Expecting to see one or both of the brothers, surprise flooded his face when he saw the black-clad figure of Sarah Hogan.

"Hell!" Cole swore, slipping his gun into his holster. He'd obviously scared the hell out of her. She'd fainted. Just what had she been thinking, barging in here like that? Only her back and buttocks touched the doorjamb, her legs stretching out before her. His eyes traveled back up her body. Her head drooped forward, and behind it a long length of wavy, tangled hair climbed the frame, the small knot at the end of it snagged on a projecting nail. This, plus his blade anchoring her sleeve, had kept her from sliding completely to the floor.

Suddenly, concern marked his face. Had he cut her? Working the hilt of his blade from her sleeve, he caught her limp figure. After unwinding her hair from the snag, he lowered her to the floor. Ripping the fabric from her arm, he saw a thin trail of blood oozing from a tiny wound. Thank God, he'd only nicked her. Using a piece of her sleeve, he wiped away the blood, then bandaged her arm with the fabric.

"Hey, what's going on?" came the prisoner's voice.

"Nothing that concerns you," Cole countered. "Shut up and go to sleep."

Glancing down at Sarah's face, he noticed her eyeglasses missing. Had she taken his advice? Brushing her hair from her forehead, he studied her pale face, noting the tiny wrinkle etching the center of her eyebrows. Cole thought her squinting had probably caused it. Her even white teeth showed through delicately parted rosebud lips. Strange thoughts ran through his mind. Had her preacher husband ever kissed her other than an affectionate peck? Had she ever known passion, white-hot and all-consuming? Irritated with the direction of his thoughts, Cole gently patted her face and quietly called her name, trying to wake her.

Wes rushed to the jail and stopped abruptly at Sarah's still figure. "Good god, Cole, what happened?"

"Don't worry, she just fainted. She'll come around in a minute."

Wes knelt beside him and noticed her bandaged arm. "What's wrong with her arm?"

"I nicked her with my knife."

Astounded, Wes exclaimed, "Why, for god's sake, did you do that?"

"She came storming in here and took me by surprise. I thought for sure Mark's brothers were coming after him."

"And they will," Mark Sheramy said from his cell.

"I hope like hell they do," Cole bit back. "Then I'll have all you outlaw bastards behind bars."

A shiver ran through Wes. He had seen Cole's accuracy with his deadly knife on more than one occasion. Yes, Sarah was one lucky woman.

"Maybe I ought to go get Doctor Mason."

"Get him out for something no worse than a pinprick?" Cole slid the fabric aside. "Look, it's not even bleeding now. Why'd she come over here, anyway?"

"Chet and Lance got into it again. She thought they were about to get into a gunfight out front." Seeing Cole roll his eyes, Wes came to her defense. "Cole, don't be so hard on her. Anyone, male or female, would've thought the worse if they didn't know the brothers. You know how those boys carry on when they get liquored up."

At that moment, Sarah groaned, and blinked her eyes.

Wes lifted her chin. A pair of groggy, glazed green eyes stared back at him. "Sarah, you all right?"

"Huh?" she asked dumbly. Suddenly her eyes sprang open in remembrance. She grabbed her wounded arm and squeezed it, sighing with relief when she found it still attached to her shoulder. The last thing she recalled was feeling something pierce her arm and seeing a knife protruding from her sleeve.

51

Shaking her head to clear the cobwebs from her brain, she looked up at Wes, not even noticing Cole on the other side of her. "What happened?"

"Just a little misunderstanding, Widow Woman, that's all," Cole growled.

Widow Woman! Fire leaped in her eyes. She whipped her head toward Cole, and raising up on an elbow she hissed between clenched teeth, "Don't call me that, you cad, you . . . you . . ." Unskilled in the art of name-calling, she let her sentence hang.

Surprise flashed across Cole's face. How strange, he mused, the lady has a temper.

He grinned, which only increased her incense. She wished for the nerve to slap that cocksure smirk from his face. "Did you do this to me?" she asked, pointing to her arm.

He nodded. "Yeah, I did."

"Is this how you greet all your visitors, Mr. Blade, or do you have some particular dislike for me?"

"Mrs. Hogan, I don't dislike *you,* I dislike the way you stormed in here. Next time, knock before entering," he returned coolly.

"Knock on the jail's door? Why, this is a place of business."

"Well, at this place of business, you knock. You knock and state your name loud and clear." Cole got to his feet and directed a backward thumb over his shoulder toward the cell. "You see that man in there?"

Sarah leaned forward and peered around him. A prisoner gripped the iron bars, a leering grin on his face. "Ah . . . yes, I see him."

"He killed a man last week in cold blood. He has two brothers as mean as he is. And I'll guaran-damn-tee you, they won't knock when they decide to save his ass."

Sarah's mouth dropped open and she sucked in her breath. Cole didn't know if it was his language she found offensive or the danger he implied that caused the reaction. He didn't care.

52

"Now, do you understand?" he asked gruffly.

She nodded slowly, giving him a look of cold scrutiny before she turned her attention to Wes. "Did the brothers solve their differences? I never heard any gunshots."

"Everything's fine, Sarah. I tried to tell you it would be."

"I know. Perhaps I reacted too quickly, but it frightened me." A frown suddenly knitted her brow. "I've lost my glasses again. Do you have them, Sheriff?" she asked accusingly.

"No, Mrs. Hogan, I don't."

"Well, they have to be here somewhere." She glanced around the floor. As she moved, she felt something beneath her buttocks. Leaning to the side, she pulled her glasses from beneath her. "Oh no, I've crushed my lenses. They're my only pair."

Sarah didn't see the pleased expressions on the men's faces.

"Is there an eye doctor here in Hazard?"

"No, I'm sorry, but you can mail-order another pair," Wes suggested.

"But that could take weeks," Sarah said with a groan. She glared up at the sheriff. "This is all your fault. If you hadn't scared me to death, this wouldn't have happened."

"You should feel lucky you only lost your glasses," Cole returned.

Ignoring him, she asked Wes, "Will you walk with me back to the saloon?"

"Of course," Wes said, helping her to her feet.

When Sarah stood up, her wealth of unbound hair fell in wild, unruly waves down her back, beyond her waist. Cole thought the weight of it might topple her backward. Never had he seen that much hair on one person. He saw Wes staring at her with that same expression of fascination.

After Sarah smoothed the wrinkles from her dress, she looked up and caught both men staring at her. "Is—is something wrong?"

"I . . . uh . . . think you lost your hairpins," Wes floundered.

Her hand flew to the back of her head. She felt like crying when she didn't find the familiar knot. Oh, how horrible she must look. Digging around in the thick mass, she found several pins buried in it. With the same skilled quickness that Cole had with his knife, Sarah gathered her heavy hair and, pulling it tightly back from her face, wound it into a thick coil and pinned it.

She smiled weakly, her face red with embarrassment. In sheer despair of anything to say, Sarah adjusted her torn sleeve. She studied the tiny wound now encrusted with blood. Her heart tripped several beats, her humiliation forgotten. If he had aimed a few inches more to the right, the blade would have surely pierced her heart. She glanced over at Cole and said icily, "From now on, Sheriff, I'll find a way to handle my problems and won't bother you."

"Mrs. Hogan, I'm here to help. That's my job."

With an unladylike snort, she turned to Wes. "Shall we go?"

Wes laced her arm through his. "Of course," he said, and bid Cole good-night.

Cole leaned against the doorjamb and passed a hot, restless hand through his thick black hair and over his forehead. "Damn, what a night."

The light from the saloon silhouetted Sarah's shapely figure as she and Wes crossed the street. Cole watched her hips swaying gently beneath her rusty black dress, a dress she had washed and mended so many times the sleeve had fallen apart like paper when he'd torn it from her arm. It had scared the hell out of him when he saw her body wilted on the floor. Thank God, he had only nicked her. Truly, he had to give her credit; she had handled it well. She was more upset with him calling her Widow Woman than she was with having the daylights scared out of her. Maybe the destruction of her gown would force her to buy some decent clothing. God knows she could afford it. James Moore had been a wealthy man. Cole grumbled, wondering when he'd taken such an interest in women's apparel. He doubted Sarah Hogan would look any better in silks and satins than she looked in her drab widow's weeds.

"You a little itchy tonight, Sheriff?" the prisoner asked, interrupting his reverie.

"I'm always itchy, Sheramy."

Sheramy chuckled. "You as fast with that gun as you are with a knife?"

With a deadly gleam in his eyes, Cole said, "It's a shame you'll never know, Sheramy."

"If you're saying they won't come for me, you're wrong—dead wrong, Blade," he stressed coldly.

Pushing away from the doorjamb, Cole closed the door. Walking slowly toward the man's cell, he stopped a foot in front of the bars. "What I'm saying is when they do come, I'll get you first."

Sheramy's face paled, his bravado vanishing like a puff of smoke.

"Now, sleep on that, you son of a bitch," Cole said with a smile that never reached his eyes.

Returning to his desk, Cole kicked back the chair and settled himself in it. Glancing Sheramy's way, he noticed his whitened knuckles as he clenched and unclenched his hands around the bars. The man turned away and paced his cell like a caged animal, looking out the tiny window several times before he finally laid down on his cot.

Sheramy closed his eyes. Suddenly his body tensed as he heard the nerve-racking sound of the sheriff's lethal blade grating slowly back and forth against the stone.

Sarah and Wes stood on the stoop at the back door of the saloon. The night was full of moonshine and the silvery light fell upon Sarah's face.

"Oh my goodness, what an evening. I ought to thank God I survived it. Sheriff Blade almost killed me, Wes."

"If that had been his intention, he would have, Sarah. But he wants to take the Sheramy brothers alive. They're working for someone, and we want to know who. I told you about the murders and robberies that have taken place

55

in the last year. The man Mark Sheramy murdered sense-lessly, George Roberts, had a sizable ranch. He was a good man, never bothered anyone. Mark said George drew his gun first, and he shot him in self-defense. Cole is wound as tightly as a spring right now, waiting for the brothers to try to break out Mark. You couldn't have picked a worse time to go running in there like you did."

"I know you're right, Wes, but he makes me so mad."

Wes chuckled. "I know where you got your temper. You are very much like your father, Sarah."

"I am?" she asked softly.

"Yes." Wes smiled. "I saw the likeness tonight. Your eyes turned a darker shade of green, real stormy looking, like your dad's." He tapped his temple with his forefinger. "And that little vein here pulsed like a mad thing."

"So that's where I got my green eyes," she said, smiling softly. "I've often wondered if I look like him. No one would ever tell me. Was he a handsome man?"

Wes laughed pleasantly. "Perhaps you ought to be asking a woman that question, because he certainly had a way with them. He was tall man, at least six foot two, lean, but not rail-thin. Before his hair turned gray, it was reddish-brown and curly."

"Like mine?"

Remembering her wild, unmanageable mane of hair, he cleared his throat. "The color's close to the same, I'd say, and he had plenty of it, but . . ." he hesitated.

"I know what you're thinking, Wes. It's a frightful mess, isn't it?" she asked with a sigh of despair.

Not wanting to hurt her feelings, he lied, "No, you just have more than your fair share of it. But tell me, Sarah, whose idea was it that you needed eyeglasses?"

"My grandfather. He said he saw me squinting at the preacher during the sermon. I argued with him that he must have been mistaken, because I could see just fine. He insisted I wear them anytime I went out of the house."

"That figures," Wes said, a shadow of a frown creasing his forehead. "Are you seeing all right without them now?" he asked suspiciously.

"I guess. It's just that I feel lost without them. But they do give me dreadful headaches if I read with them."

A sudden light kindled in Wes's eyes. He gazed at her features closely. Her face gleamed as white as marble in the moonlight. Not only did she have her father's hair and eyes, in profile she looked very much like him — a slight upward tilt on the tip of her high well-molded nose, a full lower lip, and a firm, decisive chin. No doubt, her grandparents also had seen the likeness and had tried to hide the evidence by making her wear her hair in this ungodly fashion and convincing her she needed glasses. He also suspected they wanted no one to look at her twice. When it came time for her to marry, they wanted to choose her mate for her . . . and they had.

He had seen Sarah's mother a short moment before their departure. James had said she was a beautiful woman. And she was still attractive in a remote way, but she had the stern, cold features of her parents. Thank God, James had seen to his daughter's welfare. Wes wasn't much for prayer, but he did pray they weren't too late to help Sarah.

"It's quite late, Sarah, and I know you must be exhausted. Why don't you go on to bed and let Gunter take care of things?"

"I will. My sleeve's torn, anyway, and I'd have to change. Oh, by the way, first thing in the morning I'm going to Mrs. Flowers's dress shop."

Wes smiled. "Good, I'm sure you will like her work. A lot of women in town use her."

"Thank you for talking with me. I really feel better."

"I'm glad to help in any way I can. Good night, Sarah."

"Good night, Wes."

Sarah waited on the stoop until Wes disappeared down the alley, then turned and went inside.

After she changed into her nightgown, she extinguished the lamp and climbed into bed, drawing the coverlet over her. Closing her eyes, her thoughts drifted to Cole Blade and a deep emotion stirred within her, so strong it actually startled her with its intensity. Angry, she sat up in bed. At her age and given her recent widowhood, she should not think of perfect happiness in some strong man's love. The chance to realize such hopes was a farfetched dream. And to think, when she thought of such happiness, it was a vision of Sheriff Blade that clouded her mind. How could she think these things about him when he'd called her that insulting vulgar name? Widow Woman, humph, she snorted, lying back down.

She again closed her eyes, but sleep was a long time coming. She was reluctant to give up the night for fear of what tomorrow would bring.

The next morning, Cole was in Wes's office, watching the busy street through the window. Suddenly he straightened and wiped at the dirty pane. Sure enough, it was Sarah. He watched as she disappeared into Mrs. Flowers's shop.

He smiled toward Wes. "The widow woman has just left the saloon and entered the dressmaker's shop. You don't think she's going to shed her widow's weeds, do you?"

Wes frowned at Cole's reference. "Cole, lighten up on her."

Cole grinned mischievously. "Hell, Wes, when she's riled up, she's almost pretty." When he saw Wes's eyebrow shoot up with interest, he added, "I said almost, Wes."

Chuckling, Wes said, "Let's just hope she's taking my advice. Mrs. Flowers will take care of her, I'm sure." Wes paused, and cleared his throat. "Cole, I don't like taking advantage of our friendship, but . . . well . . . I have a favor to ask of you."

"I'm all ears."

"I know your job leaves you very little time that you can call your own, yet I can't help imposing on your good nature. Would you keep an eye on Sarah?"

Cole snorted.

"I know you think she's a royal pain in the ass."

Cole rolled his eyes.

"Hear me out," Wes implored. "Truly, she is a delightful young lady. If you knew how she'd faced an entire church body in defense of a drifter she'd befriended, well, I'm sure you'd have a higher opinion of her."

"I'll admit she has spunk."

Wes paused, a concerned frown knitting his forehead. "I'm really concerned about her. After all, since Dusty Mills has been buying up all this property, the chance is even greater that he'll try to get Sarah's." Wes hesitated. "I really need to tell you something. It's confidential, but the way things are going, you ought to know. Sarah doesn't own the ranch."

"What?"

"It's the truth. James stipulated in his will that Sarah has to run the saloon a year before the rest of her inheritance is turned over to her."

"Now, wouldn't that be an eye opener for Dusty? It couldn't happen to a nicer man," he said sarcastically.

"Let me show you something." He withdrew a sheet of paper from his drawer and spread it on his desk. "I've drawn a map of the route where I think a spur would link Hazard to the rail line. I'd like you to see where the deaths and buy-out of properties have taken place so far."

He ran a finger down the line. "All this belongs to Dusty Mills. Sarah's property and George Robert's estate are right in the middle. If Mark Sheramy killed George on Dusty's orders as we're suspecting, then when George's sister arrives from England to finalize his estate, Dusty will probably approach me and make an offer—that is, if George's sister wishes to sell it. Now, all that's left is Sarah's property."

"Well, one thing's for sure. If Mills shows an interest in her, we'll know he's after her property—her assets are the only thing attractive about her."

"Damn it, Cole . . ." Wes's voice trailed off.

"I'm sorry, Wes, I shouldn't have said that, but damn it all, I came near to killing her last night, and would have if that had been my intention."

"She realizes her mistake now, believe me."

Cole pushed away from the window. "All right, I'll watch over her. That's the least I can do for James. We haven't seen Mills in quite some time. He's probably somewhere else rooking people of their property."

"I wouldn't doubt that for a minute."

"I need to get back to the jail. I don't like leaving Sheramy alone with Johnny."

Chapter Seven

The open doors and windows invited the gentle breeze that caressed the damp faces of the congregation. Sarah Beth Hogan sat up front on the second pew, her beautiful voice raised in song. She knew the words by heart.

When Sarah had entered the church, every head turned, watching her. Lips puckered like dry persimmons and brows shot up like winged birds as the members watched her take a seat.

Sarah didn't fidget or yawn or crane her neck to see who was in church. Instead, she sat quietly listening to the reverend's sermon, soaking up the message. Then the most wonderful thing happened. The Reverend Millard Perry taught of a great love and understanding. No fire and brimstone or damnation, nor was there any reference that women were no more than chattel for men.

She wished her grandfather could have heard the Reverend Perry. Then it hit Sarah like a bolt of lightning. Her grandfather's control over her life had depended on his ability to nurture fear and dark foreboding. Sarah began to look at herself in a different light. She was a woman, fully grown and mature. As Wes had told her, the power to shape her destiny was now in her hands. She was trying, but it was hard with so many changes taking place so quickly.

When the reverend called for donations for new hymnals, Sarah's hand was the first one in the air.

The members greeted her warily when the service was over and they congregated on the grounds. Sarah introduced herself and smiled warmly, never letting a glimmer of recognition show in her eyes when the women in turn introduced themselves and their husbands. At first the men downed their heads or fidgeted with their collars. When they realized Sarah wasn't going to let on that she had seen them in her saloon, they relaxed, and a burgeoning respect was born for the saloonkeeper.

Ida Flowers and Sarah left the church grounds and strolled together along Front Street, discussing the new black gowns Sarah had ordered earlier in the week.

The dressmaker beamed. "Oh, Sarah, let me tell you about this beautiful piece of fabric that arrived yesterday. You would do it proud." Warming to her subject, Ida Flowers's eyes gleamed with enthusiasm and her arms rocked with excitement. "It's a startling emerald, and when you turn it just so, it shimmers like moonlight on a still lake."

"Sounds wonderful," Sarah agreed, becoming caught up in Ida's excitement. "I promise you, the minute my mourning period is up, you can make me a gown from it," she said smiling.

Mrs. Flowers cocked a brow and studied Sarah from head to foot. "Poppycock! May I be perfectly honest with you?"

"Yes, of course," Sarah assured her.

"With your coloring, the dark fabrics you wear give you a washed-out appearance. And I mean no disrespect to your late husband, but wrapping yourself in widow's weeds is absurd. You're young, and unless you intend to spend your life in sackcloth and ashes, you need to plan for your future."

Sarah smiled warmly, not offended in the least. "You remind me of a very good friend I had back home. She said very much the same thing you've said. I'll think about it, all right?"

Mrs. Flowers didn't continue pressuring her, but talked about the other beautiful dresses she had made for various customers. Sarah knew she meant well, as did Wes, but they would just have to understand she couldn't change overnight. It would take time. My goodness, trying to get used to the idea of running a saloon was bad enough.

Suddenly, a flash atop one of the storefronts caught Sarah's attention. She dismissed it for a step or two, then it caught her eye again.

"We may not have access to all the fine fabrics the people in the East do, but I try to keep abreast of current fashion."

Something about the flashing light nagged at Sarah; she couldn't leave it alone. She continued studying the rooftop. When she'd convinced herself it was only an overactive imagination, another flash accompanied by a bobbing head alerted her that indeed something very dangerous was going to happen. Then she remembered the sheriff's warning that the Sheramy brothers would try to break their brother out of jail.

"Mrs. Flowers, I don't mean to frighten you, but I think we should get off the street."

"Why, there's not a soul in sight." Ida quickly glanced up and down the deserted street. "Everyone's having their dinner."

"Not everyone," she said, nodding toward the rooftop. "I'm going for the sheriff."

As Ida watched Sarah rush along the boardwalk, she decided posthaste to take the young woman's advice.

Sarah's heart pounded wildly in her chest as her hand curled around the doorknob of the sheriff's office. Before she pushed the door open, the vision of a knife-trapped arm and the sheriff's hateful words halted her. *Knock and state your name loud and clear.* Removing her hand, she adjusted her gloves and balled her hand into a fist. Once, twice, three times, she rapped her knuckles against the

63

door. "It's Sarah Beth Hogan," she called. This is ridiculous, she thought, lifting her hand once more to the wooden surface.

"Come in," came a distinctly smiling voice.

As Sarah reached for the knob, a shot rang out, splintering the doorjamb.

Her breath left her as she screamed and propelled herself forward on wobbly legs. A hard chest stopped her headlong flight, and strong arms moved around her.

"The Sheramy brothers! I believe they're here," she ground out breathlessly.

"I think you're right," he admitted, kicking the door shut and moving her slowly across the room to lower her into a chair.

"You knew! You mean I risked my life for nothing," she spouted indignantly.

"I am the sheriff, if you'll remember. I'm supposed to know these things." He knelt before her and brushed his fingers across her fisted knuckles. "You were very brave, and I appreciate what you did. I've been expecting the brothers to pull something. What better time than a peaceful Sunday afternoon?"

Sarah's eyes drifted over Cole's shoulder to the cell. The prisoner leered at her with an *I told you so* grin.

Her eyes shifted back to Cole and she clasped his hands. "But—but I'm stuck in here until this is all over." As the shock of her actions registered, she began to tremble.

Cole could feel the tremors that rocked her body, and suddenly wanted to protect her from her fear. When he would have enfolded her in his arms to comfort her, another shot rang out, shattering a window. Gun drawn, he sprang to his feet. Moving behind her, he took a rifle from the rack behind his desk. Flipping the lever open, he checked the chamber. Satisfied, he snapped the lever shut and cautiously approached the window, his feet crunching the broken glass. With a quick glance over his shoulder, he warned, "Don't move."

"I—I won't," she whispered dully.

"Why don't you just let me out and save yourself a lot of trouble, Blade?" the outlaw taunted.

"Don't you know, Sheramy?—trouble is my middle name." Cole answered dryly.

"Is that what you want on your tombstone, Blade?"

Sarah was scared to death, and she was quickly tiring of the prisoner's taunts. Her hands trembled as she clutched the arms of the chair and turned to face the cell. "Shut up, Mr. Sheramy. Can't you see that the sheriff has his hands full without your yammering behind his back?" she shouted.

Cole turned from his position at the window, surprised at Sarah's outburst. Her statement was so ludicrous, he had to bite the inside of his lips to keep from smiling.

There, Sarah thought as the prisoner became quiet. He was really a vile-looking man. His head looked like an orange with hair, and only on the sides. Long greasy strands swept from behind his ears over the shiny pate he tried to cover. His face made up for the hair his head refused to grow. His eyes gleamed at her with biting dislike from beneath bushy brows. A mustache of the same coarse-looking hair snaked beneath his thin nose to blend with a thick beard. She shifted restlessly as the prisoner gripped the bars and raked her body from head to foot.

"Widow woman. Isn't that what I heard the sheriff call you?"

Sarah stiffened and pivoted in the chair, not caring to discuss anything with such a blackguard.

"Yeah, me and the sheriff had a long talk about you the other night after you left."

"Shut up, Sheramy. Leave the lady alone."

"You gonna make me, Sheriff?"

"It's all right, Mr. Blade. I wouldn't believe anything he had to say anyway."

Reluctantly, Cole returned his attention to the street.

He couldn't afford to let the brothers get the upper hand—not with Sarah Hogan now perched in his office like a sparrow awaiting flight. Still, he had to admire her grit. He couldn't think of another female in town who would have risked her safety to warn him of the danger. Yeah, maybe there was more to Sarah Beth Hogan than he'd first thought.

"Ain't you the one what took over the saloon?"

She ignored him.

"Me and the sheriff has got a bet. I bet him you'd be as stiff as a dead trout in bed."

Sarah couldn't control the outraged gasp that slipped from her mouth. Her hand made its way to the collar of her dress and her fingers ringed the inside of the collar like fingers scraping an empty jar of jam.

"Now, the sheriff is of a mind that you'd be a real wildcat beneath the covers."

Her head snapped sharply toward him. "Mr. Sheramy, please."

"That's exactly what I said to him. Please spare me the details. But no, nothing would do him but tell me everything he would do to you if given the opportunity. He said after he got you out of those god-awful clothes—and he would take his own sweet time removing them—he would take down your hair and wrap a long strand around each nipple . . ."

Sarah felt the heat of the blush as it crawled up her neck and stained her cheeks, embarrassed beyond anything she'd ever experienced. She jumped to her feet. "I will not sit here and listen to any more of your disgusting jargon."

"Make you hot, hearing what the sheriff would do?"

Deciding she would put that odious creature in his place if it was the last thing she ever did, she marched toward his cell. Suddenly a volley of gunfire interrupted her course. She dropped to the floor in an unceremonious heap, appalled at her behavior.

After returning the gunfire, Cole turned his attention to a pale-faced Sarah. "Damn it, woman, you have to stay down. I can't watch you every minute and do my job."

"I'm sorry, I'm sorry, I don't know what I was thinking, to let him get to me that way." On all fours, she made her way up behind the sheriff and peered over his shoulder out the window to the deserted street. "Is there anything I can do to help?"

"Yeah, you can get me an extra box of shells. They're in the top drawer of the desk. But please stay down."

"I will." Carefully, she crawled across the floor, her progress slow because her knees kept trapping the tail of her dress, finally ripping it from the waistband in front. *Another dress. I've ruined another dress.* Groaning, she hitched up the tail and moved freely toward the desk, her knees and hands becoming bloodied from pieces of broken glass.

Cole should have had his eyes on the street, but he couldn't resist watching Sarah. She looked like a turtle with a hat on as she crossed the floor slowly but surely. Her bottom, even beneath the drab fabric, was trim and shapely. He heard the fabric tear, and watched as she jerked her skirt from beneath her knees. He'd glimpsed a length of tempting shapely legs and was reminded of the first time he'd seen her. Yet now for some reason she looked different, and she smelled different. When she'd fallen through the door into his arms and then again when she'd crawled up behind him, the gentle fragrance of lavender had teased him.

Another windowpane shattered, spraying glass over Cole. He swore violently and directed his attention once more to his job. Movement on the rooftop directly across the street caught his eye. He adjusted the rifle and watched steadily until the figure bobbed up to fire. Cole pulled the trigger of the rifle and watched as the man fell end over end to the ground.

Sarah had crawled back just behind Cole's shoulder

when he fired. She covered her mouth to keep from crying out.

"One down, one to go, Sheramy."

"Bastard," the prisoner hissed.

Cole took the box of shells from Sarah and began reloading.

"Why are you using a rifle instead of your handgun?"

"Accuracy and range."

"Oh," she said, nodding her head as though she knew exactly what he was talking about.

"I know what it is now," Cole declared, studying her.

"What?" she questioned, adjusting the hat that had become askew in her journeys across the floor.

He tilted her chin, examining her face closely. "I like you without your glasses."

"Yes, well, I've discovered I see better without them."

The creaking of boards sounded through the shattered window like the buzzing of a mosquito on a humid day. Cole patted his finger across Sarah's lips and shook his head.

They heard it clearly, but, as still as they remained, they couldn't figure out from what direction it came. They cocked their ears, listening intently. Cole pulled the gun from his holster and pulled back the hammer.

Mark Sheramy bellowed, "Come on in," and immediately the door burst open and a matched set of Peacemakers sent a hail of gunfire sweeping the room.

Sarah screamed.

Cole squeezed the trigger of his gun, and the intruder was hellbound before he could get the sheriff in his sights.

Sarah watched in a trance as Cole bounded to the dead man's side and eased the guns from the lifeless hands.

Moving from her position beneath the window to the chair she'd earlier occupied, she noticed Mark Sheramy's body sagging against the cell, his limp arms dangling over the bars, holding his body. "Cole," she croaked.

He looked up and she motioned toward the cell. He rushed to the dead man. "My god, I can't believe this. One of his brother's bullets caught him in the chest."

Several of Hazard's businessmen entered the office, slapping Cole on the back and congratulating him for a job well done. Sarah also received praise for her bravery.

She watched as though from afar, as the men examined the matched set of Peacemakers and began a discussion on the merits of various firearms. Someone pulled a wagon in front of the jail and the men took charge of the bodies. In a short time it was all over, and the men departed, leaving her and Cole alone. She looked at the empty cell with its door standing ajar, at the shattered glass sprinkling the floor, the bloodstained boards, and at last she lifted her head to Cole. He was framed in the doorway watching her, his strong arms folded across his chest.

"I'm sorry you had to witness this."

"Me too," she answered quietly. "I can't believe how quickly a life can be taken. In the space of minutes three lives are over. Why?"

"Survival. If the Sheramy brothers hadn't died, we would have. It's as simple as that, whether you approve or not."

"Oh, I know you did the only thing you could. You saved my life, and I'll be eternally grateful. It's just that one minute I'm sitting in church singing "We Would See Jesus," and the next minute I'm dodging bullets. If nothing else, it's quite an adjustment, Mr. Blade, for truly I had not thought to see *Him* today."

A lazy smile lifted the corners of Cole's mouth and his eyes sparkled with humor. "I see."

"So, you understand?" she asked, lifting her hand to push a clinging strand of hair from her face. When she lowered her hand, a streak of blood marred her face.

"You're hurt," Cole announced in surprise, approaching her. As before, he knelt down beside her. He wiped

69

the blood from her face and lifted her hands. Her gloves were damp with blood. "How the hell did you do this?" he muttered, stripping off her gloves.

Ignoring his language, she replied, "When I was crawling across the floor, my hand got in the broken glass. It doesn't hurt, really."

He shifted the chair toward the light and examined her hand. A tiny piece of glass protruded from her finger. He plucked it loose and took her finger into his mouth, sucking gently on the injury.

Sarah forgot the injury, the killings, singing in church, everything—her body centered on the explosion of pleasure spiraling through her. His tongue beat against her finger like a heartbeat and she was ill-pressed to remain upright in her chair.

"Better?" he asked, releasing her hand.

"Much," she whispered, not daring to mention her knees were also bleeding, fearing he might suck on them, too. Then, for sure, she'd melt into a puddle on the floor.

"I'll see you back to the saloon before I make my rounds."

"You're a busy man, Sheriff. Don't you ever get a day off?"

"Yeah, I just didn't want to leave the jail when I thought there would be trouble."

At the mention of the trouble, Sarah remembered Mark Sheramy's disgusting discourse. "Sheriff, it embarrasses me more than you'll ever know, but I must ask. You didn't discuss me with that terrible Mark Sheramy, did you?"

"I wouldn't even discuss the weather with that trash, much less you, Mrs. Hogan."

"Thank you."

They remained silent as they left the jail, each caught up in their own thoughts. Her skirt swished lightly against the leg of Cole's pants, and fleetingly he pondered the possibility of removing the dress and loosening her hair until it tumbled around her naked body. Then he would lift the strands and wrap them slowly around her nipples . . .

And she, against her will, wondered what it would be like to have the handsome sheriff take down her hair, combing his strong fingers through it just before he . . . No, no, she couldn't — wouldn't — let herself think about such things. How in the world could she be walking along Front Street in broad daylight contemplating such physical thoughts with a handsome man she knew nothing about? or with any man, for that matter? She'd had her fill of the intimacies shared between husband and wife, and from her experience, she had nothing to recommend the act. What was happening to her? These strange feelings and even stranger urges were something she'd never dealt with before.

As they approached the street, he placed his hand on her back to guide her across the street. Her mind went into a spin, and she was sure his handprint was scorched into the fabric of her dress. Yet, the way her blood had surged wildly through her when he'd touched her so freely, as he was wont to do, left her breathless. If a bolt of lightning had appeared out of nowhere and struck her dead, it wouldn't have surprised her. She'd be on her knees for a week seeking forgiveness for all her sinful thoughts.

Chapter Eight

One dress. Merciful heavens, I'm down to the clothes on my back. Hastening to Mrs. Flowers's shop in hopes she had something already made up appropriate for a widow, Sarah stepped off the boardwalk to cross the street. She stepped back quickly when she saw several riders galloping briskly toward her.

Behind her, a woman screamed, "Mary, come back!"

In the next instant, a toddler darted past Sarah, directly into the path of the horses. Without thinking, Sarah darted after the child. As she snatched her up and enfolded her in her arms, she saw a huge golden horse almost upon them.

Cole, leaving the general store, heard the loud neighing of a horse and glanced up the street. A horse reared back on his hind legs, his hooves flailing the air, and beneath the animal was a woman clutching a small child. Recognition struck him like a bullet. Sarah!

Running toward them, he watched helplessly as a hoof clipped the side of Sarah's head, sending her falling backward to the ground. Still holding the screaming child against her chest, she rolled quickly to her side to protect the child as the horse's hooves came down on her.

Fear and despair surged through him. God, was he too late to help them?

Agonizing pain ripped through Sarah as she felt the sharp hooves dig into her flesh. Her screams mingled with the shocked and terrified cries of the onlookers. She heard the child crying and, looking up, saw the hooves coming down again. In an instant, someone grabbed her and dragged her to safety. The child wiggled from her arms, crying out, "Mommy!"

"Someone go get Doc Mason."

"Sure, Sheriff," a man called back.

"Sarah?"

Dazed, she gazed up as Cole lowered to his knees beside her. He brushed her tangled hair from her chalk-white face and, removing his handkerchief, gently wiped the blood from the cut on her forehead. "It isn't bad, thank God."

As he tenderly stroked her face, Sarah sighed, "I'm so glad *Save Widow Woman* is still on your list of duties."

Cole chuckled. Leaning over, he whispered, "It breaks the monotony."

His warm breath caressing her ear sent shivers running down her spine. She forced her arms to remain at her sides, struggling with the urge to drape them around his neck and . . . *kiss him?* That thought brought the heat rising up her neck and onto her face.

Noticing her suddenly flush face, he asked, "Are you hurting anywhere, Sarah?"

Yes, just kiss my hurts like you did my finger and I'll lie here forever. "Uh . . . just my hip and ribs," she managed to say, although the thought of his mouth touching those barren places was almost her undoing.

"Don't move. You might have some broken bones."

No, they've already melted, along with everything else, she thought. Another voice broke into their conversation. "Ma'am, are you hurt?"

She glanced up at a strikingly handsome man hovering over her. "Just a little, but I'll be fine, thank you."

She didn't see the scowl on Cole's face as his steel-gray eyes met the ice-blue eyes of Dusty Mills. The moment he and Wes had dreaded had arrived.

Sarah judged the man to be in his early fifties. Beneath a long straight nose, a blond mustache formed a neat arc over his generous mouth, the ends waxed to a point. He wore a black felt hat, the hair around his ears and neckline a dark blond interspersed with streaks of gray. But it was his eyes that held her attention, the most intense blue eyes she had ever seen.

He saw her watching him, and smiled. "I'm sorry, real sorry, ma'am. I couldn't stop my horse fast enough."

"It wasn't your fault, Mr. . . ."

"Mills, ma'am, Dusty Mills."

"I'm Sarah Hogan, Mr. Mills."

"You must be new in town."

"Yes, I'm James Moore's daughter."

Cole noticed the shocked look on Dusty's face. So he's just learned that James has a daughter. Guess this puts a barb in his plans, he thought deviously. Cole was certain that in time, Dusty had hoped to buy Moore's property.

The commotion had drawn the employees from the saloon. Billy's heart lurched to his throat and he lit out in a dead run when he saw Mills standing over Sarah. Had the bastard killed her? He slowed his pace, his eyes scanning her still figure. He caught Cole's attention, "Is . . . she . . . she—"

"She's shaken up a bit. I've sent someone for the doctor."

Billy, along with the rest of Sarah's employees, emitted a pent-up sigh of relief as Sarah smiled up at them.

Rooting his way in beside Cole, Billy squeezed her hand. "You're a brave little gal, missy, for risking your life to save that young 'un."

Before Sarah could answer, Cole said, "Here comes Doc now. Wes is with him. You'll be in good hands, Sarah."

74

His black bag in hand, Doc made his way through the crowd that had gathered around Sarah. Doctor Mason was a young man who'd graduated from some fancy medical school back East. The citizens felt fortunate to have a man of his caliber tending to their needs. Married to a local girl, everyone hoped he'd stay in Hazard instead of moving on. When he'd first come to town, shoot-outs, fights, and killings were so frequent, it was almost more than he could handle. No one had been so relieved as the doctor when Cole finally brought some law and order to the town.

Everyone moved out of the doctor's way. Kneeling beside her, he asked softly, "Where do you hurt, Mrs. Hogan?"

"Here," she said, moving her hand along her ribs and hip. "Do you think I've broken any bones?"

He smiled. "Let's hope not, but we can't move you until I check. Now, this might hurt a little . . ."

Sarah grimaced when he pressed lightly along her ribs. When his hand brushed the undersides of her breasts, she jumped.

"Did that hurt?"

"No . . . I mean yes, a little."

"It doesn't feel like any ribs are broken, Mrs. Hogan. Once we get to your room, I can examine you more thoroughly."

"I'll carry her," Billy offered.

"No, I will," Dusty quickly interceded. "After all, it's my fault she's hurt."

"You might drop her, Mills," Billy insisted. "Me? I'm strong as an ox." To prove it, he thrust out his broad chest and flexed his biceps.

Wes's eyes cut toward Cole; he saw the scowl on Cole's face. While Dusty and Billy argued, Cole knelt beside Sarah. "Just put your arms around my neck, Sarah."

Gladly, she thought. Complying, she nestled her head in the crook of his neck, drinking in his masculine scent. Heaven . . . I'm in heaven, she thought dreamily.

After Cole lifted her, Dusty and Billy stopped arguing and stared slack-jawed, their eyes following Cole as he carried her across street. Belle and Collie went ahead of him to prepare Sarah's bed.

In Sarah's bedroom, Doctor Mason was making preparations to examine her. The only thing that covered her nakedness was a flimsy sheet. She lay flat on her back in bed, clutching the sheet beneath her chin as though it might try to fly from her. She glanced at her breasts, horrified to see the contour of her nipples beneath the sheet. She glanced furtively at the doctor as he was pulling things from his bag.

Collie and Belle brought a pail of cool water and several cloths. When the doctor asked them to stay in the room so he could advise them on her care, a tide of relief washed over her.

He saw Sarah's fright, and understood. "You've never had on examination, have you, Mrs. Hogan?"

"N-no, n-never," she wailed quietly. She was shaking so much the sheet was quivering.

"Then let me assure you, I will respect your modesty. I need to look at your injuries so I'll know how to help you."

"Don't worry so, Sarah," Belle piped in. "A doctor examined me once and there was nothing to do it. If he hadn't helped me, I probably would've died of pneumonia."

"When was this?"

"I was six, I think." A frown etched her smooth brow. "No, maybe seven."

"Thanks, Belle," Sarah said nervously. Then to Doctor

Mason, she said, "I've wasted enough of your time, Doctor. If you're ready, then so am I—I guess."

True to his word, Doctor Mason was very professional.

"The skin's not broken, Mrs. Hogan, but you're badly bruised. I'm going to apply wet, cold cloths frequently for a while and then Collie and Belle will take over with the next step."

In the beginning, feeling the cold cloths against her warm flesh was almost as bad as the pain itself. As Doctor Mason worked, he talked to her about everyday events, helping her to relax and forget her embarrassment.

"Do you have any vinegar?"

"We should. I'll have Billy get it." Collie said.

"Has somethin' bad happened?" Billy asked the second the door opened.

"No, Billy, Sarah's doing just fine. We need you to get some vinegar."

"That's all? You're sure she's all right?"

"Yes, I'm sure. Just be patient." As Collie closed the door, she laughed to herself. Billy sure was a strange one and his attachment for Sarah was even stranger.

After Billy returned with the vinegar, Doctor Mason instructed them to soak the brown paper in a solution of vinegar and apply it to her bruises throughout the night. "If she needs something for pain, you can give her a small dose of the laudanum." He turned back to Sarah. "Mrs. Hogan, you won't feel like moving around too much for the next couple of days. Belle and Collie have offered to take care of you."

"But they have to help out in the saloon," Sarah insisted.

"We'll take turns, Sarah," Collie said. "Now, don't worry about what goes on downstairs. We're capable of handling everything until you're able to help. Right now,

77

our main concern is getting you back on your feet."

"Oh, all right," Sarah replied glumly. "But being an invalid sounds pretty boring. Can I work on my books?"

Doctor Mason chuckled. "You probably won't feel up to it for the next few days. I'll come by first thing in the morning."

When the doctor opened the door, he found Billy, Dusty, Wes, and Sheriff Blade waiting for him in Sarah's parlor. He explained Sarah's injuries, telling them it would be best that she didn't receive visitors until the next day.

"Doctor, I want you to send me the bill," Dusty offered.

Cole and Wes exchanged frowns.

"Mr. Mills, you can discuss this later with Mrs. Hogan. However, she doesn't blame you for her accident."

"Tell me something, Mr. Mills," Billy put in with a nasty smirk, "if it was that little child lying in there instead of Mrs. Hogan, would you be so damned generous?"

A sudden hush fell over the room as each pair of eyes fixed their attention on Dusty. A muscle twitched furiously in his jaw as he tried to contain his anger. "I don't see that it's any of your business, Mr. Ward, but in answer to your question, yes, I would help in any way I could. Now, if you gentlemen will excuse me, I have other business to attend to."

After Doctor Mason and Dusty departed, the remaining three moved out to the hall.

"You'd better watch your mouth, Billy," Cole warned. "Dusty might just sic one of his hired guns on you.

Billy hitched up his pants and leaned one shoulder against the wall. "I don't want him messin' around here and botherin' Sarah. Son-of-a-bitchin' varmint. Pay her doctor bill, humph," he snorted.

"Just stay out of it, Billy," Wes ordered. "That temper of yours could make problems for Sarah instead of solving them. Just keep an eye on things for us, all right?"

Billy fingered the black patch covering his eye. "Oh, I'll keep an eye on things, yessiree I will. If he has any intentions of goin' upstairs again, he'll have to go through me first."

"Don't you think Sarah should have a say about who she wants to visit her?" Cole asked, hoping to dissuade Billy from taking matters into his own hands.

Billy looked at Cole in bewilderment. "You want him up here botherin' her?"

"What I want you to do is the job Wes hired you to do, Billy," Cole snapped, "which is keeping the saloon clean and helping Gunter. If that isn't enough to occupy your time and keep you from causing trouble, we can easily find someone else to replace you. Got that?"

Wes lowered his head and smiled.

"He . . . he can't do that. I'm the—"

Seeing Billy's temper rising to the breaking point, Wes interrupted, "Billy, get back to work. We'll talk later."

"Damnation," Billy swore, pushing from the wall. As he descended the steps, they heard him mutter, "Fire me! Now, ain't that the damnedest thing?"

"From the look I caught on Dusty's face earlier, he didn't know James had a daughter," Cole said grimly. "What do you think he'll do next?"

Wes scratched his chin thoughtfully. "If he's after her property, now's the time he'll make his move. He has the perfect opportunity. He can check on her to his heart's content and there's not a damn thing anyone can say. Sarah might find him a charming man . . . unless, of course, you should decide to show her a little extra attention. You could, you know?"

"Damn it, Wes, you go too far."

"You know she's infatuated with you."

79

Cole raised a questioning eyebrow.

"Oh, she hasn't told me her feelings; she doesn't have to. I see it in her eyes every time she looks at you."

Cole shuffled his feet uneasily. Suddenly he barked, "No, the answer is no! I'll watch over her, but I'll be damned if I'll lower myself to Dusty's level by deceiving her."

Wes shrugged his shoulders. "In that case, I guess we'll just have to hope Sarah can handle Dusty alone. You can't blame me for trying, Cole. James was my best friend, and I only want to protect her."

"You can't coddle her forever, Wes. Give Sarah a chance to discover what kind of rat Mills is." But for the life of him, he couldn't figure out why his gut hurt when he thought of Sarah ever being in Dusty Mill's arms.

Chapter Nine

All hell broke loose in the Do Drop In later the next afternoon. Billy was helping Gunter behind the bar when the batwing doors swung open and several women from the church marched into the room. Ed Culpepper was standing at the bar sipping on his drink when he saw his wife, Alma. The liquor spewed from his mouth seconds before he sailed over the bar, ramming his head into the shelf housing glasses. Deke Womac saw his fiancée and took a nosedive behind the piano, spraining both wrists as his hands slammed palm upward against the wall. Hank Stewart saw his grandmother and, throwing his cards, bounded from his chair, cracking his head on the table as he plunged beneath it. Some men quickly shoved the brims of their hats over their faces. Others dashed through the back door, their heads buried beneath their jackets.

As the ladies slowly perused the suddenly quiet room, some smiled in amusement, while others hissed like snakes. Then, single file, they paraded up the steps to Sarah's room. The instant they were out of sight, the saloon emptied so quickly, one would have thought someone had yelled fire.

Collie was with Sarah when they heard all the commotion downstairs. As Collie opened the door, several women were just coming into the sitting room.

From her bed, Sarah recognized the lady in front,

Alma Culpepper, the organist at church.

"Please come in," she called out, not missing Collie's frown as she stepped aside for them to enter.

One by one, they filed into her room and circled her bed, each praising her for her heroic deed and each handing her a small gift of appreciation.

After a moment, their chatter picked up.

"I know it was Deke I saw go sliding behind that piano," Tammy Sue Blakely said in a huff. "Well, the marriage is off."

"Now, Tammy," an older woman said, patting her hand, "if all we women had said that when *our* men first started going to the saloon, we wouldn't be married today."

"Yes, and Mrs. Hogan's doing a fine job watching over our men. Why, Fred's not come in drunk since she started running the place."

"And we should all be mighty thankful to her for covering those pictures of the naked women."

"Yes, especially the one named Katy," replied Mattie Ivens, a young and very pretty redhead.

Everyone's eyebrows shot up as they curiously stared at Mattie. "How do you know her name?" one of them dared to ask.

Mattie stiffened visibly. "Because my husband talks in his sleep. I refused to cook another meal until he told me who she was. Any more questions?"

Everyone burst into laughter, including Sarah, who was trying to laugh without jarring her ribs.

After the ladies and Collie left, Belle came in and told her Dusty Mills was outside, waiting to see her.

"Just a minute," Sarah said, patting her hair and adjusting the pretty gown and robe Mrs. Flower's had brought by earlier. As she started to ask Belle to see him in, Mr. Herman bounded through the open window and pounced upon her bed, curling up beside her. "All right, I'm ready."

Belle opened the door. "You can come in now, Mr. Mills." Turning to Sarah, she said, "I'll be back shortly, Sarah."

Entering her room, Dusty removed his hat. "Thank you for seeing me, Mrs. Hogan. The doctor told me you were fine, but I wanted to see for myself."

Sarah heard a low growl coming from Mr. Herman. When she looked at the cat, he was up on all fours, the hair raised in salute on his back. "Mr. Herman, is this any way to treat our guest?"

She returned her attention to Dusty. "I—I don't know why he's acting like this. Won't you please sit down, Mr. Mills?" she asked, nodding to the chair nearby.

Dusty stopped beside the bed, and a ghost of a smile stole across his mouth as his pale blue eyes scanned her face. He held out a box. "Chocolates. I hope you like them."

After Sarah accepted the box, with a yowling scream Mr. Herman leaped on Dusty's arm and clawed his way up his sleeve. Dusty jerked his head back only a split second before the cat took a swipe at his face with his sharp claws. Yanking the cat off him, he tossed him to the floor. In the next instant, Mr. Herman bounded through the window and disappeared.

Sarah stared at the window in shock.

"Does he attack all your visitors like this?" Dusty asked, disgruntled, straightening his jacket.

"You're the first," she said perplexedly. "Maybe he doesn't like chocolates."

Dusty laughed. "I'll remember that next time."

"I'm terribly sorry, Mr. Mills. Again, please have a seat." Sarah opened the box of chocolates and looked up at him and smiled. "Thank you." She closed the box and set it beside her on the bed.

Dusty sat down and crossed one leg over the other. "Now, about the accident, Mrs. Hogan. I would like very much if you would let me take care of your doctor bill."

Surprised, Sarah said, "No, absolutely not, Mr. Mills. Please don't fret so about it. As I told you, it wasn't your fault."

"Still, I'd like to do something for you."

"You have already. I love chocolate candy," she said with a smile.

For a moment, he didn't say anything, but gazed at her with those intense blue eyes. Finally, he spoke. "When I came through the saloon, I noticed you've really cleaned up the place. It looks better than it ever has."

Her cheeks flushed with his praise. "Thank you. But there's a lot more to do before I'm finished."

"I'll be frank with you, Mrs. Hogan. When I heard the widow of a minister was running the saloon, I expected you to either sell it or board it up. You've surprised me."

Feeling at ease, Sarah said lightly, "No more than I've surprised myself. But I'm actually enjoying it, now that I'm over the shock."

His eyes swept her at his leisure, then paused on her face. "I have another confession to make. I didn't know James Moore had a daughter, especially one as young and beautiful as you are. Where had he been hiding you?"

Sarah blushed to the roots of her hair. "Why—why, thank you, Mr. Mills. As to your question, I'm from Tennessee."

"Oh? But why did you come all the way out here?"

"Please, it's a long story. If you don't mind, I'd

rather not go into it. Suffice it to say, I'm now making my home in Texas, Mr. Mills."

"Please, call me Dusty. May I call you Sarah?"

"Of—of course."

"Good," he said, rising from his chair. "I don't want to tire you, so I'll go now. I wish you much success in your venture, Sarah." He nodded politely, then turned and crossed the room. Settling his hat on his head, he turned as he opened the door. "Now that I've met the charming new owner of the Do Drop In, you just might see me more often."

"I hope so. And thank you again for the chocolates, Mr.—I mean Dusty," she returned with a smile.

Later that evening, Billy brought her supper and situated the tray on her lap. He lingered a moment, as though he wanted to talk.

"What is it, Billy?"

"It's about Dusty Mills, missy. Don't let the man fool you," he urged, hoping to quench any interest she might have in the man.

"Why? He seems to be a real gentleman." She held up the box of candy. "Look, he brought me chocolates."

"Humph," Billy snorted. "He's a schemin', selfish man, full of his own self-importance." He pressed his point. "He came to Hazard less than a year ago and started buyin' up all this property. Afterwards, a rumor started that Hazard was gettin' a railroad spur."

"So, he invested wisely. Does that make him an evil man?"

"No one knows a thing about him."

"No one knows a thing about you either, Billy." She grinned mischievously. "Does that make you evil?"

Billy's mouth slammed as tight as a clamshell. For a moment he didn't say anything. "No, I just don't have nothin' interestin' to talk about, missy."

"I doubt that, Billy. Would you like to talk to me?"

"Don't have time. They've already warned me to stop interferin' in things that ain't my business. Said I'd lose my job if I wasn't careful."

"Who said this?"

"Mr. Norman and the sheriff. But, damn it—excuse me, darn it—I like you, missy, and I just thought you ought to know the man for the bast—culprit he is."

"Billy, I appreciate your concern, but I'll form my own conclusions. Oh, and as long as you're doing your work, no one will fire you."

Billy nodded. "Thanks, ma'am. Well, I'd better hurry along."

When he closed the door behind him, Sarah sank back against the pillows and smiled. She would never admit it to a soul, but as rough and outspoken as he was, she enjoyed Billy's company. Like Orie Wheeler, she knew he possessed a gentle, caring heart.

Cole paced the floor, feeling guilty that he'd not visited Sarah. Her close brush with death had frightened him. And reluctantly he admitted he missed her, her impulsiveness, her wit, and her infatuation. But he didn't want to feel anything for her, and these new feelings disturbed and confused him. Avoiding her was only making him miserable and, though he hated to admit it, lonely, damned lonely.

His eyes grave and smileless, he thought about Dusty Mills. On two occasions, he had seen the man enter the saloon early in the afternoon. By way of the grapevine (Belle and Collie) he'd learned of Dusty's gifts, the chocolates and a pair of silk gloves. It didn't require very keen scrutiny on Cole's part to arrive swiftly at the conclusion that Dusty was undeniably clever. What better way for a man to win a woman's admiration than to flirt with her vanity?

Shoving back his chair, he rose and settled his hat on his head. Outside, he glanced up at Sarah's window. *Damn it, woman, when you're not around, you make my life hell!*

Sarah lay in bed halfway between wakefulness and sleep and imagined all kinds of crazy things. For a moment she thought Cole was standing in the doorway, the sweetest smile spanning his face she'd ever seen. Later, her drowsy eyes blinked open. He was still standing there. This time he was clutching a nosegay of flowers. She rubbed her fisted hands against her eyes and took another peek. He was still there. A smile trembled on her lips as she scooted up in bed.

"I thought I was dreaming," she confessed.

"I hope it wasn't a nightmare," he teased, approaching the bed.

"How long have you been standing there?"

"Not long. Here." He extended the hand holding the flowers.

"Thank you, they're beautiful." Her hand closed around the posy and their fingers touched. Time stilled, as did their breathing. Green eyes locked with steel-gray ones and words couldn't deny the heat scorching the tips of their fingers.

"Forget-me-nots," she choked out, examining the delicate flowers.

Cole fought the raging lust battling through him. Her voice husky from sleep pulled at him like a fire on a cold winter's night. She was warm and soft-looking, cuddled beneath the covers that way. Her hair, tangled and mussed, encouraged him to lose his fingers in the unbound mane. She looked just like he knew she would, even though he'd tried to believe she held no attraction for him. Her gown was a soft white cotton, high-necked and long-sleeved, the delicate lace on the cuffs brushing the backs of her hands as she brushed her hair from her face. He knew that if he buried his face in her neck it would feel like warm sunshine.

"How are you feeling?"

"Bored, bored, bored. If they don't let me out of this room soon, I'm planning a mutiny," she teased.

"Don't do anything impulsive, Sarah. The doctor knows best."

"The doctor doesn't spend his days counting cracks on the ceiling either," she said, pouting.

Before he thought, Cole dropped to the bed beside her. "Is there anything I can get you that would elevate your boredom?"

She wanted to say *you, you, you,* but refrained. Instead she tailed her finger over the border of the sheet and whispered, "Just talk to me."

"You've been having a lot of company. Surely that helps pass the time."

"Oh, I don't mean to be unkind. Yes, I've had company. Collie and Belle stop by all the time. But they're busy downstairs."

"What about Mills? He's been a frequent visitor."

"Yes, he's been very kind." How could she tell him he was the one she'd ached to see? Now he was here and she was rambling.

He lifted her hand and fingered the delicate lace.

She pulled her hand away and wound her fingers together, twisting them nervously.

"Are you afraid of me, Sarah?"

"No." She swallowed loudly.

"Then what is it?"

"I don't know how to say this without sounding like something's wrong with me. Maybe there is, I don't know. Collie and Belle are like you. They touch and hug so effortlessly. They think nothing of laying their hand on someone s arm or hugging another person just because they're glad to see them. Even Billy Ward is quick to pat my hand or my back if he's pleased about something—or sometimes for no reason at all.

"And that bothers you?" Cole asked.

"Well, it bothers me only because it makes me uncomfortable. But I'd like to be that way. It makes me feel good when one of the girls hug me, or when Billy pats me on the back. It makes me feel like I'm part of something special. But I don't know how to hug them back without feeling awkward. And for the life of me, I don't know why I'm telling you this." She laughed nervously.

Cole's heart filled with something he didn't want to examine too closely. He knew Sarah had no inkling of the fine art of flirting, but her admission moved him. "Didn't your mother or your grandparents ever hug you?"

She shook her head.

"For god's sake, Sarah. Didn't your husband just hold you sometimes for the sake of holding you?"

She shook her head.

"Well, I'll be damned."

"Don't swear, Cole. It's not nice."

"I guess your grandfather taught you that, too?"

This time, she nodded her head.

What kind of man was her grandfather? He'd taught her not to swear, but had failed to teach her to reach out and touch another human being, had refused her the comfort of a hug.

"Am I just being foolish?"

"No." He reached for her hand and unwound her fingers. "Don't jump. I'm just going to hold your hand."

They sat there for several seconds, Cole holding her limp hand. Finally her fingers came to life and she gently gripped his hand. Several minutes passed and neither of them said anything, just continued to hold hands.

"How does that feel?" he asked.

"Good." Then she smiled. "Very good."

He dropped her hand. "Now it's your turn."

"What?"

"For you to hold my hand."

"I thought I was."

"You instigate the hand-holding this time."

She stared at the large brown hand laying palm up on her bed covers. A ripple started in her stomach and wound its way up her back to the nape of her neck. She lifted his hand and turned it over, curling her fingers between his.

"That wasn't so bad, was it?"

She shook her head.

"Now, about that hug." He scooted toward her.

She shot straight up in bed.

He placed one hand around her shoulders and the other around her back. She was as stiff as a Georgia pine. "Relax," he whispered.

"I can't."

"Just lean against me. I won't bite."

She laughed, and he felt her shoulders slump as she exhaled. He wiggled closer and rested the side of his face against hers, his chin nuzzling her neck. Sure enough, she smelled like sunshine. He lifted his hands to her shoulders and leaned back so he could see her face. Her eyes were shut and

90

the softest look encompassed her face.

She felt the lack of comfort from his body and her eyes blinked open, a puzzled frown marring her brow. "Did I do something wrong?"

"Oh no," he assured her, "you're a very good hugger."

"I am?"

"Amazing, isn't it? And you so new at it."

He tightened his arms and repositioned his head. His lips brushed the warm flesh of her neck. He heard her breath catch.

They sat very still, savoring the comfort of each other. He could feel the rise and fall of her breasts pressing against his chest as she breathed, the pulse racing in her neck. He dropped his arms from her back and leaned away. "Now it's your turn."

She lifted her arms toward him, then changed her mind and repositioned them. At last, she slid one arm beneath his and spanned his ribs before she settled her hand on the small of his back. The other arm circled his shoulder and her palm rested between his shoulder blades. She turned her face into his neck and nuzzled much as he had done earlier to her neck. Like her, his breath caught. But if she'd seen the swelling at the juncture of his legs, their lesson in hugging would have died a sudden death. She felt so good, so damn good, he couldn't control his own body.

"Are hugs supposed to last this long?"

"I guess that depends on who you're hugging."

As they separated, each felt an immediate loss and wanted to assume their former position. But it didn't seem such a good idea. The room had become unusually hot.

When Cole lifted her hand, she didn't flinch. He didn't wind his fingers through hers, but instead studied the lines marking her palm. One hand slid up the length of her arm while the other continued to cradle her hand. Slowly he lowered his mouth and kissed her in the middle of her palm. His tongue traced her life-line until the lace edging her cuff touched his nose. Pushing the sleeve up, he kissed her wrist. When he lifted his head, her other hand was extended. He took it and applied the same thorough treatment.

When she could get her breath, she asked, "What's that called?"

"Foreplay," he answered hoarsely.

"It's wonderful," she sighed.

"Most assuredly, but I can't . . ." He examined her flushed face, the brightness of her eyes, and the fullness of her mouth. There was no way on God's earth he could continue to touch her, and not sample the sweetness of her mouth. Talk about being between the devil and the deep blue sea. He felt as though he'd just been broadsided by his conscience.

"Oh hell," he growled, removing himself from the bed. Approaching the window, he bowed his arms on the windowsill and studied the street below. His mind was far removed from the activity going on below him as he tried to control the surging lust throbbing through him. Gaining limited control, he peered over his shoulder at Sarah. She snuggled beneath the covers watching him—the picture of innocence.

He felt himself losing ground. "I need to go, Sarah, I've a thousand things to do."

"Thank you for coming by, and thanks for the flowers."

"Give me a quick hug before I go."

She smiled brightly and lifted her arms.

He dared not sit on the bed again, so he bent from the waist and wrapped his arms around her. When he released her, she placed her hand against the side of his face and stroked his bristled cheek. "Thank you for everything."

"My pleasure," he admitted, taking her hand and kissing the tips of her fingers. "Anytime. Now, you get some rest."

"Will you come back to see me?"

"You can count on it." But he knew he couldn't. Sarah did things to him that he didn't want to explore.

After the door closed behind him, Sarah picked up the bouquet and studied the flowers. Strange, she thought, fingering the delicate blooms, when Cole touched her it was nothing like the girls' hugs or Billy's pats. Something wonderful happened inside her when he touched her, something she'd never felt before.

Chapter Ten

Cole turned his attention to the street, noticing a buggy drawing to a halt in front of Wes's office. He watched curiously as Skeet Weston assisted a beautiful woman from the buggy. Her clothing would evoke the envy of any woman in Hazard and would probably bankrupt a wealthy man. Her tall, shapely figure was arrayed in yards of deep blue silk with lace edging the sleeves and low neckline of the bodice. Atop a cluster of golden curls, she wore a matching hat with a long white ostrich plume curling over the crown.

Cole lifted a curious brow. "I thought you said you didn't have any more appointments today."

"I don't, why?" Wes asked, placing his pen in the inkwell.

"A woman—and a mighty-good-looking one—is walking this way. Skeet Weston just brought her in."

"Skeet? George Roberts's foreman?" Wes asked, perplexed, rising from his seat. Donning his jacket and straightening his tie, he opened the door. His eyes widened with interest as he viewed the beautiful woman standing before him. Beneath perfectly arched brows, a pair of slanted blue eyes met his. "Are you Mr. Norman, the attorney?" she asked with a soft British accent.

Wes's interest strengthened. An Englishwoman? "Why, ah . . . yes, I am."

"I'm Juliet Barrington, Mr. Norman, George Roberts's sister," she said, offering him a lace-gloved hand. "I've . . . I've just been out to my brother's ranch and learned of his death."

Wes took her hand. "I'm so sorry. Please come in, Mrs. Barrington."

"It's *Miss*," she stressed, entering the office. Her eyes darted to the window where Cole leaned leisurely against the wall. "Oh, I'm interrupting you. Shall I return later?" she asked, the gloom lifting from her face as she scanned Cole from head to toe.

"No, we've been hoping you'd show up soon. This is Sheriff Cole Blade. Sheriff, Juliet Barrington."

She smiled invitingly at Cole. "Please call me Juliet."

Cole boldly returned her gaze, his eyes lingering on her full mouth. He touched the brim of his hat and nodded. "It's a pleasure meeting you, Juliet."

"Please sit down," Wes suggested, assisting her into a chair in front of his desk. Wes leaned against the edge of the desk. "I'm sorry you had to learn about your brother's death that way. I tried to find you."

"I've been traveling extensively, and it would have been near impossible to track me down."

"We know. George told us you were coming for a visit. He was a fine man, Juliet, his death a shock to everyone in the community."

Her face suddenly washing over with grief, she whispered, "They told me he was murdered." She pulled a handkerchief from her reticule. As she dabbed her teary eyes, she glanced Cole's way. "Why would anyone want to do such a horrible thing?"

"The man, Mark Sheramy, claimed George pulled a gun on him and he killed him in self-defense," Cole said. "But if it's any consolation, George's murderer is dead now."

"Juliet," Wes interjected, "According to George's will,

you are his only surviving relative. Did you know he left everything to you?"

"No, I didn't," she said, smiling sadly. "Mr. Norman, George was my stepbrother, and I haven't seen him in years."

"No one even knew you existed until he mentioned you were coming to visit him. It's a shame this had to happen."

"Yes, I had so looked forward to seeing him again." Distraught, Miss Barrington rose and smoothed the folds of her shimmering gown. "Perhaps I should schedule an appointment so we can discuss George's will. I really don't feel up to it today. Do you think it would be all right if . . . if I stayed at the ranch for a while?"

Wes chuckled. "The ranch belongs to you now, Miss Barrington."

She smiled sadly, "Yes, I'm really not thinking too clearly at the moment." She paused. "Is there anything in town I'll need to purchase before going to the ranch?"

"No, I don't think so. The ranch hands and house-keeper have stayed on since George's death, and I've been paying their wages with monies from the estate. You should find the house and grounds in excellent shape. Now that you're here, we can settle his estate. In the meantime, if you need anything at all, just let me know."

"Thank you. Good day, gentlemen."

Wes watched Cole eye her swaying hips as he followed her across the room and opened the door. Once outside, the first person they saw was Sarah. She stopped abruptly on the boardwalk, her green eyes widening as she stared at the elegantly dressed woman. Then she looked toward Cole. "Is . . . ah . . . Wes

96

here?" Sarah asked, tripping over her words.

"Sarah, what a pleasant surprise," Wes said, stepping outside. "I'm glad to see you up and about."

Wes introduced the two women and explained Juliet's presence in Hazard.

"I'm terribly sorry about your brother. If I can help you in any way I'll be happy to," Sarah said, noting her complexion was as fair and delicate as a white rose.

"Thank you."

"Sarah's also new in town, Miss Barrington. Her property borders yours on the west side. Sheriff Blade rents her house."

"Oh? Then, where do you live?" Juliet asked.

"In an apartment above the saloon," Sarah blurted.

The young woman glanced fleetingly over Sarah's black clad figure, an amused smile tugging the corner her mouth. "Do you work there?"

Sarah's face reddened. She hurried to explain. "Yes, I—I own it."

Juliet smiled. "Oh? How interesting. Well, it was nice meeting you, Mrs. Hogan. Perhaps we can get together after I'm settled. I must be going along now. It's dreadfully hot here in the sun, and I foolishly left my parasol in the carriage." She turned to Cole and her small pink tongue ran enticingly over her rose-colored lips. "Sheriff Blade, since we are neighbors, you must stop by and have dinner with me. My door is always open."

"I'll remember that," Cole said, tipping his hat to the beautiful woman. "Good day, Miss Barrington . . . Juliet," he corrected, his eyes flickering admiringly over her shapely curves as she walked to the carriage.

Sarah's eyes followed Juliet, and she wished she didn't feel envious of the woman. Everything about her sparkled—her clothing, her eyes, and even her blond hair. Sarah hadn't missed the admiring looks that Cole and Wes had given the woman, either. She wanted desperately for Cole to look at her that way. Still, she would settle for the way he had looked at her when he'd come to visit her. But then she hadn't looked like a crow. She'd had on the pretty gown Mrs. Flowers had given her.

A pained expression gripped Sarah's features. She looked at the plain black dress she now wore, one of the new dresses Mrs. Flowers had made for her. Mrs. Flowers had added a touch of white lace and ribbons to add softness to the harsh color. She wore a black bonnet garnished with white daisies around its wide brim. Oh, she was sick to death of wearing black. If only she could. . . . No, it was out of the question.

She watched the carriage roll out of sight.

Wes noted the envy in Sarah's eyes. "Come inside out of the sun, Sarah." He and Cole stepped aside for her to enter. "How are you feeling?"

"Oh, much better. The bruises are barely noticeable now.

Wes smiled. "You're wearing a new dress, I see."

Sarah looked at Cole and caught him rolling his eyes. "Yes, I went by the dress shop earlier and picked up my new dresses."

At this, Wes's interest perked. "So you've taken my advice. I hope you ordered a green one to match your eyes," Wes interrupted with a smile.

Strange that he'd mentioned green. Mrs. Flowers still had that bolt of emerald silk and had mentioned again she'd like to make a dress for her from it. "No, Wes, I'm still in mourning."

"Still?" Cole asked mockingly.

Her chin shot up haughtily. "Yes, still."

"God forbid that you should do something improper," Cole taunted.

Hurt by his insult, Sarah turned to Wes. "If you'll excuse me, I have some more errands to run."

"I'll see you out," Wes volunteered, looping his arm through hers.

With a slight nod in Cole's direction, she said, "Good day, Sheriff."

When Wes came back inside, Cole asked, "What do you make of Miss Barrington, Wes?"

"I don't know. She's young and very beautiful."

Cole chuckled. "I noticed. Can you believe the age difference between George and his stepsister? She's young enough to be his daughter." He paused, and frowned. "Something about her keeps nagging at me, but for the life of me I can't put a finger on it."

Sarah fumed as she made her way down the boardwalk. If it wouldn't call attention to herself, she would stomp. Nodding her head and pursing her lips just so, she mimicked, "Sheriff Blade, you must stop by and have dinner with me. My door is always open." Miss Barrington had blinked her big blue eyes as if a swarm of gnats had attacked her. "Humph, wonder what else her invitation had entailed?"

Suddenly, a deep sadness enveloped Sarah. She had to admit Miss Barrington really was beautiful. The way Cole and Wes had looked at her with their tongues hanging out had only reinforced Sarah's dowdy appearance. She frowned and tugged at the ugly fabric of her new dress. The woman had forgotten her parasol. Poppycock! Sarah didn't even own a parasol. As she thought about it, there were a lot of things she didn't have. Did it make her a better person because she deprived herself? What would it be like to wear beautiful shimmering clothes?

She stopped abruptly right there in the middle of the boardwalk, and with an unladylike snort shifted directions. What was the matter with her? After facing the beauty of Juliet Barrington and then hearing Cole's insult, she'd completely forgotten her purpose for going to Wes's office. She'd wanted to pick up the saloon books that Wes had taken earlier in the week.

When she reached Wes's office, the door was ajar. As she started to knock, she heard Wes's voice.

Frustrated that Cole couldn't see beyond Sarah's frumpy clothes, Wes snapped, "You know what I think, Cole? You'd die before you'd admit it, but Sarah's caught your interest. Even those unsightly clothes can't hide the fact she's a woman, a right shapely one, too. One day soon, you're going to be in for a big surprise, Sheriff."

"Well, I'm all for surprises, but believe me, it would take a miracle to turn Sarah Hogan into a desirable woman," he said more harshly than he intended. Nothing in the world would make him admit he already found her desirable.

"Damn it, Cole, it won't kill you to be nice to her."

"Now just a minute. I have been nice. Tell me, Wes, if she decided to tackle the running of the saloon, why in god's name is she clinging to her past? She dresses like an old woman, and twists her hair around like baled hay. Women are supposed to be soft and feminine. She could be, too, if she'd only put forth a little effort and shed those damn black rags she wears."

"I know. I've talked and hinted until I don't know what else to do. I don't want to hurt her feelings and tell her point-blank how unfeminine she looks."

"What would James think of his beautiful daughter?" Cole asked sarcastically.

With her hands clasped over her mouth and tears

sparkling in her eyes, Sarah strained to hear Wes's answer. Instead it was Cole's voice that rocked through her mind.

"I'll tell you what James would have thought. She would have embarrassed him to death. All I ever heard from him about his daughter was how beautiful she was. God rest his soul, at least he was spared the shame of having to explain her appearance to his friends."

"James did set a lot of store in his own appearance," Wes added sadly.

"Damn straight he did. In the meantime, I think I'll take Juliet Barrington up on her invitation."

"You planning to play the part of Romeo, Cole?"

Cole laughed. "I've done worse things."

"Yeah, but look what happened to that unlucky bastard."

"But it could be very interesting . . . and rewarding," Cole added with a sly grin.

Blinded by her tears, Sarah stumbled from Wes's office. Why? Oh, why hadn't she listened to Wes? He'd tried to tell her, Mrs. Flowers had tried to tell her. The sad truth was, she was more like her staunch grandfather than she was like her father. And more than anything in the world, she didn't want to be like her grandfather. *Oh, please help me. I don't know what to do,* Sarah prayed as she rushed from Wes's office. Avoiding the front entrance of the saloon, she went up the back stairs. She couldn't bear it if anyone saw her in such a terrible state.

Chapter Eleven

An unusual trio made their way across town to Ida Flowers's dress shop, turning more than one admiring head in their direction. It was the richly-clad pair escorting the widow that drew their attention. Their intent was questionable, as the widow stopped her progress several times and shook her head negatively. The girls, Collie and Belle, pleaded, cajoled, and finally enticed the widow to continue the journey. Upon reaching their destination, it was several hours later when they departed the dress shop, laden with boxes of varying sizes and description. A lengthy visit to the druggist saw additional packages added to the growing number. Last, but equally important, was a stop at the bootery, where Sarah was measured for several pairs of soft leather shoes.

Sarah's soft tinkling laughter filled the room as she collapsed onto the sofa. "I never dreamed spending money was so tiring."

Collie and Belle quickly agreed, taking a seat among the various packages.

"I'll trim your hair while we're waiting for Billy to bring your bath water," Collie volunteered.

"My hair?" Sarah gulped, moving her hand to the bun that rode low on the nape of her neck.

"You can't dress in beautiful new clothes and continue to wear your hair in such an unbecoming manner."

"I know, but you mean to cut it?"

"Just trim off those dead ends, and shampoo it with something besides that horrible soap you use."

"That's all I have."

"Not any more," Collie insisted, prowling through the packages. "We have here Abe's very best almond-nut cream to soften your complexion." Collie brought forth each concoction, proclaiming its merits with the rhetoric of a seasoned huckster.

"Ah-h, here we have a wonderful buttermilk glycerine soap for your bath, and witch-hazel toilet cream for skin that is chapped and rough. For your hair, we have a fine shampoo liquor that leaves the scalp perfectly clean and the hair soft and silky."

The girls laughed and exclaimed over the worth of each preparation, not completely taken in by the claims.

From her reticule, Belle pulled out a small package and handed it to Sarah. "This is from me and Collie."

"You girls have done so much for me already. You didn't have to buy me anything."

"We wanted you to have it," Collie added with a smile.

Sarah's eyes lit up as she turned the package over several times in her hand. Very slowly, she pulled the string from the package, winding it carefully around her hand. She held her breath and push back the wrapping. Cushioned on a bed of fine Valenciennes lace was a lapidary-cut stopper bottle of diamond brilliance. Essence of Lavender, the label read. Sarah lifted her eyes to her friends. "Thank you," she whispered.

"We noticed that sometimes we'd catch a hint of lavender when you came downstairs. So we thought you might like it."

"I love it. A friend of mine back home gave me a scented bar of soap. Thank you, this is very special to me."

"Now, about your hair," Collie chimed in.

"If you're sure nothing else will do, then I guess I'm in your hands," Sarah supplied, a skeptical brow arching heavenward.

"Nothing else will do. Belle, if you'll help her out of that dress, I'll get my scissors and check on the water for her bath."

"Oh, my," Sarah moaned, seating herself at the dressing table.

She'd removed her dress and covered her mended undergarments with the ugliest wrapper Belle declared she'd ever seen. It really was ugly, Sarah decided as she smoothed the brown lapel. Old and limp, the flannel fabric was covered with tiny little balls that nothing would remove. Sarah took the pins from her hair and shook her head, sending her hair in a cascade down her back. She chewed her lips as she watched Collie lift her hair and drape a linen towel around her shoulders. After wetting Sarah's hair, Collie picked up the scissors. Sarah buried her face in her hands, her shoulders shaking.

"Sarah, please don't cry. I promise it will look better. Don't you trust me?"

Sarah nodded her head and wiped the tears from her face.

"Have you never had your hair cut?"

"Once," Sarah sobbed.

"Will you tell me about it?"

Taking a deep shuddering breath, Sarah nodded her head. "When I was a child, Mother always braided my hair. One Sunday at church, I noticed Mary McMahon and her friends. They were wearing their hair in soft curls down their backs, decorated in one way or another with pretty ribbons. Well, I thought, we're all the same age. If they'd outgrown pigtails, maybe I had too. All that following week I practiced curling my hair. The next Sunday, I brushed and brushed, trying to copy Mary's style. Although I couldn't make those smooth thick curls, I thought it looked quite nice. I rushed into the parlor to show my mother my accomplishment. My grandparents hit the ceiling when they saw it. Grandfather said I looked wanton, and took the scissors, cutting my hair almost to my ears. He said it was my shame, having my hair sheared, and that it would give me plenty of time to think about my sin before it grew back."

Collie and Belle didn't verbalize their thoughts, but the words sweeping thorough them would have kindled a fire to enormous proportion. They blinked the tears from their eyes and hugged Sarah tightly.

"I promise you'll love what I do to your hair, and if you think I'm cutting too much, just let me know and I'll stop."

Sarah watched quietly as her hair fell to the floor in little mounds. Belle applied the almond paste to Sarah's face and the witch-hazel toilet cream to her hands. Sarah's green eyes sparkled with mischief from the mask of cream as she questioned, "Is this the devil's workshop, or perhaps I have stumbled into some remote torture chamber?"

"It is torture for sure, what women must go through to enhance their beauty," Belle agreed, trimming and buffing Sarah's nails.

When the bath water arrived, Collie met Billy at the door and took charge once again, filling the copper tub and sprinkling bath salts in the hot water. Frothy bubbles danced across the surface of the water; an occasional one would become airborne and float across the room, dipping and swaying in the glistening light. Sarah waited for the girls to excuse themselves before she started to disrobe. Her friends had no compunctions about naked bodies as they pulled her from the seat and made quick work of disrobing her. Sarah blushed to the roots of her damp hair. She was not in the habit of removing her clothes in front of anyone other than her mother, and that had been only when she was very young.

She slid into the tub until the water lapped against her neck.

Noticing Sarah's discomfiture, Collie thought to ease her mind. "Sugar, don't worry about running around here buck-naked in front of Belle and me. You ain't got nothing we hadn't seen before."

Sarah sank lower in the tub, her red face glowing.

"Why, honey, you've got a fine figure, all the curves in the right places. I bet the sheriff could really appreciate the turn of your body."

"I don't see how. I don't have near as much up . . ." Sarah cupped her hands just above the water and bounced them several times.

Belle and Collie erupted into laughter.

Sarah, realizing she had just admitted an interest in the sheriff, began a stumbling denial. "No, no, I didn't mean it like that."

"It doesn't matter, honey, we know what you mean. Besides, I've been told any more than a handful is wasted anyway."

"Oh, my." Sarah's eyes slid shut and she sank lower still.

"Honey, you're going to have to toughen up if you're going to make it in this business."

"I know, and I'm trying."

"Wait until you meet Marge Tulley, and it's time for her to come into town. She and the boys make the trip in about once a month to pick up supplies. *Boys,* that's what Marge calls them, but let me tell you, those are men if there ever were any. Big ol' strapping fellows. They could snap you apart like a green sapling if they were of a mind to."

"Right-good-looking *boys*—if you ask me," Collie added sheepishly.

"Marge looks like her boys. She's a big woman and doesn't take any mouth off anybody. She's as rough as a cob and some of the things she says will curl your hair. She's a strong woman and she expects other women to be strong. If she approves of you, then you have a friend for life. If not, she just won't have anything to do with you. Her husband abandoned her with three children to raise alone. If anybody knows about hard knocks firsthand, it's Marge. Anyway, when they come into town to get supplies, Marge spends several hours here in the saloon while her boys are visiting Lila's."

"Who's Lila?" Sarah asked, soaping the fragrant shampoo into her hair.

Collie cleared her throat, and Belle busied herself laying out Sarah's new undergarments.

"She runs the town brothel," Collie said quickly.

"A house of prostitution," Sarah said without hesitation.

"You know about such things?" Belle asked, shocked.

"If it has anything to do with sin, believe me, I know about it. My grandfather preached long and hard about the sinfulness of mankind."

Belle and Collie laughed, and each reached out to touch her. "You are really something, Sarah Hogan."

"Thank you, I think. Now, back to Marge. You

mean she knowingly lets her boys frequent a place like that?"

"Here, lean over and I'll rinse your hair," Collie said, kneeling beside the tub. "Sarah, these *boys* are all looking at the back side of thirty. They're men, and men have needs—their mother knows this."

"I see," Sarah whispered, not understanding at all.

Sarah turned before the mirror, once, twice, three times. She couldn't believe her eyes. Her hair didn't look like dead grass anymore. Collie had pulled it atop her head and worked the hair into a nest of soft curls that shimmered with copper highlights when the light touched it. A few shortened strands curled in front of her ears, enhancing the sleekness of her high cheekbones. Her face was still sunbrowned, but the creams and ointments had indeed softened her skin. The dress she wore was an apple green with a high neck of cream linen lawn edged with delicate embroidery and matching cuffs. A close-fitting bodice with tiny covered buttons fit her body like a lover's hand. The deep shirring at the hem was inset with the same linen lawn and complemented with tiny embroidered ribbon tied into delicate bows. Her undergarments brought a blush to Sarah's face just thinking about them. Fine cotton embraced her body, gently whispering against her nakedness when she moved. Never had she imagined herself wearing anything so soft and delicately trimmed.

Sarah smiled, smoothing the fabric of her dress. "It does look nice, doesn't it?"

"You look wonderful," the girls cried in unison.

"It's late, and we just have time to dress. We'll meet you downstairs in a little while."

"Thank you, both," Sarah replied, and remembering the lesson Cole had given her, she unabashedly hugged her friends.

108

After the girls left, Sarah busied herself putting her things away, making a point of passing close to the mirror each time she crossed the room. She couldn't help it; she did look nice. It was true she could dress in a flattering manner without looking garish. She studied her glowing eyes and the delicate blush on her cheeks. If her father could see her now, would he be shamed by her appearance? She didn't think so. The sheriff had been right—she knew that—but, still, what he'd said hurt her deeply.

Well, she'd taken steps to correct the damage and revive the image of his beautiful daughter her father had left with his friends. Wes didn't even know about the new Sarah Hogan. She'd thought long and hard about her decision before asking Collie and Belle to help her. Even then she'd had misgivings and had tried to change her mind. The girls wouldn't hear of it. Her course was set and the girls were determined to see the deed done. Ida Flowers had been in her element and had flitted about her shop like a honeybee dipping into the nectar of flowers as she pulled out one delicate garment after another for Sarah's approval.

It was time. Sarah dreaded going downstairs as much this night as she had her first night. She could hear the tinkling of the piano keys and the buzz of conversation as the sounds drifted through her window. She checked her appearance one last time, then closed the door quietly behind her.

Chapter Twelve

From the railing, Sarah could see the back of Fancy Fingers Floyd as his fingers skimmed across the piano keys. His playing seemed to have improved with the addition of new clothes and his personal grooming habits. Sarah smiled warmly. Gunter had taken on the chore of coaxing Floyd into bathing and wearing new clothing. She didn't know how he had managed it, but Floyd was like a new person, in dark gray cassimere pants with hairline stripes of black, and a snowy linen shirt with fancy silver cuff links that sparkled in the light when Floyd's fingers danced along the keyboard. And to top off his attire was a red silk vest and a thin string tie.

Sarah hoped fervently that she hadn't overdone it by shedding her mourning clothes for a more fashionable wardrobe. Whether or not she liked it, clothes made a definite impression, and right now she needed to make a good impression.

Her hand halted on the banister for an instant as she scanned the crowd. One by one, the customers noticed her as she began her descent. All became deathly silent. One brave soul swept off his hat and pursed his lips, letting loose with an ear-splitting whistle. Suddenly the room became a roar of catcalls and clapping hands. Air kisses and generous smiles welcomed her as she entered the room. She made a point of greeting her customers with a warm smile. She didn't have Collie's and Belle's poise and charm, or their easy manner with the men, but she tried to appear comfortable. Inside, her stomach was in knots, and she wanted to clinch her hands. Billy Ward *oohed* and *ahhed* over her until her face turned crimson.

Collie joined her. "Do you remember Belle and me telling you about Marge Tulley? Well, she's here and she wants to meet you. She thought a lot of your father."

"I hope she likes me," Sarah whispered, dreading the confrontation.

"Just be yourself and you'll do fine. No, I better rephrase that, be your new self."

Collie escorted her through the crowd to a table in the corner. A large woman in men's clothing came to her feet. The hand she offered Sarah was as big as a dinner plate. Sarah smiled and shook the woman's hand, introducing herself. Marge Tulley eyed her from the top of her head to the toes of her shoes.

"You're just a tiny thing. And you're definitely not the mousy little thing I've been hearing about. Are the folks around here treatin' you right?"

"Yes, ma'am."

"Well, have a seat. If you've got a minute, maybe we can chew the fat for a spell. My boys'll be back soon and we'll have to start for home."

Sarah sat down and watched as Marge snipped the end from a cigar and ran her tongue around the dark rich tobacco before she applied a match. The woman inhaled deeply, pursed her lips, and blew a string of perfectly round smoke rings. The rings circled Sarah's head like a halo, then drifted toward the light in a widening circle. "Do you live far from town?"

" 'Bout fifteen miles west of town as the crow flies." Marge smoked her cigar and studied Sarah. "So, you think you've got the brass to run James's saloon."

111

"Yes, I think so. Anyway, I'm trying."

Sarah and Marge sat there for quite a while talking. Sarah had yet to find the woman's language crude or vulgar, just very to the point.

A mewling of sorrow erupted from a table several feet away. Sarah excused herself to see what was the matter. She hadn't taken three steps when the mewling began in earnest.

"Oooh . . . Katy," the lone man wailed, sitting beneath the sheet-draped painting.

As Sarah watched, he lifted a long thin stick toward the painting. She followed the direction of the stick. Her knees buckled, and she clasped the back of a chair. "Oh, my Lord," she whispered. Someone had cut out perfectly round circles in the sheet. Katy's large brown nipples glowed like beacons against the white background of the sheet.

The man prodded one hole, then the other, crying, "Oooh, Katy."

Sarah's back snapped straight, her arms still at her sides, and a red stain began at the base of her neck and crawled up the length of her throat. She didn't know what to do. The room was becoming quiet, and she could feel the eyes of her customers watching her. It dawned on her that covering the paintings only called attention to them.

"Shut up your caterwauling, Earl. Katy isn't the only woman in the place," Marge called to the man as she clamped a cigar between her teeth and settled back in her chair.

Earl eyed Marge's generous breasts and a smile closely resembling a leer lifted his mouth. He pushed back from the table and staggered toward her. Everyone in the room laughed.

Sarah breathed a sigh of relief and approached the

painting. With a flick of her wrist, the sheet drifted to the floor, baring Katy in all her naked splendor. A warm round of applause greeted the unveiling. One by one, the girls uncovered the paintings.

"You handled yourself very well, young lady. You might just have the brass to carry it off. If you ever need my help, just holler. James was good to me and my boys. He helped me out of a tight one once when I almost lost my ranch. I'll always be beholden to him and his kin," Marge said before she turned her attention to Earl.

Coleman Blade lifted the mug and took a deep pull of the amber brew, never taking his eyes from Sarah. God, she looked good. She had turned from an ugly duckling into a beautiful swan. Even as he admired her, one thought kept prodding through his head: Now more than ever, I'm absolutely damn sure that she has just made the job of protecting her harder. Now, every man for miles around will want a look, and maybe a feel, of the new saloon owner.

A puzzled frown marred his brow. What was it about her that drew him? From the first time he'd met her, there was something inside him that wanted to protect her. Hell, he'd never felt this way about anybody. Why her, of all the females he'd met? Was it her courage that he admired? Just when he thought he had her figured out, some new twist would lead him astray. He looked about the saloon in admiration. She'd tackled the job of cleaning the place, and by god she'd done it. Come hell or high water, she'd meant for the saloon to be clean. It was. Even Fancy Fingers Floyd had blossomed under her tutelage. The girls, Belle and Collie, treated her with respect and friendship, knowing that Sarah Hogan was as different from them as one could possibly get. Damn it, he would watch over her and do

113

his damnedest to protect her, but he wouldn't like it. And the next time Wes decided to take in a stray, he'd do well to call on somebody else to play nursemaid.

"Hello, Sheriff, busy night?"

God, her eyes were green. "Not bad, but it looks like you're doing a booming business."

"It tears at my conscience to think these men are spending their hard-earned money on drink. Still, I try to watch over them and send them home before they become inebriated," Sarah assured him proudly.

"Inebriated, huh? You mean drunk."

"Drunk, intoxicated—the list goes on—but we both know what I mean."

"So, the men of Hazard have their own little guardian angel." He lifted his hand and touched the tantalizing curl in front of her ear. When he did, his fingers grazed the side of her face and a bolt of desire shot through him. He tried to ignore it. "What about you, Widow Woman? Who watches over you?"

"You don't know it, Sheriff, but for the first time in my life I'm taking care of myself—and I can do it. I'm not a child."

"No, Sarah, you're not a child." He eyed the curves of her bodice. "And you're doing a damn fine job of running your saloon." He scanned the orderly saloon. Even Dusty Mills's thugs had toned down their roughhousing. "I think you're probably a very good businesswoman."

"Why, thank you, Sheriff. Coming from you, that means a great deal to me." She smiled brightly.

"I do have my moments."

"I believe you do," she teased.

"While I'm on a roll, let me tell you how nice you look tonight."

Sarah waited, watching him.

He waited, watching her.

She shifted.

"Well?" he asked, irritated that she hadn't commented on his compliment.

"I'm waiting."

"For what?"

"For you to tell me how nice I look tonight."

"I just did."

"No, you didn't. You said *let me* tell you how nice you look tonight."

"Sarah." His voice was threatening, but the smile he bestowed upon her took the bite from the single word.

"Okay, thank you for the compliment."

"You're welcome. I know you're busy, but walk me to the door. I have to make my rounds."

Sarah watched as Cole crossed the street. He stopped, and she wondered if something was wrong until she saw the flare of a match. As he lifted the match to the cigarette, she could see the planes of his face. Goosebumps ran over her body and she hugged her arms around her waist. He was such a handsome man. She was glad she'd worn the green dress. If she'd admit the truth, she'd done it all for Cole. "Oh, my, what am I getting into?" she whispered into the darkness.

Cole stood in the shadows and watched as one by one the lights in the saloon went out. In a few moments, a light in Sarah's apartment came on. He could see her moving about in her bedroom. It was the same every night. He felt like a peeping Tom watching her, but until he knew she was safe, he wouldn't abandon his vigil.

The first night he'd watched her, he had almost choked on the deep drag he'd just taken on his cigarette when she'd begun talking to someone. He'd peered intently into the lighted room. Did she have a man in her room? Her conversation had been animated as she'd paced the room, occasionally stopping and pointing at the bed. She'd undress a bit, then talk toward the bed again. Sometimes she'd remove a garment, and laugh and toss it toward the bed. Cole had become so angry wondering who was in her bed that it had taken him a while to notice her shapely body. When she'd approached the bed, he was ready to storm the building and drag her lover out into the street and beat him to a bloody pulp. Then suddenly there she was, standing at the window holding something in her arms. She'd leaned over and the bundle in her arms had leaped onto the rooftop and scampered away. "My god, a cat," Cole had whispered to the darkness, relief surging through him.

Cole shook his thoughts aside. He waited for her to put the cat out, knowing that when she did, it would only be a few moments before she would be safe and sound in her bed. As usual, after the cat crossed the rooftop, it made a beeline for Cole. He bent down and picked up Mr. Herman.

He chuckled. It had taken the cat only a couple of nights before it discovered Cole's presence in the shadows. Since then, the cat visited every night, rubbing around Cole's legs until he would squat down and pet it. Soon after, it would saunter away into the night in pursuit of whatever it was that cats did in the wee hours.

Cole remained in the shadows, waiting until darkness encompassed the room above the saloon, then he returned home to seek his own rest, confident that all was well.

Chapter Thirteen

From a deep sleep, Cole awakened instantly. He lay quietly, listening intently, when unexpectedly a shadowy blur shot across the bed. A melee of hammering legs and arms followed, accompanied by a chorus of grunts and groans. The combatants rolled from the bed, each struggling for control. At last Cole subdued his attacker, retorting sardonically, "You took your own sweet-ass time getting here."

"Patience was never one of your virtues, Cole," came the pert reply.

"Humph, I've made it thirty-four years without it."

Chin chuckled. "Yes, and sometimes I have wondered how." He looked up at his friend and added, "A cup of tea would be nice, unless keeping me pinned to this damnably hard floor is your intention. I have had a long journey."

"You still drinking that stump water?" Cole questioned, releasing his opponent and getting to his feet.

A match flared in the darkness as he lit a lantern. A mellow light shrouded the room, chasing the shadows into the corners. Cole picked up his discarded pants and slipped them on, watching as the little man bowed his back and sprang to his feet.

"I'll put the water on, then I'll bring you up-to-date on the happenings in Hazard." Taking the light, he led the way down a wide hallway into the kitchen.

"This is very nice, Cole," his friend said, noting the comfort of the room.

"It belonged to the man who hired me. He has since died and his daughter has taken over his properties."

Cole slid a chair from the table and straddled it. Studying his friend, he admitted, "I can tell you now, this sheriff business has its drawbacks."

"Could it be because you have a problem dealing with the limits of the law that your badge signifies, while the thieves run rampant with no regard for man or beast?"

"You do have a way with words, Chin, and a hellacious right cross," Cole assured him, tenderly stroking his bristled jaw.

"And you, my friend, have no respect for the fine teachings of an ancient art."

"If getting your brains kicked out when a strong uppercut will get the job done is disrespectful, then I'm a bastard through and through."

As the Chinaman prepared his tea, he eyed his friend and kept his comments to himself. He knew Coleman Blade better than anyone, and indeed there was a streak that ran through Cole that on occasion frightened even his friend.

"And what is my position in your scheme of things?"

"I'd like you to keep your eyes and ears open. Dusty Mills is after property, and he'll resort to any means to get it. He employs a league of men that carry out his orders."

"He sounds like a dangerous man."

"He is, and the thing that bothers me the most is the way he operates. He's a real smooth-talking charmer. Another problem is with the new owner of the saloon, Sarah Beth Hogan. She is as green as a spring apple, and her property sits right in the path Dusty Mills has woven for himself. If he sets his sights on this property, and I'm sure he has, I don't know if she can handle his charm without getting hurt."

"And you care if she is hurt?"

"Only because her father was a good friend," Cole bluntly assured him.

"Is there any evidence that a spur line is actually coming to Hazard?"

"Just speculation, as far as I've been able to tell. Still, Dusty Mills knows something. He whirled in here like a dust devil and began buying property."

"It sounds like you have your work cut out for you."

"It's not the work that I mind, but the manner in which I'm bound that rankles me."

"Why not turn in the badge and do it your way?"

"Because I gave my word."

"And your *word* means more to you than your *life?*" Chin added thoughtfully.

"I wouldn't say that."

"Why not? That is what it sounds like to me. That piece of tin you wear leaves you wide open for any kind of attack. The people you are dealing with do not have any rules. If it takes a bullet in the back, then so be it, as long as the job gets done."

Chin's outburst of anger surprised Cole. One of the many lessons the man had taught him was never to let anger overrule sound judgment. But he understood why Chin had broken his own rule: the man treated Cole like a son.

"It was my intention that you would guard my back," Cole answered quietly.

"Why did you not say so in the first place?" Chin blustered, busying himself preparing another cup of tea.

Not a hint of a smile touched Cole's face, but inside he was aglow. It was a rare day indeed when anyone caused the little Chinaman any discomfiture.

"I've been keeping an eye on Sarah Hogan, but a lady by the name of Juliet Barrington has taken possession of her late brother's property. It joins this land. If you could keep an eye on her, it would help a great deal. I can't watch both women and protect them from Dusty Mills."

Later, Chin retired to his own room, and Cole, back in bed, found sleep elusive. Instead, images of a friendless, lonely strapping youth beat to a pulp wouldn't leave him alone. It had happened a long time ago, but Cole could still remember the intense pain. He hadn't even been able to blink his eyes without pain shooting through his body.

A lady named Sally Backman had hired him to work on her ranch. He'd done the jobs no one else wanted, and he'd been at the beck and call of every hand on the place. He hadn't said much, and no one had said much to him—except to add to his list of chores. That had been fine with him; he hadn't had the time to shoot the breeze, anyway. Still, there'd been a man called Bo Allen who'd disliked Cole on sight. Cole had never figured it out. He'd done nothing to the man and had done his best to stay out of Bo's way. Some sixth sense had warned him that the man was a danger to him.

But as was the way of Cole's young life, he hadn't moved fast enough one day and Bo had collared him. When Bo had gotten him down, his rage had found a home, and he'd pummeled Cole until Cole had fallen unconscious.

Cole had never known when the ranch hands had wrestled Bo away from his broken body. Nor had he remembered the strong, gentle arms that had lifted him and carried him to a comfortable bed. His wounds had

120

been cleaned with carbolic acid, and his broken ribs swathed tightly, while eagle eyes had watched over him.

When Cole had regained consciousness, he'd uttered not a word, nor a grunt of pain as he'd shifted restlessly on the bed. But his storm-gray eyes had spoken volumes as they'd stared from his bruised and battered face. The questions posed in their depths had never passed across his swollen, distorted lips. Instead, he'd watched with wary disbelief every gesture the little Chinaman made, accepting his ministrations simply because he had no choice.

Cole had been young and the healing of his body had taken place rapidly. Yet, his spirit had been slow to respond to any form of kindness.

Cole had known who the Chinaman was—Sally Backman's houseboy. Chin, everyone had called him. Cole had never known if it was because he didn't have one, or if it was a shortened version of a longer name. Chin could enter a room so quietly he didn't stir the air. His words were few and as quiet as his movements, but when he'd talked, Cole had eagerly listened. Their friendship had begun slowly, until a trust had developed between these two unlikely comrades.

In the evenings while Cole had been bedridden, Chin had sat beside his bed, sipping green tea and extolling his philosophy. Cole soon learned he'd liberally sprinkled it with the teachings of Confucius and Buddha. At this particular time in Cole's life, moral character and responsibility had meant little to him. All he'd wanted to do was to beat the shit out of one Bo Allen. He'd wanted revenge, and none of Chin's sayings had encouraged that outcome.

Things had really become interesting for Cole when his body had completely healed. Chin had begun teaching him an age-old method of unarmed combat used by

121

Buddhist monks. Empty-hand, Chin had called it—in Japanese called Karate; in Chinese Kung fu—the use of controlled kicks or strikes with hands, elbows, knees, and feet.

At first, Cole had scoffed at the very idea that monks would have any knowledge that would interest him enough to consider learning. Hadn't Chin told him they were pious hermits?

Yet, his interest had perked when he saw the flowing circular motion that completely fooled an observer about the forthcoming blow delivered with lightning speed. Cole had become an avid pupil, taking to the ancient art like a duck to water. But he'd had no patience for the meditation. Empty-hand, yes—Cole had particularly liked the sound of that name.

Everywhere Cole had gone, every chore he'd performed, he'd approached with a flowing circular motion. The slop bucket he had used to feed the pigs became a mass of lumpy, dented metal. The chicken house had become a training ground for his chops and blows. He'd timed his strikes with the falling of eggs and had adjusted his speed according to where the yolk had splattered the wall. Eventually, he could balance an egg on the toe of his boot and send it spinning through the air in a sweeping arch, then catch it on the other foot without so much as a crack in the shell.

Chin hadn't questioned the dwindling number of eggs in the larder, but seemed pleased that he had chosen a worthy person with whom to share his knowledge.

The chickens had cackled and squawked raucously when Cole appeared, swiveling their necks and puffing their feathers in agitation. Cole had paid them little heed, for he had as yet to use his newfound skill when called upon to produce chickens for Sunday dinner.

Every week Chin had added some new instruction

until Cole's mind had been awash with *do's* and *don't's*. Still, he'd listened and had taken to heart everything his friend had told him.

And when Cole had finished his chores and darkness had halted his practice of empty-hand, Chin had brought out an abacus and textbooks. He heralded Confucius: "Any surplus energy may be used for book learning." Thus, the beginning of Cole's education. Cole hadn't taken to the book learning as he had to Chin's previous instruction until the little man had threatened the young upstart with abandonment of further advice on empty-hand.

Chin had also hinted that he was an expert with a knife. If Cole had any desire to learn the skill, he'd do well to put his nose to the grindstone and apply himself posthaste to his studies.

Again, the henhouse had become a training ground as Cole counted everything he'd come in contact with. He'd shuffled the chickens from nest to nest as he'd added, then had reversed the process as he'd subtracted. When Chin had begun teaching Cole multiplication, Cole had developed his own system, using the eggs he'd gathered. Like it or not, the hapless chickens and their product had become an instrument of education.

After continually serenading the chickens with a ditty, Chin had started teaching him the alphabet. The weary chickens completely quit laying.

When Cole had become proficient with empty-hand, and Chin was sure he wouldn't abandon his studies, he'd begun to teach him the art of knife fighting. As in his other instruction, Chin had been exacting and merciless.

On occasion, Chin had removed the rawhide strip he'd worn around his neck and had bound their wrists together. They'd then fight until one of them dropped.

123

Other times, they'd hold the corners of a handkerchief between their teeth, Chin testing the knowledge he'd shared with Cole. Even when Cole had slept, he'd not been free of instruction. Chin had thought nothing of a midnight attack.

Not only had Cole learned to defend himself with his limbs, he'd also developed lightning skill with a knife. Still, there had been more to it than that. His senses had become finely tuned to the slightest sound, smell, sight, touch, or taste.

But above all, he'd learned the pleasure of his own company.

The weeks had turned into months, the months into years, and Cole had turned from a gangly youth into a handsome young man. He'd been a dependable worker and had gotten along well with the other ranch hands, but there'd been a distance about him that hadn't invited familiarity.

And unknown to Cole, he had caught the eye of Sally Backman. She'd hired him when he was no more than thirteen, an orphan on his own. Through the years she'd paid him little attention, because he'd never caused any trouble, and he'd earned his keep. And then suddenly she discovered he was no longer a mere boy but a man.

One hot, sultry day as she was returning from a neighboring ranch, Sally had seen him replacing fence posts. She pulled her carriage to a halt, watching as he worked. The sweat glimmered in the sunlight, rolling down his shirtless bronzed back. The muscles tightened and bunched as he lifted the post and worked it into the ground. Cole noticed that Sally Backman had also broken into a sweat as she'd watched him tamp the dirt into the hole until he'd set the post satisfactorily.

That evening, she had sent for Cole. Another lesson

was in store for him, and he took to it as he had so long ago taken to empty-hand. They became lovers that same night.

Sally had been like Chin in one respect—she was exacting in everything she did. (She'd had to be to single-handedly run a ranch the size of hers.)

She had taught Cole the secrets of a woman's body, and the patience to achieve ultimate pleasure. Cole had always been a fast learner, and this school of sensual pleasure had been no different. Soon he became the teacher and she the pupil as they traversed the path of higher learning.

The ranch hands had grumbled as they trudged through the early morning mist to the mess hall. Bo Allen shoved his way through the waiting line to the front and filled his plate. Since Sally Backman's affection for him had waned, and Cole Blade had now become the center of her attention, everyone had cleared a wide path for the surly brute.

When Cole had entered, scrubbed and freshly shaven, every head turned and every hand paused, waiting expectantly. As though snapped to attention, all heads shifted from the handsome young man to the bloodshot eyes of the bristle-faced Bo Allen.

The hand paused at Bo's mouth came down on the table in a rushing blow, sending his plate flipping through the air. Eggs splattered his companions and the thick bottom of a biscuit dripping with sawmill gravy landed smartly against the side of Bo's head before it hit the floor with a splatter.

One old-timer who didn't care much for Bo anyway had piped up, "My ma always told me that old sawmill gravy stuck to your ribs, but I'll be gol-dang if I knowed it'd stick to your ear like that, Bo."

"Shut your fool mouth, if you know what's good for you," Bo had shouted, swiping at the gravy dripping from his ear.

The old-timer had chuckled merrily, returning his attention to his plate.

"You got nose trouble, Blade?" Bo had shouted when he saw Cole glance in his direction.

"Not that I know of," Cole had answered offhandedly.

"You think you're something now that you're banging the boss lady, don't you?"

"What I think is none of your business."

"You ain't hiding nothing. We all know what's going on. It was purty good stuff when I was getting it, but that was before I wore it out."

"It's still good—when you get past the *used*," Cole had added sharply.

It had then become so quiet one could have heard a feather drifting through the air as the men noted the slur on Bo's manhood. The titters began slowly, then built to full-blown guffaws.

A red haze of hatred blistered Bo's common sense and he had shoved from the table and approached Cole. He'd always hated the bastard, even when Cole had been just a kid. "I hope to hell you've got a hardy appetite, boy, because you're gonna eat them words."

"It'll take more of a man than you'll ever be to make me. You're not dealing with a kid anymore."

Bo adjusted his low-slung holster.

Chairs scraped the floor and booted feet scurried for cover as the two men faced each other.

Bo straddled his legs, positioning his hand over the butt of his revolver.

126

Cole stood perfectly still, never lifting his gun hand.

Sweat broke out on Bo's forehead, and the armpits of his shirt became stained with perspiration. His hand wavered slightly above his gun.

Cole watched until the man's hand closed around the butt of the gun and his arm began an upward arch.

Bo's gun had cleared the holster when Cole's foot caught him just under the chin, sending his head slamming backward. Everyone heard the snapping of bone just before Bo Allen crumpled to the floor in a dead heap.

The men had rushed from their cover to examine Bo. No gunfight, this—it had happened so fast they hadn't been sure of what they had seen. They'd looked from the dead body to Cole in astonishment.

"How'd you do that?" the old-timer had questioned.

"Just good reflexes. I didn't stand a chance of beating him on the draw. All I ever use the gun for is killing rattlers." He patted the holster, housing his gun.

"Well, as far as I'm concerned, you've just killed the meanest snake in these here parts, and you did it with your foot." The old-timer had scratched his jaw in thought. "I think these gol-dang eyes of mine just ain't what they used to be. But yeah, you killed him with your foot."

Cole left the mess hall and packed his gear. The time to move on had come. He had another lesson to learn, a lesson he couldn't learn here. He'd bid Sally Backman farewell, thanking her for everything. Leaving Chin was the hardest. He'd been the only true friend Cole had ever had. The mutual respect of teacher and pupil had created a bond that could never be broken.

Still, Cole had vowed when he'd stood poised before Bo Allen that he would never find himself in a situation like that again. If he was to protect himself, he couldn't depend solely on empty-hand or his skill with a knife. A fast gun was the law of the land, and he intended to be the best.

Chapter Fourteen

Twilight descended upon Hazard. Westward, the coral glow of the sunset still hung above the hills, while in the east, the moon's silver crescent was poised against the darkening blue of the summer sky. Along with the continuous whirr of cicadas rose the mimicking call of the mockingbird. Carried on the warm restless wind was the sounds of revelry drifting through the open doors of the Do Drop In.

Inside the saloon, Sarah and Billy sat at a corner table playing cards. For several days, Billy had been instructing her on card games the men played, five-card draw being her favorite. Sarah had surprised him with her uncanny ability to remember the cards played.

Billy chewed on the remnant of his stale stogy waiting for Sarah to decide how to play her hand. She looks quite fetchin' tonight, he thought, admiring her gown of cream brocade. No longer did she resemble the meek minister's widow. He'd noticed the sheriff's interest in her, too. His face had taken on a new expression, speculative and admiring, not his usual expression of cynicism or broodiness.

From a conversation he had overheard between Collie and Belle, he knew that Sarah had taken a liking for the sheriff. Billy smiled. Suddenly a frown replaced his smile. He was a little worried about her falling in love with the sheriff. From what he knew of the handsome man, he might not be the kind who'd want to take a wife and settle down. He might be quick with a gun, accurate with his blade, and a real lover, but as a husband for Sarah? He just didn't know.

Still, Billy detected a restless stirring inside the sheriff, sort of like the calm before a storm. The storm was brewing, and he knew it wouldn't be long before the town bore the brunt of it.

After drumming her fingertips on the table for several moments, Sarah pulled a card from her hand and laid it facedown on the table. "I'll take one card, Billy."

"Just one?" he asked with a smile.

"One's fine."

"Want to put a little money in the pot to make it more interestin, missy?"

"No, I'm not ready for that, yet."

"Whatever you say." After she picked up her card, he watched her mouth curve into a sly smile. "Keep a poker face, Sarah. Anybody looking at you would know you probably have good cards." He dealt himself three cards and looked at them. "I fold," he said, placing them on the table.

"Do you mind?" she asked, turning over his cards and spreading them. "You would've beat me with your pair of sixes." She showed him her cards—a pair of fours, and nothing else.

"So-o-o," he drawled, "you tried to mislead me. You learn quick. But if you were playing against a real gambler, I hope you would've folded and not bet on such nonsense."

"No, I was only seeing if I could trick you . . . and I did." She pushed her cards to him. "Now, teach me to cheat, Billy."

"Teach you to do what?" Billy sputtered.

Sarah refused to be put off. "To cheat. I know you

know how. I heard you and Gunter talking about it."

Billy sighed deeply and rolled his eyes. "Anything in particular you wanted to learn?"

Sarah leaned forward on her elbows watching intently, trying to catch Billy when he palmed a card. "You are really good," she admitted when he showed her the card.

"Maybe, but I wouldn't encourage cheating. It can get you killed."

"Oh, I don't want to cheat. I just want to know what to watch for."

"That too can get you killed, young lady."

"Will you show me again, if I promise not to call anyone a cheater?"

Suddenly the buzz of activity in the room came to a breathless pause. The look of disgust that streaked across Billy's face caused Sarah concern. His eye had narrowed to a mere slit and a sneer curled his lips as he stared behind her. With a puzzled frown, she twisted around in her seat to see what had brought on the sudden change in his expression.

Two brawny, bull-necked men stood rigidly in the doorway. Both were heavily armed, their faces sullen and threatening. Were they gunslingers? she wondered, shuddering as a chill ran up her spine.

She swiveled around in her chair toward Billy. "Who are they?"

"Dusty's henchmen—and speak of the devil, there he is."

Sarah leaned forward and whispered, "Now, Billy, I know you don't like him, and I'll admit I have my doubts about him too, but please be nice. He hasn't done anything wrong."

"Yet," Billy finished smugly. "Just give him time and he will."

"What's that supposed to mean?"

"He's looking around the room, probably for you." He patted her hand. "Stay put and maybe he won't see you. Then you'll see exactly why I warned you about the man. It might not make that box of chocolates and pretty gloves he gave you seem so special."

Dusty's deep voice drew their attention. "Mind if I join you boys for a few hands?"

Silence fell in the room until finally a man said, "Uh . . . sure . . . it's fine with me, Dusty. Caleb? Ben? That all right with you?"

"Reckon so, as long as it ain't a long evening. Got to get up early in the mornin' and repair some fences before the heat sets in."

"Hey, Belle, bring these gentlemen a bottle." Dusty kicked back a chair and sat down. "I won't keep you long . . . I promise."

Billy looked across at Sarah. "He won't keep them long because they'll be broke before the first hour's up."

Sarah glanced once again at Dusty. "Is he that good a gambler?"

Billy sneered. "No, he's just good at cheatin'."

"Cheating? If that's true, why does anyone play with him?"

"It's not that simple, missy. What are the men going to say? They're not going to come right out and accuse him—then he would kill them."

"Why doesn't Sheriff Blade do something to stop him?" she prompted.

"He has to prove it first. You don't call a man a cheater without havin' somethin' to back it up."

The sound of the piano, the hum of voices, and the clinking of coins returned, breaking the tenseness in the room. Billy left Sarah to do his chores, and Dusty's

132

employees swaggered to the table, pulling up chairs just beyond the game.

From the corner of her eye, Sarah saw a towering figure just outside the saloon doors. Cole pushed the doors and purposely made his way to the bar. The muscles in his jaw tense, his lips set, and his face hard, he didn't invite conversation. He found his usual place at the bar and shoved his hand in his pocket. Drawing out a coin, he placed on the smooth surface. "Give me a beer, Gunter."

"Your money's no good in here, Sheriff," Gunter replied, sliding a mug of golden brew across the counter.

Sarah noticed that Cole had tucked the tail of his jacket behind his holster when he removed the coin. Was he expecting trouble? She watched his reflection in the mirror as he lifted the mug and took a long drink of the beer.

Only after he'd set the glass on the bar did he turn around and scan the room. He cut his eyes toward Dusty's table, then glanced fleetingly around the room for Sarah. When he didn't see her, he returned his attention to Dusty.

Dusty rocked back in his chair and eyed Cole through the pall of smoke. A smile of malice parted the older man's lips as one hand played idly with his cards. Neither spoke, but the silence was palpable. Raising his glass, Dusty gestured a mock toast before he took a long pull from his drink.

Sarah watched the scene with interest. Well, whatever else Dusty Mills might be, he certainly has iron nerves, she thought. Cole was a man to be reckoned with.

Cole watched as the men continued their game, and Dusty raked in the money. As Dusty's pile grew, so did Cole's suspicions that something wasn't right. Then it hit him. He'd been watching the wrong man. Without appearing obvious, he shifted his gaze to Dusty's hired men, sitting behind the other players. For men who weren't a part of the game taking place, they were suspiciously intent on it.

It didn't take Cole long to figure out what was going on. Their signals were subtle enough, but they were signals no less.

Cole's movement was so unexpected that no one noticed he'd moved until he leaned over the man's shoulder. "Shooter, isn't that your name?"

The hired gunman jumped before he could stop himself. "Yeah, what's it to you?"

"Let's me and you step outside."

"I ain't done nothing," the man bellowed.

"Haven't you?" came the cold reply.

"Well, I ain't going nowhere with you."

Thinking no one was paying any attention to him, the other gunman eased his hand to his holster.

"Unless you favor a bullet through your friend's back, I wouldn't do that," Cole threatened.

"You're absolutely right," Shooter replied, the cold metal barrel resting against his spine the only encouragement he needed to agree with the sheriff. His friend jerked his hand from his gun and cupped his knees with his hands.

Shooter wilted against his chair, knowing the sheriff had no qualms about shooting him right where he sat. "Oh, hell," he mumbled as he got to his feet, casting Dusty an exasperated look.

"You men get back to your game," Cole said. "Maybe you'll find Lady Luck in your corner now." After his remark, his eyes gleamed with victory as he cut his eyes toward Dusty.

Dusty wanted to kill the man. A cold fury built in him until he thought he would smother. It was a humiliation to himself that the sheriff knew he'd been cheating a bunch of two-bit ranchers. By god, he'd get him if it was the last thing he ever did.

Every eye watched as Cole escorted the men to the door and warned them that they might live longer if they made it a habit to avoid the saloon.

The blood was roaring through Sarah's ears as she rushed to the bar, her progress so great that her shoes should have sent forth sparks. She knew little about how the cheating had been done. But something had tipped off the sheriff, and she wanted to help him. "I'll take these," she offered as Collie turned from the bar with a tray of drinks, destined for Dusty's table.

"What are you doing, Sarah?" Collie asked, perplexed.

"Oh, I just thought I'd help you out a bit," Sarah said, smiling devilishly.

Sarah hastened to the table, the tray tilting precariously in her grasp.

Cole stepped back inside just in time to see Sarah pause before the table. His brow knitted in curiosity as he watched her. There was something expectant and anxious in her face.

"Your drinks, gentlemen," she purred. "My goodness, just look how well you're doing, Dusty."

She felt the glare of the other men's eyes on her as she placed a drink in front of Dusty. "None for me, Sarah, but thank you."

"Oh, but your glass is empty." Leaning over to pick it up and put it on her tray, her tray tilted and the drinks spilled over Dusty's jacket and trousers.

"My god, watch what you're doing," he shouted as he leaped to his feet, wiping his hands across his soaked jacket.

"Oh, I'm so sorry," she exclaimed, "how clumsy of me."

When Dusty looked at her, she saw the veins pulsing in his temple.

"Here, let me have your jacket, Dusty," she said, pulling at his sleeve. "I'll have it cleaned."

"It isn't necessary, Sarah," he said, clenching his teeth.

"Oh, but I must," she insisted, trying to tug his sleeve over his shoulder.

When he resisted, she tugged harder. As he shook his arm out of her grasp, her hand slipped and knocked over a glass on the table. Startled, a drunk Ben Davis jumped up and toppled the table, sending cards, money, overflowing ashtrays, and empty glasses in every direction.

"Oh, Dusty," she said in mock apology, "I've really made a mess of things. It looks like I've ruined your game."

"Not really, Sarah, the money was mine anyway," Dusty said smoothly, trying to sound pleasant. Inside, his blood was boiling in his veins.

Cole approached them, not even glancing at Sarah. With a suspicious glint in his eyes, he asked, "All of it, Mills?"

After a dramatic pause, Dusty said, "Yes, Sheriff, all of it."

The room suddenly became deathly still as the customers waited doggedly to see what would happen next. The men who had gambled with Dusty weren't about to argue with him. They were scared, and all they wanted to do was get the hell away from him before blood was shed, possibly theirs.

Sarah grew uneasy as she watched the men, her eyes wide with apprehension as Cole and Dusty sized each other up, their hatred thick in the air.

"Then, I suggest you take your winnings and leave,"

Cole ordered.

A sardonic smile pulled at one corner of Dusty's mouth. "And if I don't?"

Sarah panicked. Dusty seemed to be purposely taunting Cole. She started forward.

"Stay back, Sarah," Cole barked.

"No!" Sarah positioned herself between Cole and the two men. She turned to Dusty Mills. "Dusty, this situation is getting totally out of hand. If I hadn't been so clumsy, none of this would've ever happened." She looked up at him pleadingly. "Please, I don't want any trouble."

A slow smile curved Dusty's mouth. "I don't want trouble either, so to prove to you I'm a fair man, I will relinquish my winnings to these men. They can divide the money between themselves however they wish."

The men's mouths gaped open in astonishment.

Sighs of relief swept through the crowd.

Then Dusty said to Sarah. "Now, I must be on my way." He took her hand and pressed it to his mouth. Releasing it, he said, "I hope the next time we meet, the situation will be different."

With a wicked gleam of satisfaction on his face, Dusty nodded to Cole. "Good evening, Sheriff."

Dusty swaggered toward the door and pushed it open. For a moment, silence hung in the room. No one could quite believe what had just happened. Cole knew exactly why Dusty had played himself up to be the hero, not the cheating, murdering bastard that he was. His eyes riveted toward Sarah, watching the play of expressions on her face. Was she so naive that she believed the man?

Sarah stood quietly beside Cole, confused by everything that had happened.

Fancy Floyd Fingers began pounding out his rendition of "Little Brown Jug," some of the cowboys began singing along, and the charged atmosphere returned to normal. Ben and the other gamblers straightened the table and chairs, then picked up the bills and coins from the floor, distributing it among themselves.

Sarah felt a hand on her arm and looked up at Cole. His face was as hard as steel. "Let's talk . . . in private."

"What . . . what about?"

Before she could protest, he took hold of her arm and began drawing her toward the back of the saloon, down the narrow corridor, and out the back door.

Chapter Fifteen

Spinning Sarah around, Cole gripped her by the shoulders and asked reproachfully, "Did you purposely spill those drinks on Dusty?"

Sarah looked off in the night. "What if I did?"

"I might just wring your neck."

"In that case, I didn't."

"Like hell you didn't!"

"That's what I said."

He raised a finger in warning, silencing her. "Don't, Sarah."

After a moment, he dropped his hand and stared at her in exasperation.

A sheepish grin curved her mouth as she said quietly, "All right, I did do it—on purpose. I thought he was cheating, and I'd hoped to catch him in the act."

He lifted a questioning brow. "And what would you have done if you had caught him?"

"I . . . well . . ." she floundered, then smiled lamely. "You're the sheriff, so I guess you would've done something."

Cole emitted a long sigh. "Yeah, I wouldn't have had much choice not to do something. I'd already caught one of Dusty's men signaling him."

"I knew something fishy was going on. That's why I decided I should do something to help you."

"Sarah . . ." Words failing him, he pushed back the

brim of his hat and studied her. At length, he said, "Sarah, honest to god, if you don't break this impulsive habit of yours, it's going to break me."

Sarah lowered her head in chagrin and clasped her hands in front of her. "I'm sorry; I don't go looking for trouble, but it always seems to find me."

Cole lifted her chin. "Yes, I know. Every day I wonder what you have in store for me. You seldom disappoint me, Widow Woman. You're always doing something—"

"To break the monotony, right?" she broke in with a smile.

He chuckled. "Yeah, something like that. But, Sarah, this foolhardy thing you pulled with Dusty tonight scared me. He's not to be trusted."

"I know. Billy told me the same thing. He said Dusty had bought a lot of property in and around Hazard because of some rumor about a railroad spur, and that he'd got it crookedly. I didn't believe him at first because Dusty's been so nice to me."

"Billy's right, Sarah."

"Yes, and so was Mr. Herman. He attacked Dusty."

Cole threw back his head and burst into laughter. "Now I know why Mr. Herman and I get along so well. We both share the same feelings towards the man."

Sarah joined him in laughter. When they finally caught their breath, she told him what happened.

"Then, the more I thought about Mr. Herman's strange behavior, I decided that maybe my cat knew something I didn't. He's always been so friendly."

On a more serious note, Cole said, "Sometimes animals can sense things—storms, danger . . . things like that. I agree with Mr. Herman, Sarah. Please watch yourself around Dusty, all right?"

"I will, Cole, I promise," she answered softly.

As she stared up at him, her shining green eyes were glowing with such innocence that it stabbed at his heart and sent his pulses throbbing. The temptation to kiss her almost won over his better judgment, but he knew by the entranced look on her face that if he kissed her just once, nothing would ever be the same again for them. Sooner or later she would get over her infatuation, if he would just leave things like they were.

Sarah couldn't account for the sudden madness that overcame her. Some feeling she couldn't recognize caused her to lift her hand and touch gently the shadow that outlined the curve of his cheek.

Cole froze, his lean muscles hardening, but he couldn't prevent the blood from singing wildly through his veins. His heart thumped in his chest and his brain began to reel as her finger moved to his mouth and caressed his lower lip. Words formed in his mouth, yet he couldn't speak them. He wanted to ask her what the hell she thought she was doing.

He was leaning very close to her when suddenly she clasped him behind his neck and brought his head down, kissing his surprised mouth. His good intentions evaporated. One hand stole to her back and pulled her tightly against him while the other slid up beneath the mass of curls at her neck. With a savage twist of his mouth, he crushed her full lips against his own and deepened the kiss.

She felt his powerful thighs moving against her, the silken garments beneath her gown grazing softly over her flesh. The effect on her senses was like nothing she had ever known when his hot tongue found entrance into the warm recesses of her mouth. Though not an innocent, Sarah was inexperienced with his kissing, but her shock was short-lived as her desire mounted apace with his. Then her arms circled him passionately in a

141

clasp that shut out the world for what might have been a second or . . . eternity.

An internal voice called out to Cole in warning. *Good god, man, have you completely lost your mind?* Cole broke the kiss. Releasing her, he turned away to pull himself together, the knot of pain in his loins unbearable.

Her face flushed with feverish passion and her chest rapidly rising and falling, Sarah watched him with uncertainty. Her mind was a labyrinth of confusion. Why had he stopped so abruptly?

"Go back inside, Sarah," he ordered huskily, his voice raw with emotion.

"Did I . . . did I do it wrong?"

His voice earnest and unusually tender, he admitted, "No, you did it very right."

"Then, what's the matter?"

"It has nothing to do with you." Hell, it had everything to do with her, he admitted silently.

"How can it have nothing to do with me when we were kissing?"

Damn, she was the most frustrating woman he'd ever met. "All right, yes, it has everything to do with you. But maybe I want more than kisses from you," he said, trying to scare her. He stepped in closer to her. "Maybe you want it too."

Sarah stepped back one step, her eyes wide.

"Do you, Sarah?" he whispered softly.

"I . . . I don't know." Suddenly feeling more sure of herself, she replied recklessly, "I do know I'm not sorry I kissed you."

"For god's sake, will you hush?" Cole groaned.

She crossed her arms, and with a determined thrust of her chin she added, "I'm glad I did it."

Cole couldn't help laughing a little. "Well, now

142

maybe you've got me out of your system. Right?"

A desire to break through his stubborn veneer sent quick impulsive words springing to her lips. "No. And I'm thinking, Cole, that you liked that kiss as much as I did."

Sarah brought her hand to her mouth and kissed her fingers, then pressed them lightly against his lips. "Good night, Cole," she quipped saucily, and opening the door, she left him standing with a nonplussed expression on his face.

"Damn it, if she's not the most infuriating woman I've ever met, I'll eat my hat." Cole vowed. Her habit of surrendering to impulses without considering the outcome of her actions was keeping his mind in a perpetual state of chaos. How was he to handle Sarah Hogan? If he had any sense at all, he'd turn tail and run. But how could he run when he was the sheriff with obligations to fulfill. And as it looked now, Sarah was his biggest obligation. He never knew from one moment to the next when she might need him — or when she *thought* he might need her.

After rolling a cigarette, he struck the match across the sole of his boot and lit it. Leaning against the post, he took a deep draw and exhaled slowly. In melancholy silence, he pondered his dilemma.

Wes had warned him she might surprise him when she decided to shed her widow's weeds, but nothing had prepared him for the incredible changes he'd seen in her. He knew it wasn't only her new clothes and her wondrous hair that intrigued him. It was Sarah herself. Feeling confident with her new image, Sarah seemed to have unleashed a myriad of emotions she'd kept bottled up inside her for a lifetime.

Cole chuckled softly. God, she hadn't known the first thing about kissing. When her mouth had first touched his lips, he could have sworn he was kissing the belly of a snake, but that sensation hadn't lasted long. Her lips had suddenly turned hot and moist, eager and willing. He'd recognized a fire burning in her that matched his own. Then he'd felt her full, soft breasts pressing against him. Restraining his passion had been like damming a river and trying to stop it before it burst. Well, it had burst, and he had let the full tide of his passion sweep over and almost destroy his reasoning. He'd wanted her so damned badly it had been a miracle he hadn't taken advantage of the moment and given her a lesson in something other than kissing. Damn, there was so much to teach her. Just thinking about it made him grow hard again.

But Sarah was green, grass-green. She'd been brought up—no, not brought up, but choked down—by a family who'd starved her soul by denying her any love or affection.

And what about him? Where was the heart of steel he'd built up over the years? To find it so easily melted by this woman's kisses troubled him worse than facing a deadly enemy. He knew how to dodge bullets—he'd dodged many—but dodging Sarah Hogan was a whole different matter.

Tossing his cigarette away, he watched its glowing tip arc through the air, then pushed away from the post and ambled to the jail.

Upstairs in her room, Sarah lay in her bed, smiling into the darkness, feeling completely lighthearted and tingly all over, just the way she knew a woman in love should feel. No man could kiss a woman like that and not feel something, could he? She felt hot all over as she relived the wonderful sensation of Cole's mouth ca-

144

ressing her own, his tongue sliding between her lips and filling her mouth with its hotness. Before that moment, she had only half realized the restlessness and yearning stirring inside her. Now she was filled with such aliveness, such energy, she felt instinctively that his kiss promised more.

Flinging back the covers, Sarah walked to the window, relishing the feel of the cool night air on her heated flesh. Her heart did a somersault. Cole was sitting on the bench outside the jail, holding Mr. Herman in his arms. Was he thinking of her as he stroked the cat? Sarah sighed wistfully, and, crossing her arms, slowly rubbed her hands over them, purring with her own contentment.

When Cole went inside the jail, Sarah climbed back in bed and snuggled deep into the feather mattress. Her mind completely intoxicated with Cole, she closed her eyes. As one hand went up slowly and touched her mouth, she made a silent wish.

I wish for him to kiss me first . . . the next time.

Cole paced the floor in front of Wes's desk, telling him about the incident with Dusty. "Now, get this. You know I've had Chin watching Juliet Barrington's house. Last night around midnight, she had a visitor who stayed for several hours. Chin got a good look at him when he left. It was Dusty Mills."

"Dusty!" Wes exclaimed. Leaning forward, he propped his elbows on the desk. "Well, I'll be damned. I didn't realize she knew the gentleman. Apparently she knows him quite well, if he's calling on her in the dead of night. This really sheds a different light on Miss Barrington. I wonder how they became so close in such a short time?"

145

"Your guess is as good as mine." Cole sat down on the edge of the desk and steepled his fingers, raking them across his stubbled chin. "You know, it wouldn't bother me at all if Mills was visiting her during the day or the evening. But that time of night? I know something's up."

"The last time I saw her, I asked her if she planned to sell her property and return to London. She said no, not at the moment. She wants to live here awhile before making any decision." Wes slumped back in his chair. "Guess all we can do is keep a close watch on Dusty and watch for any other developments."

Dusty was in the hardware store when he saw Gunter enter. As Gunter talked with the proprietor about obtaining more glasses for the saloon, Dusty slipped by him unnoticed and headed for the saloon. Checking his timepiece, he knew it was too early in the morning for anyone to be in the saloon, except maybe that bastard Billy Ward. Not knowing Sarah's morning routine, he decided to see if she might be there alone. He hoped that if Sarah had suspected him of cheating, he'd erased those thoughts when he'd left his winnings to his opponents. When she'd spilled those drinks on him, accident or not, she'd given him an opportunity to save face. But should she appear uncomfortable with him, he'd know she still didn't trust him. Damn Blade for messing up his plans with Sarah. Ever since Blade had come to this town, he'd been a thorn in his side—but he wouldn't be for long, Dusty vowed as he crossed the street.

Looking out the window of the jail, Cole saw Dusty pausing outside the door of the saloon. So he didn't take my subtle warning seriously, Cole thought angrily.

As Dusty entered, Cole quit the jail and hurried across the street.

On her knees behind the bar, Sarah was counting the bottles of liquor stored on the shelves beneath it. Her mind cluttered with figures and brand names, she didn't hear the creaking of the doors as they swung open. She continued jotting the figures down on the small notebook lying on the floor beside her.

It wasn't until she heard Cole's voice that she realized she wasn't alone.

"What's the matter, Mills? Afraid you've lost favor in the lady's eyes?"

Dusty turned, seeing his nemesis as he walked through the door. "Why I'm here is none of your business, Sheriff."

"I'm making it my business."

Cole? Dusty? Sarah remained crouched behind the bar. This time she would control her impulsiveness and stay put.

"Is there a law that says I *can't* call on the lady?"

"Maybe I need to refresh your memory. *I* am the law, Mills . . . and the law doesn't allow card cheats in this saloon."

Dusty chuckled maliciously. "Tell me something, Sheriff, is that what's really bothering you, or could it be that you have your eye on the lady, too?"

"Yeah, I have my eye on her."

His confession caused Sarah's heart to race wildly through her chest.

"Just like I keep my eye on everyone in this town," he added. "Part of my job, you know."

Is kissing the women part of your job too? she almost blurted. Then she remembered . . . *she* had kissed *him*. Well, it didn't matter. He had liked it, and in a roundabout way had even admitted it. But how foolish of her to think he'd ever admit such a thing to Dusty Mills.

"Whatever, you can't prevent me from seeing her. We became very close during her convalescence. If she thinks I cheated, I want to hear it from her mouth, not yours."

"Very well, then we'll wait on her to come down. But, Mills, anything you have to say to her, you'll say in my presence. Too bad you didn't bring flowers or chocolates. You might need them," Cole said sarcastically.

Dusty glowered. "In that case, Sheriff, I'll save my words for later. I *will* be back," he said, walking briskly past Cole and out the door.

As Cole started to follow him out, he heard a crashing sound behind him and turned abruptly, watching as a liquor bottle rolled to the end of the bar.

Cole walked around the bar and saw Sarah crouched on the floor amidst several bottles. He pushed back the brim of his hat with his thumb. "Mornin', Sarah."

"Uh . . . mornin', Sheriff," she said with a lame smile. "I . . . ah . . . was counting the inventory. I accidentally knocked a bottle against another one, and, well . . ." her voice trailed off.

"You heard?"

"Of course I heard."

"Well, for once you had enough sense to keep your mouth shut."

"It does happen occasionally."

He chuckled. Brushing his jacket aside, he rested his hands on his hips. "What are you going to do about it?"

"Start cleaning it up, I guess. Gunter'll have a fit when he gets back. He had it all sorted and—"

"I'm not talking about the bottles, Sarah. It's Mills

148

I'm referring to."

"I'm going to forget the incident and hope it doesn't happen again."

"Sarah, he was right about one thing. I can't prevent him from seeing you. If he bothers you, it's up to you to put a stop to it."

She sighed. "I know. I'll handle it . . . somehow." Settling back on her haunches, she said, "Right now, I'm more concerned about getting all this mess back in order."

"Where is Gunter?"

"I sent him to the store to buy more glasses for the bar. Afterwards, he had a few personal errands to run."

"Maybe I can help you."

Her face brightened. "Oh, would you?"

Strolling down the narrow aisle, Cole picked up some of the bottles in his path and set them inside on the shelf. Squatting, he looked along the shelf that ran the length of the bar. Only a few bottles remained standing. "Well, where do you want me to start?" he asked, and looked over at her.

Sarah was staring at him with that same star-struck gaze he'd seen on her face for the past week. It was that infernal kiss they'd shared.

"Shouldn't we get busy?" he asked with a lazy smile.

"Oh! Yes, of course. We'll start here and work our way down the shelf."

He nodded.

Side by side, their bodies touching, Sarah breathed in his heady masculine scent—a manly scent of leather, tobacco, and the woodsy-smelling soap he used. While straightening the bottles, Cole's hand closed over hers as they picked up the same one. In unison, their heads turned and their eyes locked and held.

Green fire met smoldering gray.

149

Their gazes dropped, each to the other's mouth.

As Cole's hand tightened over hers, Sarah leaned in closer to him.

Each waited, their mouths so close their quick breaths mingled.

Kiss me, she willed silently.

Kiss her, his body demanded, reacting to her nearness. His eyes lingered on her mouth as the tip of her tongue slowly ran along her lips.

Not now, not here, you fool, Cole berated himself. Suddenly he released her hand and, turning his attention back to the shelf, began righting the overturned bottles. "Where does this one go?"

"Here," she said, taking the bottle and trying to reach beyond him.

Losing her balance, Sarah fell against Cole, and both fell sideways, Sarah finding herself lying halfway atop him.

"Oh mercy, I'm sorry, Cole," she said, gazing down on his handsome face.

"I doubt that, Widow Woman." Damnation, now why the hell did I say that? he thought.

Strange, she thought, how the name leaving his lips didn't sound vulgar this time. Sarah smiled, recalling Wes's words. "I am a widow . . . and I am a woman." Suddenly Sarah's eyes widened as she realized she'd voiced her thoughts. Her face turned as red as a beet.

Cole grinned rakishly, his hungry gray eyes roaming here and there over her face. "That you are, Sarah Hogan, that you are."

Captivated by the spark of passion he found glittering in her eyes, desire raged inside him. Knowing he would probably regret it a thousand times over, Cole cupped her pert chin and lifted his head to meet her mouth.

"Got the glasses, Sarah," came Gunter's voice as he entered the saloon.

Cole rolled from beneath her and scrambled to his knees, jerking a flush-faced, glazed-eyed Sarah to a sitting position only seconds before Gunter rounded the end of the bar.

Holding a crate of glasses in front of him, his eyes darted from Sarah to Cole and then to the floor where several bottles still rested. "What happened?"

Nothing, thanks to you, they both thought in unison.

Sarah cut her eyes toward Cole and saw his mouth twitching with laughter. "I made a mess and the sheriff was helping me clean it up."

Cole rose and said, "Gunter will be a bigger help at this than me, I'm sure. See you later, Widow Woman," he said with a knowing grin.

Once outside, Cole hurried across the street to the jail. He would have laughed at her obvious attempt at seduction, but couldn't risk drawing attention to his blatant arousal.

Chapter Sixteen

Sarah made a final slow turn before the mirror. She could appreciate the steel-colored foulard gown with its flounces and lace trim, but the bustle she had to wear beneath it was another matter. Only a few of her gowns required the uncomfortable item. But today was a special occasion. Juliet Barrington had sent her an invitation requesting her to join her for tea. Recalling how the elegant Miss Barrington had viewed her with such distaste when they were introduced, Sarah would not give her the chance to do so again. She'd taken extra pains with her appearance.

Very carefully, Sarah placed the close-fitting straw bonnet on her head. The crown was high with two full-blown pink roses resting within white lace. The brim, lined with dark gray velvet, arched above her softly curled hair.

Looking forward to her outing, Sarah made her way downstairs, only to come up short when she saw Billy standing at the foot of the steps, a rifle in his hand.

"You'd better take this with you, missy. Do you know how to fire one of these things?"

"Sure," she lied.

Billy cocked a disbelieving brow.

"I do, I really do. I've watched my grandfather use his on several occasions."

"Humph. Well, it's loaded, so be careful."

Billy walked outside with her and assisted her into the buggy he'd hired for her. After giving her directions to the ranch and placing the rifle beneath her seat, he stood on the boardwalk and watched until the buggy faded to a blur at the far end of town.

With her parasol shading her, Sarah slowly drove through the countryside, taking pleasure in viewing the scenery surrounding her. A gentle wind whipped the tall bluestem grass, rolling it like waves across the prairie. Ranches scattered the area, some enclosed with barbed-wire fencing. Wes had told her only the larger ranches could afford the fencing. One of Hazard's biggest problems, as was with all Texas communities, were the fence-cutters. Small landowners didn't like having their water supply cut off for their cattle, so the larger ranch owners were constantly replacing their fences.

An idea suddenly leaped to her mind. Wes had said Miss Barrington's property bordered her own. She had never seen her property. Though Wes had offered to take her on several occasions, running the saloon had taken all her time. After her visit with Miss Barrington, she could ride over there and at least view the house and property.

As the buggy topped a small rise, the sound of gunfire ripped through the stillness. Jerking the reins to the left, she drew the buggy to the side of the road. Her horse sidestepped nervously as one shot after another rang out, the sounds drawing nearer. Sarah quickly closed her parasol and put it beneath the bench. Lifting the heavy rifle at her feet, she stepped up onto the bench for a better view. Fear surged through her. She saw a rider's horse kicking up the dust, and following closely behind him were two riders. Lying over his horse's mane, the fusillade spurring him onward, he veered quickly toward the road, heading in Sarah's direction. As he neared, Sarah recognized him. Cole! The men were going to kill him if she didn't help him. Sarah cocked her gun and braced it against her shoulder as she had seen her grandfather do. She'd wait until the men following him came closer.

Cole daringly raised his head enough to check his bearings. *No, it can't be!* He dared to look again. *Damn it, it is!* What the hell does she think she's doing, aiming that rifle at me?

Cole flattened himself like a pancake over his mount. Seeing Sarah Hogan holding a gun seemed a hell of a lot more dangerous than the men firing at him from behind. A worse fear roared through him. She was directly in their line of fire. Damn fool woman! he thought. As he neared her, his heart nearly leaped from his mouth. She took aim, fired, the blast knocking her backward over the bench. In the next instant, the mare took off, hauling Sarah and the buggy over the prairie. Cole glanced behind him and noticed one of the men clutching his shoulder. Amazement washed over his face. She had winged the bastard! The two men turned their horses around and raced in the opposite direction.

Digging his heels into the flanks of his horse, Cole took off after the buggy. Closing in on her, he saw her feet flailing the air and the lacy trim of her drawers. By God, when I catch her, she'll wish I hadn't, he vowed, planning to bare her dainty butt and give her a spanking she would never forget.

Sarah felt every rock and every hole that the wheel hit. Lodged between the front and second bench, her body rocked, rolled, and bounced. As her head banged repeatedly against the side of the buggy, her hat pin jabbed her scalp. Lord help her! Any moment now, the buggy would overturn and she would die. There was no way Cole could save her when he was running for his

154

life. Suddenly a thought more devastating than death jolted her. Eli, her staunch, God-fearing husband! God forgive her for her blasphemous thoughts, but she was not ready to join him for all eternity.

With a fortitude she didn't know she owned, Sarah decided to take her chances and jump off. Grabbing hold of the bench, she tried to pull herself up, but she couldn't move. She imagined it was Eli's invisible hand pressing against her. The wheels hit a deep rut and the buggy tilted dangerously on its side. Tears filled her eyes. She was going to die. Eli had won.

Cole noted his horse's sides were heaving and its mouth lathering, but his fear spurred him onward. In front of the buggy barely a hundred yards away was a deep ravine, invisible to the horse because of the tall grasses. If he couldn't make it in time, the horse and buggy—and Sarah—would plunge over it.

Finally Cole managed to get alongside the swaying buggy, and jumped from his horse to the driver's seat. He didn't waste time looking behind him to see how Sarah fared. In the next instant, he was atop the runaway mare, and grabbing the reins, he pulled the horse to the right seconds before it reached the ravine.

He eased back on the reins. "Easy, girl, easy," he said, rubbing the horse's sweat-laden neck, trying to calm her so she wouldn't take off again.

He heard Sarah groaning, and dismounted, his anger returning now that he knew she was safe. As he looked over the sides of the buggy, he saw her lying partially on her side, wedged between the front and back bench. For a moment he could do nothing but stare at her as she twisted about. Protruding from a heap of upswept lacy petticoats and skirt was a pair of slender, white-stockinged legs and sheer drawers. He tore his gaze from her legs and moved to her face. Her hat had slid

155

to the side of her head and two large pink roses dangled over her eyes.

Sarah didn't feel the buggy moving anymore. Had she died? she wondered, her mind dazed.

Cole tilted back his hat and wiped his arm across his wet brow. "You know something, Widow Woman? — you're fast becoming a pain in the butt."

Had Eli just asked her if she had a pain in her butt? Oddly enough that was the only place on her body where there was no pain. *Butt?* Eli would never say such a vulgar word. *Widow Woman?* He wouldn't have called her that either. Cole! Sarah tried to open her eyes, but her lids felt so heavy. Had he died too? "Cole! Did I . . . did I shoot you?"

Propping an arm across the side of the buggy, Cole glared at her with an angry frown marring his brow. "No, but you damned near did."

"Then, why are you here?" Sarah asked, completely disoriented.

"Just doing my usual thing . . . saving your ass."

Something isn't quite right here, Sarah thought, trying to understand. If he saved me, then I'm . . . Sarah raked her eyes, dragging the roses aside. The sun was so bright she could barely see him. Squinting, she asked, "I'm alive?"

For a moment Cole couldn't speak. Good god! She thinks she's dead? She's hurt worse than I thought. Leaping into the buggy, he stepped across the front bench to the second one and knelt. "Yes, you're alive, Sarah. Did you hit your head?"

Raising on an elbow, she groaned. "At least a thousand times, but I don't remember ever blacking out. I feel so stupid thinking I'd died." She smiled up at him weakly. "And I thought I'd killed you, too."

"It's a damned miracle you didn't," he replied acidly,

156

his anger surfacing again.

"Well, at least my shot scared them off, right?" she asked proudly.

"That's putting it mildly. Tell me something, Sarah. When are you going to stop meddling in my business?"

"Meddling!" She fairly tore the words from his mouth. "I saved your life!"

Oh hell, just what I need, a knight in shining armor, Cole thought in exasperation. Or did one call a woman a knightress? "Then, now we're even, because I just saved yours."

He couldn't tell her he'd been leading the men into a trap. Since the gambling episode, he'd known Dusty's men had been watching his every move, waiting for a chance to kill him. He had purposely set himself up for an ambush . . . with Chin's help, of course. There was no way he could explain this to Sarah.

"But why did those men want to kill you?"

He shrugged his shoulders. "For several reasons. I've stepped on a lot of toes since I became sheriff." Not wishing to discuss the matter further, Cole leaned over the bench and offered his hand. "Here, let me help you up."

Sarah gave him her hand, and as he pulled she tried to push herself up, but she wouldn't budge. "Something's caught."

"Let's see if I can find the problem." Cole wedged his hand beneath her back and the wide board under the bench. He laughed outright. Crossing his arms on his bent knee, his eyes twinkled with amusement. "Leave it up to the widow woman to do the unbelievable. Your bustle's jammed under the bench."

"It can't be!" Sarah shouted, her arm flying back behind her. "Oh no."

Cole clucked his tongue. "Some buggy ride, huh?"

For a few moments Sarah said nothing. Why was it that every time Cole was around, the most horrible things that could happen *did* happen? She mentally reviewed one deplorable event after the other and finally gave up counting.

While Sarah wrestled with her thoughts, Cole was having a difficult time keeping his eyes from her exposed legs. She did have nice shapely legs, tapering down to trim ankles and small feet. His eyes drifting upward, he noted the pretty rosebud embroidery trimming the edge of her drawers. From there, his imagination flowed.

"This is embarrassing," she groaned. "I wonder what the odds are of a woman's bustle becoming stuck under a bench."

"Pretty darned good if it's *your* bustle," Cole said laughingly. Standing up, he placed his hands on his hips. "There's enough wadding in that damned thing to stuff a mattress. I'm either going to have to rip apart the bench or you're going to have to take off your dress," he said with unconcern.

"What!"

"Well, do you have a better idea?" he asked cockily.

Sarah was almost in tears. Trying to think of a way to save her dignity along with her new dress, another idea popped into her head. "What if I unfasten the bustle and then you can ease it out beneath my gown? That would work, wouldn't it?"

"I doubt it, but it's worth a try."

"Turn your head, please."

Cole rolled his eyes, then turned, staring out over the prairie.

Sarah bunched her petticoats and skirt over her waist and untied the bustle. After arranging everything back into its proper place, she said, "It's unfastened."

"Good, then let's get on with it." Cole knelt and grabbed a wad of gown and petticoats and pushed them up to her waist. "Hold them out of my way."

Sarah gasped in horror when she looked down and saw her silk-stockinged legs exposed and—God forbid—her drawers, so sheer that she just knew he could see the tiny birthmark on her thigh. Even Eli had never seen her legs. They had always dressed and undressed in privacy, or in the darkness of their room. Now she was exposing her unmentionables and her legs to the leering gray eyes of the sheriff. With a quick shove of her skirt and petticoats, she covered her legs, her face so hot she knew it was blistered.

"I've already seen your legs, Sarah," he grumbled, wiping his hand across his sweaty brow. "I've *been seeing* them for the past several minutes." Again he pushed her clothing above her knees. "Now hold thcm."

Gulping, Sarah clutched the garments to her, her tongue too paralyzed to speak. She lay stiffly and tried to block everything from her mind.

Cole stepped down beside her. Removing his hat, he laid it on the bench. He pushed her rigid legs forward until he made room for both his knees.

With wide eyes, Sarah stared at him over her shoulder. Leaning forward, his chin resting on her hipbone, Cole worked both hands around her bustle and began pulling it.

Feeling the heat of his hand through the sheer fabric of her drawers, Sarah panicked. "Oh my lord," she screamed out in horror, twisting and flopping around like a fish out of water.

Cole's chin bounced on her hip. Raising his head, he snapped, "For god's sake, be still."

Sarah suddenly stopped and stiffened as she glared at him with enough fire in her eyes to burn the

159

whole state of Texas. "You're touching me!"

"Hell yes, I'm touching you. How else am I going to pull the damned thing out!"

With her face flaming a brilliant red, Sarah settled on her side again, trying to ignore where his hands were as he grunted and pulled and twisted the bustle. As he raked the back of his hand back and forth across her buttocks, she felt his hard knuckles knead against her soft flesh. *Please let me faint,* Sarah prayed. Closing her eyes, she willed the blackness to steal over her and free her from her humiliation. Instead, she felt her silky drawers rubbing over her most private place, the friction causing strange little quivers to throb between her legs.

Cole glanced occasionally at her face as he worked. Her eyes were closed and a dreamy smile tugged at the corners of her mouth. Damned if she wasn't liking it. Well, hell, he was liking it, too. If he didn't get the infernal thing out soon, he'd burst the buttons of his fly. Giving the bustle a vicious jerk, he felt it give. Collapsing with exhaustion, he rested his cheek on her hip. For several moments he lay there, breathing deeply, his senses picking up a hint of lavender. God, she felt good.

Sarah's eyes drifted open. "Did it come out?"

His mind on the hard arousal throbbing between his legs, Cole clenched his teeth in agony. "Almost."

"What?"

"Yes, damn it, it's out!"

Yanking his hand from beneath the bench, Cole rubbed the crease that ran across its surface where the board had pressed against it. Sweat had broken out on his brow and was rolling down his face. He didn't know if it came from exhaustion or from the carnal thoughts that were running through his mind.

"Well, you don't have to shout at me," she returned hotly.

Cole grumbled something beneath his breath, and dragging out the bustle, he dropped it on the bench. "I'm taking you to my house—your house, that is," he corrected, "so you can get yourself in order before I take you back to town."

"But—"

"No buts . . . you're going."

Sarah wouldn't dare argue with him. Climbing over the front bench, she sat down and waited while he tethered his horse to the back of the buggy. Then taking his seat beside her, he gathered the reins and clucked his tongue.

Sarah gripped the sides of the bench as the buggy lurched forward, again hitting the holes hidden in the high grass. Finally they reached the main road and Sarah looked over at Cole. "Wes said the ranch is still operating."

"Yes, at full capacity."

"Then, we won't be alone," Sarah said casually.

Cole thought about Chin maybe being there, but didn't want to mention him in case he wasn't. The least he had to explain, the better. "Maybe, I don't know. You worried about being alone with me, Sarah?"

"No, should I be?"

When he noted her eyes fixed on his mouth, he grinned and asked, "Were you on your way out to see me?"

"Actually, I was on my way to have tea with Juliet Barrington."

"Tea? How interesting. Just you, or with several other women?"

"I don't know. The invitation didn't say. I guess she's just wanting to become acquainted with some of the ladies. She must get very lonely, living by herself." She cast him a furtive gaze. "Of course, I'm sure, as pretty as she is, she must have several gentlemen callers," she hinted.

"Yeah, I'm sure she has," he admitted, thinking of one gentleman in particular: Dusty Mills.

"Oh," was all Sarah could reply, wondering why she bothered asking in the first place.

Chapter Seventeen

After a short time, they turned from the main road into an oak-arched lane. Wild roses bloomed in profusion over the fencing along both sides, their sweet fragrance filling the air. The lane suddenly turned sharply and Sarah saw a modestly built, white-framed house perched atop a knoll, nestled within a cluster of oaks and pines. A shady veranda encircled three sides of the house. Everything was quiet except the chirping of birds and the drone of the bees as they buzzed around a clump of honeysuckle growing from a stump.

Cole pulled the buggy to a halt in front of the house. He put his large hands around her waist and lowered her to the ground. While one hand lingered on her waist, he wiped a smudge of dirt from her cheek. "I'll take the horses to the barn and feed and water them. Why don't you go inside and look around? Everything's the way your father left it."

Cole released her and walked to the gate and opened it. Climbing into the buggy, he said, "Oh, in one of the drawers in the desk are some keepsakes of your dad's. I keep forgetting to bring them to you when I come in. He would want you to have them."

"Thank you," she said, stepping onto the porch. Sarah's hand hesitated on the doorknob. A rush of sadness enveloped her. At one time, she had lived in this house with both a mother and a father. Of course, she had been too young to remember that time of her life. Still, she couldn't help wondering how different her life might have been if her parents had stayed together and lived as a family.

Finally, she opened the door and went inside, closing it behind her. Sarah walked around the parlor, surprised to find everything so neat and orderly. She couldn't imagine a man with Cole's hectic schedule having the time or patience to clean up for himself.

The furnishings were simple, yet bespoke taste and refinement. A large oval braided rug took up the area in front of the hearth. Situated to one side of the stone fireplace was a sofa with plump floral pillows and a colorful quilt folded neatly over its back. In front of the sofa rested a low table, piled high with neatly stacked books and papers. Against the wall behind the sofa was the desk Cole had told her contained her father's keepsakes. Two side chairs with a table and kerosene lamp between them sat opposite the sofa. Over the fireplace was a thick, hand-hewn mantel containing a tall, rectangular clock and an assortment of odds and ends. A silver picture frame caught her attention. Sarah walked over and picked it up, holding the picture toward the light. Her heart skipped several beats, and she pressed her hand over her mouth as she stared at the tall man standing beside her mother. In his arms, he held an infant. Tears suddenly welled in her eyes. This was James Moore, the father she had never known. The tintype was at least twenty-three years old, she knew, because she was the child he was holding in his arms. He was probably the age Sarah was now, or thereabouts. He seemed strangely familiar, but she supposed it was because of the remarkable resemblance between them.

Suddenly a terrible bitterness constricted her heart. How could her mother and grandparents have kept her from seeing and knowing her father all these years? She struggled to keep down her rising sobs. With a trembling hand, Sarah set the photograph back on the mantel. After several moments, she turned away, her face marked with desolation. She thought of the letters she'd written her family, trying to make them understand why she'd chosen this new life against their wishes. If they had truly loved her, wouldn't they have at least answered her letters even though they disagreed with her? Even her own mother had abandoned her, and that had hurt worse than any hurt she'd ever known. Until now. Sarah felt betrayed, thinking they had only used her as a weapon to punish her father. Because he was dead, they had washed their hands of her.

As Sarah walked to the desk, she didn't see the little man peering at her through the window beside the front door.

He watched her rifling through the drawers of the desk. He frowned and scratched his chin. She had to be Juliet Barrington, the Englishwoman Cole thought was involved with Dusty Mills. Cole had told him that she was beautiful and boasted a fine figure. Yes, it had to be her, and she had been in on the ambush. They had to have captured Cole, or she wouldn't be here going through the desk.

He saw her reticule lying on the desk. She probably carried a derringer inside it. He watched her withdraw a string-tied parcel from the drawer. What was it? he wondered as he watched her untie it. He waited until she appeared absorbed in its contents, then slowly turned the doorknob.

A distinct clicking sound brought Sarah to her full senses. Her muscles hardened sharply all over as she glanced at the front door and saw the knob turning. Knowing Cole hadn't had time to tend to the horses and return this quickly, she looked for a place to hide.

Suddenly, the door swung open and a strange little man leaped through it with a bloodcurdling cry. His quick, agile movements astounded Sarah more than they terrified her. Landing on one foot, he twisted his body and drew in his other knee close to his hip, the sole of his shoe facing her.

They stared at one another, neither making a move, while he continued to balance himself in that contorted stance. She quickly noted he carried no weapon in his hands, nor did she see any sign of one. He was a slim, short man of an undetermined age, and wore dark baggy clothes and soft-soled slippers. His hair was as black as ink and braided into a pigtail, his eyes dark and slanted. She'd seen pictures of these people in books. He was Chinese.

Finally he spoke. "Who are you?" Though he spoke English, he spoke quickly, his words running into each other.

"Who—who are you?"

"Where is Cole?" he countered.

Suddenly her heart started pounding. He had to be one of the men who had chased Cole, and she wasn't about to tell him where he was. She had to get away from him and warn Cole. Moving to the back of the sofa, she placed her hands on the quilt. She hedged. "I haven't seen him."

Slowly, he lowered his leg and walked toward her. "You lie," he said, a deadly gleam in his eyes.

Sarah tried to appear cool and calm as she clutched the quilt. He was so small, she felt confident she could overpower him.

He stopped at the end of the couch and bending both arms, he held his hands stiff and erect and slightly shook them. "I could hurt you with these,"

166

Chin threatened, hoping to frighten an answer from her. Instead, she faced him with fire in her green eyes, not fear. He had never struck a woman and did not plan to do it now.

Sarah whipped the quilt from the sofa and hurled it over him. As Chin wrestled with the quilt, she shoved him over the back of the couch as she ran by him. She heard a thud as he hit the floor, and kept on running. Closer to the back door than to the front one, Sarah rushed toward it and jerked it open. Her heart pounding, she darted through a short, narrow hallway and found herself in the kitchen. The outside door was locked; he had her cornered. She grabbed the first thing she saw, a heavy iron pot resting on the cookstove. Moving quickly to the side of the doorway, she held the pot over her head. Afraid he might hear her quick pants, she held her breath.

Chin crept as quietly as a cat through the hallway, pausing outside the kitchen door. He listened for movement and heard nothing. He wasn't even sure she'd run into the kitchen. As Chin stepped through the door, his keen senses picked up her presence behind him.

As he pivoted, he gave his fierce cry the exact moment that Sarah dropped the pot completely over his head and smothered him with rice. Before he could remove the pot, Sarah grabbed a metal dipper and started banging him over his head. Chin thought his head would burst wide open as the sound reverberated through his ears like the ring of a hammer on an anvil.

How had this happened? Chin wondered, trying to defend himself. If he didn't do something soon, he'd either smother to death in rice or the woman would beat him to death. He for sure couldn't eat the stuff fast enough to get out of this mess. Staggering, Chin reached out blindly and tried to grab

167

her, but his effort proved futile.

As Cole stepped upon the porch, he heard a loud clanging noise. Damnation, what's going on now? he thought, running into the house and toward the kitchen where the commotion was coming from. Cole came to an abrupt stop in the doorway, shocked to see Sarah pounding away on Chin's pot-laden head. Suddenly Chin reeled backward and crashed against the table, then slid to the floor.

Whirling around to escape him, Sarah screamed as she bumped into a hard chest. Thinking the man's accomplice had joined him, she poised the dipper over her head. As her hand came down, Cole caught her wrist, his other arm snaking around her waist and pulling her tightly against him. "It's all right, Sarah, calm down," he urged softly.

Sarah collapsed against him. "I got him, Cole," she said, panting breathlessly.

Concern marking his face, Cole released her. He quickly dropped to his knees beside Chin and tugged the pot off his head. Gummy rice coated his entire face and hair. "Yeah, you got him all right," Cole said numbly, wondering how she'd managed to outwit Chin when he'd been trying for years.

Her green eyes sprang open. "Oh lordy, I didn't . . . I didn't kill him, did I?"

"No, but he'll probably wish you had when he comes around. Maybe I ought to deputize you, Sarah," he said with a deep chuckle. "As far as I know, no one has ever bested him—myself included."

She frowned. "You know him? Is he one of the men who shot at you?"

Cole leveled his eyes at her and a slow smile curled one side of his mouth. "No, he's my friend."

Bewildered, Sarah's mouth dropped open. "Your . . .

168

friend?"

"Yes, and also my guest." Cole almost laughed at the expression on her face.

At that moment Chin groaned. He tried to open his eyes, but the rice had matted his eyelashes together. Wiping his hands across his eyes, he gazed up at Cole. Then he saw Sarah standing behind Cole, and bolted upright. "Watch out! She's behind you!"

"I know, Chin."

Chin's face turned as white as the rice coating it. "Aren't you going to tie her up? She's dangerous, Cole. You can put her in jail for breaking and entering."

"That might be a little hard to do when she owns the house."

Chin's Adam's apple bobbed in his throat. He leaned over to Cole and whispered in his ear, "You are telling me this is not Juliet Barrington?"

"No, Chin," Cole countered. "Sarah Hogan."

Smarting from the fact that a mere woman could overpower him, Chin replied smugly, "She is most fortunate, Cole. If you had come a moment later, I might have hurt her."

Cole threw back his head and laughed. "Looks to me like it was the other way around, friend. Got more than you bargained for, didn't you?"

Chin abruptly sat up, and trying to salvage his dignity, he said, "Only because she is a woman did I allow her to live."

Wanting to make amends with the little man, Sarah said, "I'm sorry we had a misunderstanding, Mr. Chin. Did I hurt you?"

Chin stared at her in utter amazement. She had nearly deafened him, nearly smothered him to death with rice, and she called it a misunderstanding? "I am fine."

Chin got to his feet and brushed the rice off his clothing. "As soon as I get this mess cleaned up, I am going to the bunkhouse and clean myself up."

"Sure. As soon as Sarah freshens up, I'll escort her back to town. She's had a very traumatic day."

That makes two of us, Chin thought quickly.

Returning his attention to Sarah, Cole said, "I'll bring you some water and cloths. If you'd like, you can use the bedroom."

"Thank you," she said. "Oh, do you perchance have a brush? I don't have mine with me."

"Sure, there's one in the top drawer of the chest. Help yourself."

After Sarah left the kitchen, Cole asked Chin, "How do you feel?"

"My ears are ringing and my head aches like a—as you would say—a son of a bitch."

"Well, now that you've finally met her, what do you think?"

"You would not like to hear what I think, my friend. Why is she here?"

Cole told him about the incident, omitting the hassle with her bustle.

"So that's why you never showed up. Did you recognize the men?"

"No, they wore bandannas. But they're probably the same men who were with Dusty that night at the saloon. They'll try it again."

"I am sorry, Cole. I thought they had captured you, and she sneaked in here knowing you wouldn't be around to stop her."

"Next time, *maybe* Sarah won't interfere with our plans—although I've learned always to expect the unexpected when it comes to Sarah Hogan."

"I can testify to that," Chin said, his ears still ringing. He looked at the rice-strewn floor and shrugged his shoulders in dismay. "I knew I should have washed that pot last night."

While Chin cleaned the floor, Cole went outside to the well to draw water for Sarah. He chuckled. He would never tell Chin how he admired Sarah for standing up to the Chinaman as though he had been no more menacing than a pesty insect.

Also, few women—or men—would have come to his defense as Sarah had today, he thought as he lowered the bucket. He doubted she knew the first thing about the handling of a gun, yet she had tried to help him. And who knows? She might have saved his life. This morning, when he and Chin had worked up the plan, they'd known it wasn't foolproof. Cole could have easily taken a bullet in his back before he'd reached Chin farther down the road. But if they had succeeded in catching at least one of the men, one way or another, Cole would have forced the man to talk.

His thoughts turned to Juliet Barrington. Why had she invited Sarah for tea? Was it just a neighborly gesture, or was there more to it? What was there about her that just didn't fit?

At first, he had thought seriously about taking Juliet up on her invitation, thinking that maybe she would inadvertently tell him something about Dusty. But as beautiful as Juliet was, Cole felt not an inkling of desire for her.

Inside the bedroom, Sarah was removing the pins from her hair. Her eyes drifted to the unmade tester bed. He sleeps there, she thought, imagining Cole's tall masculine figure nestled within the rumpled bedclothes. Drawing a deep luxurious sigh, she closed her eyes and easily conjured up a vision of her and Cole lying there together. Then a knock on the bedroom door jolted her back to the present.

"Sarah, can I bring in your water?" Cole called.

Sarah quickly glanced at her face in the mirror. Were her thoughts still written on it? Gathering her composure and trying to control her racing heart, she returned, "Yes, thank you."

Opening the door, Cole entered with a pitcher and paused. God, she was breathtaking. Her hair, completely free from the pins that had bound it, rippled like gleaming copper strands over her shoulders and down her back. His eyes flickered over her, then came to rest on the quick rise and fall of her breasts.

Sarah stood motionless, her fingers twisted in the folds of her skirt as she gazed at him. His hard, rugged body with its uncompromising strength brought a quick surge of excitement flowing through her. He'd removed his hat, and an ebony lock of hair had fallen over his forehead, giving him a reckless appeal. Her eyes met and held with his dark ones.

A deep longing built up inside Cole, a longing to pull her into his arms and awaken the passion that was burning in her eyes. But holding his desire in check, he walked to the washstand and poured the water into the bowl, then laid a bar of soap and cloths beside it.

"Thank you," she said softly.

"Did you find my brush?" he asked, avoiding looking at her, afraid she would see the half-mad passion in his eyes.

"I haven't looked for it yet."

Cole opened a drawer and got his brush, laying it on the dresser. Instead of leaving, he positioned himself in a chair close to the window. Slouching forward, he propped his elbows on his knees and cradled his chin, studying her.

Trying to ignore his presence, Sarah picked up the

cloth and dipped it into the water. After washing her hands and face, she picked up the brush and stared at the black strands of his hair laced within the coarse bristles. Shortly, her reddish gold strands would mingle with his own. She felt a peculiar sense of intimacy knowing she would share his brush. Tilting her head, she began brushing the tangles from her heavy hair.

His husky voice filled the room as he asked, "You're not afraid of anything, are you, Sarah?"

The brush stilled in midair as she found his reflection in the mirror. "I'm afraid of everything."

"I don't believe you."

She shrugged her shoulders.

"You've taken on the running of the saloon, which was completely foreign to you. And, I might add, you've done a good job."

"I really didn't have a choice. I had to make a living."

"Everything you do, you go at with such an unselfish attitude that you inspire those around you. You think nothing of your own welfare when you save a child from certain death, or"—he smiled teasingly—"dump a tray of drinks on a man known to have a violent temper, just to save the wages of some cowhands you hardly know."

"Well, I was afraid. I was terrified to operate a saloon." It was her turn to laugh. "I was afraid of the paintings, of Collie and Belle. I thought they would resent me. I was afraid of everything."

"You're a remarkable woman, Sarah Beth Hogan."

"No, I'm not, I even cried when Collie cut my hair." Again, she lifted the brush to her hair.

He saw her wince.

"What's the matter?" he asked, concerned.

"My shoulder. I must have hurt it when I fired the

173

rifle."

"Had you ever fired a gun before?"

"No."

A look of astonishment washed over his face. Beginner's luck? It had to be. He'd never tell her she had actually winged the man. Seeing her wince again, a sudden impulse brought him to his feet.

Sarah caught his image in the mirror as he softly gripped her wrist. "May I?"

"You want to brush my hair?"

"Yes, does that surprise you?"

"Well, I've never had a man brush it before."

"And I've never brushed a woman's hair before, either," he said huskily.

Chapter Eighteen

Cole lifted a generous portion of her hair and slowly pulled the brush through it. His eyes watching her face in the mirror, he thought her the most glorious creature he had ever seen. Her eyes, now wistful and compelling, bewitched him. Her rose-colored mouth, marvelously content, beckoned him to taste its sweetness. The feel of her luxurious hair sliding through his fingers tempted him to toss the brush aside and bury his face in its silken mass.

Sarah's body tingled with a warm heat and a dreamy languor washed over her. She felt as though she had just wakened from a deep, restful sleep. A little smile touched her mouth as she reveled in the feel of his hands working through her hair.

Laying the brush on the washstand, he drew her back against him, and pushing her silken hair aside, he slowly trailed the callused pad of his finger down her sensitive neck.

For several seconds their stares held. Entranced by his magnetism, she turned in his arms.

Cole's heart stilled in his chest. His hands slid into her hair and, holding her head secure, he slowly lowered his head, his mouth claiming hers in a gentle, searching kiss. The hunger broke free, giving way to a passion that was almost violent. Sarah opened her mouth, accepting the fierce probing of his tongue.

Lifting her hands, she clasped his neck, her fingers entwining in his thick hair. She answered his kiss boldly, her own feverish passion unlike anything she had ever experienced.

Cole brushed aside her heavy hair, his warm mouth placing feather-light kisses over the ivory column of her neck. His mouth found the delicate lobe of her ear; he bit it lightly, then laved it softly with his tongue, his warm breath fanning her neck. Feeling her body grow limp against him, Cole moved his mouth slowly, deliberately across her cheek, once again capturing her lips in a burning kiss. As he explored the recesses of her mouth, his hands moved down her back, the heels of his hands scaling the sides of her breasts.

Sarah felt his hand pause, and she was fearful he would stop this wondrous pleasure. Answering the cry of her body, she pressed herself against him. Were these the forbidden desires her grandfather had preached about? A slow languor washed over her. At the moment, she didn't care; she only wanted more, more, more.

Breaking the kiss, his breathing hard and labored, Cole pulled her tightly against him. He had never wanted a woman this badly. More than anything, he wanted to teach her, show her passion. Even though he knew she'd been married, it was obvious she was truly virginal. He also knew that a passion burned in her that matched his. He'd felt it. Yet he was afraid that if he let his passion have full rein, it would scare her away, that her fanatical grandfather's teachings would swamp her with guilt. Could he teach her that these feelings were perfectly normal, that she wouldn't splatter hell wide open just because she sought a kiss? But, oh god, he wanted so much more than just a kiss. But something told him that if he took her, his life would never be the same. He couldn't, wouldn't ruin her life because he couldn't control his desire. No, at this point he needed time to think.

Resting his hand on Sarah's shoulder, he leaned over and brushed his lips across her cheek. "You might not believe me, but stopping at this moment is probably the most difficult thing I've ever had to do."

She reached up and touched her finger to his mouth. "It's okay. I don't understand it, but I believe you. Maybe it's best. There are so many things happening inside me that I don't understand," she whispered.

"I know. Let's take things one step at a time, Sarah. This is not something we should rush into just yet." He laid his hand on her shoulder and, forgetting its soreness, gently squeezed it.

She winced.

"Maybe some liniment will help. Would you trust me to apply some to your shoulder?" he asked teasingly.

"Yes," Sarah said with a soft smile.

"It's in the kitchen. I'll be right back."

Finding the liniment, Cole returned to the bedroom, where Sarah was sitting on the edge of the bed. She had managed to unfasten enough buttons so she could ease the bodice over her shoulder.

Cole dipped his fingers inside the small jar. His hand paused at her shoulder. "I'll try not to hurt you."

Sarah tilted her head to the side, her eyes flickering over his tense face. She saw a muscle twitching at the corner of his mouth as he lightly applied the liniment just below her shoulder. Looking down, she watched as his fingers gently rubbed the cooling cream over the reddened area. She studied his hands, noting how dark they were against her fair skin. His long slim fingers were so close to the swells of her breasts that Sarah

177

had difficulty breathing evenly.

For several minutes, Cole had been staring at the wall behind Sarah, not trusting himself to look down at her. When he felt the rise of her flesh beneath his hand, desire shot through him. Unbidden, he dropped his gaze to the soft crescents of her breast, his hand yearning to slide deeper within the bodice. Instead, he removed his hand completely from her flesh. "Is that better?"

"Yes, thank you. If you'll button me, I'll finish getting ready."

"Sure." When he'd finished, he said, "I'll bring the buggy around and wait outside for you."

Opening the door, Cole hastened through it, wiping the sweat from his brow as he closed the door behind him. As he walked to the barn, he hoped he could quench his desire for her before he took her into town.

Inside the bedroom, Sarah fastened the dreaded bustle at her waist and smoothed her gown over it. After pinning up her hair, she lifted her hat to place it atop her head and noted the dangling roses. She'd ask Mrs. Flowers to fix it for her tomorrow. As she started to go outside, she remembered the package on the desk that had belonged to her father. Sarah picked it up and walked out to the porch. Chin was sitting on the steps.

"Mr. Chin?"

He turned and, giving her a cool look, said, "Just Chin."

"Chin what?"

"Just Chin."

"Oh," she said, still wondering if Chin was his last name or his first. She walked down the steps and sat down beside him. "What was all that strange stuff you were doing earlier with your feet and hands?"

Chin couldn't help smiling. "That *stuff* is the ancient

178

Chinese method of fighting. Your hands and feet are your weapons. A man can kill or hurt another man easily with one quick thrust."

"Who did you think I was?"

"When I saw you rummaging through the desk, I thought you were with those men who had chased Cole."

Sarah laughed. "And I thought *you* were one of them. You scared me to death."

Sarah softened Chin with her charm, her confession doing much to repair his damaged ego. "I would never have known it." Chin studied her pensively for a moment. Cole had told him how troublesome she was, and always referred to her as the Widow Woman when he mentioned her. He'd notice Cole's face soften when he spoke of her, and to his keen ears, Widow Woman sounded more like an endearment. An idea leaped to his mind and he smiled secretly. "Mrs. Hogan, Cole is not due at the jail until this evening, and it would please me very much if you would have supper with us."

Her face lit up like a candle. "I'd like that very much, but perhaps you'd better ask Cole. He's bringing my buggy now."

Cole pulled the buggy to a halt in front of the house and leaped to the ground. "Ready, Sarah?" he asked with a smile.

Chin stood up and exclaimed, "Oh, I have asked Mrs. Hogan to dine with us, Cole. Now you will not have to make two trips into town."

Cole's glance shifted in Sarah's direction. "Won't your employees worry about you?"

Before Sarah could speak, Chin said, "The men are back. We can send one of them into town with a message."

Cole smiled. "In that case, maybe Sarah would like to take a walk around the ranch while you're getting supper."

"I would love to." Turning to Chin, she held out her belongings to him. "Would you take these inside for me?"

Taking them, Chin said, "Of course. Enjoy your walk."

For a moment, Chin watched them stroll side by side down the shady path toward the barns. Turning, he entered the house with a broad smile splattered across his face.

Cole led Sarah beneath the shade of a pecan tree. "Wait here while I go to the bunkhouse and ask one of the men to take a message to the saloon."

"All right, thank you," she said, leaning back against the tree. From her position on a small rise, Sarah had a good view of the ranch. Scattered over a broad area were many well-kept barns, stables, and various other structures. The sounds of rigorous ranch life filled her ears: the bleating cattle, the whinnying horses, and the boisterous shouts of the cowboys. In one fenced area resembling a maze, cowboys wearing leather chaps and dusty Stetsons prodded cattle through narrow aisles. Nearby in a corral, more cowboys worked diligently to control several horses as they bucked and tugged against the ropes looped around their necks. Elsewhere, she saw men working on machinery and men unloading bales of hay from wagons.

Watching as a spectator the activity going on below her, it suddenly dawned on her that all this would belong to her in a few short months.

"It's beautiful, isn't it?"

Cole's voice startling her, she jumped, then nodded her head in agreement.

"You see all that land out there? For as far as you can see, it belongs to you."

Sarah gazed in awe at the rolling plains. Without a mountain to break its vastness, the land eventually met the blue of the sky. "I can't believe my father owned so much."

"Yes, and there's more." Turning her around, he directed her toward the east. "There's miles and miles of timberland."

Sarah's eyes widened with fear.

"What's the matter?"

"It's mine," she whispered, her voice trembling.

"What?"

"All of this! Trying to run the saloon all these months, I've barely given this place a thought. Now that I've seen it, I'm terrified. I don't know the first thing about ranching."

He laughed a little. "You didn't know how to run a saloon either."

"Maybe so, but how could I possibly keep up with all of this?" she squeaked, waving her hand with a flourish.

Cole took her hand in his. "There's no reason for you to be so distressed. If you have good people working for you—which you do have now—you can successfully run it. Without them, this place wouldn't have stayed in existence after your father's death. They depend on you for a living, Sarah. Treat them fairly, pay them good wages, and they'll stick by you."

After a moment, she said, "You make it sound so simple."

"No, ranching isn't simple, but nothing worth fighting for is. This is your legacy." He tightened his hand around hers. "Tackle it with the same fortitude you've done with the saloon and you'll make it just fine."

She beamed. "Thank you for your encouragement, Cole."

"We'd better get back to the house. Chin gets his nose out of joint when I'm late for supper."

As they walked together, Sarah asked, "Where did you and Chin meet?"

"He was the cook on a ranch where I worked several years ago. We've always managed to keep in touch."

"So, you haven't always been a gunslinger and bounty hunter."

Her remark caught him by surprise. "My reputation doesn't bother you?"

"No," she said softly, "I don't care about your reputation. It's the man you are now that matters. When you took the job as sheriff, I see it as a step in the right direction for you."

His face suddenly turning grim, Cole stopped abruptly and turned to her. "Sarah, sometimes you are so damned naive. My badge is nothing more than a piece of tin legalizing what I've always done. I'm not proud of my past, but I can't change it."

"You could try if you wanted to," she returned. "I have."

"Maybe I like my life the way it is," he said, opening the back door.

Any argument Sarah might have had died a quick death when she saw Chin standing in front of the stove, stirring something in a small pot.

"Ah good, you are back. Supper will be ready in just a few minutes. Sit down at the table while I finish preparing the meal. Would you care for tea or coffee, Sarah?"

"Tea, thank you."

Sarah and Cole took their places at the table, covered with a red-checkered cloth. She noted a pair of sticks lying beside her other eating utensils. "Toothpicks?" she asked laughingly.

Chin turned and said, "No, chopsticks. In China, we eat with them. I thought you might like to try them." He brought her a cup of steaming tea and a cup of coffee for Cole. "Cole does not appreciate my tea. I have prepared you a special tea, oolong, scented with jasmine."

"Oh, it sounds wonderful."

From a deep kettle on the stove, Chin ladled soup into two small bowls and set them in front of her and Cole. Sarah dipped her spoon into the hot soup and sipped the broth. "The soup's delicious, Chin."

"I am glad you like it, Mrs. Hogan."

She saw Cole eyeing the soup strangely, a frown on his forehead. "This isn't bird's-nest soup, is it?"

Sarah's spoon paused at her opened mouth. "Bird's what?"

"You heard me right, bird's-nest soup."

Chin laughed. "It's a real delicacy in China. Sea swallows eat seaweed and other sea plants, then spit out the substance to make their nests. We take these nests and soak them overnight, then boil them to use in soups."

Sarah's stomach started rolling and lurching.

Chin went on to say, "In China, only the rich can afford to eat it. They hire girls with excellent eyesight to remove the feathers from the nests. The Chinese believe that if one eats bird's nests, they will enjoy good health, live longer, and increase their energy."

Contrary to Chin's belief, Sarah found her good health and vitality quickly diminishing. She looked down into her bowl, expecting to see feathers floating on the surface. Suddenly she remembered picking up a bird's nest when she was a little girl. Mites had crawled

183

over her hand. She shuddered. She was eating mites and no telling what else!

Chin and Cole exchanged amused expressions.

"But the nests are not found around here, so I regret I could not share with you this exotic delicacy."

Her chalk-colored face slowly regained its rosy glow. Not wanting to appear rude, she said, "I'm . . . so disappointed. Uh . . . what kind of soup is it, then?"

"It is called three-shreds soup, a chicken broth containing shredded chicken, ham, and pork."

"Oh, how nice." Trying to hide her relief, Sarah lowered her spoon again into the soup.

While Cole ate, his thoughts were on the delightfully entertaining woman beside him. Knowing Sarah, if the soup had indeed been made of birds' nests, she would've eaten it anyway to please Chin.

Pushing her bowl aside, Sarah watched Chin as he dropped lightly battered cubed chicken into a skillet of hot grease. After a few minutes, he removed the chicken and set it aside. Then taking a small handful of shelled, skinned peanuts, he dropped them into the skillet and briskly stirred through them.

After taking a sip on the strongly-brewed tea, Sarah whispered to Cole. "Peanuts? What's he cooking?"

"Beats me. He's always coming up with strange recipes."

"Do the Chinese really eat birds' nests or was he just teasing me?"

"They do eat it. Actually, Chinese food is quite good; they just don't serve large portions like the Americans. It takes at least two helpings to fill me up."

In a few minutes, Chin set a bowl of hot, fluffy rice on the table, followed by a platter containing the chicken and vegetables in a sauce.

"Pass me your plate, Sarah, and I will fix it for

you," Chin offered.

After Chin fixed her plate, he and Cole served themselves.

She picked up her sticks and stared at them. "What do I do?"

"Like this," Chin instructed.

Sarah watched Chin pinch the rice between the ends of the sticks and bring a small portion to his mouth. Mimicking him, she lifted the rice, but as she opened her mouth, it fell in her lap.

"Keep on working at it. You'll get the hang of it," Cole said, looking as much at home with the chopsticks as he would be with a fork.

Cole and Chin exchanged amused glances as Sarah tried again and failed. Giving up on the rice, she tackled a bite of chicken and stabbed it.

"It's already dead, Sarah," Cole said dryly.

She shot him a go-to-hell look before she slipped the chicken into her mouth. Her taste buds exploded as though she'd just put a fireball into her mouth. Tears sprang to her eyes. Her throat burning as she swallowed, she followed the food quickly with the rest of her tea.

"Are you all right?"

"Oh—fine," she gasped, her hand clutching her throat. "Could I—have a glass of water?"

"Sure," Cole said, sliding back his chair and going to the dry sink. Pouring her a glass of water from a pitcher, he handed it to her. She gulped it down.

After refilling her glass, he sat down again and began eating, watching her from the corner of his eyes. As he knew she would, she never mentioned the hot food, but continued eating very slowly, still wrestling with the chopsticks.

Cole fixed another plate and finished it before Sarah

even made a dent in the food on her plate. "You'll be here all night, at the rate you're going." Picking up her fork, he handed it to her.

"Thank you." Now, having no excuse to avoid eating, Sarah ate several more bites, finding that if she combined the chicken with the rice, it wasn't quite as hot.

"I apologize if it is too hot, Sarah," Chin said. "I am used to cooking for men. They have iron stomachs. One day you must come back again for supper, and I promise to omit the chili peppers."

"The flavor's good, and I really like the peanuts," she said with a weak smile. "It's only a little too hot . . . really." She wiped her mouth and set her napkin on the table. "Would you let me cook for you and Cole some evening?"

Cole's interest perked. "Can you make desserts? Chin never makes them."

"Strawberry shortcake's my specialty."

"Maybe you could fix me some," Cole suggested.

"I'd love to," Sarah said, smiling broadly. So Cole had a sweet tooth. Tomorrow she would go by the store and get the makings for strawberry shortcake.

"I'd better get back to the saloon now. Soon the crowd will come rolling in."

"I'll get my hat and jacket and join you in a minute," Cole said, backing away from the table.

When Cole left, Sarah said, "Thank you for everything, Chin. What started as a bad day for us has turned out well, don't you think?"

"Yes, indeed it has," Chin said, bowing slightly. "I look forward to seeing you again, Sarah."

Sarah left to join Cole. Tethering his horse to the back of the wagon, he stepped up into the buggy and sat down beside her. It was a happy pair who rode back to town that night beneath a star-studded heaven and a sickle-shaped moon. Sarah's spirits had elevated to a new high. When the time was right, she would ask him to run her ranch. Yes, she would give him a chance to start a new life when he gave up his badge.

Chapter Nineteen

Sarah counted the money from the previous night's business and wrote the figures in neat columns in the record book. Every morning it was the same. She counted the money, went to the bank to make a deposit, and returned to the saloon to go over the stock with Gunter. Billy Ward kept the saloon clean and was always near when Sarah had trouble making a decision. When she was alone in the saloon, Billy was always close at hand. When the other employees were present, he made himself scarce. He surprised her with his knowledge, on the one hand, and irritated her, on the other, wanting to protect her. She could take care of herself, and she told him this repeatedly.

Sarah didn't step from her apartment with a hair out of place. It had taken a lot of patience, but she had learned how to use the creams and ointments the girls had insisted she buy. Sometimes when she slid into bed greased like a hen for roasting, she wondered what kept her from sliding right off the bed onto the floor. Still, she'd kept up the nightly ritual until her face was as smooth as a baby's bottom and her hair shimmered with a healthy sheen. Gone was the stringy, dry mane she'd hated for anyone to see. She was terribly proud of her new clothes, and took pride in her new appearance. Sometimes she wondered if she was too proud. Her grandfather had been fond of warning her, "Pride goeth before destruction, and a haughty spirit before a fall."

If Sarah Hogan was nothing else, she was aware of her shortcomings and failures. Her grandfather had made sure of that. But there was a fire in her that she had banked all her life—until now. And more than she liked to admit, the fire raged, leading her to impulsive acts. Yet it wasn't wrong. It was a freedom and a discovery about herself that didn't disappoint her. She wanted to experience new things, to touch people's lives, and have them touch hers.

Running a saloon would not have been her selection of providing for herself. Still, she was doing it and doing it well. On more than one occasion, women had stopped her on the street to thank her for watching over their husbands and seeing that they hadn't spent all their money on drink or gambling. Sarah made sure that Gunter put out plenty of popcorn, not too salty, or a dish of crackers. Someone had told her that it would help keep the men sober if they nibbled while they enjoyed their drink.

She delighted in her new clothes and daily was thankful that she had a choice. She would be eternally grateful that she had overheard the painful conversation between Wes and Cole.

Sorting through the wardrobe, she chose a sheer ivory shirtwaist with a lace yoke and tiny pearl buttons running down the front. The skirt she chose to wear was black with tiny ivory flowers sprinkled through the fabric. She picked out her undergarments and studied the stiff corset for several moments.

"For heaven's sake, I'm only going to the bank," she declared, shoving the corset back into the drawer. She needed to stuff herself into that contraption like she needed another leg. She would be miserable.

189

It was already hot and muggy.

She checked her appearance one last time. A small hat with a whisper of a veil rested just above her right ear. Satisfied with the reflection staring back at her, she picked up her purse and the moneybag.

On her way to the bank, people greeted her by name and talked about the weather or made some other friendly overture. Some even made a point of telling her how nice she looked. Her—Sarah Beth Hogan. She loved it. Never at home had she experienced the feeling of belonging that these people had gifted her with, not even during her marriage to Eli.

As she excused herself to get by some men standing in front of the door at the bank, a feeling of unease rippled down her back. When she asked their pardon, they snapped to attention like taunt garters and lowered their chins, turning their faces away while pulling the brim of their hats over their foreheads.

Sarah dashed the unease away and entered the bank. She stood in line talking with Hattie Duncan about the hot weather and the hope of a rain to cool off things a bit. Suddenly the front door slammed against the wall. Three men entered—the same three Sarah had passed outside—with guns drawn and bandannas pulled over the lower portion of their faces.

"Don't anybody move!"

The tallest of the three stepped forward and tossed a flour sack toward the teller cage. "Fill this poke up."

Instead of going over the cage, the sack caught on the bars, sending a shower of powdery white flour into the air.

"Hell," the man muttered. Whipping the sack from the bars, he shoved it through the teller's window. "Now fill it up."

The little man behind the cage slowly removed his

190

spectacles, placed them before his mouth, and breathed on them until they fogged up nicely. Then, whipping a handkerchief from his breast pocket, he wiped them clean before replacing them, all the while shaking his head. "I'm afraid I can't do that."

"What do you mean you can't do that? You will and you'll damn well do it fast, if you know what's good for you."

"Mr. Robber, you'll have to understand that Mr. Johnmore Hamilton, the owner of this bank, has just seen fit to promote me to head cashier. If I do as you ask and give you the money, I'm sure Mr. Johnmore Hamilton will demote me."

"I don't give a damn if Mr. Johnmore Hamilton cuts out your heart and feeds it to the vultures. Now get busy fillin' up that poke before I lose my patience with you."

"I'm sorry, no."

"Why, you little pissant, I'll fill it up myself." As the robber stepped toward the cage, his booted foot hit the floor where the flour had settled. His feet flew out from under him and slammed against the partition separating the customers from the employees. The frightened customers had to smile when his toes cracked like someone popping their knuckles. When he got angrily to his feet, no one mentioned that his backside was coated with enough flour to make a pan of biscuits.

The customers backed out of the way when the second robber stepped forward, brandishing his gun toward the little man. "What's your name?"

"Ernest Millsaps."

"If you don't start puttin' the money in that sack, and pronto, I'm going to come back there and choke the life out of you with your fancy little bow tie, Mr. Ernest Millsaps. Then where will Mr.

Johnmore Hamilton be? Now move!"

The bow tie in question bobbed as Mr. Millsaps swallowed. "I can't."

"You'd risk death before demotion?"

He nodded stiffly.

"Tell you what I'm going to do," the flour-covered robber said, waving his gun. "I'm gonna give you one more chance. I'm gonna make it where even Mr. Johnmore Hamilton won't blame you. For every five minutes that you keep me waitin', I'm gonna shoot one of your customers."

"Please don't," Sarah said, stepping between the robber and the teller.

"What's this? A damn crusade to save the bank's money?"

"It's not the bank's money, it's our money, and we worked our ass off to make it," shouted a man from the front of the line. "Do you expect us to hand it over to a bunch of two-bit robbers without a fuss?"

"Hey, watch out who you're callin' two-bit robbers. We're gonna be the new James gang."

"Are we going to rob this bank or stand around jawin'?" the man guarding the door interrupted. "Just take the money, damn it! We don't care if Millsaps loses his job or not. Now get a move on before the whole town is breathin' down our neck."

As everyone turned to face the man talking, Ernest Millsaps eased toward the vault.

"No!" shouted the flour-covered robber.

But it was too late. Ernest pushed and the vault door slid shut, the well-oiled hinges not even squeaking.

One robber fired into the air and Ernest Millsaps's neck disappeared somewhere in the folds of his shirt. With the discovery that he wasn't shot, his neck slowly reappeared, somewhat like that of a rooster getting ready to crow. But Ernest didn't crow; he was too thankful to be alive. He turned his chalk-white face to the bandits. "I'm sorry, I just couldn't let you take the money. The vault has a time lock on it, and I can't open it again until tomorrow morning," he lied smoothly.

"There's a passel of folks headed this way. Now what are we gonna do?" bellowed the man guarding the door.

"If we're gonna get out of here alive, we need a hostage." He lunged for Hattie Duncan, wrapping his arm around her neck.

"Oh dear," Hattie wept, clasping her chest and swaying in the man's arms.

Without a thought for her own safety, Sarah stepped forward. "Please take me. Mrs. Duncan has a weak heart." Sarah knew there was nothing wrong with Hattie's heart. But by the looks of her, that possibility was looming closer and closer.

The gunshot had brought a small crowd together outside the bank, people wondering what was going on inside. Several brave souls even pushed their faces against the window to get a better look. The robbers settled the question when they pushed through the doors and ordered the people out of the way.

A hushed silence fell over the assembly and those slowly emerging from the bank as they watched the departing robbers and Sarah Hogan. Sarah rode behind the taller of the robbers, holding on to him for dear life. With every step the horse took, she bounced like a tight spring, and a cloud of flour billowed from the saddle, while her stockinged legs protruded from the horse's side like flagstaffs.

"Someone go get the sheriff," Ernest Millsaps called to the crowd. He was feeling terribly guilty because they had taken Mrs. Hogan. If he had turned over the money, none of this would have been necessary, but then he might have lost his position in the bank. And he would rather face a dozen bank robbers than his wife when he had done something to displease her. She was happy being the wife of the head teller, and God help him, but he wanted her to stay happy. Besides, the sheriff could catch the criminals without delay. They hadn't seemed very good at their profession, anyway. Something that really bothered him was that Mrs. Hogan still had her deposit with her. He hoped she took care to hang on to it, because she couldn't expect him to give her credit for a deposit she hadn't made.

Coleman Blade snuggled lower in his misery and wished a pox on whoever was making that infernal racket. When his brain finally cleared, he thought for a moment he was smothering until it dawned on him that he was clutching a pillow over his face. Pushing the pillow away, he groaned, and rolled to his side, seeking a comfortable position for his throbbing head. His leg fell off the bed and his booted foot hit the floor with a thud, rocking his head with pain. He swore softly and opened one bleary eye, the sunlight piercing his brain like a sword. When he could focus his bloodshot eyes, he saw that he had slept in his clothes, and a frowning Chin stood at the foot of the bed.

"What was that damn hammering all about?"

"A group of men from town are looking for their sheriff."

"One day! I take one friggin' day off, and they're out hunting me before the sun rises." He pulled his weary body to a sitting position and cradled his face in the palms of his hands.

"The sun has been up for quite some time, Cole. I

believe the sun had begun its ascent when you stumbled home."

"Humph."

"A wise man knows—"

"I don't want to hear it, Chin," Cole interrupted. "No matter what little tidbit of wisdom you have for me today, it isn't going to help my head." Cole took a shuddering breath. "Nothing will help my head."

"I have mixed a potion that will ease your head—if you will drink it."

"I'll drink anything that will stop this god-awful pounding."

"The taste is vile, but it will help your discomfort." Chin handed Cole a cup filled to the brim with a black-looking substance.

Cole eyed the liquid apprehensively. "It looks like there's things swimming around in it."

Chin shrugged his shoulders.

"Do I have to drink it all?"

"Every drop."

"I was afraid that's what you'd say." With all the fortitude he could muster, he lifted the cup and drained the liquid. If it was possible, it tasted worse than it looked. Cole shivered from head to foot, then flopped back on the bed like a beached fish, vowing never to overindulge again.

"The men are waiting," Chin reminded him.

"What the hell do they want?"

"Some men tried to rob the bank this morning. When they weren't successful, they took Mrs. Hogan as their hostage to get them out of town."

His headache forgotten, Cole was on his feet, buckling on his gunbelt, before Chin finished speaking. "Damn it, I knew it. I knew something would happen the minute I took my eyes off her."

After splashing water on his face and brushing his teeth, he changed shirts. As he left the room, he was pulling on a leather vest. For a second he glimpsed the badge pinned to the breast of his vest. Some damn fine sheriff I've turned out to be, he thought. I was drunker than a muleskinner when Sarah really needed me.

All the men began talking at once. Little by little, Cole got the story from them. If he could have gotten his hands on Ernest Millsaps, he would have pinched his head from his weaselly body. Who did he think he was to put the value of his position and the bank's money over a human life? Cole knew it wasn't his position he feared as much as it was that crow of a woman married to him. That bastard! If he put such store in his job, why hadn't he offered himself as hostage instead of letting them take Sarah?

He saddled his horse and packed his gear in record time.

Chin had a bundle of food ready for him. "I know you don't want it now, but later you might feel like eating something."

"Thanks. Keep an eye on things while I'm gone. I don't know how long it will take me to find them. They have quite a head start."

"You don't think this is a ploy of Dusty Mills to get you out of town?"

"No. The men who took Sarah apparently didn't know what they were doing. If they had been serious, they wouldn't have let Ernest get the upper hand."

"Then, do what you have to do. Everything will be fine here."

His head was pounding and his stomach was queasy. Still, Cole picked up the trail and followed the markings that led him toward the mountains.

It was *her* fault that he had this hellacious hangover.

If she hadn't gotten herself all fixed up and tempted him with her big green eyes and come-hither look, begging to be kissed, he wouldn't have all this stored-up lust eating away at him. . . . That wasn't completely true, and he knew it. She'd drawn his interest when she'd looked like a skinny mop. He couldn't figure it out. Why her? Maybe it was her innocence. He didn't know. He only knew she was always on his mind. Maybe, just maybe—

Damn it, he decided, *he'd do it!* And the more he thought about it, the better it sounded. He was tired of running from her. If Sarah saw something in him worth salvaging, then he'd give it a try. He would court her, something he'd never done before with any woman. He'd never taken the time to care—he'd never wanted to be like his father.

Memories of his father, broken and ruined because of his love for a woman, came sharply into focus. He'd tried to dismiss his memories, but they kept creeping back. He could only vaguely remember his mother, but her betrayal was as poignantly acute as though it had happened yesterday.

From the dim recesses of his mind came her gentle laughter and the low huskiness of her voice. Then suddenly the laughter turned bitter and her voice harsh and insulting. He'd been only a child, but he could remember huddling beneath his bed covers, trying to block out his mother's angry words. She was leaving. She hated her life, hated having tied herself to a man who would never amount to anything, and a kid to look after. She'd found a real man, a man who would dress her in the finest clothes and take her to exciting places. He'd heard his father pleading with her to stay. She'd cursed him and her child. She'd left that same night, never saying good-bye to her son. Cole remembered

197

thinking it was his fault, and he'd never have the chance to show her what a good boy he could be, if only she would stay.

His father had decided to follow her and her lover and bring her back. When several days had passed and his father hadn't returned, Cole had begun walking in the direction his father had taken. He hadn't been gone more than half a day when he'd found his father's horse. Not far from the horse had lain the crumpled body of his father. Cole had wrapped his frail arms around his father and cried deep shuddering sobs. And on that day so long ago, he'd vowed that some way he'd find the man who had taken his mother away — and kill him.

Cole hadn't lived his life full of revenge and hate. Instead he'd put the memories away, knowing that what goes around comes around. He'd have his chance to even the score. Someday.

Now, when he'd least expected it, Sarah Beth Hogan had come along and disrupted his peace of mind.

Chapter Twenty

The shadows lengthened and black billowing clouds scooted across the horizon. Cole could smell the rain in the air. The wind picked up, and jagged streaks of lightning hastened his pace. He had to find shelter. The rumble of thunder rolled through the trees like the sound of a giant clapping his hands. When Cole had given up finding shelter, he caught the smell of wood smoke. It was hard to tell the direction from which the smell came, with the wind whipping against him, and the first large raindrops funneled through the trees, distorting his vision. He could barely make out the shape of a cabin. As he drew closer, he saw a lean-to with three horses tethered inside. He dismounted and hitched his horse with the others. Carefully, he made his way around the cabin. With gun drawn, he pushed through the door.

Four pairs of startled eyes looked up. Then everyone moved at once. Chairs flipped over and the table rattled across the floor, sending playing cards in every direction. The tallest robber couldn't get his gun out of his holster; the second one couldn't find his; and the third one pulled the trigger before his gun left the holster, and blew the toe out of his boot.

"What in god's name is going on here?" Cole shouted.

"Oh my lord, I think I shot my toe off." The man

hopped around the room like a worm in hot ashes. "Somebody take my boot off. I'm afraid to look," he moaned.

"Here, sit down—I'll help you," Sarah offered, kneeling before the outlaw.

Cole couldn't believe his eyes. He kept his gun drawn, but leaned against the door watching the fiasco, having a devil of a time keeping his lips from twitching.

The other outlaws leaned over Sarah's shoulder, watching expectantly.

"Ready, Steve?" Sarah asked, gripping the toeless boot.

"I can't look." Steve groaned, burying his face in his hands. "Is there much blood?"

"I don't see any blood at all." She pulled, the boot came off, and she tossed it aside. The end of his sock was gone, but his toes were all intact, curled beneath his foot like scorched bacon. "This little piggy went to market, this piggy stayed home, this little piggy . . ."

The man called Steve lifted his head and smiled brightly.

The other men slapped him on the back, and one returned his toeless boot.

"Now, will someone tell me what the hell's going on?"

"You scared us to death," the tall man said.

"And you think you didn't scare the people of Hazard when you tried to rob their bank and then kidnapped Mrs. Hogan from beneath their noses? Not to mention you taking me on a wild-goose chase across god's country."

"Well, we apologized to Sarah for kidnappin' her, but we didn't see any other way of gettin' out of town without gettin' killed."

Sarah—he's calling her Sarah. Sounds like a pretty

tight-knit group to me, Cole thought, trying to cool his annoyance. He didn't quite make it, and barked harshly, "And that's supposed to make it right?"

"They didn't mean it, Cole. They've had a string of bad luck lately. Let me introduce you. This is Boyd." She lifted her hand toward the tall man.

"And this is Aaron."

Cole recognized him as the robber who couldn't find his gun.

"This is Steve," she acknowledged, smiling at the one with the toe of his boot missing.

"They're all cousins. This is the sheriff of Hazard, Coleman Blade."

Cole plowed his hand through his hair. "I'm afraid that it's too late for an apology. You threatened to kill the customers and do bodily harm to the head teller."

The man called Boyd lowered his head sheepishly. "We were bluffin'. Steve was the only one who even had his gun loaded," he admitted.

"Do you mean to tell me you tried to rob a bank, and your guns weren't loaded?"

"We didn't want anyone to get killed."

"God, I've heard it all now."

"It's the truth, Cole."

Cole noticed that when Sarah got to her feet, she moved very slowly. "Are you hurt?" he asked, watching her.

"I'm sore, and when I sit for any length of time, my body gets stiff. I think riding the horse did it. I'd never ridden before."

"Well, you could've fooled me. I thought you did very good. Didn't you boys think she did an excellent job ridin'?"

They all nodded their head in agreement and expounded on her merits as a horsewoman.

201

"I guess it happened when you stuck me with that hat pin, and we went sailin' through the air," Boyd offered, rubbing his backside in pained remembrance.

"I'm fine, really. I just need to sit down."

The outlaws rushed to her side to help her, bumping against each other in their haste. They righted the chairs and placed a folded quilt on the seat of the chair for her.

Cole watched in amusement, struck by the tender care the outlaws bestowed on Sarah. No hardened criminals, these. Like Sarah had said, they were probably just down on their luck. They seemed nice enough. What had happened in their lives to force them into a life of crime? Well, one thing was for sure, Cole intended to scare the living hell out of them. By the time he got through with them, they'd think long and hard before resuming their career as outlaws.

He lifted his gun. "Well, fellows, I have to take you in."

"In this rain?"

"If the good people of Hazard can build a scaffold in this downpour, then it won't hurt us to ride in it."

"A scaffold," they cried in unison.

"What they need a gol-dang scaffold for? That's for hangin' people, ain't it?"

Cole nodded his head somberly.

"You mean they're gonna hang us?"

"But we didn't even get their money."

"Doesn't matter. You broke the law and you have to pay the consequences."

"Don't we get a trial or nothin'?"

"Oh yes, you'll get a trial."

The outlaws sighed with relief.

Cole rubbed his bristled face and pondered the dilemma. "Of course, I can't say how fair it will be. I'm

202

afraid you're already guilty in the eyes of the town. They'll hang you for sure."

"Would it help if I testify in their behalf?" Sarah pleaded. "They didn't hurt me." She reached to the floor and picked up the bag holding the saloon's deposit. "They wouldn't even take my money, and I offered it to them."

Cole hated to upset Sarah, but he had no way of letting her know what he was doing. He shook his head slowly.

"Oh dear," she whispered.

"Hazard has never had a hanging, much less a triple hanging. You boys should make the headlines in newspapers all over Texas."

"Well, that's just comfortin' as hell. Too bad we won't be around to read them glowin' headlines. We'll be deader than Moses."

Cole bit the inside of his mouth to keep from smiling.

Sarah watched him with a troubled expression. She had to admit she was delighted to see him, although it troubled her to see her new friends so distraught. When they'd taken her, she'd been terrified. Yet their manner had eased her fears, and she'd decided she was more afraid of the horse than of the outlaws. Upon reaching the cabin, they'd tried to make her comfortable, and had assured her they meant her no harm. After much probing, she'd learned their attempted bank robbery was no more than an act of sheer desperation. They had owned a ranch north of a small town not far from Hazard until an underhanded schemer had taken everything they owned. To this day, they didn't quite know how he'd managed it. All they'd ever known was hard work, which pleased them just fine, and the only experience they'd had with guns had been hunting.

As she watched Cole, she noted a peculiar gleam in his stormy-day eyes. Something wasn't right. He looked as though he was struggling to keep a stern appearance. She would try once more to explain the situation to him. Maybe he would help. He didn't seem so cold-hearted that he wouldn't listen to reason—she hoped.

"Cole, please try to understand that these men have suffered a terrible blow."

"Just terrible," the men agreed, nodding their heads.

"Their ranch was literally stolen from beneath their very noses."

"Yeah. But we can't prove it."

"Isn't there some way they can get a second chance?"

"Yeah, a second chance."

They reminded Cole of a congregation *amen*ing everything a preacher said, and Sarah was their preacher. It was hard for him to concentrate on what she was saying—rather, he found himself admiring her animated face. Her hair was down, and draped her shoulders in disarray; her face was flushed with bright colors; and her beautiful green eyes were alive with her impassioned plea.

"Dusty Mills," she said.

"Yeah, that no-good varmint."

"What? Who?" Cole blurted out, shifting his attention back to the conversation.

"Dusty Mills. He's the man who cheated them out of their land."

"Well, now, that sheds a little different light on the situation."

"Do you mean we could get a second chance if we give you our word never to pull a stunt like that again?"

"Like I said, you broke the law, and I'm sworn to uphold the law. I'll have to take you in."

"Oh," they answered dejectedly.

"But if you should escape . . ."

"Yeah, *if*. And *if* a frog had wings, he wouldn't bump his little green ass on the ground."

Sarah laughed before she could cover her mouth, and Cole couldn't help the chuckle that escaped him.

"Anyway, if you did escape, I'm sure I couldn't find you. And when I return to Hazard, I'll try to convince the people it was all a mistake." As Cole spoke, he approached the table and carelessly laid his gun down to adjust his gunbelt.

"We've decided we're no good at this outlaw stuff. I guess we'll have to go back to Hazard and take our medicine."

"If by some remote chance you did escape," Cole said, "and I could clear your name, it would probably be wise if you didn't come into town until this bank-robbery business blows over." He pushed the gun farther onto the table and bent over to pick up the scattered playing cards.

It suddenly hit Sarah what Cole was doing. She glanced around the table. The men had no earthly idea what was going on and had no intention of trying to escape.

Unconsciously, Boyd leaned across the table and traced his hand along the cool metal of the trigger guard. Then sticking his finger in the guard, he spun the gun around and around as it lay atop the table.

Cole appeared to pay him little attention.

When the gun quit spinning, Boyd moved his fingers to the stag handles, studying them for some time before picking up the gun. Weighing the gun in his palm, he wrapped his hand around the butt. "You know, I believe my daddy had a gun like this," he said offhandedly, taking a bead on the door.

Cole's arms shot into the air. "Don't shoot. I won't try anything."

Boyd dropped the gun like a hot potato and rammed his own arms into the air. Cole's gun skidded across the table and into Steve's lap.

If every head hadn't turned in his direction, Cole would have rolled his eyes and shook his head. Instead his head rocked forward until his chin almost touched his chest and his breath left him in a disgruntled sigh. My god, what else can I do? he thought.

Steve had started to hand the gun back to Cole when Sarah leaned toward him and whispered, "Now's your chance to escape. Go. And Godspeed."

"But . . ."

"Go," she whispered.

"Will you be all right?"

"I'll be fine. The sheriff's a good man."

Cole arched a brow.

Steve took a firm grip on the gun. "You've left us no other choice, Sheriff. We ain't hankerin' to be Hazard's first hangin'. I hope you understand."

"Completely." Thank God for small favors, Cole thought.

"You won't try to follow us, will you, Sheriff?" Aaron questioned, as though Cole's answer determined whether or not he'd leave.

"You won't be robbing any more banks, will you?"

"Lord, no," they quickly agreed.

"Then, I won't follow you. You have my word."

"Thanks," the outlaws said, rushing to the door.

"One more thing—" Cole asked. "Would you mind giving me back my gun? We've gone through some hellacious battles together. I feel naked without it."

"Yeah, sure," Steve responded, nonchalantly handing Cole their means of escape, then ducking out the door

Cole did roll his eyes and shake his head. He holstered the gun in bewildered amusement. Lord, what a day. He lifted his head and met the joy dancing in Sarah's eyes.

"You really are a very nice person."

"I couldn't just turn them loose. I thought they'd eventually take the hint. Indeed, their minds aren't of a criminal bent, or they would've taken me the moment I entered the room, or leastwise when I put my gun on the table. If Steve hadn't acted when you told him to, I would've had to take them back to Hazard. I was running out of hints."

She laughed soundly. "You almost scared Boyd to death when your hands shot in the air, and you told him not to shoot."

"I noticed . . . when he launched my gun across the table."

"They're not really building a scaffold in Hazard, are they?"

"No, but I wanted to encourage your friends to abandon their life of crime."

"I think you succeeded. They were shaking in their boots."

When a war whoop shattered the quiet, Sarah and Cole stepped from the cabin into the rain and watched the departure of the happily reformed outlaws. They turned in their saddles and waved good-bye, then gave another shrill war cry.

Cole and Sarah stood completely still, letting the gentle rain wash over their suddenly heated bodies, each abruptly aware of the other and the isolation of their position. Cole cautioned himself to remember that she was a lady first and foremost. Yet, he'd glimpsed her passion and tasted her desire. The memory of her lips and the feel of her in his arms played havoc with his

207

reasoning power. He wanted her as he'd never wanted anything in his life. He watched, wondering if she was praying as she lifted her face to the heavens. Droplets sparkled on the tips of her lashes as the rain caressed her face and rolled in rivulets down her neck, becoming absorbed in the fabric of her blouse. Her hair lay wet and clinging against her shoulders, tempting Cole to wrap his hand in the coppery strands. His body was responding to her in ways that would embarrass her if she noticed. He couldn't help it. At this point, he had no control over his passion, and he throbbed with unquenched desire.

She turned to him, her eyes shimmering with invitation. It dawned on him that she hadn't been praying. Instead she'd been fighting the same weakness he had. Her look took care of any misgivings he had harbored. His gaze encompassed the length of her. He drew in his breath sharply, the blood bubbling through his veins like boiling water. The rain had made her blouse transparent. The fabric was molded to her breast like a lover's hand, and her nipples responded to that touch by hardening and standing erect beneath the wet fabric. He lifted his hand, cupping the side of her face, his thumb rippling across the fullness of her moist lips.

Her breath faltered, and the coolness of her flesh heated beneath his touch. She parted her lips and her tongue touched his thumb.

He groaned, "Sarah," in a harsh voice that was lost in the steady rhythm of the rain. Lowering his head, his hand worked its way to the back of her head, tilting it just so.

Her heart pounding a rapid tattoo, she reached up on tiptoes to close the distance between them. They came together like two bolts of lightning. She, in her innocence, although she was no longer a virgin; he, with the experience of a well-taught lover, yet innocent with newfound emotions. When they touched, it was as though they'd reached home after a lifetime of partings. She fit perfectly in his embrace, and there was no shame as she gloried in the feel of him. Her arms circled him, her fingers tangling in the rain-wet strands of ebony hair.

Their hands and faces shimmered with rain, their bodies with longing. He nibbled the fullness of her lips, his tongue lifting the raindrops and scattering them across her face. He skimmed the curve of her lips before penetrating the warmth of her mouth. He explored slowly, thoroughly. The tip of her tongue hesitantly touched his, evoking a legion of new emotions. He throbbed and swelled with longing as he cupped her bottom and pressed her against his hardness. She whimpered in his embrace and molded her body closer to his.

His hand skimmed the tiny buttons that scaled the front of her shirtwaist, sending a longing through her that surprised her with its intensity.

Without loosening their embrace, he shifted their bodies until he had positioned her against the wall of the cabin. His fingers, clumsy in their haste, worked the buttons free and opened her shirtwaist. His breath caught in his throat when he viewed the creamy flesh spilling over her lacy chemise. A hardness rocked through him that left him shaking in its aftermath. With trembling fingers, he skimmed the wet fabric.

Goose bumps danced along her skin, intensifying her hardened nipples. From somewhere within the depths of her consciousness came the revelation that this was passion in its rawest form, something she'd never experienced. Her husband would never have looked on her bare flesh—indeed, he'd never touched her—in such a manner. Was this love or lust? She wasn't sure. But it was wonderful, simply wonderful. Surely she must love him — if not, how could he make her feel this way?

Standing there in the gentle rain, Sarah Beth Hogan lifted her hand, and with the same trembling haste that Cole had experienced, her fingers moved to the button placket of his shirt. When she'd freed the few buttons, he leaned away from her and tugged the damp shirt over his head. She faltered in her exploration until he lifted her hands and placed them on the width of his chest. She could feel the beating of his heart, the solid muscle, and the furling of soft hair beneath her hand. She licked her lips and swirled her fingers through the hair and across his turgid nipples.

"Sarah," he growled as his lips met hers. He welcomed the heat and passion of her response as he deepened the kiss, exploring and teasing. He strained against her, the evidence of his arousal burning its way through her skirt. His mouth moved down the graceful sweep of her neck and along the smooth, wet flesh until he reached the fullness of her breasts. He tongued one puckered nipple then the other through the wet clinging fabric. The sensation of the heat of his mouth blended with the cool material of the rain-soaked chemise, and sent a ripple quivering through her body that depleted the strength in her legs. When she began sliding slowly down the wall, he scooped her up in arms and carried her inside to discover the secrets of her body and share his with her. There would be no turning back . . . this time.

Chapter Twenty-one

Cole kicked the door shut and his long strides carried them quickly across the room. Picking up the quilt from the chair, he moved to a narrow bed in the corner. Lowering Sarah to her feet, he spread the cover over the lumpy cornshuck mattress.

She couldn't take her eyes off him. His back gleamed in the soft lanternlight, his muscles swelling and relaxing as he reached to straighten the quilt. Raindrops shimmered in his hair and desire burned in his eyes. When she lifted her hands to close the front of her blouse, he shook his head and took her hands in his. "No." His voice was hoarse and filled with passion.

He lifted her hands to his mouth and skimmed his lips over her knuckles, his tongue salving the areas between her index finger and her thumb. Turning them over, he addressed the pads of her fingers and then her palms. His lips burned a path of total surrender. He kissed one wrist lightly, then the other. Lowering himself to the edge of the bed, he pulled her between his legs. He buried his head against the softness of her stomach and cupped the curve of her bottom. He didn't do anything for a moment, just held her to him, savoring the feel of her, marveling at the sheer joy of holding her.

She wrapped her arms around him and lowered her head, nuzzling against him, coppery strands blending with raven as she absorbed his warmth.

Very slowly, his hands began to glide over her. He lifted his head and his eyes collided with hers. He pulled her onto his lap and sought once more the sweetness of her mouth. He couldn't get enough of her. They became lost in their quest for fulfillment. He was eager to join their bodies. She was eager for she knew not what. Her body blossomed under his touch and her passion matched his. Buttons were unbuttoned; ribbons became tangled in his gunbelt and both slid unnoticed to the floor. Bare chests came together, one silky and creamy white, smelling of lavender, the other hard and masculine, furred with crisp hair. He touched hers; she touched his.

He lifted her from his lap and stood her before him. Slowly, he stripped her of every stitch of clothing, kissing his way from the top of her head to the tips of her toes as he discarded her shoes. When he raised his head, a spark of mischief gleamed in his eyes. " 'Do unto others as you would have others do unto you.' Is that what you told me?"

She took the hint, and moved her lips across his body with lingering perfection, stripping away his remaining clothing. Her boldness took his breath away, and her ardor fueled the flame that raged inside him. She'd never seen a naked man before, so her journey was fraught with newfound discovery. The few times Eli had bedded her—he, in a long nightshirt; she, in a heavy gown—there had been no touching, no caresses or whispered endearments, not even a kiss. He had crawled atop her, raised her gown slightly, and pressed his manhood into her, heaved and sweated over her, then rolled away. It had been painful and degrading.

Again Cole scooped her into his arms and laid her gently on the bed. He lay beside her, their naked splendor glimmering in the light. They touched and tasted, giving full rein to their passion, while beyond their nest the rain fell in sheets.

Cole trailed his fingers down her stomach and fisted his hand in the mound of coppery curls. He unwound his fingers slowly, sliding them between her legs until they were wet and slippery.

Sarah moaned.

He burrowed deeper until she arched her hips, settling his finger securely in her woman's flesh. His heated breath fanned her face as she rolled her head wildly. Sarah didn't understand the ache pulsating through her. She felt as though something wild and wonderful was trapped inside her and would give her no peace until it was set free. She couldn't believe that the sounds, the moans, and the quickened breathing were coming from her.

Taking his own sweet time, plying her with skilled strokes, Cole taught her the wonders of her body, things she would have never dreamed possible. Lust, raw and new, swept through her like a storm brewing out of control.

Cole's own control fell short of an ability to rein his desire. He wanted her, desperately. Her caresses left him with little command over his body. He lifted himself and straddled her, resting his weight on his bent legs. Cupping her breasts, he stroked them, squeezing the taut nipples as his manhood throbbed against her belly. She moved her hand over him and marveled at the heat radiating from him. He placed his hand over hers and showed her how to pleasure him. They watched as their hands moved together, back and forth, back and forth. From deep in his chest, he moaned.

Sarah gloried in his pleasure and increased the motion. He could wait no longer. Lifting her hips, he positioned himself for the welcoming journey. Her hot, wet flesh closed around him, tightening, and pulsing against him. He surged deeper . . . deeper. Her cry of sheer pleasure filled the room as her legs locked around him. She raised her head from the quilt. Sweat beaded his brow. His eyes glazed with passion and his jaw tense with emotion, he lifted her bottom higher, watching as he entered her.

A bundle of heat started at the juncture of her legs and rolled through her as he increased his force. He shifted his weight. Leaning over her, he pulled her into his arms and kissed her deeply, wildly. She answered him kiss for kiss, motion for motion, until suddenly the heat erupted, sending ribbons of pleasure convulsing through her. She tightened her legs and arms around him as he moved faster and faster until blinding pleasure ripped through him. He moaned, his body quaking against her as he spilled himself into her. They lay very quiet, wrapped in each other's arms, savoring the wondrous tremors still sweeping through them. He rolled to his side, taking her with him. Their bodies shimmered with a fine mist of perspiration. When their bodies began to dry, a chill beset Sarah and she shivered in his arms. He rubbed his hands over her naked body, chasing the chill away.

"I'll build a fire," he whispered before kissing her soundly. He rose from the bed and pulled the quilt over her.

Where his body had lain on the quilt, it was toasty warm. Sarah snuggled in the folds and watched Cole as he strode across the room, unconcerned with his nakedness.

Beside the hearth was a stack of dry firewood. He splintered enough kindling to start a small blaze and fed the fire until the flames were leaping and dancing.

He picked up their wet clothes and draped them before the fire. Picking up Sarah's drawers, he eyed them wickedly, then lifted his gaze to her. His eyes, as gray as the day outside, simmered with passion. Sarah herself tingled with renewed desire just watching him finger her undergarment. Smoldering desire sizzled between them like droplets of rainwater hitting the fire.

He winked at her, and she blushed to the roots of her hair. He was truly a beautiful man. His face was a work of planes and angles that combined in breathtaking beauty. His furred chest with soft dark curls was broad, his stomach flat and as hard as a rock. And he had handsome legs, long and supple. His buttocks were slim and firm. And his manhood — big and pleasing — were the first words that came to her mind. A tiny sprout of recrimination budded and grew. Could this be Sarah Beth Hogan thinking such carnal thoughts, indeed, relishing the thought of more of the same?

Cole saw the marked change come over her when she began questioning what they had shared. Damn it! He wouldn't let her fanatical upbringing come between them and destroy the joy of their lovemaking. He cared too much to let that happen. She was a hell of a woman, pleasing to look at, impulsive, determined — and there lurked a passion in her that took his breath away. A lesson in love was in order, and if Cole was nothing else, he'd always been a good pupil. So why shouldn't he be a good teacher? With his purpose in mind, he approached the bed. Scooping up Sarah, quilt, and mattress, he placed his bundle before the fire, and set about to fill her mind and body with only thoughts of him. When he reached for her, he saw the glimmer of tears, and cursed soundly the past that would tear her from his arms.

He rained kisses across her face and whispered words

215

of love and lust, chasing the shadows from her mind. She responded with a force and boldness that swept everything from his mind except the rushing desire to make her his once more.

Darkness settled and the rain turned to a fine mist, yet inside the small cabin it was cozy and warm. The firelight cast the only light as clothes dried in the heat of the room. A cornshuck mattress and a multicolored quilt cushioned the naked bodies of the lovers as they discovered each nuance of the other's body. They made slow, deeply satisfying love. They made fast, hard, bone-melting love that sent pleasure rocking through them.

When the embers of hot coals shifted and settled in the dying blaze, one of the lovers would rise from the bed to toss a log on the fire. The lovers were much like the embers, as their passion again and again blazed anew.

They laughed and played and teased, and dozed in each other's arms until the dawning of the day chased the darkness away. They made love in the light of day, and helped each other dress. Both bellowed with laughter when Cole couldn't find his shirt and Sarah tossed him her frilly chemise, telling him that he could borrow it until he found his shirt.

Cole loved her dry humor, her play, and her sensual body. In fact, much to his own confusion, he decided he loved her. His mind wasn't quite ready to accept this discovery, so he didn't say anything. He needed time to think this through.

Sarah, on the other hand, would have blurted out her feelings with excitement. When she tried to tell him, he put his finger over her lips and shook his head. She looked at him with hurt and puzzlement.

"Not yet, Sarah." He raked his hand through his

216

rumpled hair, then picked up his gunbelt and buckled it on. "Hell, I don't have the answers, but we can't let lust make our decisions."

"Lust," she whispered. "Is that all it was to you? Lust?"

"For god's sake, Sarah, you know it was more than that."

"Don't take the Lord's name in vain," she answered quickly. "And how do I know it was more than lust? I want to tell you how I feel, what's going on in here—" She pounded her fisted hand against her chest. Tears puddled in her eyes and rolled down her face. "I've never felt like this before."

He closed his arms around her and tried to soothe her. "Hey, baby, don't cry. I didn't mean to make you unhappy. This is all new to me, too. I just don't want to screw things up."

"Me either," she sniffled, lifting her tearstained face to his.

The temptation was too much. He lowered his lips to hers and lost himself to the welcoming response. Much later, they prepared for the journey back to town. It was still very early, and they wanted to make it back before everyone was up and about. Then they could lie a bit and put their return in vague early-morning hours without anyone knowing they had spent the night together.

Getting Sarah atop the horse was a feat in itself. She was terribly sore from the ordeal the day before. As long as she'd remained in the warmth of the cabin, she'd been fine. But the cool morning air took its toll on her sore, stiff muscles. Still, once astride, she and Cole shared a most enjoyable ride.

It took some doing, but they managed to skirt the middle of town and dodge people until Sarah could slip

217

quietly through the back door of the saloon. She watched from her window as Cole rode up the street as though he were just reporting for work. He lifted his head and smiled at Sarah, winking boldly. She hugged herself tightly and dipped about the room, humming softly one of the tunes she'd heard Floyd play on the piano. She fell onto the bed and let her memory have full rein, reliving the time spent with Cole. In only a few short moments her eyes shut in peaceful slumber, her dreams filled with a handsome sheriff and a widow woman.

Belle and Collie had known when Sarah had arrived. The previous evening, they'd sent everyone else home and had paced the floor awaiting word of Sarah. The town had been up in arms over the kidnapping of Sarah Hogan. If Billy had had his way, he would have strung up Ernest Millsaps without delay. No ifs, ands, or buts about it, the little weaselly man would live longer if he cut a wide path from the anger of Billy Ward. No one had ever seen Billy in such a rage, and his concern for Sarah had been heart-wrenching.

Indeed, of all the prayers said on Sarah's behalf, none were more beseeching than those offered by Ernest Millsaps. He knew without a doubt that if anything happened to Sarah, he would surely lose his job. Billy couldn't get him fired, but he'd sworn he would burn the damn bank to the ground if Sarah didn't return safely. Then Ernest could kiss his head teller's job good-bye. Billy would do it, too. Ernest knew he would. He'd never seen anyone with a mean streak like that — except, of course, his wife.

Belle had just gone downstairs to make coffee when she'd heard the back door open. She'd watched as Sarah had sneaked in to make sure the way was clear before Cole stuck his head in. She'd seen them as they

218

shared a long, deep kiss, their hands touching each other with familiarity.

"Get some sleep. I'll see you later," Cole had whispered.

"Will you have a chance to sleep? I know you're tired," she'd said, stroking his cheek.

"I'll be fine. Now scat before someone sees you." And he'd patted her on the bottom before he'd left.

Belle had smiled from ear to ear and had waited until Sarah had been safely in her room before she'd bounded up the stairs to tell Collie.

When Sarah awakened after only a couple hours of sleep, she felt like she could take on the world. She was sure the sheriff had spread the word about her safe return when she opened her door and found sitting outside several buckets of steaming water. She'd been on her way to ask Billy to heat water for her bath. She blessed him soundly and carried the water into her room. After a leisurely bath, her muscles loosened up some. She dressed with care, taking note that none of the passion or the explosions of pleasure showed on her face. Although, she did admit, there was a softening in her face that hadn't been there previously.

Making her way down the stairs, a round of applause from men and women alike greeted her. For an instant, the presence of women in the saloon took her aback until it dawned on her they were happy to have her back safely. She smiled warmly among hugs and handshakes, and asked Gunter to break out a bottle of fine sherry for the women.

As far as Sarah knew, the women, one and all, sampled the sherry, if only a small sip. The sheriff had explained the harrowing adventure and the long ride through the night to reach Hazard safely. Belle didn't say anything, only smiling brightly and nodding her head in sympathy. But she knew that it had rained until dawn, and that when Sarah and Cole had entered the saloon, their clothes had been as dry as a freshly diapered baby's bottom.

Dusty Mills sat behind the desk, drumming his fingers against the smooth surface, pondering the words the man before him had just related. Son of a bitch! The little fluff wasn't the lady she'd appeared, he thought angrily. "You're sure they spent the night together?"

"Hell, boss, I ain't blind. I followed them back into town. They didn't see me, but I didn't let them out of my sight. It was like watching two lovebirds. They couldn't keep their hands off each other. She was riding astride the horse with him. A couple of times I thought he was going to take her right there on that horse."

"Well, well, it appears I played the wrong cards. Instead of playing my ace, I let her bluff me."

The man standing before him scratched his ear, trying to figure out what Dusty meant. Sometimes, the boss referred to things in the terms of card games.

"How's that?"

"I treated her like a lady instead of the slut she really is. I should have made a move on her, but I was biding my time, thinking to charm her slowly so as not to frighten her away. Hell, I should have known better. Women are all the same. Sarah Hogan just managed to hide her itch better than most."

"Will that be all, boss? I've developed my own itch since watching them this morning. I thought I might ride into town and check out Lila's."

"Yeah, go ahead. And Early? There'll be a little something extra in your wages this week. If you see anything else, just let me know."

"Sure thing."

Dusty turned in his chair and peered out the window over the miles and miles of his property. Hundreds of heads of cattle grazed contentedly on the lush grasses, and fine strong horses filled the corrals. He was on his way to becoming a very wealthy man, and he relished the idea. Indeed, he deserved it. It mattered little to him who was hurt or killed as long as he got what he wanted. And damn it, he wanted Sarah Hogan's land. The bitch had fooled him. From the gossip he'd heard, he thought she was something special. He'd even altered his plan to court her. Hell, she was just like all the rest. By god, she didn't deserve any special attention.

When the railroad purchased his property, he would move on, obtain other properties, and enlarge his holdings until his name was a household word in the great state of Texas.

He had spent his life pursuing pleasure in one form or another. Women had played a vital roll in his upkeep. He had won them with his charm and good looks. When they were completely his and he knew it, that's when the tables turned. From the finest clothes and best food, to the most luxurious accommodations, they provided it all. He allowed them to dress in the very best, and taught them to play cards, and to become adept at the sleight of hand that ensured a winning hand. If they couldn't make a living at cards, they sold their bodies. They would do anything to stay in his good graces—he saw to that.

His father had taught him well. As a child, it had been only the two of them, and the women—god, the women! He remembered the big handsome man well.

As far as Dusty could recall, he had never worked Women had taken care of him, but then he'd taken car of them also ... with his body. Dusty had learned early on what women liked. His father had taught him Dusty had hidden and watched when his father had taken women to bed. His father had told him abou making love and saying just the right things — thing women liked to hear. Strangely enough, his father had scorned the very women who'd taken care of him. He' taught his son never to trust a woman: they lied an used a man to their own satisfaction. They were als shallow, vain individuals and easily manipulated by th proper word and skilled strokes. Still, he'd assure Dusty there was nothing in the world that would com pare to the pleasure of sinking himself deeply into woman's flesh.

When his father had died, his legacy lived o through his son. Only his son took the legacy one ste farther. He charmed the women, loved the women, use them, but when he was through with them, he kille them. The first had been an accident, but it ha brought him such a hard, violent climax that h couldn't get it out of his mind. After that, it becam part of his ritual. His good looks and easy manne turned the women's heads. For the most part, he preye on married women, with a few rare exceptions. When woman left her husband for another man, she becam an outcast, seldom sought out by the cuckolded hu band. The exceptions with the single women came whe they had no family ties or close kin who might try t track them down.

Through the years, Dusty's plan had worked withou fail. It was only recently that he'd decided his ag would sooner or later put an end to his comfort. As h had been trying to figure out a way to set himself u

222

for life, he'd overheard the plan about the railroad spur linking Hazard, Texas, to a main rail.

His future had fallen into his hands like manna from heaven. He'd begun to make plans. Dusty paid top wages, so he had been able to select his men carefully. Then he'd settled on the outskirts of town like an aching tooth, bringing pain and discomfort to the good people of Hazard.

He was bad, he was evil, and he didn't give a damn. He wanted wealth and, if anyone stood in his way, he didn't give a tinker's damn if he had to kill them or not. Dusty Mills always got what he wanted.

In addition to being a wealthy landowner, he'd decided he wanted Sarah Beth Hogan. And he knew just how to get her.

So she was bedding the sheriff. Well, hell, he could take care of that fast enough. And in the process he could kill two birds with one stone. Coleman Blade would hate her, and when he discarded her, Dusty would be there to lick her wounds.

He shifted again in his chair and took a key from his pocket. Anticipation swirled through him as he unlocked the bottom drawer of his desk. Taking a long wooden box from the back of the drawer, he produced another key and inserted it into the lock. He lifted the lid and eyed the contents. An evil smile twisted the curve of his handsome mouth as he ran his hand through the trinkets. Shimmering gold and silver, diamonds, emeralds, rubies, and sapphires trickled through his fingers. Each represented a conquest, a victory. A woman.

He remembered each and every one of them—their faces, their beauty, and their lying eyes. From each he had taken a token—a golden or silver chain, a ring here and there, with a variety of stones, a single diamond, or a cluster of pearls. It didn't matter, just some little memento of appreciation.

Some men notched their guns; others told stories of their triumphs. Not Dusty. He kept his victories to himself, and on occasion took the box from safekeeping and admired his trophies. The trinkets were like spoils of a battle. But Dusty was the only one who ever knew there was a war going on.

When he viewed his plunder, he became instantly hard. The blood shot through his body and settled in his loins. He unbuttoned his pants and pushed them to his knees. He lifted the box and let the trinkets slide slowly around his throbbing, straining manhood. Cool gold and silver chains tangled and shimmered as they coiled around him, and sparkling jewels and pearls glimmered in his tight curls. He brought his hand around his hardness and stroked slowly, reciting each name. "Mary Katherine, Louise, Francis, Helen," and on and on.

Lifting a gold chain with a delicately scrolled locket, he pressed it against his heated flesh and pumped faster, faster, spilling himself and the name of the owner of the golden locket — Lois Blade.

Chapter Twenty-two

Cole flipped his thumb across the head of the stem and watched the match flare. Bringing the fire to the dark rich tobacco, he inhaled deeply and rocked back in his chair. For some reason the traffic outside his office seemed heavier today than usual. Everyone and their brother had stuck their head in the door and asked how he was doing. The people of Hazard had always been friendly, but this bordered on the ridiculous. Why was everyone suddenly so concerned about his well-being? If one more person stuck his head through that door, he'd be tempted to throw something at him.

Several days had passed since he and Sarah had returned to town. They hadn't been alone, even though he'd seen her every night in the saloon. It had been all he could do to keep his hands off her. His body had reacted with pulsing need every time his memory veered to their night together. He'd never felt this way before. How had she managed it? She was so innocent, so sweet, so exciting. Even now he swelled with desire.

The jarring of the door distracted his thoughts and he looked up to encounter Wes's angry face.

"You look like somebody just stole your girl."

"I don't have a girl," Wes snapped.

"Well, you should. Maybe it would take that sour look off your face."

"Right now I have more important things on my mind."

"Such as?"

"This!" Wes slapped a large square of paper on the desk.

Cole picked up the paper and scanned the contents, his stomach tightening as though someone had just plowed their fist into his midsection.

$1,000 Reward
for the body of
Sheriff: COLEMAN BLADE
No questions asked
Payment on delivery
Hazard Post Office
Hazard, Texas

"Who?"

"I have no earthly idea, but someone plastered the damn things all over town. You must have really pissed somebody off."

"That's not unusual, although I'll admit no one has ever gone to this extreme. They normally just try to shoot me in the back." Cole laughed, and read the paper again.

"Damn it, Cole, this isn't funny. No matter how you cut it, this is premeditated murder. Someone wants you dead, and it's worth a thousand dollars to see the deed done. Every trigger-happy bastard in the state will be trying to collect that reward."

"Then, I'll have to be more careful."

"For god's sake, will you take this seriously?"

"I'm dead serious, no pun intended. But I can't crawl in a hole and try to wait this thing out. I'm the sheriff and I have a job to do. If I tuck tail and run, then whoever posted this reward will win without losing a dime."

"I've already checked with the post office, and sure enough, there's a package of money, one thousand dollars, with instructions to give it to whoever delivers your body."

"I bet Jake is quaking in his boots."

"God, he is. He wants no part of this and has no idea how the money got there. When he opened up this morning, the package and instructions were on his desk. That, in itself, was enough to shake him up, knowing that somebody was in there prowling around."

"Well, I can understand. I'll check with him later to see if I can do anything."

"I asked him to keep an eye out for anybody unusual hanging around. He's the nervous type anyway, and when he gets the least bit upset he pulls the hair out of his mustache. It wouldn't surprise me if the next time I see him the region above his upper lip is completely bald."

"The thing that gets me is that anybody brazen enough to kill me and then try to collect the reward will be arrested for murder."

"That's true, but whoever devised this scheme is clever enough to realize that greed will overshadow any wrongdoing. It's caused an uproar, and I'm sure that was the intention."

"So while I'm expecting a frontal confrontation, my back is exposed."

"That's about it. The way I have it figured is that you've become a real thorn in somebody's side. Before you took over as sheriff, this town was headed straight to the dogs. You've restored order to this town and somebody doesn't like it."

"I'd bet my last dollar it all boils down to the rumor

of the railroad spur. And we both know who that is. Dusty Mills has set up a kingdom like he's some kind of damn prince. If anyone gets in his way, well, that's just their misfortune."

"I'll say one thing for him. If Mills is behind this, he covers his tracks well. I've checked every source and I've come up with nothing."

"Who else could it be, if not Dusty? From what James Moore told me when he asked me to take this job, Hazard was a peaceful, law-abiding town before Mills moved here."

"Oh, I agree with you one hundred percent. He's the culprit—he just doesn't dirty his hands. I want you to take care, and don't make any careless moves."

"You can count on it."

Wes left a deeply troubled man. Cole's own safety didn't worry him. He'd been dodging bullets for a long time. It was his relationship with Sarah that tore at him. He would never endanger her. Whoever had put out the reward would think nothing of using her to get to him, if they thought she meant anything to him. The only way he could protect her was to stay away from her. It was like offering candy to a baby—and when the baby reached for it, jerking it away. He'd had a taste and now he wanted more. Sarah was the most wonderful thing that had ever happened to him. Now he had to deny himself the thing he most wanted. He laughed harshly. I can look, but I must not touch, he thought sadly.

That was the way it had to be, if he was to keep her safe. And Sarah was smart enough to figure out what was going on, if he didn't come up with something that would convince her that he truly didn't want her.

Cole peered through the window, never seeing the activity beyond as he pondered his dilemma. Suddenly the vision of his thoughts stormed through the door, her faced flushed, her state highly agitated as she shook a piece of paper beneath his nose and demanded an explanation.

He shrugged his shoulders and remained seated, determined not to take her in his arms and comfort her.

"Maybe it's somebody's idea of a joke," he offered lamely.

"That's not true and we both know it."

"What do you want me to say, Sarah? I don't know any more about it than you do."

"But somebody wants you dead and they're offering a lot of money to see that it's done."

"It's a free country. Anybody can post a reward, but murder is still against the law."

"Thank you for pointing that out to me. It comforts me to know that should someone kill you, they will be punished," she replied, her voice dripping with sarcasm.

"Sarcasm does not become you, Sarah."

"Neither does your attitude about this whole affair. You can't just brush it off. It's real."

"It's not the first time. And if I live, I'm sure it won't be the last."

"You make me so mad," she stormed. "How can you sit there and do nothing? What do I have to do to make you understand?" she shouted.

This was the perfect opening, and he couldn't afford to pass it up. He wanted her mad, and out of the way. It was his only hope of protecting her.

"You can leave me the hell alone. I don't need, nor do I want, you hanging around my neck whining and complaining," he said harshly.

"Whining, complaining. Me! I've never whined in my life."

"You could've fooled me. You've whined and complained ever since you stormed in here. I've got too many things on my mind right now to see to the needs of a sniveling female."

"Well, I can assure you that you won't have to see to the needs of this sniveling female. I'm sorry I wasted your time."

She slammed out the door like a tornado in search of a landing.

Cole ground his teeth and gripped the edge of his desk to keep from calling after her. It was best this way. He could deal with her anger, but he couldn't stand it if any harm came to her.

That night when he made his rounds, he stopped in the saloon, and would have sworn the temperature dropped from pleasant to freezing within the space of a few steps. Sarah ignored him completely, and when she chanced to glance his way, she looked through him. Everyone else was pleasant enough, and he was asked repeatedly about the reward. It didn't take him long to get his fill of questions—and of Sarah's refusal to acknowledge him. He called it a night and headed for home. At least Chin wouldn't hound him to death.

The night was reminiscent of Cole's mood, inky dark and blustery. After the reward, he should have been paying more attention, but instead his mind was awash with thoughts of Sarah and how beautiful she had looked, even in her anger. He'd done what he set out to do: She was angry, and he wanted her to stay that way, for a while, anyway. When this blew over, he would make it up to her. He would apologize and take her in his arms and love her until his heart was content.

From the darkness, two men emerged, guns drawn. As he drew his horse to a halt, a third man dropped from a tree limb above him. That was the last thing Cole knew, until several hours later. Slowly he came to, and had to stifle a groan as he became aware of his surroundings. Through slitted eyes, he watched as the men sat around a campfire. He watched as they passed a bottle between them and talked about how they would spend the money they had yet to collect for Cole's body.

"I've been wonderin' how we're goin' to get the money without bein' arrested."

"I reckon the sheriff'll be dead, so who's gonna arrest us?"

"That's somethin' else. Why didn't we just kill him straight out, instead of draggin' him all over the damn country?"

"Red, that's just like you. You want to take all the fun out of things." The man flipped his arm over his shoulder toward Cole. "Here we've got the fastest gun in Texas, and you'd kill him straight out. Well, I got me some plans. I figure I'm faster than he is. Anyway, I aim to find out. If 'n I could take him, just think about it. My whole life would change."

"Yeah," the man called Red huffed. "Then everybody in Texas would want a shot at you."

"Humph. If I can take him, I can take anybody else. Don't you know we could make a lot of money with a reputation like his behind us? Tell me, if you're playin' cards and you need a little help, who's gonna point it out if you cheat? Nobody, that's who. Everybody'd be scared you'd draw on 'em. Yeah, I see a way to make a lot of money."

"It's your neck," Red replied.

"Just shut up and bring the prisoner over here."

Cole closed his eyes.

Red kicked Cole in the side, then grabbed his arm and hauled him to his feet. "The boss wants to talk to you, Blade."

With his hands bound, Cole clutched his stomach and stumbled ahead of the man. Red pushed him into the campsite, almost sending him into the fire. Cole struggled to keep his balance, and kept his head lowered dejectedly.

"You don't look like a gunslinger to me. You look more like a whupped dog," the apparent boss reasoned with a hearty laugh.

Cole lifted his head. The fire burning in his eyes caused the man to take a step backward. "Now, that's more like it. You do have some backbone, don't you?"

The boss pulled Cole's gun from his waistband, where he'd put it earlier, and flipped open the chamber, letting the bullets fall to the ground. When the gun was empty, he shoved it into Cole's holster. "Now me and you's gonna find out who's the fastest. Red, you untie him when I'm ready."

"But that's cold-blooded murder, boss."

"I didn't say it was gonna be a fair fight. Now, do as you're told."

"Hell, I'll untie him, if Red ain't got the guts. It don't matter to me how he dies as long as he dies. He don't mean nothin' to me except a thousand dollars," the third man said, stepping into the firelight and placing the whiskey bottle on a rock near the fire.

Cole wasn't as cowed as he wanted the men to think. He'd studied each man and had drawn his own conclusions. Of the three men, this one was the most dangerous. Like Cole, the man had no qualms about killing another human being. Red was uncomfortable with the whole thing, and the boss was a windbag with too much whiskey in him.

The boss counted off his paces, adjusted his holster, and flexed his hand. "You boys are fixin' to see history in the makin'. Untie him, Louis."

Louis stepped to Cole and loosened the rope. Cole didn't move a muscle, except for the dangerous clenching and unclenching of his jaw. He had moved his hands as much as possible while tied, to keep the blood circulating. The boss wiped his suddenly damp brow and positioned his hand. Louis stepped to the side of Cole, and Red stood in the background whining. Cole just stood there.

The boss's fingers curled around the butt of his gun. "Damn it, you have to draw."

"Who says?"

"I do, damn it. How will I know who's the fastest if you don't draw?"

"Your logic astounds me. Either way I'm dead. Why should I give you the pleasure of testing your speed?"

"You wouldn't want anything to happen to that sweet little saloon owner, would you?"

Cole positioned his hand, never giving any thought as to how the man knew about his relationship with Sarah.

"That's more like it."

The boss prepared to draw. Cole watched as the gun filled the man's hand. Standing flat-footed before his enemies, he tilted his body to the heels of his feet and turned so swiftly he was only a blur. As he pivoted, one leg shot out and caught Louis behind the knees, sending him to a heap on the ground. The boss shifted his gun, trying to find his target. Cole's foot hit the boss's hand, the blow breaking the man's wrist before the side of Cole's hand shattered his windpipe.

Louis grabbed the whiskey bottle, shattering the bottom on a rock. He backed Cole away with jabs and swipes as he tried unsuccessfully to draw his gun. The jagged glass caught Cole in the shoulder, and Louis thought the victory was his as he moved in for the kill.

His triumph was short-lived when a gleaming blade appeared in Cole's hand one second, and was arching through the air toward Louis's chest the next. Blood bubbled up in Louis's mouth and his death mask was one of surprise.

Red, afraid to move, huddled, trembling in his own shadow as pains shot down his arm and a great weight compressed his chest. He was convinced that what he'd just witnessed had been no earthly man. Instead, he believed it was the incarnation of scriptures his mother had read him as a child—of winged men with unequaled power. He shifted his eyes to the outlying darkness to see if there were more. Just then, a stick burning over the fire split apart and fell into it, sending up a halo of sparks. Before Cole could reach Red, the man clutched his chest and wilted to the ground, released at last from his hellish existence.

Chapter Twenty-three

When the first mellow rays of the morning filtered through the curtains, Sarah rose wearily from bed and tended to her ablutions. She'd spent a restless night thinking about her argument with Cole, and had finally decided he would never have spoken to her in such a manner if he weren't under such a tremendous strain. During their journey back to town after they had spent the night together at the shack, Sarah had asked Cole if he thought the outlaws were telling the truth about Dusty. Cole had reluctantly told her that for some time now he and Wes had suspected Dusty of swindling landowners because of the rumor about the railroad spur. Dusty would probably try to buy her property, too, if he could get Juliet Barrington's property. He and Wes had kept this from Sarah because they hadn't wanted to frighten or worry her. Now that he'd enlightened her about her dilemma, he had again stressed that she use caution in her dealings with Dusty. Though Sarah was too proud to admit it to Cole, it angered her that Dusty's compliments and gifts were only a front to deceive her.

Now that she knew all this, Sarah didn't know how she should act around Dusty. If she avoided him entirely, he would surely become suspicious. She knew the only way Dusty could ever touch her property was to marry her. That problem was simple enough to handle; she just wouldn't marry him.

As Sarah dressed, a thought suddenly leaped to her mind. She remembered the strawberry shortcake she had promised to fix Cole. So much had happened since the night she had dined with him and Chin that she had forgotten all about it. She'd make it for him now and present it to him as a peace offering. She desperately wanted to bridge this gap between them.

Dusty sat in the chair at the barber shop, listening to several bystanders talking excitedly outside the door. They had just received an invitation to the Barrington ranch for supper and dancing on the ground. Except an occasional wedding festivity, seldom was entertainment given on such a grand scale in the small town of Hazard. As Dusty sat in his chair, the barber talked to another customer awaiting his turn. They were curious about this new owner of the Roberts ranch. Only a few townspeople had met or even seen Juliet Barrington. She kept to herself, sending one of her ranch hands into town for supplies. The men working for her had raved about her beauty, so the marriageable men were eager to make her acquaintance. Single women were a rarity in town, and at the moment they had two good prospects in Juliet Barrington and Sarah Hogan.

After paying the barber, Dusty headed anxiously toward the saloon. He wanted to make certain no one else got the jump on him and asked Sarah to the party before him, especially Cole Blade. Pausing outside the door, he picked a thread off the shoulder of his jacket and straightened his string tie, then entered the establishment.

He saw Sarah reading the invitation.

"I hope I'm not too late," Dusty said, pasting a

pleasant smile on his handsome face.

Sarah looked up, surprise flashing across her face. She had difficulty returning his smile. "Too late for what?" she asked, puzzled.

"If no one has asked you, I'd like to take you to Miss Barrington's party, Sarah."

Oh goodness, how am I going to handle this? Flustered, Sarah replied, "Oh, I haven't decided whether to attend, Dusty. Someone has to stay here and run the saloon that evening. Saturdays are our busiest days, and my employees have received invitations, too."

"It won't be busy Saturday. Everyone'll be at the party. You won't make enough money that day to even bother opening."

She thought about Cole. Would he ask her to go with him? Somehow, she doubted it. Even without this terrible breach between them, he would not want to risk her reputation by openly showing more than his usual interest in her. But there was no way on earth she'd go with Dusty. How to refuse tactfully was the problem.

"Well, I suppose it wouldn't hurt to close that one day."

"Good. Now that this is settled, what time shall I pick you up?"

"I doubt that I'll have the time to go."

"Why not?" he asked, noticeably upset with her reply.

"I've fallen behind on keeping my books in order, and this would give me time to get them up-to-date." She lied.

"So, you'll spend the day working while everyone else is having a great time. You probably need a break more than they do."

"No, they're hard workers. I'm glad to give them the day off. If I should change my mind, I'll see you

237

there," she said, putting an end to the discussion.

Outside the saloon, the hum of voices suddenly ceased, and an unusual calm settled over the town. Wondering what had brought on the sudden quietness, Sarah and Dusty moved outside to the boardwalk. Pedestrians and shop owners stood like statues, their eyes wide and their mouths agape, watching as the sheriff slowly rode in, pulling three horses behind him. Slung over their saddles were the bodies of their riders.

Sarah's blood froze in her veins. Cole's face showed no remorse, his features as hard as granite as he reined his mount in front of the jail and dismounted. After he tethered the horses to the railing, he untied the ropes that secured the bodies to the saddle.

"Bury the bastards," he ordered contemptuously to one of the startled onlookers.

Perhaps Cole sensed her eyes upon him, for as he started to turn toward the jail, he looked Sarah's way, his eyes boldly sweeping over her. Sarah cast him a trembling smile, her heart pounding furiously. Then she saw his eyes slice toward her companion, and his expression settled into the familiar lines of cynicism. Turning sharply on his heel, Cole swaggered into the jail.

Dusty commented, "Looks like the sheriff's been a busy man. They must've been after that reward someone put on his head."

"I can't believe someone thinks he can get by with this madness. Thank God, he's alive."

Dusty took note of her heartfelt words. Too bad they missed, he thought with a scowl.

A moment later Wes Norman left his office and entered the jail. For several minutes, she and Dusty, along with several other people, watched as two men began loading the bodies into a wagon.

Sarah saw Wes leave the jail and return to his office. "Dusty, if you'll excuse me, I want to talk to Wes and find out what happened," she lied. She was going straight to Cole, but Dusty needn't know her plans.

"Of course, Sarah. I have other business to see to before I head back home. I'll see you tonight. Maybe I can change your mind about going with me."

Sarah didn't acknowledge his parting remark, but waited until Dusty had disappeared into one of the stores up the street, and then she hurried back to the kitchen behind the saloon. Picking up the glass-covered strawberry shortcake, she set it on a tray along with a fork and napkin. Placing another napkin over the tray so no one would see what she was carrying, she left the saloon and quickly crossed the street toward the jail.

She stopped at the door, finding it ajar. "Sheriff?" she called, instead of using his first name so familiarly.

"Yeah, come in," came his gruff reply.

When Sarah entered, Cole was standing shirtless, his back to her. She paused, her eyes traveling over his broad bronze back. Immediately, she recalled how his muscles had flexed beneath her fingertips when she had stroked his back. Oh, how she longed to have him hold her again.

He turned around, holding a cloth to his shoulder. "You shouldn't be here, Sarah."

Closing the door behind her, she asked, "Were—were they after the reward?"

"Yes," he replied curtly.

"They might've killed you," she said with incalculable grief.

"Well, I wasn't, and they were," he finished abruptly, tossing the cloth aside.

It was then she noticed the blood on the cloth. She glanced at his shoulder and saw his wound. "You're

239

hurt!" Quickly setting the tray on his desk, she started toward him.

He held up his hand to stay her. "It's all right, Sarah, no more than a scratch. I'm not bleeding anymore." He knew if she touched him, it wouldn't be long before he dragged her into his arms. God, he had missed her so damned badly. "One of the men came after me with a broken whiskey bottle, but I dodged him before he could do much damage." He slipped his bloodstained shirt over his head and buttoned it.

As he approached his desk, he noticed the covered tray. "What's that?"

She smiled, and removed the cloth from the tray. "I brought you a peace offering, a piece of the strawberry shortcake I promised to make for you."

Cole's features suddenly softened. "Thanks, Sarah, though I don't deserve your kindness. I've not exactly been in the best of moods."

"I understand. I'd like to forget yesterday ever happened. We were both uptight over the reward and said things I'm sure we regret now."

He did regret his words, but not his reasons for saying them. But he couldn't send her away now after her sweet offering. Damn, she knew how to mess up his mind.

She took off the glass lid, then stepped back, clasping her hands behind her.

Cole looked down at the mound of juicy red strawberries with a dollop of thick cream on top and the thick syrup spilling over the sides of the cake. He smiled over at her. "You should've brought another fork for you. Do you think I can eat all this?"

"After seeing how much you ate when I dined with you and Chin, yes, I think you can handle it. There's more at the saloon if that doesn't fill you up." She laughed. "At least, there was when I left. If Billy or Gunter happen to see it, I can't guarantee it will still be there."

Before he sat down, he dragged a chair next to the desk. "Then, at least sit down and talk to me while I eat."

"You're sure you don't mind?" she asked sheepishly.

"No, enough people have probably seen you come in here by now, anyway. But we have to be careful, Sarah."

Sitting down beside him, she said, "That's why you jumped all over me yesterday, wasn't it? Well, I'm sorry, but that poster flew all over me."

"I know. Let's just forget it right now. I'm starving. I haven't had a bite to eat since noon yesterday," he said, picking up the fork. He slipped a cream-laden strawberry into his mouth and closed his eyes. "God, this is good. It's been years since I've had strawberry short-cake."

He pierced his fork into another plump berry and held it toward her. "Have a bite."

She laughed. "But I made it for you."

"I'm not so greedy that I won't give up one of them."

"Oh, all right, but just one," she said, opening her mouth to receive his offering.

Cole saw a smidgen of cream on her lower lip. Though he would have preferred to kiss the cream from her rosebud mouth, instead he raked it off with his finger. "Here, you missed some."

Sarah's tongue caught his finger, their eyes locking as her tongue swirled around it. A swift current of desire ran through him. Regretting his foolishness, Cole removed his hand and went back to eating, his finger still tingling from her touch.

Sarah had also felt the rush of warmth flood through her and settle in the core of her femininity. With growing apprehension, she had waited for him to speak tenderly to her, but he had said nothing.

Finished, Cole wiped his mouth with the edge of his napkin and leaned back, rubbing his flat stomach. "I won't be able to eat for a week."

"I doubt that," she said laughingly.

As he slid the tray aside, she noticed the unopened invitation on his desk. "I see you've received an invitation to Miss Barrington's party, too."

"So that's what it is." Cole opened it and briefly scanned the contents. His heart racing, he laid it aside. He arched one eyebrow. "Are you going?"

"I haven't decided yet." She paused. "Cole, Dusty offered to escort me." Seeing his face tighten, she rambled on. "I didn't accept. I hope he believed me when I told him I'd take that day to work on my books and allow my employees to go."

"It's probably better if you do stay here."

"Well, I told him if I changed my mind, I'd see him there. I didn't want him to become suspicious if I decided to go."

Neither spoke for a moment, then Sarah popped the question Cole knew she would ask. "What about you? Are you going?"

He pondered her question. God, how he wished he'd read the invitation before she'd come in here bringing him that damned dessert. Then, he would have immediately sent her out the door, telling her he didn't want a peace offering, that what he'd said yesterday still stood. Now, he knew that if he didn't hurt her further, she'd use every excuse in the book to be with him. The invitation was the perfect opportunity to put an end to their relationship. Cole wouldn't even treat an animal this cruelly, yet it was the only way. Oh, Sarah, forgive me, he pleaded, wishing he could say it aloud before he dealt her this blow.

At length, he said, "Sarah, Miss Barrington has asked me to be her escort for that evening," Cole managed to say with indifference, though all his vital functions seemed to cease.

Sarah's face paled. She thought she might be sick. "But—but you're not going to . . . accept, are you?"

"Yes, Sarah, I am."

Sarah stared at him. Only moments before, she'd felt so happy, thinking they'd solved their differences. He couldn't be telling her this, no . . . no . . .

Her throat ached painfully, her voice seeming to echo in her ears as she asked, "Cole, did our night together mean nothing to you?"

"Sarah, put that night out of your mind. I have," he lied.

"What?" she asked, thinking she hadn't heard him right. "You can't mean that . . . surely."

Cole's arms ached to go around her. In that crucial moment, his last shred of control almost snapped. For this one woman he was perfectly willing to throw everything aside. But not now. What if she had been with him last night when the men had attacked him? He tried to sound more convincing by saying, "Yes, damn it, I'm not the man for you—never was."

The fine hair on the back of Sarah's neck bristled. She leaped from her chair. "But Juliet Barrington is the right woman for you?"

"I am attracted to her, yes."

With her arms akimbo, she lashed out at him. "Tell me, Cole, have you slept with her, too?"

"Sarah, that's none of your business."

A mournful sob broke from her and her tears

243

splashed on the bodice of her gown. "And I thought you might care for me."

The anguish in her voice brought a knife-wrenching pain in his heart. He gazed into her pain-filled eyes, wishing he could express the wealth of feeling that surged up inside him. Frustrated, he raked his hand through his hair. God, what could he say to her? He was so damned sick of the lies and the pain that tore through him when he told them. Yet, if he went to her and enfolded her in his arms and told her what was in his heart, she would never leave him. He would not want her to, either.

Cole leveled his eyes with hers. If Sarah's heart weren't filled with such hurt and grief, she would have readily recognized the pain in his own face and voice as he answered, "I'm sorry, Sarah, I never set out to hurt you."

Sarah took the napkin from the tray and wiped the tears from her face. Taking a deep breath, she tried to salvage her last shred of dignity. Lifting her head haughtily, she stood as rigid as a pillar of ice. "Have a good time at the party, Cole."

Picking up the tray, she turned with a flourish and swept through the door.

Several days passed. To Sarah, time had stood still—each day exactly like the day before: days of fear, of heartbreaking grief, of false smiles, of hectic routines. Only one thing had made the endless hours endurable for her: Cole had survived. Though he had made it clear to her that he was interested in Juliet Barrington, she could never hate him. She had pushed herself into his life and had probably pestered him until finally he'd given into her just so she'd get him out of her system.

244

Wasn't that the phrase he had used not so long ago? Well, from the looks of things, it had had the reverse effects. She was left wanting him, and he wanted someone else.

Nights were Sarah's worst times. For hours she would sit by the window, motionless, staring at the jail where a thin stream of light streaked across the street. On the nights Cole was working, she'd watch him through the jail's window as he paced restlessly about the room. Other times her heart would still in her chest when he'd come outside and smoke. She always feared someone dangerous was lurking in the shadows, waiting to gun him down. When finally she would climb into bed and drift off to sleep, nightmares would gallop through her mind, giving her no peace.

Sarah's sadness had found echo in the heart of everyone who knew and cared for her. Billy cut his most amusing remarks, trying to bring a smile to Sarah's mouth. Fancy Fingers Floyd searched through his repertoire of music, playing mirthful songs to lighten her spirit. Belle and Collie flashed their most brilliant smiles, lavishing her with compliments about how pretty she looked, when in truth Sarah's waxen face and drooping posture denoted otherwise. But nothing they did seemed to lift the gloom from her heart.

And Dusty had started frequenting the saloon on a nightly basis. To her employees' knowledge, he wasn't cheating the players, and even lost an occasional hand. But after a while, it became obvious that Dusty's interest was not in gambling, but leaned toward their pretty boss. Sarah paid little attention to him, often excusing herself and going to her room. Sometimes Cole would come into the saloon and see Sarah and Dusty talking together. If he had felt any emotion at all, he had hidden it well. His aloof manner toward Sarah angered her employees.

Cole had indeed masked his emotions well, but inside he was shaking like an earthquake, and wondered how long he could carry on with this charade before he split wide open. Seeing Dusty occasionally at her side made him angry and miserable. She knew Dusty was after her property, so he hoped she had enough sense not to seek her revenge by consorting with the man. Should he have told her how dangerous Dusty was, that he'd stop at nothing to get what he wanted? Even murder? In protecting her from her own reckless nature, was he throwing her right into the hands of the devil himself?

Her vision haunted him. He saw her lovely, piquant face with its quick, delightful expressions—and her deep green eyes that emitted an ever-changing sparkle of tenderness, mischief, and intelligence.

Sarah . . . God, how he missed her.

Chapter Twenty-four

The sky was the bluest of blues, and a drop in the temperature combined with a zephyr-like breeze to make the day perfect for Juliet Barrington's lawn party.

Sarah arrived at the party after most of the guests were already there. Walking through the gate toward an impressive two-story farmhouse, Sarah noticed several people, young and old, playing croquet. Secured on the limb of an age-old oak was a rope swing where children waited eagerly for their turn. A man had brought along his guitar, and as he strummed a tune, several old-timers sitting on blankets spread beneath the trees clapped and sang along with the music. A cluster of handsome young men dressed in their Sunday best ogled some attractive girls who were giggling and whispering among themselves. She saw one boy break from his group and join the girls. With the ice broken, his friends gathered their courage and swaggered in behind him.

Flirting, Sarah thought, was an art she'd never learned. The only men Sarah had been acquainted with were members of her church. Though they'd been friendly enough, one damning look from her grandfather had always sent them in search of a warmer reception.

Today she had dressed with extreme care, hoping to attract Cole's attention. Earlier in the week, she had seen a scarlet shirtwaist with a black lace yoke in Mrs.

Flowers's shop and had commented on how pretty it was. Remembering the black taffeta skirt Mrs. Flowers had made her before she gave up her mourning, she'd bought the shirtwaist to go with it. Belle had loaned her a black velvet ribbon for her throat with a cameo in its center and a pair of dangling black onyx earrings. When she had descended the stairway, she knew she'd accomplished her goal when Billy stood mouth gaping and Floyd choked on his drink. Now, if she would only have the same effect on Cole . . .

She searched the grounds for Cole's towering figure, and with a sinking heart, she realized he had not arrived. Though she had desperately tried to drag her mind from him, she had found it a hopeless cause.

A long table stretched across the immaculate lawn, and several women gathered around the table, helping with the arrangement and serving of the food. Near the table was a roasting pit where a beef was cooking, the aroma filling the air and stimulating the appetites of the guests. Sarah saw Wes and her employees standing beneath a tree, laughing and talking. She didn't see Dusty and hoped he hadn't come.

Sarah would not have recognized Juliet without a second glance. Today, she looked much younger than the sophisticated woman Sarah had first encountered, but she looked no less elegant without the extra frippery. She wore a simple calico dress printed with dainty blue-green flowers, the hemline bordered with lace. Draped around her shoulders was a white shawl. Her unbound hair fell in golden waves midway down her back, no ornaments save a wide turquoise ribbon. Juliet was enjoying herself famously. The men hummed around her like bees around the sweetest rose, hanging on to her every word as she laughed and jested with them.

Seeing her, Juliet waved and, excusing herself from

the men, lifted the hem of her skirt and walked down the steps to greet her.

She is so lovely, Sarah thought. No wonder Cole wants to be with her. Still, Sarah would try to be nice to Juliet, though her heart wasn't in it.

Juliet took Sarah's hand. "I'm so glad you came, Sarah. I was afraid you might not close the saloon."

Sarah smiled warmly. "I believe all my customers are here. What a beautiful day for your party."

Juliet nodded. "Yes. I don't know what I would have done if it had rained. Though the house is quite large, I doubt everyone could fit inside. I'm so sorry you couldn't make it for tea, Sarah."

"You did get my note explaining I couldn't leave the saloon at that time?"

"Yes. I should have given you more notice."

"Everyone seems to be having a grand time. You have a beautiful home."

"Thank you. Would you like to see it? Maybe you can help me decide on some redecorating I was considering."

Juliet gave her a quick tour of the house, which boasted five tastefully furnished bedrooms, an immense dining room, and a large kitchen off the back. Juliet told her she was keeping all her brother's beautiful furnishings, but the actual decorating needed a feminine touch; it was much too masculine for her tastes. After they discussed the possibilities, she led Sarah into the parlor.

As Sarah gazed around the room, her eyes grew wide with pleasure. Angled in one corner of the room was the most beautiful piano she had ever seen. Immense in size, the dark casing and thick legs were richly carved in rosewood. Sarah walked slowly toward it, feeling her fingers tingling with excitement. Leaning forward, she nimbly ran her fingers through several scales, then straightened.

"So, you play?" Juliet asked with a smile.

Sighing wistfully, Sarah said, "I had lessons when I was a child, but I always yearned for a piano like this. Do you play, Juliet?"

"Oh, heavens, no. As with all the other furnishings in the house, the piano came with it. I remember George playing when I was a child. I'm afraid its only purpose now is to collect dust."

"What I would give to have this," Sarah said, then she added laughingly, "Of course, I wouldn't have any room for something this size in my apartment."

"You could put it in the saloon," Juliet suggested.

"Oh, what a horrid thought! I wouldn't dare place such a fine piece of furniture in the saloon. I can just imagine the abuse it would receive from people setting their drinks upon it and laying their cigarettes along the edges."

"If you would like to have it, Sarah, perhaps we can work out a trade," Juliet put in smoothly, delighted to have found a way to approach her without seeming too eager.

"Goodness, I have nothing this costly to trade."

"Actually, you have something worth a hundred times as much, and I'm prepared to make up the difference." Juliet walked over, coming to rest beside the piano. As she ran her hand along the carved surface, she asked casually, "Could I interest you in selling me your ranch, Sarah?"

"My ranch?" Sarah stared at Juliet with a stunned expression on her face.

"Yes. I've decided to make my home here permanently and would like to increase my holdings. You seem to have no serious interest in ranching, so I thought you might wish to sell it."

"It isn't that I don't have the interest, Juliet, I haven't the time." Sarah couldn't tell her it wasn't hers to sell right now, anyway.

"I hear you're doing a wonderful job running the saloon. With that income plus the money you'd make off the sale of your property, you would never have to worry about your future. Won't you at least give the matter some thought before you completely refuse?"

"I'm sorry, but for the time being I'll hang on to it. The ranch is running smoothly right now without my involvement. Besides, I'd like to try ranching first before I make any decisions along that line."

"Very well," Juliet said with a deep sigh. "I have guests to entertain."

After they walked outside to the veranda, Juliet paused and said, "Please keep me in mind if you should have a change of heart."

"I will, I promise."

"You can still buy the piano if you'd like."

"I'll think about it. Thank you," Sarah said softly.

Juliet's blue eyes suddenly sparkled with excitement. "Oh! If you'll excuse me, I see our sheriff's arrived. I must welcome him."

At the mention of Cole, Sarah felt her legs weaken beneath her. Turning, she watched Juliet hurry across the lawn to greet him and, grasping his hand in her own, walk with him down the path to the house. When Cole's gaze shifted toward her, Sarah swiftly looked the other way, pretending she had not seen him.

But Cole knew she had seen him. He had come to the party for only one reason, to find out something about this woman locked on his arm. In projecting an interest in Juliet, he thought he might find out what was going on between her and Dusty.

Cole saw Dusty approach Sarah and lace his arm through hers. A combination of hurt and anger welled inside him. Dusty's interest in her was as plain as the nose on his face. Cole knew in his heart that if it came down to it, he would kill Dusty before he would see Sarah hoodwinked by the likes of him. It might be cold-blooded murder and he might hang, but knowing he'd rescued her from the man's evil clutch would bring him satisfaction even in death.

He frowned slightly as he gazed down on Juliet's honey-colored crown. She had been chatting away, yet he'd barely heard a word she'd said. As beautiful and wealthy as she was, he couldn't understand why Dusty wasn't openly courting her. Dusty's late-night visit to her still had Cole baffled. If he was courting Juliet, he for damned sure wouldn't be flaunting Sarah in front of her.

The clanging of a bell and a shout of "Come an' get it!" broke through the din of laughter and conversation.

"Are you hungry, Sarah?" Dusty asked.

"Famished," she lied. The hunger that had drawn her stomach into a hard knot was not a hunger for food, but for the man who ignored her. From the looks of things, she'd have Dusty to contend with for the rest of the evening. He'd seemed so pleased she had decided to come, latching onto her the moment he saw her.

Dusty led her to the end of the line. She saw all her employees ahead of them and called out to them. They greeted her warmly until their eyes came to rest on Dusty standing behind her. She saw the marked irritation on Billy's face. He got upset every time Dusty entered the saloon, and it took a great deal of coaxing to soothe him.

As Sarah placed the food on her plate, her eyes drifted toward Cole and Juliet as they stood beneath a tree and chatted with Wes. Cole held Juliet close to his side, his arm wrapped possessively around her tiny waist. Sarah bit the inside of her lip until she tasted blood. She couldn't believe how amicable she'd felt toward Juliet earlier. And the lady had the nerve to ask to buy her property. Not only did she want her property, she wanted her man, too. Of course, Juliet could not know this, but it still didn't make Sarah feel any better.

Taking a hot biscuit from the basket, Sarah saw red as Juliet cast Cole an adoring smile and Cole returning her smile with a lusty grin. *Oh, how I'd like to stuff this in her mouth,* Sarah screamed inside, clenching the biscuit so tightly that it crumbled in her hand. As she started to set it on her plate, she realized what she had done, and discreetly let the crumbs fall to the ground.

Moving on through the line, her eyes still on Cole and Juliet, Sarah spooned food onto her plate without even knowing what she was doing. Arriving at the barbecue pit where a ranch hand was slicing off chunks of the juicy meat, she held out her plate to receive her portion. Steam billowed from her ears as she watched Juliet lean into Cole, her lips pouting up at him as though waiting for his kiss.

"Ma'am, you need another plate."

Sarah whipped her head around toward the man. "Excuse me?"

"You don't have room on your plate for the barbecue. Why don't you get another one?"

Her face turned as crimson as her shirtwaist as she gazed down at her overflowing plate. She'd taken enough food to feed a family of four and it had all run together into an unappetizing mess. The only items she could identify were the green peas and carrots, neither of which she liked. "I . . . ah . . .

really don't need any, thank you."

The man grinned at her, then winked. "Hope you left some for me."

Dusty hadn't missed Sarah's wayward eyes, and chuckled to himself. "Find us a spot while I get our drinks, dear. Lemonade all right?"

Sarah gnashed her teeth together. She couldn't handle one more "dear!" When they were out of earshot from anyone, she whispered, "Dusty, I would appreciate it if you would not call me dear, please."

"Oh, I didn't realize it bothered you, Sarah," he said softly. "It's just that having been in your company so much of late, you *have* grown very dear to me. But I think you know that, don't you?"

"No, I've only considered us friends. If you've thought otherwise, I'm sorry."

His intense blue eyes darkened as he said in a low voice, "I have every hope of changing your feelings towards me."

Sarah felt a tremor ripple through her body. "I'll—I'll find us a table."

Balancing the plate carefully in both hands, Sarah walked slowly for fear of spilling the contents on her clothing. Finding a table and bench, she set her plate down, took her seat, and waited for Dusty to join her.

How was she going to handle this situation? She had never had a man actually pursue her. With Cole, she'd done all the chasing, finally thinking she had captured his heart. Her eyes darted to the handsome couple and pain tore through her.

"I'm sorry it took me so long," Dusty said, noting her eyes suddenly shift to him. "I got caught behind a slew of thirsty children." Setting her glass of lemonade beside her plate, Dusty sat down beside her on the bench.

"Thank you," she said, taking a sip of the refreshing drink.

"The sheriff looks like he's having a good time," Dusty remarked offhandedly.

Sarah stiffened noticeably. Rather than reply to his statement, she slid her fork through the mishmash on her plate and slipped the unwanted food into her mouth.

"Do you mind if we join you?" Juliet asked.

They looked up to see Juliet and Cole at their table. Sarah's face crumbled into a thousand little pieces. She couldn't, she just *couldn't*, sit at the same table with them.

"We'd love to have you join us, Miss Barrington," Dusty said, and rose politely from his seat until Juliet had seated herself across from them.

Cole's eyes narrowed as he looked at Dusty. "Mills." He nodded briskly.

"Sheriff." There was no denying the brief spark of hatred that leaped in the man's eyes as he watched Cole take his seat beside Juliet.

Cole glanced across the table at Sarah. "It's nice seeing you again, Mrs. Hogan."

"Thank you, Sheriff," she said, then clamped her mouth shut and looked down at her plate. Oh, how she wished she could excuse herself and go home.

"Ooh . . . try this, Cole," Juliet cooed.

Sarah's curiosity got the best of her. She watched Juliet lift a generous portion of barbecued beef and slip it into Cole's opened mouth. Sarah fumed. He had a whole plate of the stuff. Juliet didn't need to hand-feed him from her own.

Sensing Sarah's eyes on him, Cole gently took hold of Juliet's wrist and guided her hand to his mouth. "Don't want to miss any of it," he drawled lazily.

255

Sarah nearly bolted from her seat, recalling him using almost those same words the day she licked the cream from his finger. If she saw his tongue touch that woman's finger, she would break every finger on the woman's hand—lady or not, that's all there was to it.

As Cole released her hand, a tantalizing smile curved Juliet's lips as she picked up her fork and began eating.

Sarah, fork in hand, sighed deeply, idly rearranging the food on her plate, her eyes occasionally lifting to find Cole closely scrutinizing her. She would not show her jealousy—if that was what he was hoping to see.

Her eyes shifted to Juliet. She saw her working the knot of her shawl. After untying it, she let it slide from her shoulders and rest in the crook of her arms. Sarah couldn't prevent her eyes widening as she noticed Juliet's low-cut bodice. Though not cut so low as to be considered indecent, her generous breasts swelled enticingly above the edge of her gown.

Cole's eyes followed Sarah's gaze. Being a hot-blooded male, he couldn't help staring admiringly at the creamy crescents. His eyes moved curiously toward Dusty. Dusty seemed oblivious to Juliet's display, his eyes never leaving his plate. Cole thought this strange indeed. What was going on here? Mills visited Juliet in the middle of the night, yet now he acted as though he barely knew her. Before Cole returned to eating, he once again glimpsed Juliet's breasts, more to tease a disgruntled Sarah than from taking any pleasure in viewing them.

Juliet turned to Cole and smiled sweetly. "Is something wrong with your food, Cole?"

Cole's eyes darted to her face. He cleared his throat. "No, not at all."

Slicing his knife through the slab of beef, he brought a portion to his mouth, his eyes meeting Sarah's green

256

ones. The iciness he saw in them would freeze hell over. He plopped the meat into his mouth. As he slowly chewed, he couldn't refrain from looking at Sarah. Damn, she looked enchanting, dressed in a red satin shirtwaist. He wouldn't have thought the color suited her, but the bold red seemed to lessen her innocence and heighten her sensuality. He noticed the dangling earrings and the velvet ribbon at her throat, the cameo resting in its midst. He had never seen her wearing jewelry. Had she changed her appearance to attract the man beside her?

Uncomfortable with Cole's steady gaze, Sarah fidgeted with the napkin in her lap. He seemed to be undressing her. A horrible thought came to her mind that he was comparing her with Juliet. Aghast, she shot Cole a nasty look. Finally he turned to Juliet and began talking to her.

Sarah suffered through the rest of the meal. If she wanted a lesson in flirting, Juliet was the perfect teacher, but it infuriated her that she had selected Cole as her subject. Sarah became so wrapped up in Cole's and Juliet's attraction for one another that she completely forgot Dusty was sitting next to her.

Chapter Twenty-five

When dusk fell, lanterns were lit around the yard, and the men who'd brought their musical instruments stepped upon the platform and began playing "Turkey in the Straw," a lively square-dancing tune. Jeremy Rinehart, the caller, also the young man who tended the livery, joined them and called everyone to grab a partner and join in the dancing. Cries of excitement ripped through the gathering as men grabbed women and hurried to take their places for the dance. A man came to their table and asked Juliet if she'd be his partner.

"Do you mind, Cole?" she asked, all smiles.

"You're the hostess, Juliet. Go ahead."

All seemed to be in motion at once: arms reached, bodies swirled, hair swung wildly, and feet kicked up, flying over the ground. The older people tottered from their benches and gathered around the circle, clapping their hands and cheering them on.

Again her grandfather's view came up short and shattered like fragile glass. He had ranted and raved about the sins of dancing, and the hell-bound destination of anyone partaking of such heathen acts. Sarah saw nothing sinful in the movements. The dances were so fast-moving, lingering touches between partners were impossible.

Could Cole dance? she wondered, gazing at his profile as he watched the dancers. Turned on the bench, he'd drawn up one leg, his arms resting casually across his bent knee. Would he ask her to dance with him? No, you silly fool, he has no interest in you, she berated herself.

Juliet had become the center of attention. Sarah noticed Cole watching her as her partner whirled her around. Her breasts bounced each time she stomped her foot. It surprised Sarah that they didn't fall out of her dress. From the looks the men were giving her, they had the same high hopes.

Juliet's partner whirled her into the arms of Fancy Fingers Floyd, her next partner. When the group formed two parallel lines, Floyd and Juliet held hands, skipping face to face down the center. Entranced by her jiggling breasts, Floyd tripped over his feet. Falling forward, his long legs stretching behind him, his arms grasped Juliet's waist in a death grip. He held on for dear life as his beaklike nose bounced off Juliet's chin and plowed deeply within the cleavage of her breasts.

"Now that's what I call gettin' an eyeful," one man called out from the sideline. The crowd burst into laughter.

Juliet tried in vain to straighten Floyd, but he continued sliding down, drawing her bodice lower with his nose. Embarrassed by the whole ordeal, Juliet gripped his shoulders and pushed him away, and poor Floyd fell flat against the ground.

Floyd wobbled to his knees and ogled the fine figure of his partner, while adjusting the cuffs of his shirt. "My apologies, Miss Barrington. Your beauty quite took my breath away."

"Beauty, my ass. It was all that bare flesh that was his undoin'," someone in the crowd mumbled.

"Oh, forgive the man," someone called, "it was an

259

accident, and could've happened to any one of us."

"Yeah, wisht it'd been me," someone put in.

Juliet wouldn't let this bungling piano player spoil her party. She smiled brightly and offered her hand to Floyd. "Shall we continue our dance?"

Floyd rose slowly to his feet and smiled sheepishly at the crowd as he clasped Juliet's hand. Before resuming the dance, Floyd clicked his heels together and gave a whoop of pure joy.

Sarah covered her mouth, her shoulders shaking as she suppressed her laughter. Cole turned on the bench, his mouth twitching, and saw Sarah's amused green eyes. Even Dusty smiled along with them.

The music changed to a waltz. Juliet returned to the table. "How embarrassing," she whispered.

"Don't worry about it," Cole put in, rising to his feet. "Come, dance with me, Juliet."

Seeing Sarah's crestfallen face, Dusty knew what had brought it on. When Cole and Juliet moved into the crowd, Dusty asked, "Would you like to dance?"

She nodded numbly.

Dusty led her to the ring of dancers and placed one hand in her own, the other at the small of her back. When he starting moving to the slow rhythm of the music, Sarah stepped on his foot. "Oh, Dusty, I'm so embarrassed. I've never danced before in my life."

"Don't worry. It's really quite simple. Just follow my lead."

Dusty began moving fluidly over the dirt-packed ground, gliding as though he were on ice skates. Sarah had difficulty in keeping her rhythm, her attention on Juliet and Cole. Several times, she stepped on his feet, and her apologies were beginning to sound trite.

Cole felt Sarah watching him, and pulled Juliet closer to him, much closer than the dance warranted. He felt

Juliet's breasts pressing against him, feeling not only Sarah's blistering gaze on him, but also those of the women bystanders. However, the men's faces contained a mixture of envy and anger, anger because Cole had monopolized Juliet from the moment he had arrived at the party.

No one was as glad as Sarah when the waltz ended. As Dusty led her away, once again the square dancing began.

Billy rushed her way and intercepted them. "If you don't mind, Mr. Mills, I'd like to ask my boss lady to dance."

"Oh, please, Billy, no! I'll break my neck," Sarah pleaded.

"Go ahead, dear," Dusty said, handing her over to Billy.

Dear? Seems to me things are gettin' a little out of hand here, Billy thought, disgruntled. Seeing Juliet pulling Cole into a group of two other couples, Billy hurried Sarah along to fill the position as the fourth couple. Sarah found herself between Cole and Billy, each clasping one of her hands. With a quick sideways glance at one another, they followed the other couples in a circle, moving in rhythm to the music. Soon into the dance after the caller had issued several formations, it was clear to the group that only one couple knew what they were doing. In confusion, Cole gripped one of Sarah's hands and Billy the other, each pulling her as though she were a stiff strand of taffy. Billy, suddenly realizing their predicament, abruptly released her hand as Cole pulled, sending her stumbling against Cole as the music stopped.

Both breathless and panting, Sarah's and Cole's eyes locked as he held her in his arms. Neither said a word, but their eyes spoke volumes. Irresistibly drawn to one another, it wasn't until the fiddler struck a chord for the next dance that they parted. Cole's eyes followed Sarah as Billy ushered her from the circle. Damn, it's hard ignoring her, Cole thought. He'd ask her to dance a waltz with him, but if he ever held her again, he might never let her go.

Dusty contemplated the scene he had just witnessed. For a second there, he thought Blade was going to kiss Sarah. When Sarah joined him, he hid the dissatisfied gleam in his eyes.

Cole followed with Juliet. "I need to talk to Wes. I'll see you in a little while."

A heavy sigh rose from Sarah's heart as her eyes followed Cole. Glancing at Juliet, she saw her staring at him, too. Who was she to think she could ever compete with such a beautiful and desirable contender? I'm a foolish dreamer, I suppose, she thought with an aching heart.

Cole found Wes standing in a group of men and told him he needed to talk to him. Excusing himself, Wes and Cole walked to a secluded place.

"Chin's waiting for us in the shed beside the stable," Wes said quietly. "Think we can get away without anyone seeing us?"

"I didn't notice any of Dusty's men in the crowd, but that doesn't mean they aren't hiding somewhere in the shadows. Surely Dusty wouldn't risk trying to ambush me here. But, with Juliet hanging onto me, it might be better if you go alone. She might come looking for me."

"Let's hope he found out something," Wes said.

"Yeah, Dusty and Juliet are doing a damned good job making it appear they barely know one another. Well, I'll get on back, and when you return, we'll talk again."

Wes waited for a moment after Cole left and, making sure no one was watching him, stole into the darkness. Strolling toward a small shed, he looked around, then stepped inside. It was pitch black. "You here, Chin?"

"Yeah, close the door. I've got something to show you."

Wes pushed the door shut, and a moment later, Chin struck a match and touched the flame to a lantern. "Is Cole not with you?"

"No, we thought someone might follow him. Find anything?"

In the dim light, Wes saw Chin grin as he reached inside his jacket and pulled out an envelope. He handed it to Wes. "I found this hidden beneath a paper that lined a drawer in her bedroom. I didn't take the time to read it for fear of someone catching me."

Wes opened the envelope and pulled out the letter. Unfolding it, he held it toward the light, first noting the letter was written by Juliet Barrington. He read it aloud.

March 18, 1885
Dear Louise,

When my letter reaches you, I pray you are in better health than me. Oh, I'm not ill, but I tire so easily of late. We've just arrived in San Francisco, and I plan to rest these weary bones a spell before going on to Texas to see George. Bernard thinks this break will be good for all of us, though Olivia does tend to bore easily.

Wes read through the rest of the letter where she mentioned the weather and points of interest during her travels, then inserted it back inside the envelope.

"Is it important, Mr. Norman?"

"Yes, at least I have this woman's address and can write to her about her friend. Miss Barrington sure didn't look unhealthy to me when she arrived in Hazard. And tonight, her weary bones seemed fit enough to me. She barely missed a dance."

"I wonder who Olivia and Bernard are?" Chin asked.

"Beats me, but they sure as hell aren't with her now. Of course, they could've accompanied her as far as San Francisco and then returned to England." Wes handed Chin the envelope. "I've memorized Louise's address. Do you think you can get back into the house without someone seeing you?"

"No problem." He grinned broadly.

"See you later. I'll tell Cole about the letter."

Wes had his conversation with Cole, both coming to the conclusion that something about Miss Barrington was strange.

Wes knew it would take some time, but he planned to go through sources in San Francisco and locate the hotel Miss Barrington had stayed in. Someone might remember her and could give them some information about this Olivia and Bernard. Also, he planned to write her friend, Louise, and ask if she had had any correspondence with Miss Barrington after March eighteenth.

Before Cole and Wes went separate ways, he told Wes he was going to take a walk and try to figure out what was nagging him about Juliet.

Dusty saw Juliet's discreet nod in his direction. He hadn't seen Blade in quite a while. He must have left, he thought, now feeling free to leave Sarah's side. "Sarah, I've rudely detained you from your friends all evening. Why don't you visit with them? There's several

264

men here I'd like to do business with."

"I will, thank you, Dusty."

Sarah didn't feel like talking to anyone. She was glad to be rid of Dusty. Earlier, Wes had called Cole aside, and after that, she'd danced several times with Dusty. Wes had returned without Cole, so she figured he must have gone home.

Anger, hurt, and jealousy flowed through her as she fixed her gaze on the woman responsible for her misery. Suddenly she felt she had to escape, go somewhere, anywhere, to get away from the music and dancing. Could she leave without someone seeing her? At the beginning of the next song, Wes took Belle's hand, leading her to the dance area, and Billy followed behind them with Collie. No one was paying any attention to her. Sarah rose from her seat and backed slowly out of the lamplight, her dark clothes blending with the night. Turning, she fled from the crowd of merrymakers.

Sarah wandered aimlessly, holding back the tears, the bright moonlight guiding her through the darkness. Her mind buried deep in thought, it was some time before she realized she had lost all sense of time and direction. She didn't care. She was alone with the sounds of the night around her. Picking up a stick, she made her own path through a section of thinly scattered woods, swiping at shadowy twigs and vines in her path, hearing the small night creatures scurrying through the underbrush. She walked until she finally came into a clearing. The moon unfurled a flood of silver upon the river in front of her.

Sarah stood there for some time, staring out blankly at the glimmering water and the soft dark sky, her heart filled with love for Cole. Through all her pain and disappointment, she managed to smile, promising herself she would never regret loving him, for he had shown her the joys of true love. For she truly loved him. If she felt any regret at all, it was that Cole wasn't willing to accept the love she offered him. All she would have of him were the memories she had collected and stored vividly in her mind.

Faint sounds of a waltz drifted her way, and rather than happy memories filling her head, Sarah recalled Cole's arms embracing Juliet and holding her closely against him. Suddenly, she could no longer hold in check the torrent of grief that consumed her. Sinking to her knees on the bank, Sarah's body shook with breathless sobbing. She buried her face in her hands, oblivious to everything but pain.

Chapter Twenty-six

Cole stepped from the shadows of the trees along the bank of the river. For several minutes he waited in the darkness, contemplating whether he should approach the weeping woman or leave her to cry in private. The moonlight spilled over her as she knelt on the bank, silhouetting her trembling figure. If she was a guest of Juliet Barrington, she had wandered quite a distance from the gathering, and he worried about her safe return.

Suddenly she rocked back on her heels and clutched her shoulders. "Cole," she whispered, his name burning her lips.

Cole? Had he only imagined hearing her call his name? She straightened and briefly turned his way, and the moonbeams fell upon her face. Cole's breath caught in his throat. Sarah . . . his sweet, lovely Sarah. The guilt he harbored welled up inside him, seeking release like a caged animal. He wasn't worth her tears, not after the way he had treated her. He gazed at her in despair, wondering what he could do to ease her pain. He had to do something.

Stepping from the shadows of the trees that grew along the river bank, he called her name in a tender whisper. "Sarah?"

Sarah turned toward the voice, her eyes filled with

wonder as Cole stepped out of her dream and into her conscious life.

Her heart pounding, Sarah rose slowly. "Cole? Is that you?"

"Yes."

"I thought . . . you'd left."

"No," he said, walking toward her. "I wasn't in the mood to socialize anymore. Evidently, you weren't either."

"I couldn't stand the pretending any longer. I—I had to get away."

Cole knelt before her and cupped her chin, raking his callused thumb over her lower lip. "Sarah, what were you pretending?"

The tears staining her face shimmered in the moonlight as she lifted her face. "That it didn't matter if you didn't care for me. That I could get along without you." Her voice broke on a sob as though someone had wrenched at the very heart of her. She shook her head. "I'm sorry, I don't mean to cry. It's obvious you want nothing more to do with me."

"Juliet Barrington means nothing to me, Sarah."

"You could've fooled me." She sniffed loudly. "She's been falling all over you tonight, and you didn't seem to mind."

"That's what I wanted you to think."

With her heart beating wildly, she looked at him in confusion. "You—you purposely set out to hurt me?"

"Yes, and I'm not very proud of it. But, Sarah, my god, that's the only way I thought I could protect you. That is truly my only sin."

Cole lifted her small hand in his, squeezing it gently. He brought it to his mouth and brushed his lips across it. "I don't want anyone else." He paused and looked into her eyes. "It's you I want, Sarah, only you."

She lowered her gaze, wishing she could still her trembling hands as he held them. "You're sure?"

He drew her against him, his arms closing around her so hungrily, so strongly, that she gasped. "As God is my witness." His eyes roamed her face. "Sarah, my Sarah, you'll never know how miserable I've been."

Her heart contracted. She spoke barely above a whisper. "Please, Cole, don't say these things to me . . . unless you mean them."

"Sarah, I only wanted to protect you," he repeated, trying to make her understand.

A flood of joy swept through her. Reaching up, she stroked his lean jaw, her eyes shining with love and contentment. "Next time let me know. Promise?"

"I promise, but . . ."

"But what?"

He drew in a deep breath and tightened his arms around her. "That's the only promise I can make for now."

Her face brightened. "That's okay."

"Will you promise to stay out of my way and let me do my job. I won't risk your life."

"You are my life, Cole," she said softly. "If you wish me to stay away from you, I will. Later, but not now." She removed his hat and dropped it to the ground. Raising on her knees, she clasped her hands at the back of his head and drew his head down to her parted mouth. "Oh, Cole, I've waited so long for this moment."

His mouth, mere inches from her own, curved into a slight frown. "Sarah, I want to kiss you, but . . ."

"Then do," she urged.

"I can't promise you I'll stop with only a kiss."

"I won't ask you to stop." With a sigh of contentment, she closed her eyes.

"Ah . . . God, Sarah," Cole groaned, knowing the instant his mouth covered her own, there would be no turning back. Too long, he had denied himself her sweet, loving mouth. Like a man who'd just found his oasis in the sun-parched desert, he savored that first taste of her lips, drinking slowly to lengthen the pleasure. His body shuddered almost violently as he felt the eager response of her tongue as it fondled and coaxed his own, the erotic play turning their mouths from warm to scorching hot.

A low groan escaped Sarah's throat as her passion burgeoned within her and sought release. She would make him love her. She knew this with every fiber of her being. Burying her fingers in his thick hair, she pressed her body flush with his and deepened the kiss. Instinctively, she rubbed her body against Cole and, wanting to be even closer to him, moved one knee between his strong muscular thighs.

Cupping her buttocks, Cole drew her against his throbbing shaft, his fingers kneading her tender flesh through her garments. His hips joined hers in a slow, taunting rhythm, rotating and thrusting, raising the fires burning within them. Tearing his mouth from hers, he kissed her cheek, her nose, her eyes. His tongue left tiny points of fire flickering here and there across her face. Lifting her hair, he kissed and nibbled at the delicate lobe of her ear, and trailed feather-light kisses across the slender column of her neck. His hand moved to her breasts and kneaded the firm mounds. Seeking and finding her passion-swollen nipple through her clothing, he tenderly pulled the hard nub and rolled it between his thumb and finger.

"Cole, I'm hot, so hot," she whispered.

With trembling fingers, Cole unbuttoned her shirtwaist and gently pushed her back against his arm. Sar-

270

ah's hands gripped his thick, strong arms, her body tingling as his mouth moved downward, his lips and tongue teasing her, scorching a path across the swollen crescents of her breasts. Through the thin fabric of her chemise, she felt his hot moist mouth explore the contours of her breasts, yet avoid their aching peaks. When finally his mouth moved to them, she moaned her pleasure, her hands pressing his head against her as his teeth gently nipped her. Sarah's legs grew weak as all the blood in her body seemed to surge through her veins and collect in the hot core of her womanhood.

His mouth left her breast and with a savage urgency came down hard upon hers. Opening her mouth, she welcomed the intrusion of his tongue with wild abandon.

Breaking the kiss, Cole's breath came in quick, short gasps. "I need—need—more from you, Sarah."

"Take more," she pleaded softly.

Sarah felt his hard arousal beneath the layers of her clothing and her hand moved of its own accord between them. When she touched him, Cole jerked in her arms. "You're asking for it, woman," he moaned.

She boldly stroked him, luxuriating in the feel of him throbbing against her hand. He was so big that she wondered how her body had managed to receive him.

"Not yet, Sarah, stop . . ." he ground out, his desire for her carrying him over the edge.

She removed her hand and gazed up at him. "Cole, I thought you liked me touching you?"

"God, yes, I like it. You see, I've wanted you so long that when you stroke me that way, I can lose control before I want to."

Sarah felt the rapid beating of his heart. "Then take me now, Cole."

Their desire too strong to wait a moment more, they

271

didn't bother to shed all their clothing. Spreading his coat on the bank, he lay down and positioned Sarah over him. Shoving her skirt to her waist, his hard, throbbing shaft found home in her warm womanly softness.

The full moon worked itself out of a cloud bank and cast a radiance of moonbeams over them as Cole took her with a violent urgency.

Replete, he held her in his arms, his hand caressing her back as she rested atop him, her cheek against his bare chest.

Suddenly Cole saw a bright red glow lighting up the black sky in the distance. His body went taut. He turned her toward the glow. "Fire, Sarah."

She raised up. "Oh, no."

"A fire out here when the grass is so dry is deadly."

Behind them, they heard the distant cries from the guests. "Good. They've seen it, too." Then he said teasingly, "Think it might have been our sparks that set it?"

Sarah giggled and, leaning down, kissed him soundly.

To make certain Sarah returned safely to the Barrington house, Cole walked her to the edge of the woods where they could see the lights glimmering on the other side of the field. Embracing her, he kissed her deeply, wishing he could hold her forever and never let her go. How long would they have to live this life of torment? Cole wondered glumly.

"Will you get someone to ride back to town with you? I don't want you to go alone."

Her eyes caressed him with a loving gaze, her complexion still containing the afterglow of their lovemaking. "Billy's already offered to ride with me. He follows me around like an old mother hen. I'm surprised I was able to escape him."

"Yes, we took quite a risk tonight," he whispered,

drawing her against him one last time. "Will we never see an end to this hell, Sarah?"

Resting her head against his chest, she felt and heard his wildly beating heart, a heart that now held within it a special place for her. "Yes, I have faith that someday we will, Cole."

He chuckled sadly. "Then you'd better have enough faith for both of us, baby, because sometimes I have my doubts." Breaking the embrace, he said, "I'm going to ride out and check the fire. I'd say several men have already left the party and are heading that way."

"Where's your horse?"

"Still at the Barrington place. I'll give you time to return before I leave, so no one will suspect anything. Sarah, I'm sure Dusty's looking for you. Don't—"

"I can handle Dusty," she interrupted.

When Sarah arrived at the house, she noticed that only a few people remained at the party. She was grateful to see Billy waiting for her beside her hired buggy, and told him she'd be ready to leave after she thanked their hostess. Not feeling threatened by the beautiful woman would make her task easier. She found Juliet standing with Dusty on the veranda. Oh, how she wished Dusty would take an interest in Juliet and leave her alone.

"Where've you been? I've been looking everywhere for you," Dusty said, noticeably irked with her.

"I took a walk," she said, unruffled. "When I saw the fire, I came back." Turning to Juliet, Sarah said, "I must be leaving now, but I wanted to thank you for inviting me, Juliet."

"I'll take you back to town," Dusty said quickly.

"No, it's out of your way. Billy's riding into town with me." Wanting to sound polite, she added with a smile, "Thank you for keeping me company and, of

273

course, for dancing with me."

"My pleasure. I'm glad you decided to come."

"Good night, Juliet . . . Dusty."

As Sarah walked away, Dusty's eyes followed her. He suspected she had been with the sheriff. While searching for her, he'd seen Blade's horse tethered a short distance from the horses of the guests, and realized Blade had not left the party as everyone had thought. Out of curiosity, Dusty wandered through the darkness to where he'd last seen Blade's horse. As he neared, he saw the sheriff mount and disappear into the night.

So, Sarah won't sell her property, he mused with a twisted smile. If Blade wasn't in the picture, Dusty knew he could win her affection. But having to deal with two women simultaneously was a complication he'd never encountered. Still, Dusty accepted this problem as a challenge. Nothing would interfere with his plans to have Sarah Hogan's property.

As Sarah and Billy journeyed to town, Sarah heard little that Billy said to her, her mind filled with thoughts of Cole. She understood why Cole couldn't make promises. As long as there was a reward on his head, he couldn't think of a future.

An inkling of an idea began to sprout as Sarah wondered what kind of person would pay to have another's death on his hands. Could she put a stop to this madness? What would happen if someone offered a reward to see that Cole stayed alive? Well, two people could play this game. She wondered why she hadn't thought of it sooner. She had the money, and by golly she would use it, every last cent of it, if it would keep Cole alive.

Later the next day, new posters began appearing all over town.

$2OOO.OO REWARD
For the safety of:
SHERIFF: COLEMAN BLADE
No questions asked
Do-Drop-In
HAZARD, TEXAS

Chapter Twenty-seven

"For god's sake, what next?" Cole asked, ripping the poster from the outside wall of the jail. He read the reward again to make sure he had read it correctly. With his face turning red with a mixture of embarrassment and anger, Cole folded the paper and shoved it into his coat pocket. Hearing the *tap, tap, tap* of hammers echoing off the buildings, he glanced up the street. Billy was on one side of the street and Fancy Fingers Floyd on the other, nailing more of the fool things on storefronts and posts. Shopkeepers stepped outside their stores, their mouths gaping as they perused the posters.

Pivoting on his heel, Cole marched toward the saloon. Pushing through the doors, he entered the saloon. With his hands fisted on his hips, he searched the room for Sarah, but didn't see her. Gunter stood behind the bar while four men were playing cards. They looked up from their game and grinned from ear to ear.

"Afternoon, Sheriff. You seen this?" one of the men asked, waving the poster.

"Yeah, I've seen it," Cole said, his mouth pulled so tight his lips were bloodless.

"We've been talkin' about teamin' up and helpin' ya out a bit. Frank and Lester, here, says they'll split shifts from midnight until noon, and Harry and me'll split the noon-to-midnight shift. That way, we can keep an eye on you real good."

Cole felt a low growl building up from deep within his chest. When they saw the sparks glittering in his dark eyes, they lowered their heads and returned to their game.

Turning his attention to Gunter, Cole heard him snickering as he polished the bar.

Walking over to him, Cole hissed quietly, "Where is she?"

"Who?" Gunter asked casually.

"You know who, damn it. Sarah!"

"Oh, her." Gunter smiled sheepishly. "She ain't come down yet."

With brisk strides, Cole crossed the room, taking three steps at a time as he scaled the stairs. Not pausing to knock on Sarah's door, he barreled into her sitting room and, not finding her there, stopped before her bedroom door. The door was slightly ajar. As he started to call her name, he heard her talking to someone.

"Isn't he going to be surprised?" he heard her ask.

No one answered.

"You can bet your sweet paws, Mr. Herman, this will make those horrible gunslingers think twice before they try to kill him. Yes, I think I had a very good idea. Cole ought to like it too."

Cole pushed the door open, and it slammed against the wall. "He doesn't," he growled.

Sarah's head popped up over her dressing screen, her eyes widening when she saw Cole's towering figure swallowing up the doorway. His deadly expression sent apprehension surging through her. Why was he angry with her?

"Good—good morning, Cole," she said weakly.

"It started that way. Whatever got into your head to pull a foolish stunt like this?" Removing the poster from his pocket, he crushed it into a ball and pitched the wad of paper toward the screen.

After it dropped to the floor, Mr. Herman bounded from the bed and pounced on the wad, then batted it here and there throughout the room until it came to rest at Cole's feet. Recognizing his friend's scent, the cat weaved his body between Cole's spread legs, rubbing against him and purring.

Cole gazed down at the cat. "You know something, Mr. Herman? Your mistress has gone completely off her rocker."

Mr. Herman settled back on his haunches and looked up at him and meowed.

"He agrees with me."

"I thought y-you'd like w-w-what I did for you."

Cole picked up the cat and shut the door behind him. Rocking back on his heels, he stroked the cat, all the while studying her. At length, he said, "Don't you remember a thing I said to you last night?"

"Yes. You've been avoiding me to protect me. Well, I decided I'd protect you. With everybody watching out for your safety, a gunslinger will have a hard time trying to shoot you. See?" she asked, smiling proudly.

"Sarah, I can guaran-damn-tee you I won't know my protector from my enemy. What if I kill an innocent person?"

She shrugged. "Oh, you shouldn't have that problem, Cole. My reward's a thousand dollars more than the one offered for your death. Anyone who had thought to kill you before will decide he'd get more money if he prevented your death. Who knows, your enemies might end up killing each other trying to save you."

She saw his tongue rolling against the inside of his cheek as he contemplated her reasoning. His temper mellowing, he said, "Your logic leaves a lot to be desired, but I do see your point. Still, it isn't foolproof. My question is this: How many two-thousand-dollars rewards can you afford to pay? They might bring in several bodies a day."

He saw her eyes soften as she gazed at him from over the screen. "As long as I can come up with the cash, I'll pay the reward."

A slow grin curved his mouth as he said jokingly, "Before all this is over, you might have to sell the saloon and your property to come up with it, too."

"If that's what it takes, I will," she announced adamantly. "Anyway, Miss Barrington has already offered to buy the ranch."

Cole's smile faded. "When did this come about?"

"Last night after I arrived at her party, she took me on a brief tour through her house. Afterwards, we went into the parlor. We were discussing her beautiful piano, when out of the clear blue, she said we could work a trade." Sarah laughed. "I told her I had nothing that valuable to trade. That's when she mentioned she'd like to buy my property."

"What did you say?"

"Of course I said no. At any rate, she said if I should ever change my mind to sell, to let her know." She paused, her eyes aglow with love as she added, "Cole, I'd sell it in a second if I could keep you from harm."

"Damn, you make it hard for me to stay angry with you. Come out from behind there, woman."

"I'm not dressed." Her eyes darted anxiously toward the door. "And someone might come in."

He gave her a one-sided grin. "In that case, I'll join you. You can hide me."

Tossing Mr. Herman on the bed, Cole came around the screen.

"Cole," she said laughingly. Dressed only in her chemise and drawers, Sarah crossed her arms over her breasts.

"Don't. It might be a while before I'll see you like this

again." Unfolding her arms, he held them close to her sides, his hot gaze roaming slowly over her then coming back to her face.

For several moments, they stood there, their eyes locked. She saw in his face an expression of mingled tenderness and desire, causing a glowing warmth to flow through her. Suddenly she flung herself against him, her arms circling his back, and pressed her body close to his. "Oh, Cole, it's so unfair."

"Unfair, yes, but necessary." His hands slid deep within her hair as he tipped back her head. Sarah closed her eyes as his mouth came crushing down on hers with an almost desperate hunger. Then, pulling his mouth from hers, his lips trailed softly across her cheek and brushed her ear. Holding her tightly against him, his hand stroked her back.

After several minutes, he pulled away and placed his hands on her shoulders, gazing down at her. "Sarah, if you do pay any monies on this reward thing, I'm paying you back. Also, I promise you this: If I ever hear of you selling any damned thing to protect my hide, I'll toss my badge and get the hell out of Hazard so quick it'll make your head spin. You hear?"

Sarah knew he meant it. She reached up and pressed her finger against his lips. She smiled coyly. "And I'll promise you something else. You wouldn't get far, Cole, before I'd find you."

He twined a thick strand of her hair around his finger and chuckled. "Yeah, you probably would."

His eyes left her face and glanced down, seeing her creamy breasts swelling enticingly over her lacy chemise. At another place, he would have taken her, his desire for her was so great. But lust played only a minor part in his feelings for her. That anyone could love him so deeply, so completely, and would give up everything for him, was the most precious gift he had ever received from anyone.

"I'd better go before one thing leads to another."

When he reached the door, he asked, "Oh, did anyone tell you it was Marge Tulley's barn we saw burning last night?"

"Wes told me this morning. I'm so glad it wasn't her home."

"Yeah, we all were. The folks are planning a barn-raising."

"Good. Marge has been very kind to me. I'll be glad to help in any way I can."

He paused. "Sarah, because of your reward, we have to be doubly careful now."

"I know, Cole. If anyone asks why I did it, I'll just say Hazard doesn't want to lose the best sheriff they've ever had."

"You're something else, Widow Woman," he said with a wink before he left her room.

Several days later as Sarah was leaving the post office, a rider came galloping through town, announcing the coming of Buffalo Bill Cody's Original Wild West Show. After tethering his horse in the center of town, the man gave several children handbills to pass among the pedestrians and storekeepers, tossing them each a coin for their help.

Sarah read the handbill listing all the spectacular events that were to take place on the outskirts of town beginning the next afternoon. The star of the show was a young woman named Annie Oakley, also called Little Sure Shot. According to the handbill, she was the greatest female sharpshooter the West had ever seen. Other members of the troupe were Indians and cowboys, and there were several highly trained horses that performed tricks and danced.

Clusters of people were grouped on the boardwalk,

discussing the big event. Upon hearing real Indians were in the show, children performed their own renditions of Indian dances and war whoops. She heard one man say that nothing like this had ever come to Hazard, and that he expected to see a deluge of people pouring into town that night.

Sarah hurried into the saloon and called all her employees together to discuss how they could make preparations for the crowd she anticipated. Gunter assured her that they had enough liquor, but that they might run short on help to tend the tables. Collie and Belle said they knew a couple of girls working at the hotel who needed the extra income. Billy would help Gunter behind the bar, or anywhere else they might need him.

Knowing they wouldn't have customers during the show, they decided to close the saloon the next day and open afterward.

Early into the evening the Do Drop In was crowded. Cole leaned against the far end of the bar, watching for anyone who might cause trouble. He thought the walls might burst if another person came through the door. The smoke created such a heavy, choking fog that Billy began opening all the windows so they could breathe. Sarah, Belle, Collie, and the girls they'd hired to help them wore paths around the room, delivering drinks. They'd brought in more tables and chairs and had even set some up on the stage. Billy helped Gunter tend bar, and washed and dried the glasses as the girls brought back the empties.

Dusty was also there, but the men he gambled with were his own employees. Cole watched Dusty eye Sarah as she flitted about the room. On several occasions he'd tried to draw her to his table, but Sarah had ignored him, sending one of the other girls to tend to him.

As Sarah was setting drinks on a table, one of the men said, "Well, I'll be damned, just look who's here."

Turning, surprise flashed across Sarah's face. She immediately recognized the man she'd seen depicted on the handbill, Buffalo Billy Cody. There was no mistaking his identity because few men boasted a white, neatly pointed beard. Beneath a wide-brimmed hat, his long wavy white hair fell to his shoulders. Beside him stood a petite young woman dressed in a dark brown skirt and ruffled shirtwaist. She wore a hat atop unbound chestnut hair, close to the color of Sarah's own. A tall, handsome man towered behind her, his hand on her shoulder.

"Excuse me," Sarah said, and made her way through the thick crowd to greet them.

Cole was already talking to them when she arrived and introduced her to Buffalo Bill Cody, Annie Oakley, and Frank Butler, her husband.

"Pleased to meet you, ma'am," they said in unison.

"I'm so glad you've honored us with your presence," Sarah said, shaking each of their hands. She couldn't believe that these famous people were actually here in her saloon, and she was meeting them face-to-face. Even the customers had stopped talking and were staring at them in awe.

Buffalo Bill smiled kindly and took her hand. "The sheriff told me about your father's death, Mrs. Hogan. It's been several years since I last saw him, but he seemed to be fit as a fiddle. It was because of his invitation that I am here in Hazard."

"You knew him then?" Sarah asked with surprise.

"Yes. We met in Wichita at one my first Wild West shows and became good friends right off. He said if my troupe was ever out this way, he hoped we'd perform for the people of Hazard. Usually we give ample notice before our show, but it wasn't until I looked on the map that I realized how close we were to Hazard. We'd just finished a show in Dallas and were on our way East."

"Well, on my father's behalf, I thank you for remem-

283

bering his invitation and coming here to entertain us. Would you like to sit down?"

"No, but thank you. Our day'll start early in the morning and we need to get a good night's sleep. I only wanted to come by and introduce Annie and Frank to your father. They've recently joined my show. You won't see a sharpshooter around that's as accurate as our little missie here."

"Hey, little lady," someone called out, "just how good a shot are you?"

All heads turned as a stranger slid back his chair and stood up. He reeled sideways and quickly balanced himself. Cole studied him. There was something familiar about him, but Cole couldn't place him. His face was ruddy and pitted, covered with a week's growth of stubby beard. His black eyes were beady beneath scraggly brows. Worst of all, he was drunk.

"How 'bout givin' us a preview?" he drawled.

"Sorry, but we don't give previews," Buffalo Bill intervened. "Come to the show tomorrow, and you'll see what a crack shot she is."

"I ain't gonna pay 'til I see she ain't a hoax." Coming around the table, he knocked against several customers as he made his way towards them. Stopping in front of them, he swept Annie's five-foot figure with an insolent sneer. "Why don't me and you step outside, small fry, and see who's the best shot?"

With her gray eyes snapping, Annie taunted, "And just what would we use for targets, mister, the stars?"

Sweeping his jacket aside, the man rested his hand on the hilt of his Colt. "So, we'll do it in here."

Before Cole could get a word in edgewise, Annie said, "As drunk as you are, you couldn't hit a target if it was held smack dab in front of your face."

His eyes turned deadly. "Why, you little—"

"Enough," Cole said, stepping between Annie and the

284

drunk. "How about you and me going over to the jail. I have an empty cell where you can sleep it off."

"I ain't sleepin' nothin' off. She insulted me, and by god, I'm gonna do sumpin' 'bout it." With that, he whipped his gun from his holster, the sudden motion causing him to stagger backward. Righting himself, he curled his finger around the trigger. He aimed it toward Gunter and Billy as they stood like statues behind the bar. "You two, start tossin' them glasses in the air."

Everyone in the room scrambled from their tables, but it was so packed they couldn't find any place to go. Some ran hastily through the swinging doors while others covered their heads and fell to the floor.

"Oh, please don't," Sarah pleaded.

"Give me the gun, mister," Cole said calmly, reaching out his hand.

The stranger grinned maliciously at Cole and raised the pistol above his shoulders. "Try to take it and see what happens."

Cole felt that same sense of familiarity. He knew this man, yet he'd met so many like him, he couldn't place him. Regardless that the man was drunk, Cole knew he had a mean streak in him that went clear to the bone. Drawing on him would only increase the chance that someone would be shot during the melee.

With an unbelievable swiftness, Cole twisted his body, his right leg shooting high, his heavy booted foot striking the man's wrist. The gun sailed across the room and slammed against the wall with a dull thud. For a moment, the drunk stared in amazement, clutching his aching wrist.

Heads popped up from behind the tables as Cole pulled his gun and ordered, "You've caused enough trouble for the night. You're coming with me. I'll even tuck you in."

"You'll be sorry," the man said, his lips tightening into

a thin white line.

As Cole turned to leave, he said to the dumbfounded threesome, "See you folks tomorrow at the show. Sarah, I'll be back after I settle this man in for the night."

After Cole left, everyone in the saloon began talking at once, no one quite believing the scene they'd just witnessed.

"I wonder where he learned to do that," Buffalo Bill said, scratching his chin through his well-kept beard.

Sarah knew exactly where he'd learned that trick. Chin. She smiled. "I don't know, but I'm glad for it. I hate to think of what might have happened if the man had started shooting."

"It was my fault," Annie apologized. "I should've known better than to taunt a man in his condition." Her chin shot up. "But, drat it, he made me so blasted mad."

"Well, I've learned a lesson from all this too," Buffalo Bill said with a chuckle. "You're a novelty, Annie. There just aren't many women sharpshooters around. I won't put you in this situation again, I promise."

Sarah felt badly that the incident had happened in her saloon. "I'd never seen that man before tonight, Buffalo Bill. Please believe me when I say we run a tight saloon here, and the men who frequent it would never accost a woman as that man did Annie."

"Don't worry, Mrs. Hogan, we won't let one bad apple in the bunch change our opinion of your saloon. I've run into this problem many times in the past. If you can shoot, there's always someone wanting to challenge you. More often than not, someone is killed in skirmishes like this one. The sheriff's a smart man, and handled the situation very well."

To Annie and Frank, he said, "We'd better get back to the hotel. Mrs. Hogan, it was indeed a pleasure meeting you. You will be at our show tomorrow, I hope."

"Yes, I wouldn't miss it for the world."

Dusty was having his own thoughts about the scene he'd just witnessed. Blade was a hard man to kill, but he was made of the same blood and sweat as any other man.

The reward Sarah had put on the sheriff's safety had fouled up everything. Dusty had noticed several men hanging around outside the jail. On several occasions, he'd seen men following Blade at a distance in town, their eyes scanning rooftops and alleys, their hands always close to their guns. Dusty's employees had reported men following him home at night. In fact, one night the sheriff had come close to killing a man who was protecting him.

But in a crowd, no one would ever know who'd fired the shot that killed the lawman, would they?

Chapter Twenty-eight

The next afternoon, everyone gathered at the end of town. Members of the show directed the people into a large circle, making an arena around the site of the show. Several families stood in their wagons and buckboards so they could see over the heads of the crowd, and small children sat atop men's shoulders for a better view. Billy and Gunter had loaded several chairs from the saloon into a wagon and set them up in the front row. Sarah sat between them and scanned the people, looking for Cole among them. She saw him standing next to Juliet Barrington across the circle from her. For a moment, her pulse beat erratically as she watched them talking. Stop worrying, she told herself. He told you she didn't mean anything to him. He's just socializing . . . that's all.

Dragging her gaze from him, she glanced up at the sky where thick clusters of fluffy white clouds floated slowly across the blue horizon. As she watched them, one particular cluster caused a shiver to ripple through her. The cloud was in the form of an arm with the hand holding a gun. Not one to be superstitious, Sarah couldn't help wondering if perhaps it was a bad omen. After last night's incident at the saloon, she decided her imagination must be playing tricks on her.

"Cole told me about your trouble last night," Wes said. "He let the man out of jail this morning and told him to get out of town."

Sarah's heart leaped in her chest. She quickly glanced up at the cloud, noting that the form had dissipated. "Oh, I wish he hadn't," she whispered.

"You should've seen him, Wes," Billy said, leaning forward so he could see Wes on the other side of Sarah. "He's as fast with his feet as he is with a gun and knife. A long time ago, I saw a man break another man's neck with that same move."

Cheers and applause halted their conversation as Buffalo Bill, astride a magnificent white horse, galloped at brisk speed and came to a halt in the center of the arena. Removing his hat, he waved it in the air and announced in a robust voice, "Citizens of Hazard, welcome to Buffalo Bill's Wild West!"

Excited cries burst from the spectators as a stagecoach careened into the arena surrounded by whooping Indians in their war paint and tribal dress, waving tomahawks and firing guns at the cowboys closing in on them. The coach came to a halt and passengers inside screamed as an Indian jerked open the door. Atop the coach, the driver wrestled with an Indian until a cowboy fired a shot and the Indian tumbled to the ground. When the mock battle was over, Buffalo Bill opened the door of the coach and the passengers stepped down and, along with the rest of the cast, bowed before the crowd.

After Buffalo Bill had cleared the arena, cowboys filled the circle, some doing skillful acts with their lariats, while others performed elaborate feats on horseback. Following this, one event flowed into another. When Buffalo Bill introduced the Sioux medicine man, Sitting Bull, the children stared awestruck at the proud Indian as he rode astride a large gray horse into the arena and stopped. With his back ramrod-straight, his weathered face expressionless, he indeed appeared fearless. Wearing a white beaded costume and full feather headdress, he paraded around the circle, pausing several times to have his picture taken for someone in the crowd. Everyone knew he had been at the battle of the Little Bighorn where General Custer and his entire troop were killed, but they responded with curiosity rather than anger.

After Sitting Bull left the arena, Buffalo Bill announced with great fanfare, "And now, ladies and gentlemen, the Wild West is proud to present a newcomer to our show, the greatest female sharpshooter the West has ever seen. Little Sure Shot, Annie Oakley!"

The crowd went wild with acclamation as the young woman, astride her western pony, came forward into the ring with a springy gait. As the horse danced, she swept off her hat and urged her mount into a deep bow, bringing enthusiastic applause from the spectators. Suddenly a cowboy appeared in the ring, and as he rode past Annie, she leaned from her horse and scooped up a pistol from the ground, firing at six glass targets that he tossed into the air. Her six quick shots brought screams of fright from the women, but the screams were soon lost in their applause. Next, the cowboy spun a wheel holding six fiery candles. Annie fired rapidly, snuffing the flames. Again the crowd cheered, marveling that this tiny girl was such a crack shot and skilled horsewoman. Next, her assistant held up his hand with four dimes positioned between each finger. Annie shot each dime out from between them, never even touching the man's fingers.

The clapping and cheering were deafening.

Sarah looked around, her gaze settling on a man on horseback, a good distance behind the spectators. As she scrutinized him, recognition dawned—the drunk at the saloon. But Wes had said Cole had told him to get out of town.

Nudging Billy, Sarah said, "Billy, see that man over there on the roan?"

"Yeah, what about him?"

"Isn't he the drunk Cole put in jail last night?"

With his one good eye focused on the man, Billy said, "I think so . . . Yeah, it is him. What's he doin' here?"

"I don't know, but I don't like it one bit."

"Now, ladies and gentlemen," Buffalo Bill shouted above the din, "our beautiful young lady will shoot out the center of this playing card." He removed a long hunting knife from its sheath, and as he held it above his head for everyone to see it, the sun glinted off the bright blade. "But, as added entertainment, Miss Oakley will use the gleaming blade of this knife as a mirror. With her back turned, she will shoot at the card from over her shoulder." He paused, his eyes sweeping the spectators. "Is there a man among you brave enough to hold the card?"

Like puppets on a string, heads turned and feet shuffled as each man waited for someone else to volunteer.

After several moments, Cole lifted his hand and said, "I'll do it."

Sarah panicked. He'd be a clear target for the man if he wanted to shoot him. Sarah jumped from her chair. "No, I will."

A hush fell over the crowd.

"You can't do that," Billy scolded, grabbing her wrist to pull her back down in her chair.

"What if she misses and hits you?" Wes countered.

"You've seen her shoot. She won't miss." With that, she turned and walked briskly toward Buffalo Bill.

"Wait a minute, missy, I'll do it," Billy called out, jumping to his feet.

"Sit down, Billy, and let Cole handle her," Wes ordered.

Sarah's eyes widened as she saw Cole leave Juliet's side. As he walked toward her, she noted his eyes were glowing dangerously and his nostrils were flaring. Now she knew how Daniel felt when they'd thrown him to the lions. If Cole could devour her, he would.

They met face to face in front of Buffalo Bill. Annie was standing beside him. Buffalo Bill looked from Sarah to Cole, then cocked his head in amusement. "Should we draw straws?"

"It isn't necessary," Cole said calmly, though inside he was mad as hell. "Sarah, I don't want to cause a scene. Get back over there where you belong."

Sarah fisted her hands on her hips and shot back, "I have as much right to be here as you do." Leaning forward, she whispered, "Besides, that man you sent out of town didn't go very far. If you go out there, you'll give him the perfect opportunity to gun you down."

"Where is he?" Cole asked, searching the crowd.

Sarah turned and looked for him. "I don't see him."

"Are you sure you didn't just think you saw him it?" Annie asked.

"No, he *was* there. Billy saw him, too."

Buffalo Bill intervened. "Look, I heard about the reward on your head, Sheriff. Maybe we ought to get someone else."

"No. If he does plan to cause trouble, we can't be sure if it's me or Miss Oakley he'll choose. We both riled him last night. She might need me if there's gunfire. You'd better be prepared to use your gun, too, Buffalo Bill." Turning to Sarah, he said softly, "We're delaying the show. Please return to your seat, Sarah . . . and thanks for the warning."

Knowing she would never convince Cole to change his mind, Sarah conceded. The cloud in the sky . . . a bad omen . . . Please don't let the man kill him, she prayed.

Walking back to her seat, Sarah saw Dusty standing behind her chair. Irritation whipped through her. She just didn't want to deal with him right now. She had a horrible premonition that something was going to happen and she was helpless to do anything to prevent it.

292

After she took her seat, Dusty patted her shoulder. "You did a very brave thing, Sarah."

Sarah snorted with disgust. She wanted to tell him to shut up—that bravery had nothing to do with her action. The man she loved could die in a few minutes because he was as stubborn as a mule. Instead she threw up her arms and dropped them into her lap, exclaiming, "I can't believe it! With as many men here at this show, and only one had the courage to hold that card."

"Now, hold on a minute, missy," Billy snapped. "I said I'd do it."

"Yes, after the sheriff and I both volunteered," she countered with a snort of disgust.

"Well, she's a woman," he argued. "And women are as skittish as colts. What if somethin' scared her the second she fired that gun?"

Sarah sighed. "Forget I even mentioned it."

As Cole walked beside Buffalo Bill to the point where he was to stand and hold the card, they both saw a multitude of hands on the sidelines moving quickly to the hilts of their guns.

"What the hell are they doing?" the showman asked uneasily.

Cole laughed. "They're my protectors . . . I hope. Mrs. Hogan had this bright idea that if she posted a two-thousand-dollar reward for my safety, she would void the one-thousand-dollar reward put on my life. Only time will tell, I reckon."

When they stopped, Buffalo Bill gave him the card, instructing him to hold his arm straight out from his body. "Good luck."

"I trust Miss Oakley," Cole said with a lazy grin.

"It isn't Annie I'm worried about." Then, to the crowd, he said, "All right, folks, we're about ready to start. Now, for safety purposes, all of you standing behind the sheriff, please break the circle and form a line."

When Buffalo Bill walked back to join Annie, Cole searched the crowd again, seeing several unfamiliar faces. One gunman he could handle, but how many more were out there lying in wait for him? He caught a movement from the corner of his eye. Cole saw a man sitting on his horse, slowly circling the outskirts of the arena. The man wore his hat low over his brow, and kept his face straight ahead. Casually glancing over his shoulder, Cole saw him stop a good distance from the end of the line.

My back will face him as I hold the card, he realized.

Sarah saw the man and tried to catch Cole's attention. When he never looked her way, her heart grew cold with fear. Her hands became clammy, and perspiration beaded on her brow. She had noticed several men's hands resting on the hilts of their guns. Some had already removed the weapons from their holsters. Could they keep Cole from harm if the man decided to shoot him? She felt the tenseness in Wes and Billy as they tightened their hold on her.

"All right, Little Sure Shot, we're ready," the showman shouted.

Sarah's head jerked toward the young woman. Turning her back toward Cole, Annie positioned the hunting knife with one hand and aimed the gun over her shoulder with the other.

The air was charged with anxiety, everyone holding their breath.

It happened so quickly. One second Cole was holding the card and in the next instant, he dove to the ground as two shots blasted the stillness.

Sarah didn't scream, as many around her did. She couldn't move, but she sat profoundly still, hardly breathing as she watched Cole lying flat and motionless. For a moment, her face was ghastly white and unconsciousness had almost seized her as she looked for the slightest sign of life. Then Cole moved and, rolling to his feet, slapped his hat against his thigh to remove the dust. When he looked her way, she saw a grim smile at the corners of his mouth.

"He's dead, Sheriff," someone called from the group of men surrounding the body. "Never had a chance to even fire his gun."

No one noticed Dusty Mills as he and his men mounted their horses. His face burned with rage that Blade escaped the bullet again. Three thousand dollars he'd offered the man, and he had failed just like all the rest.

Sarah rushed toward Cole, with Billy and Wes behind her. Sarah had expected Juliet to join them, but saw her turn away and climb into her buggy.

"Oh, Cole, are you all right?" Sarah asked, her eyes searching his towering figure for a gunshot wound.

Still holding his smoking gun, he smiled appreciatively at Sarah. "Yes, thanks to you, Sarah, I knew to look for him."

Annie and Buffalo Bill joined them.

Annie's face was white as she said, "I—I aimed for his gun, but—"

"You did hit his gun, Miss Oakley, but I killed him," Cole assured her. "We hit him within a split second of one another. How'd you know to fire at him?"

"I caught his reflection in the blade and saw him raise his gun."

"Sheriff, if you ever want another job, come see me," Buffalo Bill said. "We could use a man with your wide range of skills."

"Thanks for the offer, Buffalo Bill. I'll think about it," Cole said, seeing Sarah frown at him.

"Tell me something, last night when you kicked that gun from the man's hand, it wasn't just an ordinary kick. Where'd you learn that method of fighting? Empty-hand, I believe it's called."

"You recognized it?"

"Sure, in my business I run across all kinds of oddities. Not many white men ever use it."

"Oh, it was just something I picked up while working on a ranch," Cole said, grinning. Then he added, "Actually, a Chinese cook taught me."

"He taught you well."

"Thank you."

"Well, this turned out to be quite a show. Maybe we'll see you folks again sometime."

"I certainly hope so," Sarah said. "Thank you so much for coming. I wish my father could've been here to watch your performance."

"Yes, me too, Mrs. Hogan . . . me too." He paused and smiled. "He's got a mighty fine daughter. She's got spunk just like her daddy," he said with a wink.

"Yeah, she does, doesn't she?" Billy piped in.

Wes nudged him sharply in the ribs. "You didn't know her daddy from Adam's house cat."

"Oh, Buffalo Bill, this is Billy Ward, my employee, and Wes Norman, my friend."

Buffalo Bill shook both men's hands, then studied Billy a moment. "Haven't we met before?"

"Don't think so."

He shrugged. "You sure look familiar. Well, guess we'd better start packing up so we can head out before dark."

"Good-bye, Miss Oakley," Sarah said, offering her hand to the young woman. Closing her tiny hand in her own, Sarah patted it. "I wish you all the success in the world."

"The same to you, Mrs. Hogan," she said with a smile.

The crowd broke up and started heading for home. Members of the troupe returned to their tents and wagons. Billy, Fancy Fingers Floyd, and Gunter began loading the chairs into the wagon.

Cole noticed his deputy approaching him. The man

pulled a horse behind him with the body of the dead man slung like a bag of feed over the saddle.

He stopped his horse beside the sheriff. "Thought you might want a look at him before we buried him."

As Cole lifted the man's head by his hair, Sarah turned her head from the sight. This could've been Cole, her mind screamed.

"Now, I recognize him," Cole said, dropping the man's head. "Name's Dallas Tate. One night a long time back, I ran into him in a saloon. He was drunk and drew his gun on me. I didn't want to kill him, so I winged him instead." He glanced over at Sarah and saw her shoulders trembling. "Revenge was his mission, the reward only sweetening the pot. Go on and bury him."

After the deputy took the man away, Cole went over to Sarah. He placed his hands on her shoulders. "It's all right, Sarah. I doubt I could have survived the day without that reward you posted. Any other enemies I might have had didn't have the courage to fire when every man in Hazard had his gun drawn."

Turning, her warm smile greeted him. "You really think so?"

"Yeah, I do. The only problem I see coming from all of this is how you're going to pay each of them two thousand dollars."

Sarah frowned thoughtfully. "Hmmm, that's a problem." Then her eyes brightened. "But I won't worry about that today. You're alive—that's all that matters to me now."

Chapter Twenty-nine

Dawn broke across the Texas horizon. The jingle of harnesses and the creaks of wagons, loaded with timber and various building supplies, shattered the quiet. Baskets of food and tempting desserts accompanied the lumbering caravan. Wide-awake children fidgeted and made plans for the exciting day ahead. The work would be hard, the hours long. Still, it was almost like a holiday. Everyone for miles around would join in to help the Tulleys rebuild their barn.

Marge and her boys had cleared away the burned remains and marked the boundaries for the new barn. The men unloaded the wagons and fell to the task of rebuilding. The rhythmic fall of hammers blended with the fluid motion of saws and the buzz of conversation as the women set up long tables in the shade. An occasional bellow of profanity went unnoticed when a thumb or finger got between a hammer and a nail. Children scampered across the fields, laughing and playing, and the women had a quantity of gossip to catch up on since Juliet Barrington's lawn party and Buffalo Bill's Original Wild West Show. One of the men's favorite topics of discussion was Sheriff Coleman Blade and the reward that Sarah Hogan had posted to protect him.

Ernest Millsaps stood on the perimeter of the gathering, his wife, Cora, standing beside him, her face wreathed in disapproval. Her lips puckered repeatedly like a nursing baby, as she perused her skittish mate. Her fisted hand gripping the picnic basket was bloodless. "Ernest, if you get up there and break your neck I'll never speak to you again."

"No, I guess not," Ernest replied solemnly.

"That's not what I mean. You're not a carpenter and we both know it."

Sweat popped out on Ernest's brow as he watched the men scale the high sloping rafters, heaving long boards into position and nailing them down. After a weary sigh, he responded, "If the truth was known, I'm not much of anything, Cora. But, I mean to change all that today."

"By getting yourself killed?"

"I'm not going to get myself killed. Instead I'm going to prove to these people I'm a man."

"That's obvious, Ernest." She wrinkled a furrowed brow. "Besides, you don't have to prove anything to these people. You're the head teller, and you were only protecting the bank's money. That's what has you in such straits, isn't it?"

"I'm just tired of everyone snickering behind my back. I know what they say. They think that I hide behind your skirt tails."

Cora snorted. "Forevermore, Ernest, that's the most ridiculous thing I've ever heard. I think you've been in the sun too long." She lifted her hand to test his brow.

He pushed it away and adjusted the galluses of his new store-bought overalls, the first he'd ever owned. Ernest had put a lot of thought into this gathering today. He'd gone so far as to take part of the day off from his job as head teller, another first for him. He wanted the people of his community to accept him. He wanted them to be his friends, and he, theirs. The first thing he'd tackled was his appearance. Hence, the new denims—he wanted to look like the other men. Instead, he stuck out like a sore thumb. His legs felt like they were encased in stovepipes, and he walked with a stiff-legged gait. But his heart was in the right place, and he was going to share in the work of building Marge Tulley a new barn.

"If you're determined to carry out this foolishness, then I will not be a party to it. I shall return home to wait for you to come to your senses and apologize to me for this inconvenience."

"You do what you got to do, Cora, and I'll do what I got to do," he said, turning and walking away.

"But, Ernest," she called. Standing there, slack jawed in the beating sun, Cora took a quick inspection of her husband. For the first time in their married life, he hadn't backed down. This new side of Ernest surprised and thrilled her. He normally gave in to her regardless of the situation. This transformation had developed after the kidnapping of Sarah Hogan. The whole affair had upset him. He'd chastised himself repeatedly for putting the bank's money over the welfare of one of the town's citizens. There had been nothing Cora could do or say to put an end to his brooding. Maybe . . . just maybe Ernest was right. It would be nice to have friends. If nothing else would do him, then she, too, would put forth her best foot and see what happened. Besides, she would love to have Marge Tulley's recipe for her brown-sugar apple fritters. Cora, herself, was a fairly good cook and Marge had hinted in the past that she'd like the recipe for Cora's Indian corn relish. Maybe it was time to share not only her friendship, but her recipes as well. In the meantime, she just hoped Ernest didn't break his fool neck crawling around on that barn. To her knowledge, he'd never built anything.

Ernest plowed through the gathering, smiling from ear to ear, calling out greetings and waving his hand like a handkerchief blowing in the breeze. Brows winged upward and hesitant smiles creased many a face as the people of Hazard wondered what Ernest was doing. Still, his enthusiasm was infectious, so they extended their hands and their greetings with only slightly less enthusiasm than Ernest.

Outfitting himself with nail apron, nails, and a hammer, Ernest proceeded to lift an awkward timber and shift it over his shoulder. Three men's heads bobbed like corks afloat as they tried to dodge the swaying board. Caleb Dotson, taking the opportunity to fill his jaw with his favorite chew, didn't see the board. It slapped him on the back, and when he yelped in pain, the freshly placed tobacco lost its mooring and slid down his throat.

Caleb coughed and gagged and spit and belched until the men standing around him doubled over with laughter. Ernest dropped the board and began pounding Caleb on the back, apologizing for any discomfort he had caused.

"Gol-dang it, Ernest, will you quit beating me on the back? It's my throat that hurts. It feels like I just swallowed a bucket of hot coals."

"I'll get you something to drink. Maybe that will help." Ernest charged through the crowd intent on his purpose when an arm shot out and grabbed him.

"Here, give Caleb some of this. It should clear out his throat."

"What the hell is his problem?" Caleb questioned when Ernest was out of hearing distance.

"He's just trying to be helpful," one of the men answered.

"Here, this should do the trick," Ernest called out, rushing through the crowd. Uncapping the jar, he handed it to Caleb.

Caleb lifted the jar to his lips and took a long pull of the clear liquid. Once again, he sputtered, and his face turned a fiery red. Sweat popped out on his forehead and he eyed his benefactor with red-rimmed eyes. "Are you trying to make a fool out of me, Ernest?"

301

"Why no, not at all. I'm just trying to make you comfortable."

"Then by all means, join me." Caleb shoved the jar toward him.

Hesitantly, Ernest lifted the container to his lips and, mimicking Caleb, took a hefty swallow. His eyes teared and his Adam's apple bobbed incessantly as he swallowed rapidly, trying not to embarrass himself further by throwing up. After a few moments his stomach quieted and fingers of warmth spread through him.

The men watched, waiting to see what the straight-laced Ernest Millsaps would do.

He surprised them all by lifting the jar and proclaiming, "To Marge Tulley's new barn." Then he took another drink of the fiery liquid. Everyone agreed, and the jar of Kentucky 'shine passed among the men until it was empty.

Ernest, stove-pipe legs and all, made it to the skeletal rafters. He worked side by side with the men without so much as a whimper. He hammered until he thought his arm would fall off—then he hammered some more. His arm had never suffered such abuse, and he knew without a doubt that he would not be able to lift a pen the following day. The inside of his mouth was raw where he bit it as he pounded the hammer. And his privates, lord, he knew they would be black and blue from jostling against the rafters. He wasn't as agile hanging in midair as the other men, so he wrapped his legs around the timbers to secure his position. But never once did he mention his job as head teller.

When they broke for dinner, it took two men to unwind Ernest's legs and help him from the roof. Proudly, he showed off his swollen thumb, garnering a burgeoning respect among the citizenship of Hazard, Texas.

Cora watched as the men laughed with her husband, not at him. He walked as if he were ten feet tall, if a bit

302

stiffly. She was very proud of him and what he'd accomplished. Cora didn't realize it, but those standing around her noticed. When she looked at her husband with such tenderness, it softened her features considerably. She would never be a pretty woman, but the tenderness negated the old-crow appearance.

"Ernest," she called softly.

He looked up in surprise. "Cora?"

"I've fixed you a plate," she offered.

Smiling from ear to ear, he approached her. "I'm glad you stayed," he whispered.

"Me too," she admitted. "You didn't really think I would abandon you, did you?" she asked gruffly.

"I didn't know," he answered truthfully.

"Now you know."

He placed a quick wet kiss to her cheek. "Thanks."

"Ernest." Cora blushed to the roots of the harshly knotted hair lying at the nape of her neck. Never had her husband made such a public show of affection. Instead of displeasing her, she decided she liked it immensely, just like she did this new side of her husband.

As they found a seat in the shade, she noticed the grimace that stole over Ernest's face when he sat down. "Are you okay?"

"If you want the truth, my butt feels like someone used it to plow a field. And these new britches have rubbed every bit of the hide off my legs. I'll probably walk straddle-legged for a month."

"So you've decided not to take up carpentry on a permanent basis," she teased.

"Lord, no, I'll probably have to spend tomorrow in the bed, recuperating."

"Not a bad idea," she replied boldly.

It was Ernest's turn to blush. He leaned close to Cora and gave her an explicit account of his privates.

Her eyes sparkled with tears of laughter and her shoulders shook with merriment.

"Looks like you two are having a good time," the sheriff called as he passed the couple.

"We're discussing the future of our children," Cora told him.

It wasn't until the sheriff had passed the couple that it dawned on him that Cora and Ernest had no children.

Cole leaned against a tree and scanned the area until he spotted Sarah. She stood with the other women dishing out food as the line of men passed. She talked comfortably with the men, occasionally replying with her own brand of dry humor. Cole would be the first to admit that she looked beautiful. Hot and beautiful. Loosened strands of hair clung damply to her neck and her face was flushed with heat. Pride swelled in him as he watched her. He loved looking at her. He loved touching her and he loved sinking deeply into her welcoming flesh. Her breathless moans and cries of passion could send the blood soaring through his body even now as he thought about their lovemaking. It was a powerful thing, their lovemaking. He'd never experienced anything so vibrant and passionate. In his lifetime he'd spent many a long sleepless night outdoors. He'd pondered the star-studded heavens, and, on occasion, watched a single star soar across the darkness. That's what their lovemaking reminded him of—two stars soaring across the heavens then coming together in an explosion of fire and light.

"Damn!" he muttered, raking his hat from his head and swatting it against the tree. My god, what had she done to him? Here he stood in the middle of a barn-raising, with dozens of the townspeople present, and all he could think about was taking Sarah to bed.

He'd tried, damn it, he'd tried to stay away from her. That hadn't worked. Hell, he'd been miserable, she'd been miserable. The only thing he could do was keep a closer watch over her. He'd been doing that for so long that it came as naturally as breathing. Only lately had he turned her protection over to Chin. At any cost, he didn't want her caught in the crossfire by someone trying to make a name for themselves by taking him down and collecting the thousand dollars. At any cost, he thought sadly, not completely . . . He couldn't deny himself the pleasure of her company.

Sarah felt his gaze even before she lifted her head. He was standing in line with the men talking and laughing, but his eyes caressed her. He winked boldly and a warmth spread through her like honey on a hot biscuit.

"That's enough, Sarah," the man before her said, interrupting her thoughts.

"What?" She shifted her gaze to what she was doing. Jerking the ladle from over the man's plate, she stammered, "Oh, I'm so sorry." The thick brown gravy ran over the mound of potatoes and the fingers gripping the plate, then dripped onto the table.

"No harm done." He smiled and moved on down the line.

Sarah could have died of embarrassment. She shot a look at Cole. He slouched against the table, the epitome of innocence, only the telltale arching of a brow giving him away.

Sarah adjusted her thinking and avoided looking at him as she ladled the gravy carefully into the men's plates.

"I think I'll have some of that fine-looking gravy," Cole drawled, standing before her.

She looked up at him and asked sweetly. "And where would you like it, Sheriff?"

"Anywhere you'd like to put it," he answered calmly.

"Stop that," she whispered, grabbing his plate.

"What?" He leaned over the table until the only thing separating them was his plate.

"Looking at me that way. It makes me feel like you're contemplating eating me instead of the food."

"That's a thought," he answered boldly.

She flushed anew, thankful that he was the last in line, lest someone overhear their conversation. She poured the gravy over the fluffy potatoes and handed him his plate. Their fingers touched and their eyes locked.

"Hey, Sheriff, did you ever find out who put that thousand-dollars reward on your head?"

The spell was broken. Sarah pulled back her hand and wadded her fingers into a ball that she rested before her lips as she watched Cole walk away.

"Not yet," Cole answered as he sat down among the group.

"Well, me and my brothers are looking out for you. Must be some kind of lunatic who'd pull a trick like that. But I'm sure that reward Mrs. Hogan's put out—" he nodded toward Sarah—"ought to ease your mind a bit."

Sarah blushed and lowered her eyes meekly.

"Yeah, it has," Cole returned, smiling at Sarah.

After the men finished eating and returned to work, the women fixed their plates and sat down to eat before tackling the job of cleaning up. Sarah couldn't eat for watching Cole as he scaled the timbers and began nailing the tin covering in place. She knew she should be ashamed of her thoughts, but she had passed those feelings after their first night together and had left her recriminations behind. It didn't do any good to scold herself, or to lie to herself that she wouldn't do it again. Given the opportunity, she would go to him, anytime, anywhere.

For the first time in her life, she was in love, deeply, completely. Their romance wasn't the conventional courtship, yet what she felt she couldn't dismiss lightly. It was the strongest emotion she'd ever experienced.

When Cole stood atop the barn and removed his shirt, Sarah almost came off the bench. Her heartbeat picked up and a fine sheen of perspiration dampened her face. She watched as he mopped his face and chest with the shirt and then tossed it aside. The sun gleamed off his ebony hair, and his golden back flexed with strength. His movement seemed effortless as he applied the hammer time and again.

He was a darkly handsome man with an equally dark past. Sarah knew very little about him, but that didn't keep her from loving him. She hoped someday he would share his secrets with her. One would think the rumors attributed to the man would have frightened the women away. Instead, it drew them like honey. Sarah had seen them falling all over each other to get his attention, or cross the street just to get to speak to him as he sauntered by them. Young and old, ugly or pretty, he treated them all the same. Cole's behavior lately had given credence to the reputation that followed him.

She shuddered when she thought of the day he'd brought the lifeless bodies of three men into town, slung over their horses like sacks of potatoes. The look on his face had been as stormy as his gray eyes. And the incident with the gunslinger the day of the Wild West show, still frightened her, bringing home to her just how deadly he was. There were so many sides to him that she wondered if she would truly ever know him. He called it a job, yet how could he touch her with such tenderness one moment, and in the next, kill with such savageness? Every day she witnessed a different facet of Coleman Blade. The people of Hazard accepted him as a part of their own, regardless of his reputation, much like they had accepted her. Both were a link in this tight-knit community.

Her daydreaming shattered when a commotion began on the barn. A man lying spread-eagle on the roof had

Cole's leg, pulling and tugging.

"Damn it, let go of me," Cole stormed out.

"I thought you was a goner, Sheriff. Can't have you fallin' and breakin' your neck."

"I just dropped a couple of nails. I wasn't falling, I was picking them up," Cole answered stiffly.

"My mistake," the man answered sheepishly.

Damn it, Cole thought. He didn't know which was worse, somebody trying to kill him, or somebody trying to save him. The problem had gotten so bad he was afraid someone would kill him trying to save him.

Chapter Thirty

A cheerful roar of approval sounded as the men and women stood back and admired their handiwork. It had been a long day, but the finished product more than made up for the aching muscles and sunburned faces. As the sun sank in the west, its orange glow silhouetted the sleek lines of the new barn.

Someone brought out a fiddle, another a harmonica, and before long an odd assortment of musical instruments comprised a lively ensemble. Their execution was off-key for a while, but when they got warmed up, the notes rippled though the evening shadows like a gentle breeze.

Sarah watched the people with admiration. She'd thought that after the completion of the barn they would fall exhausted into their wagons and head home for a much-earned rest. Instead, the hard work had only whetted their appetite for a celebration. They strung brightly-lit lanterns to ward off the encroaching darkness, and built a huge fire with scraps from the building materials.

Marge Tulley produced a bowl of lemonade punch, and the men groaned about the sissy punch and produced their own refreshment. The laughter and backslapping was contagious. As the men sought out their wives to whirl them about the hard-packed earth to a rousing tune, it was a celebration indeed.

Collie and Belle, who'd stayed behind to keep the saloon open, showed up, telling Sarah that the town was dead. They'd closed the saloon and had come to join the fun. It wasn't any time at all until two of Marge's sons had noted their appearance and taken it on themselves to entertain the girls. A rush of gladness warmed Sarah as she watched her friends. The same tinge of sadness that Sarah associated with Collie, still lingered in her friend's eyes, but when she looked at David Tulley, a genuine glow of happiness showed in her face.

Belle was the same beautiful, happy-go-lucky friend Sarah had learned to love months ago. She had her eye on Vince Tulley, and there was no denying it, no matter how hard she tried.

Sarah hadn't talked to Cole since dinner. She'd watched him escort one female after another through the lively dance steps, and was beginning to doubt she would get to spend any time at all with him. She moved through the crowd, getting caught up in the fun. Before long, she was also whirling about the hard-packed earth. She laughed and talked and danced, quenching her thirst often with Marge's lemonade punch.

Sarah looked at the people around her. They were good, hard-working, God-fearing people. She delighted in watching the fun they shared after working to help a neighbor in need.

Ernest Millsaps buzzed through the crowd like a bee dipping and sipping; he was the life of the party. Cora was at his side, not as jubilant as her husband, but just as sincere. That Ernest had sampled the men's brew was quite apparent when he slapped Cora on the bottom and ushered her through the rousing steps of a square dance. He'd apologized over and over to Sarah about the kidnapping, and she'd assured him repeatedly that everything had turned out fine. She wished she could only tell him that in truth the kidnapping had been the most

310

wonderful thing that had ever happened to her.

When the children became tired, they bedded down in the wagons beneath warm quilts. The moon shone brightly and sparkling stars dusted the sky as lilting notes filled the air.

Cole excused himself and scanned the crowd looking for Sarah. She was the only one he wanted to hold. He needed her, to touch her, to know she belonged to him and no other. Throughout the day, he'd caught glimpses of her, yet when the dancing started he'd been unable to get to her. He'd done his duty and played the gentleman to the hilt. He'd smiled and danced and shared the men's liquor, when all he'd wanted to do was have Sarah to himself. She'd whirled by him on the arms of other men and he'd had to grin and bear it. It was all he could do to keep from dragging her away. At last, he spotted her on the arm of Porter Goins. The man was not known for his gracefulness. He swung her to and fro like he was wringing the neck of a chicken. The force of *to* slammed her against his chest, and the momentum of *fro* almost jerked her arm out of its socket. Her coppery hair bounced in the lanternlight, and the smile on her face rivaled the bright moon overhead. He noted her relief when the strains of the music ended. He watched her as she declined an invitation to resume dancing and moved to the sidelines. He couldn't take his eyes off her. This need, this passion he had for her, was like nothing he'd ever experienced.

Lifting her hand, she tried to smooth her tangled hair. Across the heads of the dancers, their eyes locked. Her hand remained poised in midair and the breath became trapped in her chest. He was the most handsome man she'd ever seen, relaxed and confident. Still, she could see the fire burning in his smoky eyes. Her body tingled with the warmth of his gaze, and she wanted nothing

311

more than to touch him. He was not alone in his quest to solve this newfound emotion. Sarah's own passion surprised and shocked her. Her upbringing had not encouraged this behavior, yet she had no control when it came to Cole.

The lifting of a brow and a barely perceptible nod sent more heat rushing through her. She watched as he turned and disappeared into the shadows. Sarah scanned the crowd to see if anyone was watching her, then skirted the dancers and drifted into the darkness. She became bewildered when she couldn't find him. She was sure he had meant for her to follow him. Hadn't he? she wondered, standing in the shadows of a copse of trees. Suddenly a warm breath caressed her ear as Cole lifted her hair and placed his mouth against her neck.

"Oh," she whispered, turning in his arms.

His mouth moved across hers with the familiarity of a lover as her arms locked about his neck. He tasted the way age-mellowed whiskey smelled, mingled with a trace of tobacco.

He moved against her as their lips sought the sweet nectar of their joining. He could never hold her close enough or kiss her deep enough, unless they were making love. Then and only then was he confident that she was his.

Their tongues touched and retreated, touched again. He cupped her face with callused hands and traced the sleek lines of her jaws silhouetted in the shadows. "I've missed you," he moaned into her mouth.

"Didn't look like it," she teased, nuzzling his hand.

He lifted his head and peered at her, his brow arched in askance. "Look who's talking. You've broken more hearts here tonight than . . . well, nothing comes to mind just now. I can't think straight when you look at me like that. But believe me, you have."

Suddenly the night was alive with the melody of a waltz. Sarah knew even with her limited experience that the way Cole was holding her and moving against her to the rhythm was not proper. Yet, how could she resist him when he felt so good. She wrapped her arms around him and let him guide her through the night. He moved them deeper and deeper into the trees until they could barely hear the strains of the music. In the lee of an ageless oak they renewed the passion that always simmered just beneath the surface. He nibbled her neck and placed hot, wet kisses across her face, his lips teasing hers into bold response. He loosened the ribbon from her hair and let the sweet-smelling tresses cascade around them like a silken curtain. "Do you have any idea what you do to me?" he whispered huskily.

"What?" she whispered heavily.

He took her hand and placed it at the front of his pants. His swollen manhood throbbed against her hand, the heat emanating from him warming her hand. Through the fabric she stroked him, bringing a hoarse groan from him that was lost in the heat of her mouth as his lips closed over hers.

Her arms became trapped when he loosened the buttons of her dress and pulled the bodice to her waist. Her creamy flesh gleaming in the faint light played havoc on his control. He teased first one darkened nipple then the other, just barely grazing the delicate fabric with his tongue. Sarah worked her arms free of the confining material and placed her hands on the back of his head, drawing his head to her breast. She strained against him until his mouth closed over a sensitive nipple, then she became perfectly still as he seduced her with pleasure. When he moved from one aching breast to the other, the cool fingers of night air touched the damp fabric and blended with the heat of her passion.

He propped a booted foot atop a decaying stump and pulled her between his legs. She tugged his shirt from his waistband and ran her hands beneath the fabric. Spreading her fingers, she furrowed the springy curls on his chest and trapped his nipples between her thumb and forefinger, then wiggled her thumb.

He groaned, and ripped the shirt over his head so he could feel her against him. Again their mouths united in a bone-jarring, knee-weakening fusion. Their fingertips touched briefly before they passed on to other explorations. Even as their passion soared, they took the time to relish the special pleasures of the other.

Cole's hands found their way beneath Sarah's dress and petticoats. He stroked the inside of her legs and teased the warm flesh just beneath her drawers, his fingers flirting across her womanly softness. His hands moved over her like the shadows of darkness, seeking and finding all the secrets of her body. He cupped her bottom and lifted her until she rested against him.

Her body flooded with eagerness. She could stand it no longer as she moved her hands until they were between their bodies. Her hand overflowed with his fullness. She had to touch him. She loosened the buttons of his pants until his manhood sprang free. His flesh was hot and pulsing as she wrapped her hand around him, her fingers stroking the fullness. He rocked against her in rhythm with the motion and slid his fingers swiftly into her welcoming body. Moans of pleasure mingled with the night sounds and their bodies sought to assure each other of the words neither spoke.

With her dress bunched around her waist and her drawers cast onto the forest floor, Cole positioned her beneath the limbs of the oak and entered her mightily and swiftly, plunging deeply and rapidly. Sarah never knew if they stood there an hour or a few moments. She

314

only knew her body surged with heat, and Cole was the only one who could quench her fire. They burned together until the fire raged out of control and consumed them. Then suddenly the flames dwindled, and she was aware of sweat dripping from Cole onto her breast. She lifted her face to him and licked the salty beads from his flesh.

His forearm rested against the tree, and when he moved it, she saw him grimace. She turned his arm over to see raw skin. "It's nothing. I just got carried away," he said.

Sated as they were, Cole still couldn't resist the warm softness of her body. He lifted her hair from her neck and kissed a path to her lips. "We'd better get back before we're missed," he whispered against the pulse beating erratically in her neck.

She nodded and began adjusting her clothes.

"I'll do that." He turned her around, and repositioning her dress, he buttoned her up slowly, stroking her bare skin as he anchored each button.

"You're very good at undressing me and very slow at dressing me," she teased over her shoulder.

"It's just that once you're dressed, I don't know how long it will be before I get to undress you again."

"I'm at your beck and call, you know that."

"Yes, I know, and I'm sorry, but for now that's all I can offer."

"I'm not complaining," she whispered, turning in his arms. She kissed him in a way that made up for all the lonely nights, the confusion, and the promises he never made.

He walked her back to the edge of the trees and watched as the darkness claimed her, then the light, as she rejoined the gathering.

Guilt ate away at him as he pondered their situation.

315

What had he done to Sarah? Where was he leading her? He was hellbent for destruction and he didn't want her hurt in the process. She was a good woman, a hard worker, honest to a fault, and completely loyal. He took her body and offered nothing in return. She deserved *more* and he sure as hell wasn't the *more*. He was everything she didn't need in her life. He was the bad man, a drifter, a killer, and his loyalty was to no one. It was only after coming to Hazard that he'd lost some of his cynicism and had developed what he might term as friendship with the late James Moore and Wes Norman. Oh, he was pleasant enough, and when it suited him, he could charm the birds out of the trees. But for the most part, it had never suited him to develop friendships. Chin had always been the only person Cole could truly call friend.

He often wondered if he'd seen too much death, or killed too quickly to experience the joys of living. Sarah Beth Hogan had offered him a glimpse of happiness, and, whether or not he wanted it, the fringe benefits of trust. She regarded him as special. Hell, he'd never been special to anyone. And god, the way she looked at him, heated his blood, and fueled his desire. She didn't badger him about his way of life or try to change him. No, Sarah had accepted him the way he was. When she feared for his safety, she set about in her own way to help him. The reward she'd offered had been the damnedest thing. But it was her way. She'd seen him at his worst, yet in truth, his worst might be his best. He was fast and deadly and no one could surpass his reputation. Money had never been a problem for him—a hired gun brought good money. He'd never squandered his pay, and his needs were few. Blood money, that's what it was—but hell, it spent just like anybody else's dollar. Still, lately that had begun to bother him. Was that what he wanted, for his fellowman to fear him, to leave a legacy of dead bodies and nameless faces?

Sarah moved through the crowd reluctantly. She didn't want to be with anyone right now. She wanted to be by herself so she could think about Cole, to relive every breathless moment she'd spent with him. Her fingers skimmed her lips, puffy from his hungry kisses, and her skin tingled just thinking about him and what they had shared. She felt things with Cole that nothing could have prepared her for. It amazed her when she thought of the way just a look from him could send her blood singing through her veins. Even more astounding was his response to her slightest touch. It was wonderful to have the ability to give him such pleasure, but the delights were twofold because he held the same gift. Right now she would settle for the stolen moments they could have, but someday she wanted more, much more.

Chapter Thirty-one

Sarah dressed with care, hoping she would see Cole sometime during the day. She had errands to run, and she wanted to visit with Wes for a while. He was busy and she was busy. Still, they were good friends and she missed his company. The time was flying by, and her year would be up before she knew it. Who would have ever thought Sarah Beth Hogan could, or would, run a saloon and make a profit? Did she want to give it up after a year? She didn't know. She kind of liked the responsibility. Everything depended on the sheriff. She would give up anything to have him.

All of Sarah's life she'd daydreamed and pretended. Coming to Hazard hadn't changed that; she still fantasized. She dreamed of being married to Cole and living on the outskirts of town, running the ranch together, the way it should be. He wouldn't have to hire out his gun any longer. He could settle down and raise cattle, and she could take care of him and their home, and someday their children. Their life would be perfect. She would make him happy; she knew she could.

Before she reached the foot of the stairs, she saw the girls and Billy talking with Cole. Her heart turned a somersault. Billy said something and Cole threw back his head in laughter. She always got a warm feeling of family when she saw her friends and the man she loved talking and laughing together. Everything had always been so serious in her grandfather's home. There was no time for laughter, only work and worship. Idle hands were the devil's workshop, and her grandfather had been determined the devil would store none of his tools in their home.

Thank you, Lord, for bringing me to Hazard, Texas, Sarah thought.

Cole saw Billy shift his attention toward the stairs, and followed his gaze.

Sarah . . . the beat of his heart. Her eyes sparkled when she met his burning look. He'd had no sleep since they'd parted the night before. After leaving the Tulleys', he'd spent a restless night trying to get his life and future in perspective. He didn't claim to know the future by any stretch of the imagination. But he did know Sarah was part of it. He was ready to make a commitment. She'd put his life on an even keel. Without her, he was the gunslinger, the drifter, and little else. With her, he was a man with purpose.

He lifted his hand toward her. She placed her fingers against his, and a ribbon of warmth flowed between them. He studied her face before his eyes drifted over her. She was a vision in a dress of ivory and lace. A delicate gold chain caught his attention. He followed the length of chain to a golden locket resting between her breasts.

He could feel his blood turning cold and hate erupting in his heart as he wrapped his hand around the locket. He closed his eyes, trying to control the violence surging through him. The muscles in his jaw jerked spasmodically as he opened his eyes and turned the locket over. Etched on the back were the initials *L.B.*

Suddenly, the memory of another woman plagued him. He could see his father, pleased with a locket he'd gifted his wife with, and brushing her hair aside to fasten the clasp. He could hear her laughter and pleasure as she

319

exclaimed over the gift. Then he heard her sharp voice as it rang through his head. "I don't want you or the boy. I've found a real man, a man who will buy me nice things and take me to exciting places."

"Cole, what's wrong?" Sarah asked, placing her hand on his arm.

"You," he answered harshly, dropping the locket and knocking her hand aside.

"What have I done?" she pleaded.

He grabbed the locket, causing the chain to dig painfully into the back of her neck.

"Where did you get this?"

"From my father's desk. I must have overlooked it earlier. I found it this morning. What does it have to do with anything?"

Bitterness turned the corners of his mouth into a mockery of a smile. "Like you . . . it has everything to do with my past."

"I'm not part of your past," she replied softly.

"You are now," he answered coldly before turning on his heel.

"Cole," she called.

But it was too late. He was gone. The only evidence of his presence was the fanning of the batwing doors.

Tears streamed down her face, and her chest heaved in agony. "What happened?" she sobbed brokenly as Billy took her in his arms and tried to comfort her.

Collie and Belle were stunned as they also tried to make heads or tails of what had taken place.

"You say you found this in your father's desk?" Billy asked, turning the locket in his hand.

"Y-yes," she cried, taking the hanky Belle handed her. "I thought I'd gone through everything in the desk. The locket must have been stuck in there somewhere, and when I was going through the drawer, I knocked it loose. This morning, when I pulled out the drawer, there it was.

I didn't know what the initials on the back meant, but I thought the locket was beautiful."

"Well, it's for damn sure it meant something to Cole, something very painful," Billy said, studying the locket with a puzzled frown.

In the space of a few moments, Cole's world had unraveled. He'd known, damn it! He'd known she was too good to be true. She was just like all the rest; her packaging was just different. What kind of fool was he? James Moore. Damn, what a laugh! He'd respected the man, gone as far as to become friends with the two-faced bastard. And all that time James had known who he was. He'd said he wanted the best, fastest, meanest gun in Texas. When Cole thought about it, it was really ironic: James Moore, in a roundabout way, had created what Cole was today. He'd taken his family from him and stolen his childhood. Cole had always known that someday he would find the man who had taken his mother and who'd been responsible for his father's death. His hatred had been like cold ashes from a dead campfire, lying undisturbed and doing little damage until rain soaked the earth and leached the minerals, spreading them into the earth. Seeing his mother's locket had leached his soul, spreading hatred into every pore of his body. He'd never felt such betrayal, such disgust. Sarah Hogan was James Moore's daughter and James Moore was his worst nightmare.

Cole kicked the door open and looked around his office. Everything was the same. Funny, he thought, things should be different. His whole life had changed.

"I've a craving to march into his office and give him a piece of my mind," Collie snapped, wringing the cloth out and placing it on Sarah's puffy eyes.

"No, promise me you won't do anything. I have to talk to him."

"Do you think that's wise? I've never seen him so angry."

"I have to know about the locket. Do you know where my father got it?"

"Beats me. I've never seen it before."

"Do you think the *B* stands for Blade?"

"Could be. That might explain his reaction when he saw it."

"Maybe it belonged to his mother or a sister. I wonder if he has a sister."

"No one knows anything about him, except his reputation. He's always been friendly enough, but as far as volunteering anything about his past, to my knowledge he hasn't," Collie said, pacing the floor.

"I love him, Collie," Sarah sobbed anew.

"I know you do, sugar, and I believe he loves you."

"Oh, Collie, what if he has a wife and the locket belongs to her? I've never thought to ask him if he was married."

"That still wouldn't explain how it came to be in your father's possession."

Sarah pushed herself from the bed and picked up her hairbrush. "I'm going to see him, Collie, I have to know. Will you hand me that ribbon."

When Sarah left the saloon, twilight was fast approaching. The only indication of her sorrow was the redness of her eyes. She didn't stop and talk to the storekeepers as they locked their doors for the day, or pass a few words with the children playing in the street. Her step was brisk and her purpose determined as she marched across the street. The afternoon had passed in a blur. She'd wallowed enough in her sorrow. She wanted some answers, and by golly, she'd resolved to get them.

They might not be what she wanted to hear, but her heart was involved and she couldn't live with the uncertainty. She couldn't fix it if she didn't know what was broken. And she had every intention of trying to fix whatever it was that had put the anger and hatred on Cole's face.

As she reached the jail, she lifted her hand to knock, then decided against it. After the look on his face this morning, she knew he would turn her away if he had the opportunity. She stiffened her back, took a deep breath, said a hasty prayer, and pushed open the door.

The room was a network of shadows, and cigarette smoke drifted like flat clouds close to the ceiling. Cole sprawled in a chair, his legs stretched before him across the corner of the desk, his hand rested loosely around the neck of a whiskey bottle that tilted precariously against his stomach.

Through slitted eyes, he watched her cross the room. When she reached the front of his desk, he lifted the bottle as though in salute or mockery—she couldn't tell which—and tilted it to his lips. Never taking his eyes from her, he took a long drink, then swiped the back of his hand across his mouth.

To her dying breath, Sarah would never know why she did what she did, but if Cole wanted to be a horse's ass, then she'd show him she could be one also.

"May I?" She leaned forward and peeled his fingers from the bottle.

He watched her closely, his brow raised in surprise.

Lifting the bottle to her mouth, she placed her lips where his lips had been only scant seconds before. She could smell the strong liquor before it ever touched her tongue. Willing her stomach to accept the substance, she tilted the bottle and, mimicking Cole's actions, she took several gulps. The liquor scorched all the way down, and she knew for sure the lining of her throat and stomach

323

had burned away. All she wanted to do was throw up, but her pride wouldn't allow it. The only evidence of her struggle was the tearing of her eyes, and her rapid swallowing. She handed the bottle back to him and brushed the back of her hand across her lips.

"Ahh . . . I needed that," she lied, when she could get her breath.

"May I ask when you took up drinking?" In spite of himself, he had to struggle to keep the humor out of his voice.

"Today," she answered truthfully.

"Would you care for another?" He offered her the bottle.

"No . . . no, I've had my quota for the day.

"It does quite well numbing the mind for short periods of time."

"Would you tell me why you want to numb your mind?"

It was as though someone pulled a mask over his face. His features became harsh, his eyes distant.

"I made a mistake," he answered shortly.

It was an ominous beginning, but nonetheless it was a beginning.

"Would you care to elaborate?"

"No."

"You're not going to make this easy for me, are you?"

"I'm not going to do anything," he replied remotely.

"Well, at least you're talking to me. That's more than I expected after the scene this morning. Now, let me see if I can figure this out," she said, pacing the room.

Cole couldn't take his eyes off her. But he wouldn't let himself feel any of the tender emotions he'd felt for her earlier. She was James Moore's daughter. She was his revenge. He tilted the bottle to his lips.

"Are you married?" she blurted.

The lip of the bottle cracked against his teeth and the

liquor spewed from his mouth. "Am I what?" he bellowed.

"Married."

"God no, I haven't completely lost my mind."

Sarah's mouth curled up in a grimace even as relief poured through her. She pulled the locket and the delicate chain from the pocket of her dress and tossed it to Cole. "I don't know what this means to you, but I want you to have it."

The muscles jerked in Cole's jaw as he rubbed the chain between his fingers. He lifted his head to Sarah, and the look in his eyes frightened her. "Just get out of my sight and leave me the hell alone."

"Why? What have I done?" she pleaded.

He pondered the question for a moment. "I guess I owe you that much, although I don't know why. But I want your word that after I tell you, you'll leave me alone. There's no place in my life for you, Sarah."

Tears sparkled in her eyes and she tried valiantly to blink them away. "Did you mean anything you said to me, or was it just words to get me in bed?"

"Just words," he answered coldly, holding up the chain. They both watched as the locket swayed in the faint light. "This belonged to Lois Blade . . . my mother."

"I'm sorry," Sarah admitted, but she didn't know why.

"I helped my father pick it out. We were so pleased with the gift and so anxious to give it to her, we couldn't wait for her birthday." His fingers closed around the swaying locket. "She liked nice things."

"What happen to her?"

"She found someone who could give her nicer things. *Things* meant a hell of a lot more to her than her husband and son," he said bitterly.

"I'm sorry."

325

"Why? It was your father who offered her nicer *things*."

"I don't believe that," she sobbed.

"Well, it's the damned truth. You said you found this in his desk." He shook the chain at her. "How the hell do you think it got there?"

"What about your father? Maybe he got rid of it after she left," Sarah asked wildly.

When he looked at her, the hatred roiling in his face would have sent a lesser opponent to his knees. "That's not likely. My father died pursuing her and her lover."

Sarah knelt beside his chair. When she would have touched him, he pushed her hand away and stood up. "Don't."

"Please, Cole. Even if what you say is true, and I can't believe it is, it's not my fault."

"When I found my father's body that day so long ago, I swore then that someday I would have my revenge. I knew I would find out who took her, and who was responsible for my father's death. I've always known I'd find out."

"But James Moore is dead," she implored.

"You're not, and you're his daughter."

"Then, take your revenge. If it will make you feel better, take your pound of flesh."

"I already have," he said quietly.

When his meaning registered, her heart wept in her breast as she recalled her eagerness, her abandonment when they made love. Never had she thought to deny him. She loved him. She had opened herself to him, taking only that which he offered, yet all the time hoping for more. She studied him as he stood in the shadows, his face cold and foreboding. And at last she admitted to herself that he meant every word he'd said. There was to be no reconciliation, no happy-ever-after. This was life and this was real, and all she had left was her pride,

326

though tattered and torn. As she'd done so many times when she'd confronted the wrath of her grandfather, she relied on her inner strength. Cloaking herself in what little dignity she had remaining, she rose from beside his empty chair. Squaring her shoulders, she made her way across the room to the door. It was the hardest thing she'd ever had to do. And she'd never *ever* forget forcing herself to put one foot in front of the other, as every touch, every kiss, every word she and Cole had shared, rolled through her head like moving pictures.

She closed the door quietly, and at last her shoulders slumped and her tears fell freely. She was trying to decide her destination when something hit the window beside her. Turning her head, she saw the gold chain and locket slither down the glass, twinkling in the shadows. She'd give anything if she'd never seen that evil thing. It had ruined her life, her happiness.

The air was cool and complete darkness was quickly approaching as Sarah made her way through the cemetery. Weathered tombstones emerged from the ground like battle-scarred soldiers guarding their positions. Sarah knelt at the grave of her father, running her hand over his tombstone, the graying wood smooth beneath her touch. She felt bereft and deeply saddened that Cole thought her father could do anything so cruel.

But could he? She hadn't known him. Still, something inside her wouldn't let her believe her father would stoop so low, not a man who had kept yellowed photographs of a daughter he hadn't seen since she was a baby. Her tears rolled unchecked down her face as she poured out her heart, leaving out nothing. When she finished, she felt no comfort or peace. Instead her burden weighed heavier than before. Her heart was broken and there was nothing she could do.

For one heart-stopping moment, a step behind her frightened her until Billy's soft voice shattered her fear.

"Sarah, I've come to take you home," he volunteered. "I was worried about you."

"Thank you. I guess I let the time get away from me. I just needed to be by myself for a while. How did you know where I was?"

"Just a lucky guess. Would you like to talk about it? I'm a good listener," he offered.

Hesitantly she began talking, and before long, the whole story came tumbling out. She told him about her lonely childhood, her grandparents, and her browbeaten mother, her father's will, and the fear of doing as he requested. She told him about Cole, and how she felt. Then she told him that the locket had belonged to Cole's mother.

Billy listened intently and offered his opinion when the discussion warranted. His interest was sincere, and surprisingly, his advice was sound. Before he answered her, he put a great deal of thought into his response. He agreed that he didn't think her father would pull a stunt like the one Cole accused him of, just from what he'd learned of James Moore since coming to Hazard.

Oddly enough, the comfort she'd been denied from the graveside came in volumes from the ragged Billy Ward.

The pain of rejection was still there, and her heart still wept with misery, but there in the darkness and chill of the cemetery a new and growing respect blossomed. And an odd kind of love developed for the slovenly Billy Ward that she would carry with her always.

Chapter Thirty-two

The only happy face in the Do Drop In was the handsome face of Dusty Mills. He had a kind word for everyone, and his generosity quirked more than a fair share of brows. Belle was quick to note that he reminded her of the Cheshire cat, but in truth he was probably as mad as a March hare. It was as though he went to bed one night as a rejected suitor, and woke up the next day as the happy groom. His attitude caused Billy unlimited stress and a horde of sleepless nights.

Everyone's concern was for Sarah. She presented herself well, but, like Dusty, she was well-versed in hiding her true feelings. When Sarah heard Belle describe Dusty as a Cheshire cat, she couldn't help pondering the similarity between herself and Alice of *Alice's Adventures in Wonderland*. Instead of following the rabbit into a hole as Alice had done, she had followed Cole and would have continued to follow him—anywhere he wanted to lead her. But he didn't want her under any circumstances.

The hours became days, and the days, weeks, as Sarah and Cole tried to get on with their unhappy lives. And everyone suffered their pain.

Shimmering auburn hair spilled over the pillow and passion lit the green eyes with a budding fire as she arched her hips, welcoming him. Cole stroked a throbbing nipple with lingering fingertips as he prepared to plunge himself deep inside her. Suddenly he shot up in his lonely bed, wild-eyed and wide awake, the dream vanishing like a mist. His breathing ragged, he was drenched in sweat and his heart pounded a reckless beat. The bedclothes were twisted and tangled, and he was deeply disappointed that he had awakened. It was only in his dreams that he could hold Sarah, touch her the way he wanted to touch her. When he was awake, he wouldn't allow himself the luxury of thinking about her. Oh, she was always on the fringes of his mind, but that was as close as he would let her be. Her memory was like an elusive shadow that followed closely on his heels. He couldn't put his hands on her, yet he knew she was always there. It was only when the darkness claimed the shadows of his mind that he could hold her.

He fluffed his pillow and leaned against it, dragging his tobacco and matches from the night table, knowing sleep would elude him for the rest of the night.

Sarah was there in everything he did. He saw her every day, sometimes from a distance, sometimes across a crowded room. Still, they could have been in different worlds, for all the encounters brought them. No matter how she tried to hide it, he saw the hurt, the longing. Yet his pain was too fresh to bridge the gap he'd created. Sarah had caused him to do something he'd never done. She'd made him care and that made him vulnerable. He hated the way his stomach lurched every time he chanced a glimpse of her, or heard her sweet lilting laughter.

Trying to stay away from the saloon was like keeping one's tongue away from a chipped tooth. He couldn't do it.

Wes had given him what-for because of his treatment of Sarah, and Collie and Belle were very cool toward him. Even Billy gave him the cold shoulder every time the opportunity presented itself. Cole hadn't said anything to anyone. He was silent and brooding, and kept to himself. One look from his stormy eyes warned any observer to cut a wide path.

The hardest thing for Cole to swallow was the constant presence of Dusty Mills. Mills had made himself the saloon's best customer. Something about the smirk in Dusty's eyes didn't set well with Cole. It was as though Dusty knew everything that had happened and was using it to his advantage. Cole didn't like the idea of Sarah sharing her problems with Mills. He was never far from Sarah's side, pulling out her chair when she sat down, and bringing gifts to her. The saloon looked like a friggin' funeral parlor with flowers scattered about the room. Billy told Cole the flowers were from Dusty, as were candy, a bit of lace for a bonnet, a bolt of shimmering fabric, and on and on.

That was fine with Cole. He wanted Sarah to get on with her life and he would get on with his. He truly wanted this to be so, but he couldn't help wondering why he had this gaping pain inside when he saw Dusty touch her.

Giving up any thought of sleep, Cole pushed the covers aside and began his day.

He'd had a rough day and was in a foul mood as he stood in the doorway of the jail, listening to the music coming from the saloon. The crowd was larger than normal and unusually loud. A team of wranglers had turned up in town, ready to spend their payday and have a good time. From the looks of things, they were accomplishing their goal.

Cole pushed away from the doorjamb and paced the darkened streets of Hazard to his last stop, the Do Drop In. He found his usual spot at the bar and ordered a beer, exchanging small talk with Gunter as he eyed the crowd. Sarah wasn't in the saloon, and he felt a pang of regret that she was absent. Collie and Belle spoke as they picked up trays of drinks, but didn't linger to talk.

The expression on Collie's face caught his attention, and he watched her closely. If he didn't know better, he would think she was frightened. Her face was pale, and she kept glancing toward the corner table. Cole followed her glance. Nothing unusual seemed to be happening at the table, other than a lot of drinking. The men were some of the wranglers who had come into town that afternoon. There were three of them, and they were laughing and talking among themselves. One of the men caught Cole's attention. He didn't bother with a glass, but drank straight from the bottle and watched every move Collie made. His look was sullen and mean. When Collie took a fresh bottle to their table, the man grabbed her arm and said something to her. Cole saw her wince with pain and shake her head furiously.

He saw the tears sparkling in her eyes and her step falter when she approached the bar. "Are you all right, Collie?"

She only nodded her head.

"Is that man giving you a hard time?"

"N-no, everything is fine," she answered too quickly.

Something wasn't right, and Cole knew it just by looking at her. There was always something elusive about Collie, but tonight Cole could smell fear. He'd been in enough situations to recognize the culprit immediately. When he questioned Belle, she didn't know anything, but she agreed that something was going on between Collie and the man in the far corner.

When he asked her where Sarah was, she shrugged her shoulders. "Why do you care?"

"I don't."

"Then, why don't you stay the hell out of her life?"

"I'm trying."

"Not too successfully, I might add."

It was his turn to shrug his shoulders.

"She's with Dusty. They went for a starlit buggy ride," Belle admitted.

Cole swore soundly. "Doesn't she have any better sense than to get mixed up with the likes of him?"

"You, him, what difference does it make? She's headed for hurt either way."

"He's just after her property. He doesn't care about Sarah."

"And I suppose you do?"

Cole dodged her eyes and picked up his beer.

Belle propped her arm on the bar and studied her hands for a moment before turning her attention back to Cole. "You know, your attitude just surprises the hell out of me. You want her, you don't want her. How can you turn your emotions on and off like that? I'd like to know, when all is said and done, what price are you willing to pay to exact your revenge?"

Before he could answer, Collie interrupted them.

"Belle, will you cover for me? I have to get out of here for a little while."

"Sure, honey. Is anything wrong? You look like you've seen a ghost."

"I can't talk about it now. I'll tell you later."

Cole and Belle watched, puzzled, as Collie hurried through the crowd and out into the darkness. Cole

333

turned his attention to the table in the far corner. The man who had grabbed Collie shrugged to his feet and followed her.

"He's trouble," Cole admitted.

"Who is he?" Belle asked, following Cole's gaze.

Cole drained his glass and pushed away from the bar. "I don't know . . . yet."

"But you plan to find out?"

Cole didn't answer as he made his way through the crowd. He stepped out into the darkness and scanned the street. There was no sign of Collie or the man. Leaning against the wall, he took a tobacco pouch from his pocket and rolled a cigarette, his mind awash with the things Belle had said to him. She'd not said anything he hadn't already thought about. The jingle of harness and quiet laughter caught his attention. He didn't have to look to know it was Sarah's tinkling laughter. He'd always loved to hear her laugh. Smoke swirled around his head as he took a deep pull on the cigarette and squinted into the darkness, watching as the buggy came into view. Dusty Mills's laughter joined Sarah's. Cole could see Dusty lower his head and speak softly to Sarah, their two heads bobbing like corks on a pond as they talked. Cole couldn't stand it. With confusion and anger soaking through him, he turned and braced a hand on the saloon door just as a curse rocked the stillness.

"No, please," a voice cried before the sound of a scuffle came from the alley beside the saloon.

Cole threw his smoke to the ground and bounded into the alley. The back door of the saloon was open and cast a dim light. The sight that meet his eyes sickened him. Huddled against the wall, Collie pleaded with her tormentor not to hit her again. Her fingers trembled as she wiped the blood from her mouth and tried to push her tangled hair from her eyes.

"I've not done anything wrong, I'm just trying to make a living."

The man grabbed her by the hair and jerked her from the wall. "Like hell! Admit it, Collie, you like it when the men rub you on the ass as you go by their table."

"No, Sam, you're wrong. They don't do any such thing. I just serve them drinks. That's all, please," she begged, trying to loosen his painful grip on her hair.

"You lying bitch." Before Cole could move, Sam drew back his hand and let go with a roundhouse punch that sent Collie to her knees.

The bloodlust that shot through Cole demanded retribution at any cost. He couldn't believe any man was low enough to hit a woman, for any reason. Cole grabbed the man by the nape of the neck and swung him around.

Surprise flashed across the man's face when he noted the rage in Cole's eyes. "Hey, this is none of your business, Sheriff."

"I've just made it my business," he answered coldly.

Shoving the man aside, he knelt by Collie's crumpled body. Pushing the tangled hair from her face, he smoothed his hand over her battered face. "I'll take you inside. Can you put your arms around my neck?" he asked softly, his throat hoarse.

"Please, just help me up, and I'll be fine. I don't want anyone to see me like this."

"Take your hands off her, Sheriff. I'll take care of her," Sam said.

"Haven't you done enough?" Sarah sobbed, running toward Collie.

Cole looked up in surprise when he heard Sarah's voice.

335

"No! Leave her alone," Sam bellowed. He lunged forward and grabbed Sarah, his arm coiling around her neck like a deadly snake. His revolver rested against her temple. "Back away, Sheriff, or I'll kill her."

A cold fear like nothing he'd ever known surged through Cole when he saw the gun at Sarah's head. "I'll see you in hell first," Cole vowed.

Everyone knew of Cole's reputation, and they knew how fast he was with a gun. But nothing prepared the gathering crowd for the swiftness of the hand wielding the gun that killed Sam Stevens. That their famous sheriff could get a shot off as he knelt at Collie's side was unthinkable. It happened so fast that no one had time to take cover. They stood there slack-jawed, holding their breath as the man called Sam wilted to the ground, his lifeless arm still coiled around Sarah's neck. She fell screaming to the ground. Cole bolted to his feet and caught her up in his arms, his body shuddering with pure terror. She sobbed against his chest until his gentle coaxing quieted her.

Collie was very still as she huddled against the wall, tears streaming from her swollen eyes, her chest heaving with anguish as she stared at the lifeless body.

"It's all right, Collie. He can't hurt you anymore," Sarah assured her in a voice choked with emotion.

"It doesn't matter. He's hurt me enough to last a lifetime," Collie cried. "He always thought the very worst of me, and I didn't do anything to deserve his accusations. The only thing I ever did was love him."

A shocked gasp left Sarah. "You knew him?"

"He was my husband," Collie sobbed.

They settled Collie in bed and sent Billy for the doctor. After Doc left, Sarah and Belle sat by her bed long into the night, listening as Collie told them about Sam.

Their marriage had been a marriage of false hopes

336

and dreams. Sam couldn't control his wild imagination. When he thought of something, it ate away at him until jealous rages consumed him. Collie had tried to love him enough to prove that she would never want anyone but him. This had only made him think she was trying to cover up her indiscretions.

The first time he'd hit her, he had cried and sworn he would never do it again, and he hadn't again for a long time. But out of the blue, something would always set him off, and he would go wild, hitting and kicking and cursing her as though she were less than human. Collie had done everything she could think of to help him, but something had tormented him, something she couldn't understand. Finally, she had realized that the only way to protect herself was to leave him and her shattered marriage behind, because she knew that one day he would kill her.

So unlike his life, Sam's funeral was quiet and peaceful. Collie's black-net veil couldn't hide her distorted features, or the mass of bruises that covered her face. Yet, she mourned the man as though he'd been the finest of husbands. When Sarah offered her time off from work with pay, Collie refused, saying she needed to be near her friends and she wanted to stay busy.

Cole helped with everything. He was there with a gentle word and a helping hand. Still, he felt like he viewed the happenings from afar. Something inside him wouldn't turn loose of his fear. Over and over, he saw Sarah with the gun resting at her temple. He brooded until he wasn't fit company even alone, and he wore a path in the pine floor at the jail. Collie's bruised and battered face stayed alive in his memory.

Plagued by his treatment of Sarah, he found no rest. Wasn't he doing the same thing to her, except in a different form? Was it his place to pay for the sins of his father, or, in this case, the sins of his mother? Could he blame Sarah for the sins of her father, expecting her to pay for something of which she had no knowledge? Revenge was a cold bedmate, and its arms bound with bands of steel. Did it comfort him with its embrace? No! It smothered and spread like a poison eating away at the goodness and love he so desperately wanted to share, and he'd have no more of it. He'd made his bed, but he would be damned if he would lie in it.

If Sarah would forgive him, he would try to make things right for them.

He decided a change of clothes and maybe a bouquet of flowers would soften her up for his confession.

Chapter Thirty-three

Sarah sat in the shade of a cluster of trees and watched a furry caterpillar crawl over her skirt, her mind dwelling on anything other than her broken heart.

A bittersweet smile played at the corners of her mouth. From all the sadness and confusion something good had emerged: The sadness in Collie's eyes was gone. A glimmer of hope and happiness shone brightly from her eyes. Cole had put that look on her face. It had taken a violent act to shatter Collie's fear—but, then, it had been violence that had put the fear there in the first place. Collie had told Sarah she'd always known Sam would show up someday, and every day of her life she had lived with that fear. She was ready to get on with her future. She couldn't let *what if*s rule her life. She'd done everything to make her marriage work and make her husband happy. Collie told Sarah that life had a funny way of getting one's attention. After all the heartache, she could take pleasure in the simple things—a friendly smile, the sun on your face, good friends, and most of all, the attention of David Tulley. He'd made several trips into town only to see Collie. And the glow of happiness on Collie's face pleased Sarah immensely.

The attention of Dusty Mills had quickly tired her. She'd wanted nothing to do with the man, yet every time she looked up, he was there with a gift clutched in his hands. Somewhere along the line she'd decided to accept his attention in hopes of gaining information about him, and finding out if he'd placed the reward on Cole. So far her plan had failed miserably. She knew no more about him now than she had previously.

The sound of a carriage interrupted her thoughts. She watched as the driver pulled the horses to halt. An elderly lady emerged from the buggy, brandishing a cane as if it were her link to survival. The gentleman driving the carriage didn't appear any younger than his passenger. The cracking of bones and grunts of exertion saw the lady to the ground. With her cane in tow, she approached Sarah.

"Young lady, could you please tell me if we are within a day's journey of Hazard, Texas? I fear we've become lost and will wander around here in the wilderness until we are only shells of our former selves."

"Yes, ma'am, you're just on the outskirts of town," Sarah said, rising to her feet. "Can I help you?"

"If you don't mind the intrusion, could I join you for a few moments. I've bounced on that seat until my posterior will never fit properly in a decent chair again."

"Yes, please do. I would enjoy the company." Sarah couldn't deny the smile that brightened her face.

"Bernard, my chair, please."

With knees and arms cracking, the man pulled a chair from the boot of the buggy and placed it in the shade for his mistress. "Would you care for a spot of tea? I can build a fire in no time flat, and you can enjoy your tea before we continue our journey."

"Only if you will join us, Bernard," the lady responded.

"My pleasure, ma'am. I'm as dry as a buzzard's gullet."

As Bernard picked up twigs and limbs for the fire, the elderly lady watched him with a twinkle in her eyes. "A buzzard's gullet? My, my, he has developed the most unusual form of expressions since traveling in the West. Quite delightful, if I do say so, and I must admit it leaves you in no doubt of what someone means."

"You're English?"

"It couldn't have been the accent, could it?" the lady teased.

"Odd that you should say that. I'd never in my life met anyone from England until recently. Now I've met two people in the space of a couple of months."

The lady's brow quirked oddly. "Is that so?"

"Yes, ma'am. A very beautiful English lady has just recently inherited property in Hazard."

"Did you hear that, Bernard?"

"Yes ma'am."

"What's this young lady's name, if I may be so bold?"

"Juliet Barrington," Sarah said hesitantly.

The cane hit the ground with a resounding thud.

"I heard, I heard," Bernard called as he bent over the small fire. He placed his hand at the small of his back and rose like a spring uncoiling by degrees, then shuffled to his mistress. His watery blue eyes took in her distress. He placed a weathered hand on her shoulder, patting her several times. "It just isn't so, miss. This is Juliet Barrington."

"What?" Sarah's confusion was rampant.

"Yes, Juliet Barrington. I'm afraid what it all boils down to is that my maid, Olivia, is passing herself off as me."

His anger fueled, Bernard interrupted. "That little twit was no more than a scullery maid when Miss Barrington took her under her wing and trained her to be

341

a lady's maid. Milady even taught her how to talk. When she joined us, her brogue was so thick you could cut it with a knife. And how did she repay the hand that fed her? She stole Miss Barrington's identity, as well as her betrothed, leaving Miss Barrington here at death's door." It took several seconds for Bernard to catch his breath after his loquacious speech.

"It's true, my dear. She was taken by my Andrew the first time she laid eyes on him—as was I. You see I am quite a bit older than my betrothed. And I fear the adage that 'love is blind' has its merits."

"Humph, you were the best thing that ever happened to that backwater varmint," Bernard intoned harshly, shuffling back to the fire.

"You'll have to excuse Bernard. His views are a bit one-sided. He's been with me for years. And I fear if he were younger, he would have set out to defend my honor. But I was so terribly ill for a while, he wouldn't leave my side."

"He must care for you a great deal." Sarah whispered, aware of how Cole had abandoned her at the first opportunity.

"He's devoted to me, but I assure you, his devotion is returned. I couldn't get along without him."

Sarah was having a devil of a time sorting out the astounding news. "Why would your maid take your identity?"

"There are several reasons: wealth, position, and the most important, love. Andrew was a very persuasive man. He was very attentive and full of plans until I became sick. In truth, the doctors didn't believe that I would live, given my age and rundown condition. I fear I tried to keep up a pace that was detrimental to my health. Women are such foolish creatures when it comes to men."

"Amen," Sarah agreed before she could stop herself.

They eyed each other in agreement and suddenly burst out laughing. From the small fire where he was tossing twigs on the blaze, Bernard chuckled.

A frown darted across Sarah's face. She leaned forward whispering, "If your maid would pull a trick like taking your identity, there's no telling what else she might do if she's forced to face you. Your life might very well be in danger."

"You're right. What do you propose that I do?"

One idea after another popped into Sarah's head, yet she hesitated to express any of them. The thought that this could be a life-threatening situation caused her to consider her actions carefully. She couldn't let an impulsive act endanger the lady and her servant. After much consideration, she jumped to her feet and dusted herself off. "I'm going to take you to see the sheriff. He'll know what to do."

"What if Olivia should see us?"

"I've thought of that. You and Bernard can ride inside the carriage, and I'll drive you into town. I'll go into the sheriff's office and make sure he's alone, then I'll see you inside."

"Thank you. You're very kind to take on the problems of someone you've just met. I don't even know your name, yet I trust you. Isn't that strange?"

"Sarah Hogan's my name, and sometimes things like that just happen."

"Again, thank you, Sarah Hogan. I don't know what I would have done if I hadn't met you?"

"Don't thank me yet."

"Your tea, ma'am."

The dusty carriage sat before the sheriff's office.

Sarah darted from the buggy to the sheriff's office and back again. No one paid any attention to her odd behavior, instead just chalking it up to her saddened condition of late.

Cole snapped to attention and looked on in confusion when Sarah rushed into his office, and just as quickly disappeared after instructing him not to move—she'd be "right back."

At first, his heart had swelled with happiness when he saw her. He thought she'd received the flowers and the note he'd taken to the saloon earlier. Now he didn't know what to make of her odd behavior. Leave it up to Sarah to keep him completely confused. The door swung wide as she quickly ushered a lady and elderly gentleman into the office. At once, she locked the door and began lowering the shades. Cole watched in amazement as she seated the couple and placed herself behind them as though protecting them.

"Cole, I have brought you a tremendous problem, and we need your help." She squeezed their shoulders as the pair nodded their heads in agreement.

Cole smiled in amusement, wondering what Sarah had got herself into this time.

Sarah took a deep breath. "This is Juliet Barrington and her companion, Bernard."

"What?"

"This is—"

"I know what you said," he growled. "I only wonder why you said it."

"Because it's the truth."

The pair nodded their heads again.

Cole shook his head and plowed his hand through his hair, totally confused. He lifted his hand toward the lady. "This is Juliet Barrington?"

"Yes," the trio chorused.

"Then, who is the lady living at the Roberts ranch?"

"My maid, Olivia."

The palm of Cole's hand hit his forehead and he shook his head in disbelief. "You're the weary bones," Cole blurted out.

Sarah gasped. Bernard cleared his throat and Juliet Barrington's laughter filled the room. "Indeed, I am."

Embarrassment flooded him. "My apologies, ma'am. I meant no disrespect. It's just that I've always been suspicious of the Juliet living at the Roberts ranch. In truth, I had a friend search the house. He found the letter to your friend, Louise. I read it, and you mentioned weary bones. It struck me odd at the time that Juliet Barrington would refer to herself that way."

"Apology accepted. I did say that, and it's completely true."

Sarah looked on in shock. And all the time she'd thought his interest in Juliet had been romantic.

"Maybe you should start at the beginning," Cole requested.

No one said anything as Juliet shared what had happened to her. Occasionally Bernard would snort, but otherwise kept his comments to himself. Sometimes the chain that Cole twisted idly in his hand would tingle against the locket. Sarah wanted to jerk the hateful thing out of his hand and stomp it. But she didn't dare. Juliet also watched the swaying of the locket as she told her story. Cole himself was completely unaware that he even held it in his hand.

"Were you betrothed before you reached San Francisco?"

"Oh, dear me, no. I met Andrew at a party I was attending. He was so charming and such a gentleman. He absolutely swept me off my feet."

"Did any of your friends know that you had a

brother in Texas that you planned to visit?"

"Yes, it was the topic of many a conversation. Everyone warned me that Texans were terrible braggarts when talking about their state. I wasn't in San Francisco long before I met Andrew. He was very attentive until I became ill. When the doctors told Bernard there was no hope that I would recover, Andrew disappeared and so did my maid, along with my papers and money. Bernard and I had to live off his savings until I could make arrangements to transfer more funds."

"But, Miss Barrington," Sarah said, "if your maid is the imposter, she's working alone. As far as I've noticed, she has no male companion—with the exception of our fine sheriff here."

"I wouldn't have thought she had the get-up to carry off something like this alone. She's a bit on the lazy side."

Cole didn't mention that Chin had seen Dusty Mills leaving the young lady in the middle of the night. He needed more facts before he shared his knowledge. There was still a big piece of the puzzle missing.

"Sheriff, may I see that locket? Juliet asked.

Puzzled, Cole looked at his hand and saw the chain draped between his fingers. "Yes, of course." He untangled the chain and handed it to the lady, casting Sarah a look of apology and a shrug of his shoulders.

Juliet examined the chain, then the locket, nodding her head all the while. "I thought so," she mumbled.

"Have you thought of something else?" Cole asked.

"No, it's just that I thought this locket looked familiar." She looked around at the eager faces, waiting for her response.

"I'm truly ashamed to tell this. It only verifies what a nosy old lady I am. Anyway, one night I couldn't sleep, so I walked down to Andrew's room. We were staying

346

in the same hotel. I hated to disturb him, but he'd always said anytime I needed him, day or night, not to hesitate to call on him. The door was open and I saw myself in. He was enthralled—yes, that word fits perfectly—completely enthralled in this box he was going through. When I made my presence known, he snapped the lid shut, but I saw the irritation that flashed across his face before he could conceal it. When he left the room to fix me a cup of tea, I couldn't resist looking in the box. It was filled with beautiful jewelry. I particularly remember this piece because of the initials. At the time I wondered if maybe he was seeing someone else and the locket was a gift for her."

Oh please, God not my father, not again, Sarah prayed.

James Moore? Cole thought. He couldn't believe it. And James wouldn't use a phony name. Why should he?

"What did your Andrew look like?" Cole asked.

What a sensible question, Sarah thought. No wonder he's the sheriff. He's so very good at his job, she thought proudly.

"He's medium-built and has a head full of blondish white hair and the most intense blue eyes I have ever encountered."

Sarah's mouth was gaping. Cole scooted to the edge of his chair.

"Oh, yes, and he is very good at any kind of card game. It is truly a joy to watch him play, unless you're the opponent. He's very good."

"Dusty Mills," Cole and Sarah shouted.

"No, Andrew Milhouse," Juliet corrected.

"Dusty Mills," they said, nodding to each other.

Relief poured through Sarah. Then, the locket didn't belong to her father. But how had it gotten in her room, in her father's desk?

Cole's mind was as cloudy as Sarah's, and he thought his heart would surely explode. How had the locket come to be in Sarah's possession?

"Dusty Mills," they whispered in unison.

Completely confused, Miss Barrington shouted, "Who is Dusty Mills?"

"Andrew Milhouse," the happy couple replied.

Cole wanted to draw Sarah into his arms and kiss her until they were both breathless. But there were so many things to do. He couldn't keep this quiet. He needed help; he needed a meeting. And he needed it now.

Cole walked Sarah outside and praised her for bringing Juliet to him, while his mind rallied with the fear of what might have happened if Sarah had taken it into her head to take care of the situation herself. Miss Barrington's life was indeed in danger, and she needed protection. He also intended on asking her if she would accept his apology. He wanted nothing more than to get this rift between them settled, yet so many other things required his attention. Still, he would allow himself just a few moments alone with her. He had to know.

Something about the tilt of her head and the spark in her eyes didn't encourage familiarity, yet he couldn't help himself. He lifted his hand and touched the side of her face.

She turned away.

"Sarah?" he whispered.

"Don't."

"Why? I want so badly to touch you."

"Because I can't handle it."

"But I thought, maybe—"

She snapped around, her attention fully on his handsome face. She wouldn't let that face and winsome smile deter her. "You thought what, Cole? That since

348

we know my father was innocent of the things you accused him of that I would fall in your arms like some dimwitted, lovesick fool? Well, *not* today, my handsome sheriff."

"Would tomorrow be soon enough?" he teased, before he understood that she was spitting mad. He realized his error soon enough.

He saw stars and his ears rang like chapel bells when her hand landed with a resounding wallop against his face.

She was mortified that she had done something as irrational as striking another person, especially the one she loved beyond all else. "I'm sorry. I didn't mean — yes, I did. I meant it. You deserved exactly what you got, and I'll not apologize."

"Maybe I should be the one apologizing. It's just that when I make up my mind about something, I can be as impulsive as you are."

"And what have you made up your mind about?"

"Us. I decided we weren't responsible for the sins of our parents. That we had our own lives to live, and I wanted to get on with living them. I want you Sarah, any way you'll have me."

"Damn you, Coleman Blade."

Cole's brows shot up in astonishment. *My god, she is serious.* He'd never heard Sarah swear, regardless of the situation.

"What do you think I am?" She flicked her hand against the badge he wore. "I'm not like that piece of metal you put on and take off at will. I can't turn my emotions on and off like you do. You want me, you don't want me. I never know from one day to the next what to expect from you. First, you stay away from me to protect me. We worked through that. You don't want me because you think my father was responsible for the death of your father. And now that Miss Barrington has enlightened us on the locket, you're ready to pick up where we left off. What will it be next week, next month, or next year, Cole? I wanted you to love me before you found out the locket had nothing to do with my father."

"I did, Sarah."

"I wish I could believe you."

"The choice is yours. I'll be here when you decide. Right now I need to get back inside with Miss Barrington. If you'll get Wes and have him come by the office, I'd appreciate it."

"I'll see you later, Cole."

"Think about me."

"I will. I've hardly thought of anything else since the day I wore the locket."

"Me either," he admitted. Hoping, just hoping, he watched her walk away.

Sarah went for Wes. Wes sent for Billy Ward, and Billy sent for Chin. Things were moving quickly, quietly, and efficiently.

It resembled a town meeting at the jail, except there was no teasing or backslapping. The faces were very solemn, and the business at hand very serious. Wes Norman rifled through papers. Sarah sat protectively next to Juliet Barrington and Bernard. Cole paced the floor, and Billy leaned against the door looking outside. It had stunned Sarah when Billy showed up. Cole also had given him a puzzled look, and then something seemed to click in his head, for he had nodded at Billy. Billy had returned the nod as though they shared a secret, and then busied himself watching the street.

Sarah was bursting with happiness, yet now was not

350

the time or the place for her and Cole to discuss their personal affairs. A quickly mouthed *I love you* had been her only concession.

When she'd returned to the saloon, a bunch of smiling, tittering employees had met her.

They couldn't wait to present her with a bright bouquet of forget-me-nots and an accompanying note. "It's from Cole," they chimed, beside themselves with excitement.

She'd torn open the note, and the boldly scrawled words had taken her breath away.

Sarah,
My words can't take away the pain my foolish pride has caused you. But my heart is truly in the right place and my direction is clear.
If there's still room in your heart for me, I would like to move in . . . forever.
Faithfully,
Cole

Sarah had had a hard time controlling the stammer in her voice when she'd asked, "When did he bring this?"

"Right after you left," Gunter had said, beaming from ear to ear. "Is it good news?"

"The very best," she'd admitted. Cole had brought it before he'd even known the real Juliet Barrington existed.

Wes's voice broke her train of thought, and she shifted in her chair. She didn't want to miss a word.

"From the little information I've gathered, it's likely that Dusty Mills overheard your brother talking about your visit and acted on that information. Tracking you down and charming his way into your life, Miss Bar-

351

rington, fits his normal pattern, according to the information I received from outside sources. And I've no doubt that had you not fallen ill, he would have proceeded to return to Hazard with you. When he learned you wouldn't recover, it was probably a blessing for you, Miss Barrington—although a painful one, I'm sure. His plans went awry, and he had no choice but to come up with a new solution. He wanted your land and he wanted it fast. If you had died, it could have taken months to clear up your estate and offer the land for sale, if ever. He was in a hurry. He had to have the land before the railroad offered to buy it. In order to do this, he needed you, or, in this case, someone everyone would think was you. I have no idea what he has promised Olivia, but if it is in our power, we plan to foil his scheme. We have no proof of wrongdoing. He's a very clever man, but I have devised a plan—"

Billy jerked the door open and Chin escorted a very disgruntled former Juliet Barrington into the room. She pulled her arm from Chin's grip and opened her mouth to deliver a scorching setdown, her eyes scanning the room.

Her mistress came to her feet. "Olivia, you look well," Miss Barrington said with all the authority her position signified.

Olivia's face became stark with fear and a slow tremble beset her limbs. Chin helped her across the room and into a chair.

"This is the plan . . ." Wes continued.

Chapter Thirty-four

The town of Hazard was buzzing with the news. Every doorway and street corner was alive with people passing on their rendition of the gossip. Even a few brave souls paused before the doorway of the Do Drop In, craning their creamy necks like cattle trying to eat through a fence, hoping for a glimpse of Sarah. They didn't see her anywhere.

Dusty pulled the sleek palomino to a halt before Mrs. Flowers's dress shop and looped the reins over the hitching post, vaguely wondering about the curious glances cast his way before he entered the dress shop. He wanted to pick up a pair of riding gloves for Sarah. Women's dress shops always inspired him. He liked to touch the delicate trims and smooth silks and satins.

As he stood before the counter fingering the fringe on a bonnet Mrs. Flowers had displayed, he could hear her talking with another customer. "I can tell you one thing, she'll be sadly missed. I've never met a more caring person."

"She's done more to bring the people of Hazard closer together than anyone I know. Why, all the reverend has to do is make a suggestion and her hand is in the air, either volunteering her time or money," the customer put in.

"That's true. I've never met a finer Christian. I don't

care if she does own the saloon," Ida Flowers added vehemently.

Dusty's elbow cracked the top of the counter and the moisture in his mouth completely evaporated. *What the hell is going on?*

"Are you all right, Mr. Mills? You look a little pale."

"Nonsense, I'm fine."

"Isn't it just terrible about Sarah?"

"I'm sorry, I don't know what you're talking about."

"She's leaving Hazard, going back to Tennessee."

"Why?" he asked, hardly able to control his excitement. Now he was certain he could get her property.

"I guess she misses her family. I haven't talked to her since I heard the news. So much has happened in the last few days, I'm having a hard time keeping up with all the news—the wedding taking place so quickly, and now Sarah selling everything and leaving town. I'm just a bundle of nerves, Mr. Mills." She stacked her hands and rested them on the counter. "Now, what can I do for you?"

Dusty's stomach suddenly dropped. He had an idea he wasn't going to like the answer to the question he was getting ready to ask. "What do you mean when you said that Sarah is selling everything?"

"Oh, I'm sorry I've confused you. Like I said, I'm just a nervous wreck. She's already sold everything."

Dusty had known he wouldn't like it.

"Billy Ward bought the saloon. Can you believe that? Who would have thought he had a dime to his name?"

"What about her property?" Sweat was beading his brow.

"I just told you Billy—"

"Not that property. Her ranch."

"Oh, that property. She sold it to our handsome sheriff. Now he and his wife's property will join."

354

Dusty's hands were now trembling uncontrollably. "What wife? He's not married."

"He will be soon. And they make such a lovely couple, don't you think so?"

"I have no earthly idea what you're talking about, Mrs. Flowers."

"You haven't been in town for the past few days, have you, Mr. Mills?"

He shook his head along with his hands.

"Well, like I said, the news has been flying all over town. I'll try to catch you up on what's been happening. Cole Blade and Juliet Barrington are getting married."

His blood froze in his veins.

"Sarah Hogan has sold everything and is returning to Tennessee."

Dusty turned and walked out of the shop. He couldn't bear to hear anything else. Hadn't he planned this down to the last detail? What the hell had happened? Surely he wasn't losing his touch. Wait until he got his hands on that two-faced, two-timing Juliet Barrington. She'd better watch her p's and q's or he would expose her for what she truly was. He knew the truth, and damn it, he'd use it if he had to. He'd made her, given her a new identity, dressed her in the finest cloths, and damn it, she owed him. And he always collected. But first, he would see Sarah Hogan and try to sway her into letting him have the property.

Dusty forced himself to contain his anger. Pasting a smile on his face, he entered the saloon. He wouldn't let himself look to the corner at Sarah's favorite table. Instead, he ordered a drink and lifted it to his mouth before he turned to peruse the room. She was there where she always sat, head bent, sifting through a stack of papers. Dusty had to clench his fists and grit his teeth to keep from pounding her head against the table-top. "Would you like some company?"

Sarah lifted her head, a pleasant smile on her face, "Hello, stranger, I haven't seen you for a while."

"I've been very busy. But I must talk to you, Sarah. I've heard some distressing news."

"Please, join me."

After positioning himself at the table, he lifted Sarah's hand and studied the satiny smooth texture of her skin. He wanted to crush her fingers in his hand until she bent to his will. "Is it true that your property's for sale?"

"Not any longer. I've sold everything." She squeezed his hand. "Isn't it wonderful, Dusty?" She drew her hand away and flipped through the papers in front of her. "Look here, maybe you can help me decide. I'd like to travel awhile before returning to Tennessee, but I can't make up my mind where I want to go."

He'd like to tell her where to go, but he didn't dare, not yet, anyway. "Sarah, I must admit that I was interested in your property."

"Why, Dusty, I didn't know. You should've said something."

"I realize that now. Is it too late? I would be willing to pay whatever you ask plus a sizable bonus, if we could work something out."

"I'm sorry, but we've already completed the deal. I couldn't possible break my word."

You stupid bitch, he thought, gnashing his teeth. He wanted to break something, but it wasn't her word.

"I'm sorry, Dusty."

"It's just that I can't imagine you selling to the sheriff."

"Miss Barrington mentioned, the day of her party, that she would like to buy my place. At the time, I'd never considered selling it. But the more I thought about it, the better I liked the idea." She laughed softly. "The good Lord has given me many things, yet I fear the ability to work a ranch is not one of them. Yes, it is better this way."

"What about the rumor of a spur coming to Hazard? Doesn't that interest you?"

"Not particularly. If it is good for the people of the community, then it will be wonderful. But to my knowledge, it's only a rumor. Cole will have to deal with it, if indeed it's true."

"I didn't realize the sheriff was interested in settling in Hazard."

"He is the sheriff, and since his recent engagement, he wants to make this his permanent home."

"But I thought you and the sheriff were . . . involved."

"Just an infatuation, Dusty, nothing more."

He knew it had been more than infatuation. Maybe she was in the habit of crawling from one bed to another. Hell, women! Who could figure them out? The sweat dried on his body and a chill beset his limbs. He had to get away and plan his next move. There was a solution to this turn of events; he just had to figure it out.

"Is everything all right, Dusty?"

"Yes, I'm just in a hurry, that's all."

"Maybe we can get together later if you're still in town. With Billy taking over the saloon, I find myself with very little to do."

"If you wanted to do something for me, you'd sell me your property." He couldn't keep the bitterness out of his voice as he rose.

The usually immaculate Dusty Mills was beginning to look a little frayed around the edges. His step wasn't as

357

brisk as normal when he left the saloon, and he looked a little piqued. His henchmen fell into step beside him when he walked outside, and exchanged puzzled frowns when Dusty had trouble remembering where he'd left his horse.

His intention was to confront the two-timing, double-dealing Juliet Barrington before he heard any more news. After rapping his knuckles against her door until they were near bloody, one of her ranch hands informed him she hadn't been on the place for a couple of days. Dusty was beside himself. How could he punish the bitch if he couldn't find her? Sheriff Cole Blade was the crux of his problem. He knew it as well as he knew that Juliet Barrington was a phony. Everything had run smoothly until Blade had taken over as sheriff. Something had to be done about that man before he fouled up everything. But Blade was a hard man to kill. He'd tried repeatedly. The thousand-dollar reward he'd offered had turned into a joke after Sarah put up her reward for two thousand dollars. And that was something else. Why would she try so hard to protect the sheriff if all she felt for him was infatuation? Infatuation, my ass! He wasn't buying that for a minute. The sheriff had seen a way to become a rich man, and he was taking advantage of it. He couldn't have both women, so he'd played both ends until he got what he wanted. Smart man, the sheriff. But Dusty was smarter. He'd make them wish they'd never heard the name Dusty Mills. Damn it, he'd make them all sorry.

Dusty's employees watched him warily as he mumbled to himself and paced the room in decreasing circles. The men were as accustomed to his fits of temper as they were to his spells of happiness. Neither lasted very long, but the man paid top wages and the work suited them. Still, this side of Dusty didn't set well with the nerves. He was downright scary.

The dreams began that night . . .

Warmth flooded his body as he drifted on a fluffy white cloud. Pleasure shot through his limbs until he was arching his body reaching for more . . . more. It was when he moved that the terrifying pain ripped through him. "No, no," he screamed, trying to recapture the pleasure.

His voice was like a catalyst that brought forth the faces from his memory. Beautiful golden hair, ebony black, shimmering chestnut, and honey brown created a veil that surrounded him. Every lovely face he'd ever known looked at him with adoration and trust, each a jewel in her own setting. The temptation to reach out and touch, to stroke the loveliness, was more than he could bear.

His torment began the instant he lifted his hand. The faces laughed and tossed their heads. Everywhere the glorious hair touched his body, his flesh ripped open, spilling precious gems, and gold and silver. The pain was excruciating, his screams filling the house and beyond it.

The employees who heard him couldn't get their gear together fast enough. Those who hadn't heard listened to the account of Dusty's strange behavior and his blood-curdling screams. Then they also were packed and on the road before the dust had settled from the preceding employees.

Dusty woke when bright sunbeams of light danced across his face. The sheet was in shreds and tangled across his body. When he called for his morning coffee, silence met him. After several attempts to get someone's attention, he tossed aside the sheet and got to his feet, mumbling his displeasure. As he passed a mirror, his step faltered. He backed up, his blood frozen. Angry red welts covered his body. The skin was broken in various places and dried blood crusted his flesh. He lifted his hands and saw that his nails were broken and bloodstained. Suddenly his dream was as vivid as the hands he held before him. He bolted through the house shouting for someone, anyone. Silence. No one was there. He peeped out the window. The yard was empty.

Rushing back to his bedroom, he jerked on his clothes, the same clothes he'd worn the day before. He pounded his feet against the floor trying to get his boots on. He couldn't stand the quiet.

He ran to the bunkhouse, hoping to find someone, but there wasn't a sign of his employees. Where were the men he'd paid to protect him?

As he entered the stables, he could hear the sound of *scrape, plop, scrape*. He followed the sound. At last he found someone—the oldest man on the place, a man who had worked for the previous owner. Dusty had kept him on to clean the stables. Now, what was his name?

"Mornin'," Dusty called.

"Same to you," the man answered without looking up from his chore.

"Where is everyone?"

"I reckon yore caterwaulin' last night scared them all away." The man lifted the pitchfork and plunged it into the muck. *Scrape, plop, scrape*.

"It was just a nightmare," Dusty snapped.

"Sounded like the hounds of hell was a-nippin' at yore heels, if'n you ask me."

"Then, why are you still here if everyone else was frightened away?"

The man paused in his labor and lifted his head,

360

studying Dusty for a spell. "The devil don't scare me none. We've been nose to nose and eyeball to eyeball on more'n one occasion."

"You think I'm the devil?" Dusty asked in amazement.

"That ain't what I said. But that's what yore men said, and they wasn't havin' none of it."

"Then, I'd say you're smarter than most. If you'll saddle a horse for me, I'll be on my way. I have some things to do in town."

It wasn't until Dusty was on his way that he remembered something eerie about the man cleaning the stalls. He'd reached to the button placket of his shirt and had pulled a chain from beneath the fabric and continually rubbed an ornament hanging there. Suddenly it dawned on Dusty that the ornament the man wore was a silver cross. A chill swept through him. He hoped the man would be at the ranch when he returned. He didn't like being all alone with his memories right now. It was the first time in his life that his memories hadn't brought him great pleasure.

He gave his horse full rein, anxious to see Juliet. Maybe she had a reason for her betrayal. If she played her cards right, he might give her a chance to explain before he dealt her punishment. When he reached her ranch, he was met with the same locked door as the day before. A mighty kick left the door tilted awkwardly on its hinges. He searched the rooms one by one, her things appearing in order. Her clothes were there in the wardrobe, and hairpins, hairbrush, and perfume bottles littered her dressing table. Where the hell was she? There was only one way to find out, and he had every intention of getting the answers.

As he passed through town, people stared at him curiously. It never crossed his mind that he was a far cry from the richly attired Dusty Mills. He desperately needed a shave, his hair was mussed, and his clothes looked like he'd slept in them. And something about his eyes frightened them.

The fine palomino's sides heaved and his beautiful coat gleamed with perspiration as Dusty reined it before the jail. Hitting the ground at a dead run, he bolted into the office.

Cole sat behind his desk, whistling as he whittled a smooth stick of cedar.

Whistling, for god's sake. Dusty couldn't believe it.

"You seem to have everything under control, Sheriff." Dusty couldn't keep the sarcasm out of his voice.

"I believe you're right," Cole answered as he turned the sharp blade, adding a fine point to the whittling stick. He tossed the stick atop his desk and snapped the knife closed. Lifting his hips, he shoved the knife into his pocket. At last he turned his attention to his nemesis. "What can I do for you?"

Dusty eyed the piece of cedar as it rocked slowly on the desktop before it became perfectly still. Much to his consternation, it reminded him of a stake. He had to clench his hands into fists to keep from grabbing up the stick and breaking it. First a silver cross and now a cedar stake. For some reason, it seemed the people of Hazard were trying to ward off evil.

Oddly enough he wondered if he was the evil they feared.

As Cole's question penetrated his contemplation, he snapped to attention. "I know we've had our differences in the past, Sheriff, but I was hoping we could bury the hatchet. I wanted to wish you congratulations on your upcoming marriage. You're getting a lovely wife." Dusty couldn't believe the words dripping from his mouth. Maybe he should have considered a stage career.

"Yes, I'm a lucky man." Cole answered civilly.

"Could you tell me where I can find Juliet? We have some personal business that needs to be taken care of before the two of you marry."

"Your guess is as good as mine. She has breezed through here several times today on her way to arrange for all the pomp and ceremony of a wedding."

The words didn't set well with Dusty.

Suddenly laughter drifted from the boardwalk, then filled the sheriff's office as the two lovely ladies stepped inside. Sarah and Juliet, behaving as though they were the closest of friends, could barely see over their armloads of packages. For a split second, fear darted across Juliet's face. She spoke to Dusty, then leaned toward Cole and rested her cheek against his.

Sarah turned her head and began stacking her packages on the floor. "I'll send someone for these later, if it's all right. My arms are breaking. I've carried them all over town."

"That's fine," Cole answered as he helped Juliet with her packages.

"Oh, Dusty, I finally made up my mind where I would vacation first," Sarah said, drawing his attention.

"Where?"

"San Francisco. It sounds like such a lovely place. I couldn't resist the lure."

"It's a beautiful place," he agreed offhandedly.

"You've been there?" Sarah asked, surprised. "I didn't know that."

"There's quite a bit you don't know about me, my dear," he bit out sharply. At the time, his usual charming manner was sadly lacking. Pity was, he didn't care how hateful he sounded. All he wanted to do was get his hands on Juliet. She'd pay. There was no doubt in his mind. He positioned himself between her

363

and the door; she wasn't going to escape him.

The moment she stepped away from the desk, Dusty wrapped his hand around her arm in a painful grip. "I need to talk to you, Juliet. It's a personal matter," he informed the occupants of the room. "If you'll step outside with me, it shouldn't take but a few moments." He increased his grip.

Again fear washed over her face. Cole nodded ever so slightly, and Juliet appeared to overcome her fright. Dusty saw the exchange and didn't care for it one bit. He propelled her hastily toward the door, his heart beating wildly with excitement as he contemplated his victory. When he jerked the door open, a passing carriage caught his attention as the driver dipped his head in greeting. The blood drained from Dusty's face and his painful grip became slack. His suddenly damp fingers dropped to his side. He shook his head in puzzlement and raked a trembling hand across his face, craning his head. *It couldn't be,* he whispered.

The occupants of the jail watched in amazement as Dusty stumbled from the room and along the boardwalk.

He searched the street, trying to catch a glimpse of the carriage. It was nowhere in sight. Turning into an alley, he rushed headlong into a group of boys. Questioning them proved futile—they'd seen nothing. Dusty backtracked. It was as though the carriage had vanished. He knew what he'd seen—and he'd seen Bernard, Juliet Barrington's manservant—the real Juliet Barrington, the woman he'd left for dead. But how could that be? If Bernard was around, then so was Juliet. No, surely he was mistaken. It was the lack of food causing his mind to play tricks on him. He couldn't remember the last time he'd eaten, and of course, he'd had very little sleep the night before because of the news he'd heard and the terrible nightmare. Just as soon as he finished his business with that two-faced bitch, he'd have a good meal at the hotel.

A little more flushed and a little less composed, Dusty returned to the jail. Other than Cole sitting behind the desk whistling and whittling, no one else was there. "Where'd Juliet go?"

"She left," Cole said absently.

"But I told her I wanted to speak to her."

"When you took off like a bat out of hell, she decided you'd changed your mind."

"Do you know where she went?"

Cole shook his head, his lips pursed in the ditty he seemed to be so enjoying.

Dusty bolted out the door, rattling the windows when he slammed the door.

Cole laid the whittling stick aside and ceased his whistling. The smile that spanned his face would have done the Cheshire cat proud.

Chapter Thirty-five

Dusty ordered his dinner and propped his elbows on the table, his manners all but forgotten. From the corner of his eye, he caught a glimpse of the waitress serving a couple across the room. The gravy dribbled from his gaping mouth and the fork clattered to his plate. He jumped from the chair and pushed through the room, knocking diners and tables aside in his rush. People balanced their plates, watching in disbelief as the man charged through the dining room. When he entered the kitchen, he sent a waitress and a tray of food spilling onto the floor.

"Where'd she go?" he bellowed.

The cook and the girl picking herself up from the floor, put as much distance between themselves and the man as they dared. "Who?"

"The other waitress. I saw her come in here."

"You—you're mistaken, sir. Evelyn's the only waitress, and I'm the only cook. Do you have a complaint about the food?"

"No, I saw her."

The cook shook her head. "You're welcome to look, but you won't find anyone else here."

Dusty was sweating profusely. He couldn't stand there and argue with the woman. But he knew what he'd seen . . . and he'd seen Olivia serving the customers

366

much the same way she'd served her mistress before he had turned her into Juliet Barrington.

He stumbled from the building on wobbly legs. Walking around to the back of the hotel, he checked every door and window, mumbling all the while about deceitful women. Still, he didn't see a sign of the waitress.

Inside the hotel, the cook and waitress began cleaning up the mess. Every time they passed each other they smiled nervously.

Again on his way home, Dusty stopped at Juliet Barrington's house. The door was still tilted awkwardly, and the place was as quiet as a tomb, not a ranch hand or an animal to be found anywhere.

When Dusty reached home, nothing he did gave him any comfort. Only after exhausting every other outlet did he pull the key from his pocket and enter his office. This was what he needed, truly wanted. The trinkets sparkled through his fingers as he shoved his hand into the box. Suddenly a frown marred his brow. The locket was missing. He wanted it back. Did Sarah still have it or had she given it to her lover? He'd planned everything so carefully, knowing Cole would turn from Sarah when he recognized the locket. Had his plan backfired? Hell, something had gone wrong. Maybe the loss of the locket was the cause of all his problems. Yes, he had to get it back, then everything would be all right. Maybe it wouldn't be that hard to retrieve.

That night Dusty slept in a chair with his beloved trinkets spread across his stomach. The dreams were worse, the faces clearer, and the voices louder. When he woke the next morning, the jewels sparkled about him like sunshine reflecting off the morning dew. His neck burned like fire, and when he examined it in the mirror, a narrow strip of red circled his neck. It felt like a rope burn, but Dusty knew better, for behind his chair where his head had rested lay a shimmering chain of gold.

His mind was in a whirl as he plotted the recovery of the locket. From his position in the alley, he could see anyone coming or going from the saloon. The girls, Collie and Belle, walked right past him, never looking in his direction. Billy Ward was in and out of the saloon several times. At last, he saw Sarah come out of the saloon. He flattened himself against the side of the building and watched her head bobbing like a damn float as she greeted friends until she entered Wes Norman's office.

Dusty moved cautiously, straining and pulling until he reached the rooftop adjacent to the saloon. Slowly he pulled himself along until he reached Sarah's bedroom window. He knew exactly where he was going. The last time he'd entered her room he'd had the protection of darkness, but this time he couldn't wait for darkness. He had to find the locket.

As he slipped through the window and his feet touched solid footing, a godawful squall pierced the air. Dusty cracked his forehead against the window sill, leaving a pump-knot the size of an egg. Before he could balance himself, he saw Sarah's cat poised for attack, its hair raised for combat as though someone had doused it with starch and put it in the sun to dry. Dusty swallowed loudly, not knowing what to do. He'd never faced a situation like this.

"Nice kitty," he cooed, leaning toward the cat and extending his hand.

Mr. Herman hissed a warning just before his paw left a path of stinging scratches across the back of Dusty's hand. Before he could pull his hand away, the cat leaped through the air using Dusty's back for a springboard as he bounded to the window and escaped the room. Dusty slid to the floor in profound relief. After getting his breath, he searched the desk from top to bottom. Nothing. He looked everywhere. Nothing. At last he admitted what he had dreaded most. Sarah must have given the locket to the sheriff.

Deciding a bath and a shave were in order before he faced the sheriff again, he prepared to crawl through the window. Scouting the street below, a well-dressed lady caught his attention. All he could see of her was her back as she looked at the window display. Something about her looked so familiar. When she lifted her hands to adjust her bonnet, he could see her reflection clearly in the window glass. Juliet Barrington! He would recognize the old lady anywhere. Hadn't he promised her the world on a silver platter if she would only marry him? What the hell was she doing in Hazard? He thought she was dead. The doctor told him she wouldn't last more than a few days.

He scrambled through the window and returned to the alley. When he left the alley, he could still see her. She had moved on up the street, but if he hurried, he could catch her. He rushed across the street, never taking his eyes off her back. Just a few more steps and he would have her. Thank God, he'd found her! She could answer so many questions that were plaguing him.

He lifted his hand and grabbed her arm, pulling her around. "Juliet, wait."

"I beg your pardon," the lady said.

Dusty had never laid eyes on this woman. "What did you do with Miss Barrington?" he shouted, drawing the attention of several pedestrians.

"I don't have the faintest idea what you're talking about. Take your hands off me this instant."

Dusty dropped his hand like a hot potato. "My mistake. I thought you were someone else."

As the woman hurried away, he gently stroked the

369

pump-knot on his forehead. That's what it was. The lick to his head had caused his vision to blur.

He left the bathhouse feeling somewhat better. Yes, a shave should boost his spirits even more.

Dusty cautioned the barber not to touch his injured head as the man placed a steaming towel over his face. The wet heat felt good. A voice from his past penetrated his thoughts. The voice asked how long it would be before he could get a shave. The barber answered, then Dusty heard footsteps before the door opened.

He lifted his head and pushed the clinging towel aside. "Hey, wait a minute," Dusty shouted.

The man nodded in his direction. "Dusty," he said softly before walking away.

Dusty scrambled from the chair. The barber watched him closely. "Do you know who that was?"

"Who *who* was?" the barber asked quietly.

"That damn man you were just talking to. I'm not blind."

The barber looked around the empty room. "Of course you're not, Mr. Mills, but you're the only customer I have."

"I know, but the man who just left was James Moore."

"James Moore is dead," the barber assured him, carefully backing away.

"I know that," Dusty shouted. "But, damn it, I just saw him as plain as day, and he wasn't dead."

"Whatever you say, Mr. Mills," the barber agreed, thoroughly frightened now. He lifted the straight razor, making sure Dusty saw it and knew he could defend himself if the occasion warranted.

Dusty was far more concerned with the appearance of James Moore. He stared at the closed door wondering what he should do. Something in his mind snapped. He turned to the barber with his eyes glittering wildly. "He wants the locket, but it belongs to me." Spittle had begun to collect in the corners of Dusty's mouth as he babbled. He rushed from the shop, vowing James Moore would never have the locket.

The barber flipped over the closed sign and pulled down the shades, needing a few moments to quiet his nerves and his trembling hands. If he tried to shave someone at this point, he would surely cut their throat.

After scouring the town from one end to the other without a sign of James Moore, Dusty purchased a shovel and headed for the cemetery.

He pushed the bouquet of flowers from the mound and began to dig. Hours passed, and still he rammed the shovel into the earth and tossed the dirt aside. Sweat poured from his dirt-streaked face. His clothes were rank with the smell of perspiration and three days of wear. He ranted and raved as he emptied the grave, swearing that James Moore would never have the locket.

At times, he seemed perfectly lucid, wondering aloud why he was wasting his time digging up James when it had been his most heartfelt wish that James Moore be dead and out of his way.

He'd made sure he was dead—because Dusty had taken it upon himself to kill James. One night he'd waited until the saloon closed and James had headed out to the ranch. He'd bushwhacked James, clear and simple. He'd seen his body fall to the ground. He'd even watched from a distance as Wes Norman made arrangements for the man to be buried quietly. Now here he was digging up the bastard.

"Dusty? What are you doing?" the sheriff asked. "Don't you know it's against the law to violate a grave?"

"No, you can't stop me," Dusty sobbed. "I have to find it." He fell to his knees and began digging furiously with his hands.

"Why would you want to dig up James? He's been dead a long time."

"I know how long he's been dead, you fool. I killed him." Dusty stopped his digging and eyed Cole furtively. "He's not dead, you know," Dusty whispered. "None of them are. They've come for the jewels, but they can't have them. They're mine."

"I see," Cole answered.

Dusty seemed to regain a bit of sanity when next he faced Cole. "I'll tell you something else. Your Juliet Barrington isn't at all what she seems. I saw the *real* Miss Barrington today. She's here in Hazard, and so is her manservant, Bernard. The doctor told me she was going to die. And god, Bernard, I thought he would've died months ago. Why, he's as old as Methuselah."

Cole smiled. He had to agree with Dusty.

Dusty again began digging in earnest.

"Is this what you're looking for?"

Dusty lifted his dirt-streaked face. Dangling from Cole's fingers was the golden locket. "Did you kill her for it?" Cole asked. He had to know for his own peace of mind.

"No, she gave it to me. They all gave me gifts." Dusty began to sob. "Now they want them back. They attack me when I'm sleeping, thinking I won't know what they're doing."

"Did you kill them?"

"I had to," he admitted, eyeing the locket. "Can I have it? It belongs to me."

Cole let the chain slide through his fingers.

Dusty caught it before it hit the ground, and held it to his chest much like a child clutching his favorite toy.

Before the sun set on Hazard that day, they had made arrangements to transport Dusty Mills to a sanatorium far away. He sat in the barred wagon with a wooden box in his lap. As he sifted through the box, he talked quietly to the contents. Had he had any wits about him, he would have thought some of the onlookers peculiar.

Juliet Barrington and the lady standing beside her were dressed in identical dresses. The lady patted Juliet's hand as they watched the departing wagon. Olivia stood on the other side of her mistress, wearing a waitress's outfit from Chapel's Hotel. The other waitress and the cook kept smiling at her encouragingly. Bernard stood behind his mistress, an aged and arthritic hand resting on her shoulder. The barber appeared still a trifle nervous as he watched the proceedings. Ida Flowers was as pleased as punch; she'd never experienced such excitement. Collie and Belle stood with Vance and David Tulley, and Marge watched them proudly.

Marge had had her hands full for the past few days taking care of her guests. Cole had known she could be depended on. Juliet, Bernard, and Olivia had been under her protection. But she'd loved every minute of it. And her third son, Evan, the youngest, couldn't take his eyes off Olivia. At first, Marge couldn't figure out if it was the girl's accent, or her shapely body that drew the boy. She finally decided it was a combination of both. The accent had intrigued him, but her body had fired his blood.

Billy Ward slumped beside Wes and Chin, talking quietly. Cole and Sarah stood closest to the wagon, hands clasped, grateful the ordeal was over. Cole squeezed her hand.

When she lifted her face to him, she encountered a

373

seductive smile and a slow wink. A hot rush of blood filled her veins. She returned his smile and his wink.

He couldn't wait to get his hands on Sarah.

As the wagon bearing Dusty crested a small rise and soon disappeared, a round of applause swept through the town. The people of Hazard, Texas, breathed a sigh of relief and vowed to be eternally grateful for their sheriff, Coleman Blade. It hadn't taken Cole long to convince Olivia that her future depended on her participation in the conspiracy. After a vivid description of prison life, Olivia was begging to be a part of the plot and redeem herself in Juliet Barrington's eyes. Cole had organized the scheme and set Wes Norman to carrying out his plan. The hard-working people had banned together to rid their town of the black-hearted Dusty Mills.

When the crowd began to disperse, Cole dragged Sarah into his office and proceeded to kiss her breathless. She returned his ardor with equal enthusiasm. Hair pins fell unnoticed to the floor as he plunged his hands into the copper tresses. He clasped her hand, and their fingers tangled and held. They needed to touch each other, to taste each other. But there was just so much touching and tasting they could do in such a public place.

"I've missed you so much," she whispered to his nose as her lips moved across his face.

"I don't ever want to be separated again," he swore.

"Me either," she agreed.

"Marry me, Sarah. Will you?"

"Yes, yes, yes," she responded as she delivered hot, wet kisses to the meanest, fastest gunslinger in the great state of Texas.

Chapter Thirty-six

The creak of the door as it swung open startled them. They quickly broke their embrace. Billy stood just inside the doorway, a sheepish grin on his face. Sarah's hand went swiftly to her unbound hair, her face turning crimson with embarrassment.

Running his hand beneath his stiff collar to loosen it, Billy cleared his throat. "I . . . ah . . . should've knocked. I just wanted to talk with Sarah a minute, but I can come back later."

Cole grinned. "Whoever heard of knocking at a place of business?" he asked, winking at Sarah.

Sarah stared at Billy, first noticing he'd shaved his beard. He wore a new suit, too, and his white shirt was freshly starched and wrinkle-free. Next, she noticed how tall and straight he stood—his usual stooped posture was gone. In fact, if he weren't wearing the familiar slouch hat and the black patch over his eye, she might not have recognized him.

"You look real nice, Billy," she praised.

"Thank you, missy." He winked and grinned. "Since I'm now the owner of the Do Drop In, I figured it was time I spruced up a bit."

"I'm sure you'll do a good job of running it, too," Cole replied, then drew Sarah close to his side, draping his arm around her waist. "You said you wanted to see Sarah?"

Billy swallowed deeply and shuffled his feet. "Uh . . .

yes." Finally, he clasped his hands behind his back and blurted, "Sarah, I've lied to you. Please don't hold it against me, because it was necessary."

"Lied?" she asked in puzzlement.

"Yes." Without another word, Billy removed his hat and tossed it on Cole's desk. Sarah stared curiously at his copper hair laced with strands of silver. Hadn't it been dark brown like the beard he used to wear? Next, he slid his finger beneath the band securing his patch and drew it over his head. Then, walking toward her, he glanced at Cole before he took her hand in his large one and placed his other hand over it.

Sarah felt uneasy as she looked down at his hands, seeing the neatly manicured nails, hands she'd never seen until this moment because of the tattered gloves he'd always worn. Gazing back up into his face, she looked straight into his green, green eyes. A picture from the past flashed through her mind: the tall, lean, handsome man holding the infant, and on his face a smile of contentment—the same smile that was smiling down at her now.

For a heart-stopping moment, she thought the man was . . . no, it couldn't be him.

Billy caught the astonishment on her face. "You're right, missy, I'm not Billy," he said softly. "You know who I am, don't you?"

She spoke barely above a whisper, her voice quivering as she answered, "You can't be. My—my father's dead. I've been to his grave, and—"

"No, he didn't die, but he had to make you believe he had."

The lie was almost more than she could bear. "Why? Why!" Hurt and anger overpowered those tender emotions of joy and love that lay so close to the surface of her heart.

She jerked her hand from his and lashed out at him. "You brought me all the way out here under the pretense that you had died? What an uncaring, horribly selfish thing to do to your own daughter."

Her words stung him like a whip. As he spoke, his voice was hoarse and shaking. "I've always cared, Sarah. From the very moment you came into this world, not a day has gone by that I haven't wished to have my daughter with me."

"Then, why didn't you write me long ago and tell me you cared?" she wailed, tears blistering her eyes.

He laughed bitterly. "I did. Once. Your mother told me she'd burned the letter. Do you know how I managed to get all those pictures of you? I threatened to return to Highridge and live there so I could see you."

"Why didn't you?"

"I loved you too much. My presence in your life would have only confused and humiliated you, because your mother would never have consented to living with me instead of with your grandparents. It was better to wait until you were old enough to make your own decision. But I waited too long to force the issue. Before I knew it, you'd married the preacher, and I thought I'd lost my chance to be a part of your life. When he died, I swore I'd not waste a moment more."

Some of her anger evaporated, but a lingering trace remained close to the surface. "Were you afraid I wouldn't come out here any other way? My goodness, to pretend you had died? Isn't that carrying it a bit too far?"

James Moore hesitated. "I almost did die, Sarah, by Dusty Mills's own hand."

Sarah's face went white as a sheet. "Dusty tried to murder you?"

"Yes. It happened after I hired Cole to become our

sheriff. Dusty knew I was on to him and didn't like me bringing in someone who'd interfere with his plans. So one night he bushwhacked me and left me for dead. During my recovery, Wes and I decided I should stay 'dead' until he and Cole could prove Dusty guilty of other murders we suspected he was guilty of committing. It was during this time that I came up with the idea of the will, leaving you my estate."

Sarah drew one shuddering breath. Still miffed, she snapped, "The least you could've done was tell me the truth after I got here."

"No, Sarah. If you'd known I was alive, you might have behaved differently around me and let something slip about me in Dusty's presence. There's no telling what the man would've done to you, if he'd found out I was still alive. The way it was, I had Cole, Wes, and even myself to protect you."

"Humph," she snorted. "You'd have really been up the creek if I'd decided to marry Dusty, wouldn't you?"

"I wouldn't have let that happen," Cole put in, a lazy smile tugging one corner of his mouth. "I wanted you for myself, Widow Woman."

"Cole Blade, you knew about this all along, didn't you?"

Cole raised his hands in mock defense. "No, Sarah, believe me, I was as shocked as you are. It wasn't until we started planning Dusty's ruination that I guessed it, then Wes confirmed my suspicions. How James pulled it off without someone in town, especially his employees, recognizing him is amazing."

"I should've known a long time ago," Sarah said with a soft smile, walking toward her father. Stopping in front of him, she stared up into his green eyes and saw her reflection mirrored in them. "As Billy Ward, you filled a special place in my heart. Even with your gruffness and unkempt appearance I felt a closeness with you." With tears filling her eyes, she said, "I forgive you, Father, because . . . because I love you."

"I love you, too . . . daughter." James's eyes were as misty as Sarah's as he drew her into his arms. "Damn, you don't know how many times I've almost pulled you into my arms like this and confessed my deceit."

For a long moment Cole watched them, feeling his heart about to burst with joy. If he was fortunate enough to claim even a tiny portion of the love Sarah felt for her father, he would have enough to last a lifetime.

Sarah turned in her father's arms and reached her hand to Cole. He took it and walked slowly to her side. She gazed up at her father. "Cole has something he wants to ask you, Billy"—she laughed—"Oops, excuse me . . . Father. Forgive me, but it's going to take me a while to get that name out of my mind."

James chuckled. "At least you liked the son of a bitch." Realizing his error, he apologized, "I'm afraid Billy and I did have one thing in common. Swearing. I'll try to learn to curb it."

"Don't worry about it," she said laughingly. "After working in a saloon, I got used to a lot of things. In fact, just living in Hazard has been a real eye-opener for me."

"Then, you're glad you came?"

"Yes, very much. If I hadn't come, I would never have met Cole." Turning to Cole, she said, "Ask him."

"Ask him what?"

"You know," she urged, nudging him in the ribs. When he looked confused, she leaned into him and whispered, "A man's supposed to ask the father's permission to marry his daughter."

"Oh, that."

"Yes, that."

"James, I mean, Mr. Moore—hell, what do you want me to call you?"

"Depends on the question, Sheriff," James said slyly.

Cole cleared his throat several times before he finally asked, "With your permission, I'd like to marry your daughter."

James beamed. "From the first moment I saw you together, I had a pretty good idea this would come to pass." Then, with an air of fatherly authority, he stated, "Now, Sheriff, being as I'm Sarah's father, it's my duty to question my future son-in-law's plans. You know, things like . . . What do you plan to do for a living?"

Cole saw James's eyes fixed on the five-star badge pinned to his vest. With a crooked grin, Cole replied. "You hired me, so you have the authority to help me make that decision, don't you?"

"Damned right I do. You're fired, Coleman Blade. Now turn over that badge."

"Gladly," Cole said, unpinning it from his vest and dropping it on the desk.

Sarah ran into Cole's arms and embraced him with a fierce hug. "Oh, Cole, I'm so happy."

Holding her from him, he frowned down at her. "Even if I don't have a job?"

Behind her, she heard her father say, "Run the damned ranch, that's what you're going to do."

They both turned, their mouths gaping in surprise.

"And in between tending to the ranch, I hope you'll find some time to give me a grandchild or two." With his hand on the doorknob, he said, "Oh, after you marry my daughter, just call me Dad." After those suggestions, he opened the door and quit the room.

A lusty gleam filled Cole's eyes before he turned

from Sarah. Walking briskly to the window, he pulled down the shade. Next he turned the key in the lock.

"Why'd you do that?"

"Taking my future father-in-law's suggestion. All that ranching might tire a man out. We certainly don't want to waste this precious free time, do we?"

"Here!"

"He fired me, remember? If duty calls, I can ignore it," he said devilishly. Drawing her into his arms, he kissed her, his mouth never leaving her own as he walked her backward toward one of the cells.

"Cole," she whispered laughingly when he eased open the cell door and gently placed her on the cot.

The news spread like a grass fire. Coleman Blade and Sarah Hogan were getting married. To a rare few, it was very confusing. Couldn't the sheriff make up his mind who he wanted to marry? It had only been a matter of days since word had spread that he was marrying Juliet Barrington. Or was her name Olivia? Yes, the privileged took great pleasure in sorting out the confusion.

As it turned out, Cole's engagement to the young girl had only been a farce to draw out Dusty Mills. Anybody with any romance about them at all knew that Cole's heart—and, truly, his love—had always belonged to Sarah Hogan.

Epilogue

A gentle breeze whipped the sheets as Sarah anchored the clothespins and stood back to admire her work. She loved the everyday chores of running her home. It had taken the threat of another pot of rice over Chin's head before he would agree to let her help him with the wash. Men! Sometimes Cole and Chin took their position of protectors a bit too far, even if her belly did look like a pumpkin ready to explode. She was only pregnant. Other than that, her faculties were still intact.

Waddling across the lawn to a grouping of chairs, she lowered her bulk into a rocker. Stacking her hands on her protruding abdomen, she lifted her face to the warm sun and closed her eyes. Wasn't life wonderful?

Sarah Hogan Blade had so much to be thankful for—and she was—everyday. She'd discovered heaven on earth. She smiled. Things had a way of working out for the best, but the lessons learned in the process she held dear.

Her father visited daily, anxiously awaiting the birth of his grandchild. The ranch house was now truly a home filled with love and laughter.

The rumor of a railroad spur had indeed come true. Ironic, the way it had turned out. Instead of the spur crossing where Dusty had thought in all his scheming and dealing, it had gone through the lower end of Marge Tulley's property. She still had her ranch and was financially set for life.

Sarah had given the men of Hazard a choice in splitting up her two-thousand-dollar reward. They'd all agreed to donate the money, plus Dusty Mills's unclaimed one-thousand-dollar reward, to the building fund for a new school in Hazard.

Her head began to tilt as she dozed in the sun. A husky whisper and pair of slow lips trailing across the column of her neck sent ripples through her body.

"Hmmm . . ."

"Are you happy?" asked the happy voice.

She nodded, and wrapped her arms around her husband. "As happy as anyone could be . . . *this side of heaven.*"

FIERY ROMANCE

CALIFORNIA CARESS (2771, $3.75)
by Rebecca Sinclair

Hope Bennett was determined to save her brother's life. And if that meant paying notorious gunslinger Drake Frazier to take his place in a fight, she'd barter her last gold nugget. But Hope soon discovered she'd have to give the handsome rattlesnake more than riches if she wanted his help. His improper demands infuriated her; even as she luxuriated in the tantalizing heat of his embrace, she refused to yield to her desires.

ARIZONA CAPTIVE (2718, $3.75)
by Laree Bryant

Logan Powers had always taken his role as a lady-killer very seriously and no woman was going to change that. Not even the breathtakingly beautiful Callie Nolan with her luxuriant black hair and startling blue eyes. Logan might have considered a lusty romp with her but it was apparent she was a lady, through and through. Hard as he tried, Logan couldn't resist wanting to take her warm slender body in his arms and hold her close to his heart forever.

DECEPTION'S EMBRACE (2720, $3.75)
by Jeanne Hansen

Terrified heiress Katrina Montgomery fled Memphis with what little she could carry and headed west, hiding in a freight car. By the time she reached Kansas City, she was feeling almost safe . . . until the handsomest man she'd ever seen entered the car and swept her into his embrace. She didn't know who he was or why he refused to let her go, but when she gazed into his eyes, she somehow knew she could trust him with her life . . . and her heart.